THE FIGUREHEAD

The FIGUREHEAD
OWEN BURKE

COLLINS
St James's Place, London
1979

William Collins Sons & Co Ltd
London · Glasgow · Sydney · Auckland
Toronto · Johannesburg

First published 1979
© 1979 by Owen Burke
ISBN 0 00 222230 2
Set in Baskerville
**Printed in Great Britain by
T. J. Press (Padstow) Ltd., Padstow, Cornwall**

For
JACQUELINE
who launched it

You never enjoy the world aright,
till the sea itself floweth in your
veins, till you are clothed with the heavens,
and crowned with the stars: and perceive
yourself to be the sole heir of the whole
world . . .

Thomas Traherne

One

Lodestar

THE FIGUREHEAD dipped and swung gracefully to port, her slim arms reaching along the bowsprit as if to pull free and dive towards the dock entrance ahead. Canvas billowed, boomed in a flurry of wind, and collapsed in on itself. Gulls that had been greedily swooping low went up in a screaming turmoil, circled, and came back again. A gust of sleet whipped across the choppy water from the far bank of the river.

A steam tug fussed in like a cheeky, dirty little terrier beside the tall clipper. On the pier the dock master was shouting instructions to men waiting with warp lines.

Nell Meredith took her grandfather's arm. It was a cold day and his lips were blue but he had stood here, his stick rammed down against the flagstones, with unwavering patience from the moment they had first glimpsed the proud three-master riding upstream from the bar. One felt that in half an hour's unblinking assessment he could count the crew, weigh the cargo, and appraise the success of the entire voyage out and home.

On the opposite pier stood another man: younger, taller, more erect than old Jesse Bostock, but equally absorbed. On first noticing each other they had raised their tall stovepipe hats and exchanged slow, courteous nods; then returned to their mutual obsession.

"Got their own berth now, I see."

Bostock might have been addressing the smoke trailer from a ferry-

11

boat puffing in to the landing-stage. But a dutiful voice from behind answered, "And a leased warehouse. No more leaving their cargoes out in all weathers."

Nell did not look round. It was a voice she detested, and she had no wish to see yet again the sly, brutish face that went with it.

"Doing nicely for themselves," said her grandfather.

"And right next door to us, sir."

Ripples slapped against the green slime and trailing tendrils of the dock wall. The sharp clipper bows were almost upon them. A varnished wooden face smiled a mysterious half-smile, still yearning forward.

It was unlike any other figurehead Nell had seen. Instead of the usual floridly painted, plump-bosomed shape it was somehow Eurasian in character—dark gold, quite naked, slim, and with small breasts but sharp and heavily tinted nipples. And the expression was not puffy and complacent as on so many models. Here the lips were slightly parted, and slanting eyes seemed to challenge the waves to smash up and over her. Churned up by a sudden tumult of the tug's paddles grinding into reverse, a whip of spray was thrown glistening along her left temple. Moisture trickled from face and breasts, and dripped from the groove where her loins blended into the sharp rake of the ship's stem.

"She's beautiful," Nell murmured.

"Beautiful, aye." Jesse Bostock was staring not at the slender figure but up into the rigging. "Dying, though. Sail won't last your lifetime, girl. And the Greshams must know it."

"The Greshams?"

"Old Gresham left his two boys a solid business, but they're not ones to take anything for granted. Two boys," he repeated bitterly. His thumb jerked towards the tall young man who had now taken a step along the quay as if to touch the vessel reassuringly the moment she was moored. "That's the older. Edmund Gresham."

Nell was silent. Already she had heard a dozen times the implied reproach that was none of her responsibility, yet which stung.

There appeared to be some argument going on with a Customs officer. Then a cry from the rail caught Edmund Gresham's attention. A younger man leaning over and waving exuberantly was so obviously his brother: the same craggy brow and spiky chin, the same sandy hair. But the differences were as marked as the resemblances. The older's smile as he looked up was slow and earnest; the younger's irrepressible, liable at any moment to crack—as all at once it did—into irrelevant but infectious laughter. The one was correctly attired as a respectable merchant; the other wore a seaman's guernsey, and his face was seamed and reddened by weeks at sea.

The gangplank rattled down. The Customs officer went aboard, followed by Edmund Gresham with black frock-coat swinging to the confident length of his stride.

Still Bostock waited, unhurried, adapted to the rhythm of this way of life.

Then came the first hint of impatience. Over his shoulder he snapped: "You didn't tell me they were buying that warehouse."

"Leasing it, Mr. Bostock."

"Leasing it, then. Staking a claim on it. Right across where *we* may want to expand."

"But Mr. Bostock," Hesketh's rasping voice protested, "I did tell you. More than a week ago I told you."

"D'you think I'd have sat tight and done nothing?"

"I told you, sir. And twice I asked if you wanted anything done about it. You didn't seem to know."

Bostock stared implacably into the shrouds above his head. "Are you telling me my mind's wandering, man? You think I'd forget a thing like that? Think I'd not be able to make up my mind?"

The only reply was a faint, resentful intake of breath.

Two figures appeared at the head of the gangplank. One was the younger Gresham. The other . . .

Nell caught her breath.

Following him was the ship's figurehead brought to life: sleek varnished timber transformed into sleek flesh and blood. She was simply dressed in what looked like a loose silk gown, owing nothing to the fashions of this year of 1855; but Nell was sure that beneath the shapeless garment the woman's shape would be just as the carving was.

Her grandfather snorted. "Young Malcolm. And what game's he playing this time?"

"The figurehead must have been modelled on her."

"Figurehead's been on the *Naomi* this last couple of years and more. First time I've seen it walking about."

"But she's so like it."

"Something that took his fancy out East, I suppose. Probably came fairly cheap. Don't know if he's hoping to sell her off at a profit."

The two were descending to the quayside. Workmen began swinging bales ashore, and the bustle of activity hid the couple from Nell.

"They're the ones we've got to beat," said Jesse. "The Greshams. Beat 'em or go into partnership with 'em."

"It sounds simple enough," Nell ventured.

"Not to me it isn't."

"What's wrong with a commercial partnership?"

13

"And who'll be the Bostock partner when I'm gone?"

"Grandfather, nobody's talking about you going."

"Not in my hearing, no. But I'm not immortal, and I certainly don't feel it. So who takes over? Your father? And after him, does Bostock disappear under the Gresham flag?"

It was still too intensely proud and possessive for Nell. Ships and their cargoes, florid lettering over doorways, a flag, a red band or a blue star on a funnel or fluttering from a top-gallant: how could such things occupy their every waking thought?

Yet looking at the lines of the clipper and at the forest of masts beyond, the great stretch of pulsating harbour and township, she had an inkling of how much it might matter if one let its spell take over.

Someone else might easily let it. Nell Meredith intended to preserve her immunity.

"We could share our trade with the Greshams on this end of the docks," her grandfather was thinking aloud. "Them for the East, us for the Atlantic, spreading our risks. Or we could combine and concentrate. If I could be sure of having enough time left"—he tightened his grip on the stick, but gusting wind brought a tear to his eye and he had to wipe it away—"I'd know how to deal with it. I'd decide which it was to be. But who else has the feel of the business?"

Between a raised hatch-cover and the deck-house Nell glimpsed Edmund Gresham, one arm out-thrust to direct the handling of a large crate. Her grandfather had seen him, too. He grunted to himself, then said:

"You'd best marry that one."

"Marry?"

"Edmund Gresham. And have a few sons, and be quick about it."

"I've never even met the man."

"Soon remedy that."

"We'll be going home in a few—"

"You're going nowhere, girl. Here's where you belong. It's marry into 'em," said Bostock, "or beat 'em."

"Then you had better beat them."

"A girl of spirit like Miss Meredith," said Hesketh's intolerable voice behind them, "could maybe manage to do both."

She had loathed the man from the first moment she saw him in that smaller seaport, on that different coast: feared and loathed him without knowing who he was or what he would bring. It was nothing to do with his movement, his face or, at first, his voice. The stillness and heaviness and silence were somehow worse than an impertinent remark or a grab at her arm would have been.

He stood late one afternoon under a gas lamp by the trawl dock. The same man, she was sure, who had dogged her footsteps the previous morning to find out where she worked, and who now knew her route and where to intercept her.

So far he had not spoken. Perhaps he never would. Nell tried to convince herself that he was just another of the sad middle-aged men who often showed up in Lowestoft when the holiday season was over, the bathing machines had been wheeled back up the sands, and lodgings were cheap. Discouraged by their landladies from staying indoors between meals, such lonely folk could find few entertainments other than staring at the busy life of the quays and, awestruck, at the Scottish fisher girls who invaded the town for a few frantic weeks to sing and shriek and laugh as they gutted and barrelled the autumn herring.

But there was nothing small and furtive about this man. In his chocolate brown bowler, broad-shouldered cape and sturdy boots he looked so solid and sure of himself.

15

Nell put her head back in the hope that the line of her chin would look severe enough to drive the fellow away. Then she had to make an undignified grab for the edge of her bonnet and thrust the hatpin more firmly home as a lash of east wind whipped across the harbour.

It proved a quiet morning in the circulating library. Mr. Trigg turned down the gas jets illuminating the darker bookshelves at the back of the room, and moved to one side of his desk to make the best possible use of the steely October daylight.

At eleven o'clock the door opened to admit a stab of cold air and Mrs. Upcraft.

"Ah, Miss Meredith." She raised her veil and set two thick volumes on the counter before Nell, conveying a severe accusation in her greeting. "This"—a wrinkled finger, freckled with a brown discolouration, tapped the cover of the uppermost book—"was a grievous disappointment."

"I'm sorry to hear that, Mrs. Upcraft."

"And I, Miss Meredith, am sorry you chose to issue such a distasteful story to me."

"You did particularly ask for the latest Charles Dickens."

"But how was I to know that Mr. Dickens had sunk into such gloom and unpleasantness? Really, if you cannot pay more attention to the contents of the volumes you offer, I shall seriously have to consider cancelling my subscription." Mrs. Upcraft tilted her head to read the titles of a consignment that Nell had just unpacked. "Is there nothing new from that admirable Miss Yonge? An author whose work can with perfect propriety be left open on the drawing-room table. One does so appreciate a story embodying fine principles, the fitness of whose ending can be foreseen."

For myself, thought Nell rebelliously, I'd rather not know the ending. There'll come a day when I shall walk through that door and down the street and board a ship without asking its destination or the length of its voyage. And somewhere there'll be an ending—or a beginning—that will take me by surprise. And *someone* who'll take me by surprise.

Instinctively she looked past Mrs. Upcraft as a shadow fell across the window. The man was there, his face as uncompromising as his stance: a weather-beaten face with hard, ugly lips. He was studying her and the surrounding bookshelves as if to memorise every detail of herself and her setting.

"Miss Meredith." Mrs. Upcraft demanded her attention.

The man contemplated the black bombazine back, and strolled on. Nell at last despatched Mrs. Upcraft with two novels by authors who, if neither original nor stimulating, were at least as innocuous as the lady's drawing-room table merited.

16

At four o'clock Mr. Trigg decreed that the library would close. The gas jet by his desk had already been lowered to its faintest practical glow, and there was no reason for further wastage.

"No lady will be venturing out at this hour. And I fancy you would do well to hurry home, Miss Meredith, and avoid any awkward disturbances."

"Disturbances?"

"The recruiting sergeant is in the town. I believe some Radicals may be declaring their opposition by the railway station. It will all end in an excuse for strong drink and fisticuffs."

Nell was glad to be out of the library. Then, emerging from the side street on to the crowded road above the station, she was less glad. He could be waiting for her, could be anywhere in the throng or in the shadows of any one of the alleys beside her.

Traffic from the bridge was forcing runnels around the military band and the resplendently attired sergeant in the centre of the usually open space. Above the clatter of wheels and hoofs rose a stentorian voice offering the Queen's shilling and the promise of dazzling adventure.

"Are we goin' to let them Russians bully us?"

"Never!" shouted the bandsmen in well-drilled chorus.

"Come and join the colours, lads. Come and show the Russian bear what the English lion's made of. You there—you're a fine-looking lad, you'll be a wonder in uniform. Your sweetheart'll love you. And the Queen'll be proud to have you."

A small group of men moved out from the shelter of the railway station. "Don't join. Don't be tricked. The cause is wrong—it's wicked."

"Treason! That's treason, that is."

There was a scuffle on the fringe of the crowd. A cane swung and a man went down; and another. The band struck up a rousing march. Nell quickened her pace up the hill. It was difficult not to keep step with the beat of the music.

A fisherman who must have started his drinking early in the day came reeling out of a doorway and caught her arm to steady himself. His breath and body stank, but under the flickering light his smile was young and cheerful and struck an answering smile from Nell. They were a rough lot, the roaring boys of the east coast, but in some way which she could not admit to herself she envied them and their raucousness and the rough girls who went with them.

"Fancy him, then?" He nodded towards the distant figure of the sergeant, bright in the naphtha flares set about the concourse. "Fancy a soldier boy?"

"No, nor a sailor boy."

17

He slapped her amiably on the hip, swayed, and blinked at the traffic.

"Here, come along." Nell reclaimed his arm and steered him through the tangle of carts and carriages. He chuckled, leaning more heavily on her than was necessary.

She kept close to him when they reached the other side. People walked up the slope and eddied about them, but she could not pick out her disquieting shadow.

"Oh, yes, and what d'you call this, then?"

A girl with a shawl pulled about her thin face set herself on the pavement before them. She glared into Nell's face, and her right hand fidgeted, ready to slap or claw.

"There you are." The fisher lad was still cheerful and still swaying gently. "Wondered where you'd got to."

"Where *I'd* got to? I like that!"

Nell said: "It's all right. We just bumped into each other." She stood away from the young man, who happily lurched towards the other girl and propped himself against her. "He's a nice chap. You'd better look after him."

Before the girl could argue further she was tugged away up the hill. Twice she looked back at Nell, obviously asking surly questions, but the fisherman urged her on. Nell waited until they had got a good start, then followed slowly.

She was shocked by her own reaction. The young man was a stranger who meant nothing and could never have meant anything to her. Yet there had been an instant when, absurdly, she might have found herself fighting with that girl: fighting as the men and so many of their women fought along the quayside, or in the steep narrow alleys known as Scores that plunged from the high town to the older fishing village below. Nell sensed, to her own alarm, the terrible appetite for such a confrontation.

Ahead of her the couple turned down the Score beside her father's bookshop.

By the time she reached the corner they were no more than elusive phantoms across the green sputter of lamplight at the foot of the cobbled slope. There was a giggling scuffle, a squeal of protest channelled up between the high walls, then a rhythmic grunting and a whimper that might have been of pleasure or pain or both.

One light burned low in the window of the shop, but the interior was dark. Perhaps her father, like Mr. Trigg, had decided that nobody would be interested in books today.

Nell stood for a moment in the side doorway, reluctant to go in. Through the narrow cleft of the Score, beyond the rooftops of the lower town, she could see a sullen pewter streak along the horizon. Against it

18

stood the axe-head silhouette of a barge's topsail. And beyond that she saw in her mind's eye a great four-master riding over the edge of the world into some unfathomable ocean, towards another, unexplored world.

Nell let herself in.

Her mother called along the passage: "Owen, is that you? I've been sitting here worrying myself silly. How could you . . ." She stopped as Nell entered the tiny living-room. "Oh, it's you. And where do you suppose your father might be?" Nell thought apprehensively of the shouting and jostling outside the station, but before she could either answer or evade the question her mother went on: "He'll be out with those agitators, I know it. He has no consideration for my nerves. None at all."

Julia Meredith still boasted dark brown hair without a fleck of grey, and finely arched eyebrows that were almost black. She could have looked as young and trim as her daughter; but perverse melancholy had bitten sharp little lines into her face and sketched thin webs of discontent around the corners of her mouth. By firelight she still looked beautiful— if only, thought Nell with a familiar exasperation, she could have been persuaded to sit upright instead of dramatising that discontent into a slump forward, head drooping and shoulders sagging.

"When I think of what I gave up for him. But then, I've never reproached him. I've only myself to blame. Only myself. But all the same, he might make *some* effort . . ."

She stared into the flames. Nell wondered what she really saw there, and how true any of it was in her own mind or in the real world.

As a little girl, Nell had asked why lots of other children had grandparents and aunts and uncles, while she seemed to have none. Her father had quietly explained that his mother and his father, a notable preacher, had died years before. Julia had first brushed aside questions—"You wouldn't understand, you're not old enough"—and then one day, with one of her distraught gestures, lowering her head and clutching her left temple, she had said that it didn't bear talking of. Her own mother had died long ago and her father was as good as dead—"Or *we're* as good as dead." Then much later, in dreamy mood, she indulged in vague fantasies of a sheltered upbringing and a gracious way of life from which Owen had somehow snatched her, depriving her of all they had been used to. "But I'll never let a word of blame pass my lips, he knows that." Once she said, out of the blue: "Poor Eleanor, you could have been an Honourable, or something like that, if I hadn't been so . . . but no, there's no point in talking of might-have-beens."

Nell was left with an impression of a lost fairy-tale world through which she and her mother might have floated in fine silks, rustling out from a gracious home across acres of gracious parkland on which the sun always shone. Instead of which they passed their days in gale-bitten streets and this draughty little house; and at night Nell huddled into a flannelette nightgown.

As she grew older the roseate vision dimmed. Her mother was, she suspected, like other disgruntled boasters of the town: boys bragging of their fathers as skippers of great ships in the eastern trade when in fact they served as downtrodden mates on shabby coasters, or the girl who had explained her father's two-year absence as being due to a prosperous engagement in the spice trade when everyone knew he was serving a Dutch gaol sentence after a drunken brawl. Yet, having once been lured into Julia's nostalgic romances, Nell still half-believed there must somewhere have been some grain of truth in it. One day she might find that truth: if not the country mansion which was so often implied, at least a dignified, well-appointed retreat in some picturesque village.

There was a swirl of cold as the outer door opened and closed again. Nell's father came into the room, taking off his rubbed, shiny overcoat.

"So you're back at last! Don't you know how worried I've been?"

Owen Meredith hung the coat in the alcove by the door, stooped towards Nell to peck at her cheek, and then kissed his wife and patted her head.

"Nothing to worry about," he said.

"Nothing to worry about? You've been down at that wretched meeting, haven't you?"

"I observed the deplorable methods of recruitment, yes." He still had a strong Welsh lilt, the cadences of the preacher he had never become in spite of his father's years in the ministry. "Deplorable. And in defence of the Turks, of all people."

"We'll be in trouble." Julia stared into the bars of the grate. "Sooner or later we'll be hounded out of this place, or it'll be burnt round our ears."

"Oh, come now!"

Owen smiled dismissively and settled on the other side of the fireplace. Julia gripped the poker and drove it between the bars. Wearily Nell recognised the storm signals. She got up. "Father, I do think the window needs rearranging. Things are all over the place."

Her mother, caught in preparation for another petulant jibe, gaped. "At this time of day?"

"Some of the pamphlets are going yellow round the edges. And there are several books nobody's ever going to buy. Why don't we deal with it now?"

Her father, puzzled, was reluctant to get up from his chair. But Nell

20

nudged his shoulder; and, belatedly awakened to the impending squabble she was anxious to avert, he got to his feet and followed her into the shop.

"You'll never see reason, will you?" said Julia as they left the fireside. "Heaven knows where it will end."

Owen risked a rueful grin at his daughter, but Nell carefully did not respond. She had learned while still a child not to take sides. Keeping a balance between her father's inadequate idealism and her mother's bitterness was a precarious task. She would not, if she could help it, tip that balance one way or the other. At the same time she wanted to seize them and shake them and, young as she might be, tell them to grow up. She was tired of making decisions for them, smoothing things over between them. If only there could be someone else to make the decisions—and make them correctly.

She turned up the light in the window. They leaned over the gently sloping frontage to reclaim some books that had slid against the glass. Behind them they heard Julia approaching, and pretended to be engrossed in their work..

"And what time will you be ready to eat?"

Then Julia screamed.

Nell's gaze jolted upwards. A man's face swam through the evening haze. She felt her heart pound; but was somehow not at all surprised.

"He's only looking at our stock," said Owen.

"No," said Nell, "he's only pretending to." She turned away with a pile of books and set them on the counter.

"Whatever do you mean, Eleanor?"

Keeping her back to the window, Nell told them in a few terse sentences.

"I knew it!" cried Julia. "I knew it would come to this. A government spy. You can tell by the way he's looking at those books."

They turned with one accord towards the window again. The man had disappeared. But then came the scratch of wire inside the wall, and the tinkle of the front door bell.

"Don't let him in."

"We shall have to," said Owen, "to find out what he wants."

Julia reached out a fluttering hand but did not grip his sleeve or try to hold him back. It was as if she wished all her direst prophecies to be fulfilled.

Owen opened the door.

The stranger took off his hard-crowned bowler and dipped the briefest of bows. "Mr. Meredith?"

"That is so."

"And"—he looked past Owen—"Miss Meredith. And . . . it used to be Miss Bostock, didn't it?"

Julia let out a little moan.

His eyes were as Nell remembered them from that morning: aggressive yet warily respectful; assessing and calculating. He went on: "My name's Hesketh. Your father sent me, Miss Bostock . . . Mrs. Meredith . . . to see how fortune was favouring you. How you were all getting on."

Owen said, "After all these years?"

"There's been many a tide making and ebbing, yes, true enough. You might well say there's one on the turn right this very minute." Hesketh plodded into the shop, looking about it with the faintest twist of that dour mouth. He wasted no time in continuing. "You had two brothers, Mrs. Meredith."

"Making themselves rich, no doubt. If my father allows them to participate." Julia was making a shaky attempt to sound disdainful.

"They are dead, ma'am."

"Dead—both of them?"

"Both. Your older brother died in a skirmish off Shanghai. Some sort of clash over opium smuggling, we heard."

"And Harry?"

"His wife died in childbirth. Very sad. He joined the army. Mr. Bostock didn't much care for that, but Mr. Harry went anyway, and not many months ago he was off to the Crimea. Died of the fever in Bulgaria before he got there."

"And their children?" asked Owen in a mild tone, which Nell sensed must conceal some important realisation.

"Mr. Arthur never did marry. And Mr. Harry, with his wife dying the way she did . . . no, none."

"I see."

"Do you?" fidgeted Julia. "What do you see?"

Owen was sizing Hesketh up. "You've come to claim all of the family that Mr. Bostock has left. That's it, isn't it?"

"More or less, sir. That was the idea, more or less."

"I take it you've been studying us from a distance before making up your mind as to whether we deserve this reconciliation."

"Mr. Bostock instructed me to see how you were getting on before I declared myself."

"I can imagine that. Yes." Owen was pale with a taut anger that he showed rarely on anything other than the most controversial social issues. "He hasn't changed, has he? Everything organised on his own

22

terms, with his slaves dancing to the tune as usual—even those he threw out twenty years ago."

"Home," Julia marvelled. "He wants us to come home."

"Assuming," said Owen, "that Mr. Hesketh condescends to give us good marks."

Hesketh's laugh was half-deferential and half-derisive. "Mr. Bostock did rather hope . . ." He stopped, tantalising them.

Owen took him up. "Mr. Bostock did hope there would be a grandson."

"I won't deny that, sir."

"Then we'll be a big disappointment. You'd better tell him the worst, and we can forget the whole thing."

"I don't think he'll want that, Mr. Meredith. I'm sure that the way I report back to him, he'll be glad to see you all again. And I hope you'll remember me, and what I've done for you, Mr. Meredith."

"Home," said Julia again.

Owen said: "You have been following my daughter about, spying on her and on us, setting yourself up in judgment, and now you're suggesting we should—"

"Mr. Meredith, please. I've had a job to do, and I've done it. I've worked a long time for Mr. Bostock and I know his ways, and how he'll take things. You'll be all right, that I promise. But there's things he'll stand and things he won't stand, so for your own sakes I'll give you a word of advice here and now. Miss Meredith'll do nicely, very nicely. But what Mr. Bostock won't care for is all those revolutionary sentiments of yours. They won't do for him."

"They never did," said Julia plaintively.

"Best keep 'em down a bit, if you want to be comfortable."

"The question won't arise. We're not going."

"But of course we're going." Julia held out her cotton skirt and swirled it from side to side, seeing herself dancing and pirouetting in richer silks, with lace about the hem and looped ribbon at her waist. She waltzed closer to Nell, putting a hand on Nell's shoulder and squeezing it. "We're going home."

BOSTOCK'S BROW was not the home that Julia had conjured up in Nell's imagination. A massive sandstone house on the crest of a hill, its domination of the crowded terraces and warehouses below had all the lowering imperiousness of her grandfather's bushy right eyebrow.

Thick shrubbery guarded house and grounds from the road. Beside the entrance gates squatted a sandstone lodge with podgy crènellations. The front door of this cottage was nearly always open, and inside sat a man wearing a gilt-braided blue uniform and peaked cap, which gave him something of the air of a retired sea captain. Occasionally he left his post to patrol the grounds, but managed to be back at the gate whenever a visitor's carriage or tradesman's van sought admission.

Along the western rim of the lawn, the high protective hedge sank abruptly—clipped low to preserve an uninterrupted view, even from the ground-floor windows, over roofs and chimneys, of the traffic on that wide, grey, clamorous thoroughfare that was the river Mersey.

On the afternoon of her first day Nell was taken by her grandfather to the large drawing-room on the first floor. A telescope was permanently mounted in the central window embrasure, with a heavy oak chair close by: not for sitting in, but so that Jesse Bostock, pushing himself across the room with the aid of his stick, could lean against its high back while sweeping the river prospect through his glass.

"Well, what do you make of it all, girl?"

He spoke as if it were all his personal domain: the entire port, the river, both banks of docks and yards, and the low hills beyond.

What *did* she make of it?

Nell had not known what to expect at the end of their journey. She remembered her mother's daydreams and her own vague picture of a country house, sunshine, and green meadows. But the reality was another town at the water's edge: no romantic rural landscape but grimy, bustling Liverpool.

"Well, then?" demanded her grandfather.

No suave aristocrat or country gentleman this, but a stocky, bull-headed merchant with large hands and a large voice. His heavy tweed jacket hung askew from his left shoulder, dipping always towards the silver knob of his stick; his neckcloth was knotted with the thickness of a mooring warp.

Nell peered through the telescope.

At the northwesterly limit of its arc began a huge granite wall, sheltering acres of docks and plantations of masts. From one copse of bare timber she saw sail billow in the breeze as a ship manoeuvred slowly out into the tideway. A paddle tug was hauling a brace of small three-masters downstream, another towed a string of coal flats in towards a quay, and in and out of the main traffic scurried ferry-boats, which let out spasmodic gusts of black smoke as they swung to stem the tide at the landing-stage. Nell scanned the far bank, which bristled with chimneys and funnels often indistinguishable one from another, the teetering derricks of shipbuilding yards, and an occasional forlorn church spire. Canvas blurred across her vision as a large barque rode proudly into midstream.

At her shoulder Jesse Bostock said: "They're running up a signal on Bidston. Whose is it?" Standing back so that he could see the glass, she watched the jerk of his blunt chin, heard the grunt of recognition in his throat. "Mm, yes, one of MacIver's."

A burgee fluttered on a tower across the water, close to a hilltop lighthouse. Old Jesse straightened up with an involuntary wince, and explained.

"Whole chain of semaphore stations, all the way from Holyhead. The moment a ship's sighted and identified, a signal starts on its way. Gives the owner or charterer time to work out when he'll need to be on the dock to clear his cargo."

From between two ranks of warehouses rose thick gouts of smoke, as if three or four old men were surreptitiously smoking their pipes in the lee of the towering, pitted red-brick walls. The extent of it all was unnerving after the compactness of the fishing port Nell had so recently left.

"Well, then." Bostock sounded grumpy. Perhaps he was impatient with her inability to say what he wanted or expected of her. He stumped to the door. "Let's try the library. Maybe find your mother and father there reminiscing, eh?" When she still did not respond he waited for her to draw level and snorted: "What do you say to taking up where your father left off? How would you like that?"

"I don't quite know what . . . I mean, when you say he left off . . ."

"You mean they never told you?" He saved his breath on the way downstairs, thumping stick and feet heavily on each tread. At the bottom he went on: "You don't know the romantic story—how your father met your mother and took her away from me?" They reached another of the house's imposing doors, adorned with a convolution of gilded scroll-work. Bostock rested his weight on the ornate octagonal knob. "Supposed to be cataloguing my library. That's what I engaged him for. Spent all his time making up to my daughter and in the end ran off with her."

Julia opened the door from within so that he was caught off balance. "We didn't run off, father. You drove us out and told us never to come back."

"Well, I've brought you back now." He waved Nell on into the library. "But I'd say one of you owed it to me to finish the job properly. Hesketh reports you've been working in some sort of library, Eleanor, so it should suit you."

The rows of books behind glass doors looked less like a personal choice than a mass purchase of bindings to give the room the air a prospering merchant desired.

"Until you get married," he added. "Only this time there'll be no running off with some penniless ne'er-do-well."

Without consulting their wishes he decided that now was the time for a conducted tour of the house. Julia did not protest, happy to reminisce: "Oh, do you remember when I fell off the rocking horse and you were so angry . . . and fancy this urn still being here . . . and this mirror, how I used to stop every time I came along and . . ." She stared at her reflection and at Nell's beside her. The gaiety faded. Creases tightened about her mouth. She drew a fingernail across a stain below her right eye that would not be rubbed off. Nell saw her own face new and unfamiliar in this unfamiliar setting: framed within the mirror's white and gold frame by a helmet of mahogany-coloured hair streaked with bronze; blue-grey eyes so cool and so remarkably assured when in truth she was sure of nothing.

At some stage of the proceedings her father joined them. He was very subdued, glancing out of every window they passed and not liking what he saw.

"We'll have tea now." A silver tray was waiting for them in a small sitting-room opening on to the terrace. "Tomorrow morning," said Bostock as Julia poured from the silver pot, "a couple of girls'll come in from the workhouse. Good school for female servants there. A maid for you and one for Eleanor. If you don't like 'em, send 'em back and I'll find another two. And tomorrow afternoon the dressmaker's coming."

Owen said, "If my wife is in need of new clothes, I—"

"A coming home present." That was that. Bostock jabbed a thumb at Owen. "While you come and have a look at the docks with me. Get some notion of what to do when your time comes to take over."

"We do have business of our own to get back to," said Owen stiffly. "We've managed all these years our own way—"

"Bostock Navigation will be yours when I'm gone. You can manage *that* your own way. And afterwards"—he glanced at Nell—"well, it's a pity you couldn't have managed a boy, but there we are. She can marry soundly. We're not sunk yet."

Nell, incensed by her father's inadequacy and her grandfather's assumption that a mere snap of his fingers would command obedience, burst out: "If you hadn't managed a girl yourself, you'd be left with nothing now, wouldn't you?"

"Nell, how dare you speak so cruelly to your grandfather?"

"Whatever it is you want of us, you'll have to take what's ours to give." Nell thought of the old ladies at the circulating library who demanded happy endings after peril and misunderstanding, all smoothed out for their sensitive palates. "Once a story's in print," she said boldly, "there's little chance of getting the author to rewrite the ending."

Bostock's face burned purple. "You've got a salty tongue." Then a laugh snorted itself out like a bung forced from a barrel. "You'll need it in these parts. Ha! Should have been a boy." This time it was meant as a clumsy compliment. Before she could argue this, too, he went on, "Tell you what, girl. Come with us tomorrow. Start learning what you'll need to know about the river, if you want to make some man a good wife."

"If I make any man a wife, I trust I'll find something more interesting to talk about than the river."

"If you're not interested in the river," said her mother with arch flippancy, "you'll get no conversation in this town."

Bostock rapped his stick on the parquet flooring. "Anything this town's got comes from there. Don't any of you ever forget it. Plenty of folk are getting too high and mighty, playing at being public benefactors, keeping themselves to Lord Street and Bold Street instead of walking the docks every day. Or attending to the news on Exchange Flags every day. They only breathe and eat because of that river and what it brings and what it carries away. The day Liverpool forgets that, God help the place— or the devil take it."

Julia nodded, anxious to placate him and cancel out the years of estrangement. But his words really meant nothing to her. House and grounds, comfort and spaciousness and prosperity: these were what counted, uncontaminated by the squalor and bustle below. The bad days were over. Nothing must be allowed to spoil the days to come.

The following morning Julia was happily braced to meet the workhouse girls and find fault with them. And Nell felt that the dressmaker, poor woman, was doomed to a gruelling afternoon.

For herself, she settled in the brougham beside her father, facing her grandfather across the narrow gap. The old man's knee repeatedly jarred against her father's, and several times his stick rapped Nell's ankle. They braced themselves as they went down a steep hill with the brake shoe rasping a spasmodic shudder beneath them. After a short, level side street there came an even more precipitous descent. High buildings closed in, then parted again to release the carriage on to a broad parade bathed in damp, wintry light.

Down here the whole perspective changed. The port was no longer a vast panorama etched with spars and sails, funnels and streamers of smoke, but a rowdy congestion of carts and sheds, men and beasts and bundles, of vessels grown suddenly large and warehouses rearing up into the sky. A few steps to her left and she could have walked straight off the quay into the water. Men in cloth caps, with sacks over their shoulders, trotted dizzyingly along the edge. Somewhere a bell was clanging insistently. From the far end of a roofed storage area came the clatter of gangplank chains.

Bostock, levering himself down from the carriage, waited for the other two to join him and then limped purposefully over the stone setts of the roadway.

"The Goree Piazzas." He waved proudly up at the towering storeys on the landward side of the thoroughfare, lettered with the names and slogans of English and American passenger agencies.

"Under which," said Owen quietly, "the traders of this town kept slaves by the thousand chained in cellars, waiting to be shipped off to misery."

"Never was as bad as you would-be reformers painted it. A lot of those darkies are happier in America, and a damn sight warmer, than the Irish we've got crawling about the cellars of Merseyside."

"Every brick in this city," Owen insisted with the preaching fervour of his Welsh ancestors, "every filthy brick, was cemented with the blood of a negro."

28

Bostock stumped on to the perimeter of a wide basin opening directly on to the river. Nell caught him up. Side by side they went round the inlet to the river wall. Ahead ran a marine parade with seats facing out over the Mersey: deserted, for it was a working day and a cold one.

Small waves lapped against stone and timber. Fingers of weed dangled from landing-stage chains. A packet boat flying the Stars and Stripes was mooring to an iron buoy in midstream. Before the operation was half-completed a little steamer went bustling in to collect mail bags.

Nell listened to some of Jesse's barked explanations, and let others roll over her. She was acutely aware of her father's aversion to grappling with the jargon of this world where he had never belonged and to which he had never expected to be summoned back. Rather than look at his glum face, Nell turned her attention to a timber boat being brought to in the reach by Brunswick Dock; watched canvas take the breeze as a tall ship set out towards far oceans. One furled its white splendour; others rode at anchor in the bay, waiting for tide or tug.

All her poor father wished was the draughty seclusion of his Lowestoft bookshop and discussion with kindred spirits.

When they turned back from the promenade it was to see a dingy two-master berthing. Noise blew along the wharf like a storm-tossed wave, and with it came the smell. Cattle and sheep groaned and stamped and bleated as hatches crashed back. Their stench mingled with a stench of sickness; squeals and bellows made a chorus with human moaning and retching.

"From Dublin." Jesse Bostock regarded that as sufficient explanation.

As soon as the craft was secured, windlasses began to lift animals out of the hold like so many bales of cotton. Human beings packed tightly on deck were squeezed aside to allow clearance for the cargo. Then, as clumsy and unsteady as a flock of stampeding beasts, men and women began reeling down the gangplank. Nell saw incredulously that while four-legged travellers had been sheltered below the deck, these other stumbling wretches must have crossed the Irish Sea without cover: hair was dank and matted, the smell of sodden clothes seeped through the smell of drink and vomit; a child in a woman's bedraggled arms was shaking as from the ague.

"They're allowed to travel like that, worse than cattle?"

"It's their choice. They pay enough for a place to stand, and that's what they get."

As the sick, dizzy Irish came off the boat they were surrounded by a horde of predators. Shouting men waved tickets or pushed carts into the throng, snatching up pitiful bundles of luggage before the owners could protest.

"This way, come on, get you the best lodgings in town."

"Tickets for tomorrow's sailing, good and cheap. No, don't pay no attention to that thieving bugger over there . . ."

"Come on, then, come *on*, if you want a bed at all . . ."

An emigration officer and a police constable tried to push through and wave the parasites off. But they circled around, dodged in again, chose the flesh from which to draw blood and skilfully lodged their barbs.

"Can't someone stop it?" Nell was almost sobbing.

She heard her father draw a shivering breath of disgust.

They had both seen cattle manhandled across Lowestoft quays and along miry streets, often enough, and seen fishermen blundering tipsily ashore after days in a North Sea gale; but never anything so frightening as these wan, undernourished creatures without the stamina, surely, to undertake any longer sea crossing.

"They'll get over it," said her grandfather. "The next stage is easier. A sight easier than it used to be." He contemplated, unmoved, a woman shrugging a shawl up over her neck while stooping to keep the cold wind off a child at her side. "Five or six weeks it used to take by sail, in tubs worse than those Dublin cattle boats. Could be half as much again, sometimes. Now those of us who've introduced steamships have cut that to twelve days or so. Twelve days—and we'll cut that down, too, before we're much older!"

The three of them stepped back a few paces as the human tide beat around them and then flowed on towards the town. A score of stragglers limped in the rear, or put their bundles down for a while until they could get their land legs. One couple leaned together, afraid to move apart: the woman bracing one leg against an old leather bag, the man dwarfed in a threadbare overcoat with sleeves down to his fingertips.

Impulsively Nell moved to pick up the bag. "Let me help. If you can tell me where you're going—"

"They're goin' wi' us."

Another woman had appeared on the scene, her hand closing on the bag to tug it away from Nell. Behind her, two men were closing in.

Nell said, "This lady isn't well. I'm sure she—"

"She'll be all right when we've settled her in."

"If you know her—"

"This is *our* stretch, allus has been, so hands off."

Nails stabbed at Nell's wrist just above her glove, so that she gasped and let go.

Her grandfather let out an ominous growl. He and her father came forward, but the two men met them and jostled Bostock to one side.

Owen slid and fell with his right shoulder against a bollard. Half a dozen dazed and cowering onlookers edged back out of harm's way.

Nell, feeling blood trickle warmly into her glove, lashed out in fury. The woman released the bag, but one of the men grabbed it and held on. Nell made a lunge at him.

"Look, I'm warnin' yer . . ."

Somebody sprang from a stone step above, landing between the two men. He swung a neat, unhurried punch. The one with the crumpled leather bag swore and doubled up. The other wiped a fist across his nose and raised it high.

"If you're interested in warnings, here's one from me to you." The newcomer's cool American accent was more effective than any ranting anger would have been. "None of you's going to make one cent out of this. Tomorrow's ship goes under the United States flag. Anyone I choose to identify at embarkation as an undesirable runner or crooked money-lender doesn't get his victims aboard. You hear me, sir . . . lady? Stay clear of them, whatever they tell you. If they come near, we apply for their prosecution by the Liverpool authorities, and we check money and tickets and the belongings of every passenger, and track down anyone who's rooked them."

"Which'll take you all of a fortnight," the woman rasped scornfully.

"Which we'll take if we have to." The young man eyed the fist threatening him, until it slackened and fell to the man's side. "We're aiming at having clean ships on our Atlantic run, and a clean departure from this side. So clear off, you three, before you're in real trouble."

There was a moment's suspense. Nell felt her own hand clenching within her glove. Then, covering their departure with a jangle of laughter, the two men and their woman swaggered away.

"I'm obliged to you." Jesse held out a hand. "Mr. Whitlaw, isn't it?"

"Paul Whitlaw, sir. Yes. Good of you to remember me."

"Good of you to be here," said Jesse with a hard-lipped grin. "Well, Mr. Whitlaw, I don't think you know my son-in-law. Mr. Meredith."

"I've not had the pleasure, no, sir."

"And my granddaughter, Eleanor."

The young man's handshake was firm and sure. His pale, serious face was capped by hair as flaxen as that of any of the Dutchmen who had appeared so frequently in the streets of Lowestoft. But many of those visiting Dutchmen had proved hard, quarrelsome drinkers. It was difficult to imagine this staid, clear-eyed Mr. Whitlaw drinking at all freely or relaxing the stiffness of his manner—or of his high collar and neatly buttoned suit.

31

His smile, too, was formal; but frankly appreciative as he looked into Nell's eyes.

"Thank you," she said, "for coming to the rescue."

"It's not often I get presented with the chance to save English ladies in distress."

Slowly he relinquished her hand.

Jesse, abruptly grumpy, said, "I didn't know you had the authority, Mr. Whitlaw, to lay down what would be and would not be permitted on embarkation of one of your craft."

"I haven't, sir."

"You sounded most convincing a few minutes ago."

"I didn't fancy any display of violence. Not before this lady." Nell was sure this winning phrase had struck him on the spur of the moment. He looked a trifle too pleased with it. But it was flattering that he should want to preen himself before her. "I thought I'd try rough talk first. Praise be, it worked."

"So you're not in shipping after all, Mr. Whitlaw?" asked Nell politely.

"Only in what you might call a supporting role. My line is merchant banking, Miss Meredith. I'm over here on two years' study with the American Chamber of Commerce."

"Whose main purpose," said Jesse, "is to feed its homeland with news of our cargoes and financial transactions so they can learn how to cut our throats. Stealing ideas for steamboats from the Birkenhead yards—"

"I'd take the liberty of reminding you, sir"—a faint flush etched the pale, reserved features—"that steamboats were pioneered on our own Mississippi."

Bostock slapped his shoulder. "Well, I'll say it again. We're obliged to you, Mr. Whitlaw."

Owen, nursing his injured arm, winced as Paul Whitlaw shook hands with each of them again. The young man's respectful tone was touched with an awkward condescension as he turned away to the shivering pair who crouched, still fearful, over the bag they had so nearly surrendered.

"If you'll come with me, I'll direct you to a reputable boarding-house not ten minutes from here. And I guarantee you'll not be fleeced."

They watched him go, matching his step to that of his charges with a sort of rigid gentleness. Some fifty yards away he looked back once and, smiling, raised his hat to Nell.

Jesse Bostock grunted. "Well, I'd say that was enough for one day." With some relish, enjoying the incident in retrospect, he began to hum tunelessly to himself and led the way at his steady shuffle back along the waterfront to the waiting carriage. It was where he had decreed it should be. Everything was where Jesse Bostock decreed it should be, for so long as he was alive.

That evening the two men sat late over the port. And the next evening, and the one after that. "I do hope your father will make an effort to live up to his responsibilities," said Julia fretfully. "Such an opportunity, he mustn't be ungrateful this time, he *mustn't*." But Nell felt sorrier than ever for her father in the mornings. Unused to drink but not quite ascetically sure enough of himself to refuse it, he suffered excruciating headaches. In spite of this his father-in-law callously, almost vengefully, heaped piles of reports and old ledgers on him—"These'll give you some idea of what I was talking about"—until, at the beginning of their second week, he unceremoniously commandeered Nell's company and took her out on her own, leaving Owen behind.

This was the day on which her attention was forcibly drawn to Edmund Gresham for the first time. She was in no hurry for a second glimpse. Her grandfather's blunt suggestion, little less than a command, rang in her ears for the rest of the day, jarred into dissonance by the echoing undercurrent of Hesketh's obsequious support.

And late in the afternoon, as dusk robbed the grey river of its last glow, he came out with it again. "Your father's not up to it, you know. Waste of time. Never really supposed he'd take the helm."

"Grandfather, if you have so little faith—"

"I've got faith," he said fiercely. "Faith in what's left to be done, what can still be done. But I've told you, it's not up to me any more. It's all for . . . for somebody else now. So . . ."

He might have been speaking to the statue of a woman some yards from them, an almost faceless statue on the half-tide basin pier, nose and lips scoured by the salty wind, peering with forlorn eyes forever westward. But Nell knew that every word was directed at herself.

"Think on," he said. "It's all up to you now. Has to be."

Already he had virtually discarded her father. Convinced his time was running out, he was impatient for the future to be shaped according to his own dictates. There was only one reason for the Merediths staying on now: that his granddaughter might yield herself to a dynastic union like those of all the acquisitive kings and queens and petty princelings throughout all the greed and conflict of European history.

Nell vowed quite calmly and resolutely that nothing in this world would ever induce her to marry Edmund Gresham.

EDMUND GRESHAM glanced reluctantly up at the clock over his desk. It was time to go back to the house and change. He would sooner have stayed here with bills and manifests and the bulky Gresham ledgers than turn his attention to dressing up and going to the ball. But on this occasion it was advisable to be seen. He pushed back his chair.

Outside, a raucous shout down an alley provoked a gruff answer. The end of the alley also caught the clang of a fog bell as some craft made its way up river. From the window he could see yellow wreaths of fog and a slimy gloss on the cobbles. In here it was warm and cosy, more a home than the imposing house in Falkner Square could ever be: warm and still haunted in the friendliest way by the jovial ghost of their father, thumping this same desk and declaiming, planning, building castles in the air . . . and factories and warehouses in the Far East. In this musty room with walls painted the drab brown and green of some Nonconformist Sunday School the plans had been made for Gresham's part in breaking the East India Company's monopoly through Indian ports, and forcing new trade on China up the Yangtze. Here "Grinder" Gresham had leased ships, found cargoes for export, and reached out over the world to build up a network of agents who would ensure that return cargoes were waiting. Here he juggled with fluctuating demands for seasonal goods and with the vagaries of freight rates. Letters of credit and discounted bills were weighed in the shrewd balance of his mind. When things turned out well he had a rich, gratifying laugh; if they went wrong he still laughed, moving at his usual pace and showing no fear.

When the time came to buy his own ship, instead of chartering, Edmund's father did not hesitate but bought two. He was happier taking all his own risks than he had ever been transferring some to other shoulders. Three ships, four ships—and instead of being a liability the fleet was soon self-financing.

Edmund had been young during the times of greatest struggle but remembered the tense, exhilarating atmosphere of those decisive days. It had never quite seeped away from the counting-house. He still found the office as invigorating as his younger brother was to find the ragamuffins of the back entries and, later, the girls streaming every day off the ferry or serving in basement chop-houses. Many an hour Edmund had spent, rapt, on the stool in the corner while his father talked rumbustiously to himself, concluded contracts with a slap of the hand, interviewed visitors, berated his staff or boomed encouragement at them, ignoring his son for an entire morning or, on impulse, drawing him into a discussion and asking—with growing attentiveness as he grew older—for his opinions. Edmund remembered the day when they decided to finance their own lighterage company; remembered them putting in hand an ambitious building programme in the shipyards across the river; remembered a thousand excitements, doubts, and disappointments.

Many a merchant who had bought a fine house for his family in Rodney Street or further out on the fringes of the town maintained a little apartment over his counting-house, excusing overnight absences with stories of night arrivals of delayed cargoes, sailings postponed because of storms beyond the bar, and sudden needs to assemble emergency crew. Most of the stories were true: wind and tide made rigid timetables impossible for sailing ships, and even the new generation of steamers could run low on fuel because of unforeseen gales, depleted supplies at coaling stations, or engine failures when it became necessary to hoist sail and limp shamefacedly home. And the merchants loved their sanctuaries and the pipe and cigar smoke, the boasts and excuses and tall stories from far corners of the world. They were more at home with their rowdy neighbours in teeming warrens behind Dale Street and Howard Street than with the occupants of those imposing mansions that testified to success without contributing to it.

Some men, it was true, had been known to profane those sanctuaries by sharing their nights with women who would not have been invited to Abercromby Square or the houses of Prince's Park. Edmund suspected that Malcolm had more than once brought some of his conquests here.

Uneasily he tried to envisage what happened, and where—on the old leather couch, or perhaps in some strange contortion in . . . no: he preferred, after all, not to imagine it. For Malcolm it was so cheap and casual and easy. Everything had always been too easy for Malcolm.

Methodically Edmund locked each drawer of his desk, turned off the light, locked the office door and went out into the courtyard. Light glowed through the archway from the ornately engraved window of a public house on the corner. He made his way past it to the livery stable beside the Custom House, where the Greshams had a standing arrangement for stabling the horses on which they rode in every morning.

As he turned the bay's head uphill, the eerie throb of a steamer's gong followed them through the fog. Edmund glanced back into the dun haze. He would have done better to keep his evening clothes in the office and change there. In Falkner Square he felt less and less at ease, with that creature of Malcolm's padding about and Malcolm forever shamelessly touching her.

Lights glowed in all the front windows as he reached the square and rode down the passage to the stables. Another of Malcolm's extravagances—turning the gas up full as he entered a room, and leaving it burning when he left.

Edmund let himself in from the stables by the side door. He needed no more than a glimmer of light from above to guide him upstairs. Knowing every tread and turn, he could in the event of a gas failure have walked through the house, just as through his counting-house, without grazing a corner of a single piece of furniture.

On the first landing he turned towards his room. Before he could reach it, the bathroom door beside him opened. A shadow drifted past him under the subdued landing light, crossing the corridor and taking on substance: taking on flesh and becoming Poppy, Malcolm's woman. She was naked, and her bare feet went gliding over the carpet without a sound. Finding Edmund nearby, she did not flinch. Only when she reached the door of the room that Malcolm had given her—their mother's old room—did she pause and turn.

"Good evening." She enunciated it carefully as if she suspected the words might, after all, be a joke that Malcolm had slyly foisted on her.

"Good evening." The musky scent of her sleek, ochre body taunted Edmund's nostrils. He looked away, just as Malcolm emerged from the bedroom that had been their father's, also barefoot but wearing black trousers and a frilled white shirt open to the waist, doing up the buttons as he came.

"Edmund. Torn yourself away from the figures? Time for a drink before we go, then." Malcolm glanced at the girl and said something in a language that meant nothing to his brother. She went on into her room, closing the door behind her without the faintest click. Malcolm said, "That last consignment of Madeira was a fine one. When you've dressed you'll find me downstairs, with a glass ready poured for you." He caught Edmund's involuntary glance at the adjoining door. "Not shocked, are you? She's so very decorative, walking about the house like that."

"Mrs. Earnshaw's the one who'll be shocked. I wouldn't want us to lose a housekeeper that good—or old McGrath."

"Do 'em good. Might put ideas in their aging heads." When Edmund was silent, Malcolm went on, "You wouldn't raise an eyebrow if she were a classical statue, all meditative in marble at the end of the banisters, would you?"

"She's not a classical statue, and she's not marble."

"No, by God, she's not, is she?"

Edmund's heart was beating fast as he shut himself in his room. It was not the brisk ride from the office to Falkner Square, nor the climb up the stairs. He leaned back against the door. *Not marble. No, by God, she's not.* She moved and breathed, and danced—to Malcolm's tune.

He took out his square-cut black dress coat with its close-fitting sleeves, and the strapped black trousers with which he had managed all these years. There were so few social functions he needed to attend: really needed to attend, that was.

When he entered the front drawing-room, Malcolm was standing near the wine cupboard. He turned with a glass in each hand, holding out one to Edmund. At the same time he summed up Edmund's clothes. Over a year ago he had jokingly said that no one under sixty could possibly wear an outfit of that vintage. Today, attired in a midnight blue jacket, silk waistcoat and trousers that Edmund had thought to be black but now seemed darkly to echo the blue, he made no comment at all; and the fact that he did not smile made it worse.

Edmund said, more curtly than he had intended, "I'm still waiting for the rest of your report on the Canton situation."

"I thought I'd finished it."

"Not a word about the negotiations with those new agents. We do have to make some decisions."

Malcolm raised his glass. "Canton's a long way away. We could easily have been five or six days late in arriving, or been blown off course on our way back. Let's pretend that happened, and I promise to work hard next week after I've rested and cleared my head."

"You call it rest?"

"You don't honestly blame me, do you?" Malcolm looked contentedly into the gleaming depths of his glass. "Funny, you know. The more you strip her down, the more mysterious Poppy becomes."

"Mysterious—to *you?*"

"Yes, to me. All those weeks on board, and now back here, and she's still a mystery."

"Is her name really Poppy?"

"Haven't the faintest idea, old lad. I called her that because her mother was involved in some opium smuggling trouble. A bit of a fracas on the wharf. If I hadn't whisked her away they'd have hauled her off with the mother."

"You just took her like that: simply took her aboard?"

"Better than leaving her to what they might have done. Someone said something about her father being French. Not been seen for years. There's a lot of anti-European feeling up the Yangtze again, and they could easily have picked on her for that on top of everything else."

"So you shipped her home purely out of gallantry?"

A few remaining drops of ruby liquid swirled in the glass. "It was the resemblance, as much as anything. The *Naomi* figurehead—astonishing. I felt it had to be an omen."

"Not the sort I'd have thought the crew would care for."

"Bad luck to have a woman aboard? Oh, but Teddy, there are two sides to that tale. They don't mind a wooden woman for'ard: she conquers the waves. So I showed them the resemblance between the two, told 'em she wasn't an albatross but an extra safeguard. And we did have a lovely run home." Malcolm beamed. "I convinced them."

Yes, he would have done that. One could almost hear the persuasive ring of his words as he talked them into it.

"This opium business," said Edmund grimly. "Did she tell you—"

"Can hardly tell me anything. I've picked up only a few words of the lingo, and she only knows what English I've taught her."

"What would that amount to?"

"Precious little. Don't want her to learn too much too soon. It would spoil that mystery we were talking about." He reached for the decanter. "I pass on a few words she needs from time to time, that's all."

"Words such as . . . ?"

"Oh, Teddy, I wouldn't want to turn your delicate ears pink." Malcolm glanced at the door. "I wonder how long she'll take to get ready. We ought to be leaving fairly soon."

"You're bringing her to the ball, then."

"Did you think I wouldn't?"

38

Of course Edmund had thought no such thing. But he had hoped. He said, "I'm not sure it's quite fitting."

"It's the Young Foreigners' Ball, and what's Poppy if not a young foreigner?"

Edmund thought that many of the ladies due to attend the function might have their own answers to that. But reproof at this stage would merely add a more defiant sparkle to Malcolm's effervescent mood.

"After all," Malcolm added, "we can make a virtue of displaying our trademark to the public."

"What trademark?"

"I've been meaning to talk to you about that. Or would you prefer it submitted to you in my very best handwriting?"

"Go on. Tell me."

"I've already told you I couldn't resist her because she was so like our *Naomi* figurehead. The crew felt it too. So I'm of the opinion we should make that the Gresham trademark. On our letter headings, bills of lading, invoices, everything. A sculpture over the new warehouse, maybe. That kind of thing."

"We'd be a laughing stock."

"Oh, no. Folks would be startled. There'd be a harvest of dirty jokes, no doubt. But that would do us no harm at all."

Edmund said, "Do you propose to marry her?"

The door opened with the faintest rattle of the handle.

Poppy wore scarlet silk, its bodice with points at the waist, back and front, cut away from her smooth shoulders. Her skirt flared out but did not, even to Edmund's inexperienced eye, attempt to emulate the wide swing of the fashionable crinoline. Its very simplicity made it more disturbing than any florid riot of flounces would have been: its austerity was stark and sensual.

"Shall we go?" Malcolm took her arm.

In the brougham he contrived without warning to seat Poppy beside Edmund, then amused himself in contemplation of the two. Edmund sat erect, aware of her perfume and the gentle pressure of her shoulder whenever they turned a corner. Her profile was impassive against a background of shifting lights, blurred by fog: low forehead, shallow nose, and those thinly parted lips.

What had Malcolm taught those lips to murmur?

She looked so demure. Yet that was the wrong word. Resigned . . . humble . . . servile . . . or deeply confident in her acceptance of what she was and whatever might happen to her?

They drove to the superb sprawl of St. George's Hall, still shining and

39

new in the old murk of the town, looming out of the haze like a great galleon as yet unmarked by the battering of seas and weather.

Edmund sprang down and offered his hand to Poppy. For the first time he detected a hesitation in her, and was absurdly gratified. Then she rested her hand on his and stepped down.

The sheer size of the entrance was breathtaking, and the brightness of the great hall within was a sparkling affirmation of civic prosperity and pride. Malcolm's pace quickened. He came up beside his brother and Poppy, impatient to be in the middle of it all.

Edmund said, "I think I'll go up to the gallery for a while, and see what's going on."

"Always watching through a telescope, old lad? Never going to risk putting out to sea like the rest of us?"

Malcolm again captured Poppy's arm in his, and led her towards the radiance of the glittering chandeliers.

THE YOUNG FOREIGNERS' BALL had become one of the great events of the
season. The original idea of arranging an annual social evening for
young men and women stationed in Liverpool by foreign firms or government departments, and thus creating political and commercial goodwill, had soon been allowed a lax but agreeable interpretation: you could
be classified as young if you were still capable of breathing, and as for being foreign . . . well, *someone* had to look after the foreigners and make
them feel at home. Older representatives of the Corporation and town
merchants kept a benevolent eye on visitors entrusted to their care.
Chaperons past their first youth regarded an invitation to the ball as a
sign that they had attained a certain level in Liverpool society.

Among those truly young and truly foreign were the ambitious sons of
timber merchants from the Baltic and Canada, coffee and flour shippers
from Brazil, agents of New Orleans and Charleston cotton merchants,
Italian and Spanish fruit importers. Dark features of a Mexican girl and
a Portuguese heir contrasted with the finely chiselled faces of sober
young men from Philadelphia and New York. Consulates were dip-
lomatically represented by younger staff with a leavening of watchful
seniors: the Dutch consul brought his tribe of daughters, and the Brazil-
ian consul was invariably present though in fact he was a Baptist minister
of Liverpool birth.

A hoary joke that went the rounds each year was that even a few

41

young folk from Manchester had been admitted: for was not Manchester foreign? "The Manchester man and the Liverpool gentleman," distinguishing between the mere manufacturer and the superior merchant, was a jibe that could usually be relied on to provoke an argument or even a scuffle. But not this evening, and assuredly not on these premises.

It was the first time the function had been held in the great hall of this palatial new building. Edmund Gresham was not the only one who, for a while, preferred to study the high vaulted roof with its tritons and mermaids, the ornate marble panels in the walls, the splendour of the organ gallery. The orchestra was dwarfed by granite columns and soaring arches. Even those already dancing looked up and around rather than at their partners, risking dizziness in that multicoloured swirl of crinolines against great coloured expanses of marble and plaster.

Footmen in the town livery stood in each corner of the hall, their jackets laced with gold and their white silk stockings in bright contrast to the dark trousers and shoes of the male guests talking, sauntering, or dancing.

Nell Meredith looked up into the sumptuous curve of the ceiling and let her gaze be tempted down the parabola of a gambolling mermaid. She found herself looking into the eyes of Edmund Gresham, and looked hastily away.

"But really, father." Julia's agitated hands waved and jabbed to where Jesse Bostock stood planted against one of the corner pillars, a squat statue in quite the wrong colour scheme, his face carved out of mottled Merseyside sandstone rather than fine marble. "Can't you introduce Nell to someone? We can't have her wilting there in such gaucherie." The word took her fancy. "So gauche, it really won't do, you know."

"Mother, I've no need of anyone thrust at me. I'm quite content for the moment."

"When I was your age I had the pick of a dozen . . . a score . . . "

The evening had begun with a set of quadrilles, followed by waltzes. After a short break there were more quadrilles. Julia wanted to take part in all of them; then, finding herself growing too warm, fanned her flushed, ecstatic face and said she must rest, but where were the right people to talk to? People seemed to have lost the art of conversation since her day. Nell had to smile—to smile with her mother rather than at her. This blaze of colour, counterpoint of voices, rustle of fabrics and heady music: these were what Julia had missed for so long.

But if Julia was radiant, Owen was glum. A poor and reluctant dancer, he gradually backed away from his wife at the edge of the dance floor and retreated under the shadow of the balcony.

Nell looked down at her green brocade dress and plucked at a thread that had come loose from one of the rosettes of purple ribbon. She had a picture of Kitty, the maid selected for her by her mother, on her knees smoothing back each petal and letting out little gasps of admiration. The girl had a wide, plain face, and thin mousey hair drawn up under her cap; hands with short fingers and easily broken nails, which were nevertheless gentle and skilful. Her adenoidal tone would have been jarring if it had not expressed such affection and willingness to please. Several times while dressing, Nell had wanted to nudge the girl away and finish the lacing and buttoning herself; but Kitty longed to display her competence, and regarded the coming evening with such glowing anticipation that Nell felt she ought really to have been the one to attend the ball.

There came another set of waltzes. Matrons with young ladies in their charge nodded approval. A trifle overenergetic it might be, but at least in the waltz there was no changing of partners, and one did not have to have one's eyes everywhere at once.

A burst of laughter close to Nell's shoulder heralded the arrival on the floor of a young man she recognised as the younger Gresham. At his side was the unruffled face of the girl Nell had seen coming ashore like some exotic bird brought as a souvenir of a far tropic shore. Where the other young women had sought to outdo one another with billowing crinolines, laced bodices and velvet knots, this one had a simple scarlet dress falling away from her burnished throat.

Malcolm Gresham laughed again, exultantly, and spun his partner out into the throng. Her face remained calm. She fitted her steps to his without once appearing to glance down or at the movements of other couples on the floor.

Heads turned to follow her progress: men's heads, in every part of the hall.

"How very vulgar," said Julia.

The music lilted high and skittish above their heads. Girls without partners chattered a music of their own and, when a young man came within range, raised their voices half an octave and fussed with their plumage.

A man was approching the Bostock group. From the corner of her eye Nell became aware of a lank figure with a slightly mincing gait, his shoulder jerking as he slowed and stopped in front of her. He looked at her with a sort of faded insolence, as if seeking an automatic acknowledgment, his eyelids drooping and then lifting indolently again as he glanced past her.

"It can't be!"

Julia was all at once beside Nell, opening her arms and then letting them fall gracefully to her sides. The newcomer extended a limp hand.

43

"I was not mistaken, then. My dear Miss . . . oh, dear me, but that was such a time ago, wasn't it? It must be Mrs. . . . "

"Meredith," said Julia apologetically. "Of course, you never met my husband." She looked into the depths below the gallery, but Owen had his back to them. "Oh, it's too bad, really it is. But this is my little girl, Eleanor."

"Who else could it be, indeed?"

"Eleanor, you must meet a very dear old friend of mine. Viscount Orrell."

"I'm afraid my father died some years ago, so—"

"So you're Lord Speke now?"

You could have been an Honourable. Surely not, thought Nell: surely this epicene creature with sallow complexion and bleached eyes could not have been one of the lingering romantic figures in her mother's memories?

"And"— Julia was studying the near and distant faces—"Lady Speke is with you?"

"Since the death of my mother there has been no Lady Speke." He gave a little shiver, of sadness or of some obscure distaste.

In his face Nell recognised the down-turn of disillusionment she had often seen her mother affect. Was it a mannerism she had consciously adopted from him in days gone by, or had she acquired it without recalling its origin?

"Miss Meredith." It was another voice, crisper and more vigorous. "I had a kind of feeling," said Paul Whitlaw as Nell turned, "that we might meet here."

"Mr. Whitlaw."

Nell was sure her mother would be waiting to learn who this young man was, would be sizing him up and making one of her usual impulsive judgments in the first second. But when she stepped back to introduce them, Julia was already moving away: her hand on Lord Speke's arm was forcing him towards Owen, against the wall.

Paul Whitlaw said, "Well, now. I was about to ask your mother if I might dance with you."

"She's rather . . . occupied, at the moment."

"Then would it be correct, or not too incorrect, for me to ask you right out?" His direct smile and the staid set of his head were both reassuring and inviting. "In return for the small favour I had the privilege of according you the other day," he said engagingly.

"A debt I'll be delighted to pay," she said.

They were caught up in the revolving gaiety of the waltz. Paul Whitlaw's awkwardness as a dancer matched her own. But his arms were strong, his polite voice gained an agreeable warmth as they circled the hall, and he gave off a crisp smell of clean linen.

For a minute or so they danced in silence, concentrating on the actual steps. Then Nell ventured, "We really were most grateful for that small favour, as you call it. I had no idea . . . "

Another couple collided with them, and it was not until they had edged away and recovered the rhythm that he prompted: "No idea—about what?"

"That poor immigrants were treated so brutally. Is it always like that?"

Paul Whitlaw seemed to be weighing his words. Very carefully he said, "It's not for a guest in your country to criticise your methods, Miss Meredith."

"They're not *my* methods, I assure you. And not yours, I imagine?"

"At New York," he said, "we used to have similar problems. All the land sharks you could invent, and quite a few you wouldn't even dream of. Waiting to take the skin off every immigrant's back and the last cent out of his pocket. Now we've got a properly administered clearance centre where the rogues can't get in."

"Then why not here, in England?"

"You'd better ask your own folk that, ma'am. Too much money, too many powerful interests. Enough money to pay for Government indifference."

"But it's monstrous."

She had gone so rigid and indignant that they were tripping over each other's feet. Quietly he said, "I told you, Miss Meredith, it's not for a visitor like me to lay down how you should run your affairs. And if we no longer have that particular problem on our side of the Atlantic, let me tell you we've got plenty of others."

He drew her closer, but was looking beyond her. As they spun in the centre of the floor, Nell found they were close to the younger Gresham and his partner. The girl's remote gaze met her own; and remained distant and unseeing, blankly smiling—was it really a smile?—with lips as dark as a bruise.

All the moths of men turned towards the glow of her.

When Mr. Whitlaw gravely returned Nell to the corner from which they had set out, she found her mother leaning on Lord Speke's arm, teasing him with snatches of reminiscence and brittle smiles, trying at the same time to keep Owen and old Jesse snared in her conversation, so that passers-by should see it as one of the important, dominant groups of the evening.

When the music began again she shrilled, "But whatever are they playing? I don't recollect anything of the kind when you and I were last at a
ball . . . Adrian."

"The polka, I believe."

Paul Whitlaw said, "In Philadelphia we consider that kind of dance too
extreme. And in New York, too. Families like the Schermerhorns and
the Bristeds don't care for their guests getting carried away like that."

"How do they keep them under control, then, young man?"

Julia was evidently prepared to invite this personable newcomer into
her coterie. She drew breath and waited, perfectly poised, until Nell had
introduced Paul; then waited invitingly for Paul to continue.

"Our latest craze," he said, "is all for the cotillion. What you might call
a dandified version of musical chairs, I guess. Mind you, it goes on for a
mighty long time." He sounded precise and pedantic, but there was a
contradictory gleam in his eyes. Again he was looking past Nell to follow
the movements of someone among the dancers. Without so much as a
glance around she knew it must be the same someone. And all the men
here, all the same! "That young lady over there," he said as casually as he
could achieve: "a most unusual complexion, wouldn't you say? Maybe
the daughter of some eastern trader on a visit?"

"Chinese, I believe," said Nell coolly.

"Result of a Gresham barter of some kind." It was her grandfather's
first real contribution this evening. "I don't suppose *she* would be approved of in Philadelphia, Mr. Whitlaw? Or New York."

Nell's attention floated away from them, up into the hall's improbable
sea-girt heaven. She looked again at the riotous ceiling, and the balcony;
and again into Edmund Gresham's eyes.

Seen from the gallery where he stood, the floor was a kaleidoscope of
reds, greens, mauves and innumerable clashes of blue rhythmically in-
terweaving, colliding and bouncing away. Golden hair and raven black
hair moved together; and parted. An occasional bald pate glistened in
the light of the crystal chandeliers.

Edmund's gaze had repeatedly picked out two distinctive splashes of
colour. They swam in and out of his vision, advancing on each other
from opposite corners of the hall, bobbing for a moment to the measure
of the music, and then separating. One was the scarlet dress sheathing
Poppy, the other a whirling skirt of green brocade and purple ribbon,
worn by a young woman with a proud head and rich brown hair.

At his elbow the brogue of Patrick Roscoe, agent for a Dublin spice
dealer who often shared a Gresham cargo, said, "I suppose you'd be noticing old Bostock's daughter has come back to the old place?"

"Hoping she'll present him with a grandson?"

46

"A bit late for that, I'd say. But there's a fine old promise in the granddaughter, don't you find?"

"I haven't met her."

"And is that so, then? You seem to have been following the way of her with some interest."

Roscoe pointed discreetly at the girl in green and purple, now at rest and talking with an easy, relaxed smile to a straight-backed young man beside one of the pillars.

"I didn't know that was her."

"It won't take long before you do. You'll be invited to meet her before this evening's done, never fear. Bostock probably has just the likes of you in mind."

"The likes of me?"

"Ah, me boy, you'd make a lovely stud for the breed."

"You're a mischief-maker, Paddy."

"Or a matchmaker?"

"That could be the same thing."

"Sure and don't you take the cynical view of things?"

Now Edmund made a point of not looking at the young Bostock girl, whether her name was Bostock or whatever. And once he caught her averting her head in what looked like answering disapproval. But then he found that old Jesse Bostock himself was staring up as if anxious to join the subject under discussion.

Edmund decided to go down when it suited him, neither nudged by a meddlesome friend nor silently summoned by old Bostock. He was not at ease on a dance floor and not in any mood to be inveigled into other people's plans.

Trios and quartets of male voices mumbled familiar melodies in alcoves below and along the gallery behind him.

"Had to lie off Hoyle Lake the best part of twenty-four hours. Those damned sandbanks . . . "

"Until they cut a new channel through the bar . . . "

"Cost half my profit to transfer that last shipment to barges and get 'em round Black Rock."

Coming round with his bony Gallic nose like a prow into wind, Jesse Bostock luffed heavily towards an old rival. "If you've a mind to keep on handling that soda ash, all right, we won't quarrel—but if you think you can buy up half Wigan under my nose . . . "

To the older men it was sweeter music than anything the orchestra could provide.

At the end of the supper interval it happened as Nell had feared it must. Groups formed and reformed, the noise grew louder as bottles were emptied and glasses were replenished, emptied, and replenished; and her grandfather paced towards her with a tall companion. His introduction was implicitly a command.

"Been telling you about my granddaughter Eleanor, Mr. Gresham."

"Miss Meredith."

Seen at close quarters Edmund Gresham was more handsome than her memory, irritated by what was so crudely expected of her, had allowed. He had wide brown eyes in strikingly dark contrast with his sandy hair. His eyebrows ran thick and straight, almost parallel with one frowning crease across his brow—a line of worry or concentration that somehow added definition to an expression Nell found surprisingly lacking in confidence. It was not that his eyes were evasive or his manner at all awkward: just that he was, she suddenly grasped, shy. He smiled and suddenly she thought how easy it would be to like him. But she had no intention of liking him.

Her grandfather backed away but continued to observe them, as patient and unblinking as when he watched a ship entering or clearing the port.

"You're enjoying your stay in Liverpool, Miss Meredith?"

So he took it for granted that she was here only on holiday. She hoped he was ignorant of her grandfather's expectations. It would make conversation easier. She said something about the east coast, and Gresham mentioned having traded through Ipswich, and they agreed that the climate here was damper than there. He was stolid but attentive, and at least had the courtesy not to keep glancing, as all the other men did, at the Chinese girl in the circle of his brother's friends.

"And you're enjoying our great social occasion of the year?"

"Even on such an evening," said Nell, "most people seem still to be talking about ships."

"It's a topic on which there's always something new to be said." He looked more animated, perhaps hoping to be done with social platitudes and to draw her into just such a conversation.

Malcolm Gresham's laugh erupted. The girl in scarlet obediently laughed with him. One man put an arm round Malcolm's shoulders as an excuse for leaning closer to Poppy. In that group, at all events, the talk was not about shipping.

Edmund Gresham was still politely at Nell's side when the master of ceremonies announced the lancers. Her grandfather had contrived to nudge others into position, so that four couples found themselves ready when the conductor tucked his violin under his chin and raised his bow. Owen, shaking his head, had refused to venture out on the floor, so the far from unwilling Julia was partnered by Lord Speke. Malcolm Gresham brought Poppy to stand beside his brother and Nell. Paul Whitlaw had not so much chosen as been chosen by the flaccid, expensively attired daughter of a leading Castle Street insurance broker.

The bow struck down across the violin strings. Again the tide of changing colours flowed and ebbed across the floor.

Nell and her partner spoke little. His set expression as he guided her, left her to move mechanically through the changing formations, and then returned, was laughable, yet comforting. Occasionally the younger Gresham moved in towards her, flicking his wrist and sporting an amiable grin as if to seek some complicity with Nell; but she did not respond. And Edmund Gresham made no similar grins and winks in the direction of Poppy. Not once did he even glance at her. It was only as they reached the final sequence that Nell was struck by the incongruity of his completely ignoring the girl. Such forced indifference threatened to make him as conspicuous as those who shamelessly could not keep their eyes off her.

At the end of the lancers Edmund bowed very correctly, took a courteous farewell of old Jesse, and walked away.

Nell saw his brother catch him up and touch his arm. As another waltz began, Malcolm pulled Edmund and Poppy together, peering mischievously into first one face and then the other. He spoke slowly and distinctly so that Nell could almost read his lips.

"Or else I shall take it as a personal slight . . . "

Any other man would have welcomed the opportunity. Perhaps that was why Malcolm had not offered her to any other man. He watched, his head tilted mockingly to one side, as his brother led Poppy on to the floor, every movement stiff and embarrassed.

Without warning Malcolm turned towards Nell, and without more than a cheeky nod at Julia, who was too engrossed in conversation with Lord Speke to pay any heed, he said, "Ah, Miss Meredith. I think perhaps we might take a turn around the floor?"

"I'm . . . rather tired, thank you."

"My brother was such a violent dancer? But surely if you favour the elder, you must be kind to the younger."

"I favour nobody, Mr. Gresham."

"I implore you, don't break my heart."

Words and a brash smile came so readily to him. He was utterly unlike his brother save for that fleeting physical resemblance. An inch or so shorter, and lighter in weight, he was nevertheless somehow more substantial, more immediately there and striking an immediate resonance.

49

And too sure of himself. Within a moment or two, thought Nell, he would too easily make her laugh—and then congratulate himself on another easy conquest.

Paul Whitlaw said, "It's uncommonly warm, don't you think? Perhaps you'd care to accompany me while I order a cooling drink, Miss Meredith?"

She turned gratefully. "I'd like nothing better."

"Nothing?" She could not even be sure that she had heard Malcolm Gresham's whisper aright, but he was grinning unrepentantly as she walked off with Paul. She had been right: if a conquest were not easy and automatic, he would at once turn his attention elsewhere.

Already he was bending attentively over a young woman a few yards away.

By the close of the evening there were ranks of carriages forming along Lime Street and down the slope beside the hall. Light spilled over the wide steps, slippery with a grease of fog. Skirts were fastidiously lifted; a man who had drunk too heavily slipped and fell, and some of his companions began to bellow a song as they heaved him to his feet; the damp Liverpool accent whined through voices that had been kept primly correct through the earlier hours of the evening.

Jesse Bostock gathered his family about him, watching thoughtfully as Lord Speke took an effusive farewell of Julia. Owen rubbed tired eyes and clearly thought only of sleep.

"Well." Jesse's hand settled Nell's cloak over her shoulders. "What did you make of him?"

"Of Mr. Whitlaw? A very agreeable young man."

"None of that nonsense, girl. I'm talking about Edmund Gresham, and well you know it."

"I found Mr. Whitlaw more congenial."

"I don't believe a word of it. In any case we're not going to have you running off to America. What use would that be? I'm not selling out to any Yankee."

"Grandfather, I've no intention of going to America, any more than you have of selling your name to them. The question doesn't arise."

"I should think not."

"Nor," she said, "does any other question, at this moment."

Shouted goodnights mingled with a staccato tut-tutting of older women trying to direct their charges to the right coaches.

Edmund Gresham drew a deep breath, savouring the sour, inimitable taste of Liverpool's night air. As the Bostocks passed him he raised his hat, catching a glimpse of Eleanor Meredith's face before it stiffened into unexpected hostility. He was surprised; and surprised how clearly he remembered her blue-grey eyes, so cool until she grew animated, when they had momentarily taken on flecks of shifting, unidentifiable hues like opals warmed to iridescence by contact with the skin.

The vision was obliterated by the smouldering recollection of Poppy and her closeness to him. Tomorrow he must make arrangements to leave Falkner Square. Under the same roof with his brother and Poppy his imagination would give him no rest. He would move out—there was nothing else for it—and live over the counting-house.

THE LIBRARY was one of the quietest rooms in the house. Even when the maids were dusting along the adjoining passage or the gardener was clipping hedges outside, the room's lack of regular use gave it a silence and solitude all its own. Sails and funnels on the river below seemed, through these windows, to drift rather than thrust forward. Even those few bound reports and annual registers that Jesse Bostock did favour with occasional attention were somehow distanced and detached from the gritty reality of the port.

Nell had been working her way along the upper shelves, carrying three or four volumes at a time down the library ladder and stacking them on the table. Some of the bindings were very fine, but she did not suppose her grandfather had ever been tempted to open them. Six volumes of sermons would hardly have been his favourite reading matter. Turning a few pages, blowing dust off them, Nell read some lines extolling the virtue of humility and patience. No: if the meek were indeed to inherit the earth, Jesse Bostock was unlikely to get any very substantial legacy.

Three or four times an hour Nell found herself straying from her task to the windows. What was the use of cataloguing all these books? In this house they performed no real function; and even if she completed the work efficiently it was unlikely that her grandfather would live enough years to take advantage of it. She looked out at the skyline with which she had become so familiar these last few months, at the thousand and one details of roofs and waterfront which were now no longer a baffling maze but a pattern she understood.

Her father was somewhere down there, trying to grapple with the ceaseless challenges of Bostock business, as dissatisfied down there as she was bored up here. While her mother hummed and primped and fussed through the house, went on expensive shopping expeditions, or drove out on silly, self-indulgent flirtations with Lord Speke.

Nell constructed another pile of books and opened the top one. *A New History of the Commerce and Township of Liverpool*—and it was in fact fairly new. She ran her eye down the list of subscribers at the back: Allday, Enoch, Mayor of St. Helens . . . Antwistle, Harold, Oldhall-street . . . the Athenaeum Newsroom, Church-street . . . and the name she expected—Bostock, Jesse, & Sons, Water-street.

Bostock and Sons . . .

That, too, was history now.

Several pages stuck together and had to be peeled apart. Nell flipped through at random, until one folio fell open on a sketch showing the cross-section of a slave ship, with tiny matchstick figures laid prone in every available space. There was no suggestion of a human element in the closely packed lines: it was simply a matter of the most logical mathematical arrangement.

The sound of a stick thudded out of the silence along the passage. Its rhythm and aggressive impact threatened an outburst of bad temper.

"Look at this." Her grandfather stamped into the room, waving a long roll of cartridge paper. "Your father's gone off without the plan. How does he think he's going to manage this afternoon? How can he give instructions in the yard without this in front of him?"

He threw the roll down on the table. One end of it uncurled. Looking across the open book, Nell said, "It doesn't look much different from this, does it?"

"What's that? Hm? Dammit, girl, are you suggesting my new steamer's just another slaver?"

Nell indicated a space filled with little dots and numerals. "Steerage passengers?"

"Of course."

"Packed in and left to fend for themselves, like those Irish we saw—"

"No such thing. They're sheltered, they've got their own galley, bunks, decent partitions. We separate the single men from the rest, supply cubicles for families. Used to be no discrimination at all."

"It still looks a bit spartan."

"If people choose to go, that's up to them. Nobody's forcing them to leave England. We give safe passage at the cheapest price that makes sense."

Nell unrolled the plan a few inches further.

"These cabins—"

"For second-class passengers."

"More emigrants?"

"If they can afford it."

"They don't look all that roomy, either."

"They don't need to be. Somewhere to lie down, a washstand—not many want more than that. If they do, they can bring their own things."

"Wouldn't it be better to furnish them adequately in the first place?"

"Good God, Nell," old Jesse exploded. "D'you think we're running a . . . a smart hotel?"

"Why not?" She smiled into his irascible face. "Why not make it exactly that—a floating hotel? Build everything in, supply chambermaids, stewardesses: call them what you will. It doesn't have to be expensive. And travellers would pay for it, I'm sure. Make travel itself a pleasure instead of an ordeal."

"You'd better find yourself a job with Inman. Or Cunard. *They* have notions like that."

"And are they doing well?"

"Well enough," said Jesse grudgingly.

"Then let's put our mind to it, and do better."

"Ours is a different sort of operation." He snatched the plan from her and rolled it up again. "Your father'll have to have this before the end of the morning. I'd take it down myself, but . . ." He thumped the table, nearly tipping himself off balance.

"Grandfather, are you all right?"

"Accursed leg. Playing me up today." Tight-lipped, he said, "Be a good girl and take it down for me, will you? So I can be sure it gets there. They'll be at the Regent Street auction. Behind Clarence Dock, you know."

"Yes, I know."

His lips quirked, losing their tightness. "It's all coming to you, isn't it?"

Owen had driven down that morning in the brougham, and it would not be sent back until he had been delivered in due course to the ferry for his shipyard visit. Nell took the gig. As she trotted it round to the front of the house, Jesse was waiting to see her off.

"I've half a mind to come with you after all, just to be sure."

"I'll manage well enough on my own, grandfather."

"That you will."

As she drove away she could feel his ache to be down there in the thick of it, with his finger in everything.

His high-handed attitude to everyone and everything continued to incense her. A number of times in recent weeks when he had tried to impress her she had made a point of looking critical and disapproving, and was childishly delighted when she could make him fidget with unaccustomed doubt. Yet there was no escaping the sheer weight of his authority. Would she have driven alone so confidently into the heart of the port if she had not also been confident of the Bostock name behind her? She was accepted now as Jesse's granddaughter: she had needed to accompany him only a couple of times, and she was known and deferred to. She had met shippers and ships' masters, warehouse managers and chief clerks, summoned peremptorily by her grandfather. She had been introduced to Customs officers, pilots and dock superintendents. And repeatedly she had met Hesketh, forever at his employer's heels or snarling off to work his bidding. She came to dread the man's laugh, half-servile and half-contemptuous, indicating that Hesketh knew his place but knew everyone else's as well and thought highly of none of them.

"He's so dreadful," she once complained to Jesse. "Do you have to let him spend so much time with father? They're not cut out for each other. He's so . . . such a bully. In everything."

"I'd sooner he was a bully for Bostock than against us," said her grandfather dismissively.

Nell took the gig down from the summit of Bostock's Brow into the canyons between interminable walls of red brick and pockmarked sandstone. Some dripped a sour green, smeared over by gouts of seagull droppings. Warehouses with jutting pilasters and deep recesses for hoists marched away into the distance, with factory chimneys so close behind that it appeared they could not wait for goods to be delivered but must press ever closer to the water's edge and gulp in supplies direct from the ships.

And everywhere, riding mysteriously between raw red buildings, seeming to chisel out thoroughfares further and further inland, were the ships themselves: tall masts and sooty funnels, manoeuvring from river to basin and from narrow channel into broad dock. The waterways formed a honeycomb of streets joining at unexpected angles, opening from viscous main roads through narrow passages into spacious squares.

Traffic managers shouted; donkey engines coughed into life; hawsers groaned, rope and wire squealed through iron sheaves.

You could hate the turmoil and dirt and brutish energy of the waterfront; or, like old Jesse, you could love it. What you could not do was avert your eyes and ignore it—though Nell's mother, she thought ruefully, was certainly doing her best.

Her father and Hesketh were standing outside the auction room when she arrived. Neither appeared to have much to say to the other. Hesketh did not look pleased to see Nell, but when she handed over the rolled plan he smirked with malicious pleasure.

"You've bid for the property?" Nell asked.

"Not yet." Owen sighed. "There's been a delay over an earlier lot—a warehouse, some quibble about access and rights of way. We could be here another half-hour before anything happens."

Once in the alleys behind Regent Street and its neighbours there had been shops supplying leg irons, handcuffs and chains for slavers. Now they sold food and bedding and cooking pots for emigrants. Regent Street itself had become a mixture of tall lodging-houses and general ships' chandlers. Today two blocks were up for sale: one of them scorched and with a roof damaged by fire. The death of the owner in the blaze had put both buildings on the market. Jesse Bostock wanted the sounder property as crew accommodation. "We'd have a lot less men jumping ship or falling into the hands of crimps ten minutes after they've come ashore," he had lectured Owen and Nell at the dinner table, "if we could establish our own lodging-house. Some of our hands have homes of their own to go to in Liverpool, but there's plenty who haven't. Scattered all over the place, and hard to round up. Offer them good plain accommodation while they're in port and we can keep crews together. In the old days you signed on anyone you could lay your hands on at the last minute. But regular passenger services need dependable crew. It may not work, but . . ."

There was no real force in the "but." Jesse had decided it ought to work, and it would be made to work.

Nell asked her father casually, "Are the two buildings going in one lot, or separately?"

He glanced along the street. "We're hoping to split them. We've no use for the damaged one."

Her gaze followed his. Dependable accommodation for dependable crew: it was commonsense. And suddenly, blindingly, she knew what else could go with it. *Must* go with it. Too many powerful interests against the idea, Paul Whitlaw had said. But if Jesse Bostock put his powerful interest *into* it . . .

She said in a rush, "Father, you have authority to buy both properties if that strikes you best?"

"Well, I suppose so. Yes. But"—he consulted Hesketh—"we don't think it best."

56

"You must get both."

Hesketh said: "Now just a minute, miss, I don't know what you're thinking—"

"I'm thinking," said Nell, "that the time has come for emigrants to be treated as sensibly as the crew."

"Oh, now—"

"Now," she insisted, "is the time to establish a centre for people who have to stay a night, two nights or more, while they wait for a New York sailing."

"Oh, that old notion. There's been talk of it before. Never got further than talk."

"A clearance centre for general use—that was overridden, yes. But why not a purely Bostock enterprise, for Bostock passengers?"

"You'd get every kind of scum in there, that's why not. Steal everything that could be shifted, wet the beds, wreck the place."

"We're talking of decent people who are off to America in search of a decent life. Treat them properly, and word would soon get round. Don't you see how much better it would be for everyone? Tidier and more economical in every way. We would be able to offer a single ticket link-up right through from the Continent—from Hamburg, from Sweden, or for that matter from Dublin—all the way to New York. A reliable place to stay. A reliable price, with no extras."

"There'd be no end to the extras," growled Hesketh. "Including funeral expenses. The last man who tried to cut out the runners and their pals ended up dead in the Pool."

"You're easily defeated, Mr. Hesketh."

Hatred simmered in his eyes. "I like to know the odds before I get into a fight, miss. And I know what the odds'd be round here."

"Do you realise"—Nell could not contain herself now—"that German ships are coming into the trade, sailing direct from German ports? The competition could become serious."

"It's still quicker to cross the German Ocean and come on to Liverpool by train. And we've had years of experience in dealing with them."

"To fight off that competition we have to deal even better with them. A single ticket," she repeated, "covering everything. Guaranteed price and guaranteed services right through: ship to Hull, train to Liverpool, accommodation in Bostock-managed premises, an assured berth aboard the Transatlantic steamer."

From inside the auction rooms came the thud of doors being thrown back. Half a dozen men came out into the street, shrugging philosophically. Two who had been waiting on the far pavement now hurried across the street towards the entrance.

57

"This'll be ours." Hesketh was virtually ordering Owen to accompany him indoors.

Nell hesitated for the briefest instant, and followed them. She said, "Father, you can get that second building cheap if you bid for both at once."

"Miss Meredith, we don't have the time to—"

"Do you have the authority, Mr. Hesketh, to overrule any of my father's decisions?"

"Well . . ."

"You're here to advise, and no more. And your advice is rejected."

"When Mr. Bostock hears what you've been up to—"

"Then it will be duly dealt with."

She was the only woman in the room. Men settling on to chipped, peeling leather chairs glanced round; and glanced again. A bawdy joke died in mid sentence.

Owen murmured, "Eleanor, I'm not sure if we ought to take such a step without consulting your grandfather."

"There isn't time. It's your duty to act."

Owen flinched away from her gaze and turned pleadingly to Hesketh. "It really is a first-rate concept, you know." Hesketh resolutely kept silent.

The auctioneer stepped up to his high desk.

"You must, father," Nell breathed.

That evening the storm broke at seven o'clock. Nell had gone to the library knowing that this was where her grandfather would seek her. Better a clash here than in the dining-room, with her father crumbling before the onslaught and her mother punctuating every remark with complaints and protests.

"A fine mess you've let me in for, young woman." Jesse slammed the door. At least he was addressing her as a young woman, no longer a girl.

"It will work out splendidly," said Nell, very steady.

"Splendidly? Since when has Bostock Navigation been a charitable institution?"

"We're not talking about charity. We're talking business. If we build up a reputation for dealing fairly and intelligently with our passengers, steerage or cabin class, accepting responsibility for every leg of the journey from the moment they set out from Europe—"

"And charging them for it? Do you know what this folly will cost?"

"Less in the end than the confused, disorganised way things are handled at present."

"You sound pretty sure of yourself."

"Yes." She threw it out as confidently as she dared.

Jesse's stick thrummed against the floor, shaken by a tremor that ran down his whole body from his shoulder. He said, "You should have got word to me. Should have hired a messenger and waited for my approval."

"There wasn't time."

"You went over my head, frightened your dithering father into doing as you told him—"

"It was my fault, yes," Nell admitted. "Father wasn't sure we ought to go ahead."

"He wouldn't be. Hasn't the mettle."

Having said this, Jesse seemed to have run out of words. He stood with shoulders heaving, glaring down into a polished corner of the table.

Nell broke the silence. "So I suppose you're going to—"

"I'm going to let it go ahead."

"You mean . . . you don't mean you'll authorise the emigration centre?"

"You'd prefer me to countermand it—sell off the property for what I can get—make you look a fool?"

She was trembling as uncontrollably as he. "We can really do it?"

"I'm not repudiating you. Bad for our reputation."

"Grandfather . . ."

She found herself running round the table, which so far she had kept defensively between them. She flung her arms round him and kissed him. He tried to jerk away, then laughed and groaned, and hammered the floor again with his stick.

"But I'm not letting you take charge." He bellowed it close to her ear. "Your father will attend to the details. It'll take hard bargaining and some hard words with some hard men. Your father will handle it the way I tell him to. Not woman's work."

"Grandfather, I insist—"

"You've done enough insisting for one day. I still give the orders. Your father is in charge of the new dosshouses."

"A woman's work is in the library?" She looked desolately back at the tiers of bookshelves.

His eyes and mouth shaped a wicked grin. "I don't think you can do anything useful here. I've a mind to let you try putting some of your other ideas into practice. Only in this case you'll report back to me before you sign anything, or spend a penny, or issue any orders."

"Report back?" she said. "From where?"

He kept her waiting, tantalising her. With galling slowness he said,

"I've been thinking over what you said about shipboard accommodation. High time you found out what a ship looks like. If you can think of some way we can win paying traffic from Cunard and Inman, I'll listen."

"You want me to—"

"To inspect the cabins, the saloons, the galleys and anything else you like on the ship we've got in service. And sketch out any ideas you like on the new one before her fitting-out. Tell me what you fancy. And I promise to turn down nine out of every ten extravagant notions you come up with."

"And the tenth?"

"Try to get it past me," he goaded. "But don't run wild. Nothing is to be purchased or commissioned until I've approved it. I'm still in command."

"Yes, grandfather."

"If you want to take the helm, you'll have to wait." He glared in mock anger; but all at once she was engulfed by the awareness of his grouchy, awkward fondness for her, and found her eyes pricking with tears. "Wait," he said quietly. "My girl . . . Nell. Your time will come soon enough."

FRED HESKETH had had about as much as he could stand. His orders had been to keep an eye on old Jesse's son-in-law and help him get some grasp of what went on in the port and where Bostock Navigation belonged in it all. That had been bad enough, for a start: you couldn't tell a man the whole story in a few months, even if he was ready to learn. And Owen Meredith wasn't ready and never would be. It had taken Fred Hesketh half a lifetime already—and what he learned hadn't come from books or talk but from living every rough, cold or sweating minute of it. It took years for it to work its way into your bones.

"According to what I've been reading about the new Passenger Acts . . . "

According to what *she* had been reading! The useless father was bad, but the girl was worse, forever pushing her nose in and dreaming up high-flown schemes as if every ill on the riverside could be tidied up by a few airy notions. Setting herself up over men who had slaved their way barefoot out of the savage back streets and studied every trick of the trade until they knew how to make them work every time.

With the minimum of schooling, Fred Hesketh had achieved quite a wide education in his thirty-five years. He knew not only the workings of the port, every deceit and brutality of the docks, but also more about the social strata in which his so-called betters liked to move than they knew themselves. If you wanted to get on in the world you had to know where you stood, and where everyone else stood—and when it was right to move, and which way. You had to know who to bow and scrape to, who to treat with just the right mixture of cheekiness and respect; and who you must kick and spit on if you wanted to win respect for yourself.

There were precious few aristocrats in Liverpool, but by God, didn't a lot fancy themselves that way? Men whose grandfathers had scraped and cheated for a living round the Old Dock now swaggered across Exchange Flags in morning coats and high hats, dressed in the evening for concerts in the Philharmonic Hall, attended genteel dancing performances, and spoke big of international commerce in imperial expansion and the nobility of their own philanthropy; but never actually of *selling* anything. To be a Liverpool cotton man was to be a lord. To ship tea or sugar in great quantities was to be a dignified merchant; to scoop it into small screws of paper and sell it across a counter was to be a tradesman.

Hesketh knew the distinctions and knew just how far he stood a chance of climbing. Some heights were beyond him, though he didn't often let himself admit this. If the Greshams and the Bostocks could get where they had got in two generations . . .

Bostock he could stand. He and old Jesse were two of a kind. If he had to knuckle under to the old man, well, he was well paid for it; and as manager was usually allowed to manage. Bostock raged when things went wrong, and as likely as not went on raging after they had been put right. But at least Hesketh was given a free hand when it came to putting those things right: a hand he could clench and swing just as it suited him. And now, after all that, here he was saddled with a limp rag of a man and a girl who looked like taking over his dominion and wrecking it.

He could show that Meredith girl a thing or two. Not what she thought she was asking for, but what she was really asking for. One fine day he'd put her where she belonged.

Her voice rang on in his head. *According to what I've been reading about the new Passenger Acts . . .*

Did she suppose that the land sharks would all turn belly uppermost and die just because a load of new laws had been passed? New regulations and increased supervision meant only that the runners and baggage-snatchers, the sharp brokers and lodging-house touts who met the trains and boats had been forced to find more cautious ways of netting their prey. Everyone along the line still made his profit, and that was how things ought to be. A dozen Nell Merediths could wreck this town if they had their way. Like the religious cranks who had done away with

62

the slave trade and handed over the profit to other countries. Handing out money to this, that and the other—and who had made that money for them in the first place?—wagging their whiskers when preachers thundered against the wicked trade in Africa and America, and sending out money and missionaries to convert the traders. And if they succeeded, then what? Liverpool without cheap cotton from the American slave states, Liverpool pampering emigrants and not squeezing every penny that could be squeezed from them, Liverpool . . . living on *what*?

Hesketh stumped away from the quayside, past the end of one of the rope-walks stretching behind the main streets of the town. The smell of tarred rope mingled with the gust from a tavern as its door swung open. He rarely went in for a drink at this time of the morning: one pot of ale and a pie or chop at noon was his usual dinner, or occasionally an "ordinary daily" around one o'clock in a dining saloon to show that he could step up a rung when it suited him. But today he had need of a genever to settle his curdling anger.

Damn that girl. Damn her and the rest of them who talked good works and did nothing but damage.

He had a second gin, ate a pie without noticing its taste, and went off towards the edge of the Devil's Acre.

These tangled streets behind Salthouse Dock had been his playground as a child. Later he had lived through the violent days when thousands of navvies labouring on the growing docks had taken over whole streets and courts, rampaging through the town every Saturday and Sunday night, carrying their spades with them everywhere—for work and warfare—smashing up anyone who came too close. He had survived; and by knowing when and where to make himself useful to the gangers had climbed his first step up out of the gutter.

At a familiar crossroads he stopped. From the washhouse on the corner came the usual buzz of voices and an occasional raucous cackle. The place had been started by his mother. Widowed, she had for a while kept her and himself by labouring in a nail factory until the hot metal scorched her fingers so badly that she was no use to her employers and was dismissed. She could just afford to buy a mangle, and began taking in washing. A local churchwarden, anxious to be elected to a club run largely by richer philanthropists, made a big show of setting her up in larger premises where she and other needy widows could handle bigger piles of laundry and do their own washing at the same time. Every day there was the scratch and thump of scrubbing, the bawdy shriek of voices, and the harsh soapy smell cutting through the air.

Fred Hesketh stood in the doorway.

An elderly woman screeched an obscene welcome. Two others looked furtively round and then pretended they had not noticed him.

A younger woman, new to the place, glanced up once and redoubled her efforts with a scrubbing-brush. The droop of her head caught at his guts. Just the same sort of age as that Nell Meredith, and a face not unlike her, either. Christ, if ever he got the chance . . .

He went in and stopped casually beside her.

"Now then, Mr. Hesketh." It was the worst old bag of the lot, old Mrs. McCreedy. "Keep out from under our feet, eh?"

"And our skirts."

The girl's hands were a harsh red but her thin bare arms were still young and smooth. Hesketh said, "Not been here long, have you?"

She shook her head.

"I think I know your husband. Tommy Connor, right?"

This time she was startled into glancing at him. "That's right . . . sir."

"It was me got him that berth on the Dublin run."

"Oh, you're Mr. Hesketh, is it? Yes, he did say something, like."

"Don't dirty your clean hands on him, Emily." A bellow from the far side of the room bounced off the damp stone floor.

He lowered his voice. "Haven't been married all that long, have you?"

"No, Mr. Hesketh."

Under the thin cotton dress there wasn't much of her, but enough to tug promisingly at the material. She was as pale as any of them brought up in the rookeries, but exertion in the washhouse had coloured her cheeks, and the way he looked at her made the colour flow down her throat.

Oh, she'll do. Give me the chance, and she'll do. Feel lonely, the nights when Tommy's away? He nearly said it out loud and then was conscious of flickering glances all about him—glances of suspicion and contempt, but all touched with fear. They might shout jokes at him, but he had moved up beyond them and they knew it. Shore Manager for Bostock Navigation. He often said the words over to himself just to be sure of them: Shore Manager. He had a hold over most of these women or over their menfolk. There wasn't one would dare cross him.

He nodded to the girl, and she knew what he meant, and she wouldn't risk saying no. Sooner or later the chance would come.

Like there had been with the girl he'd been made to marry. Forced into it by his mother and that canting old swine the churchwarden, because he'd got her with child: and then the kid had died anyway, and the next one died of diphtheria, and that was all he'd ever had out of that

64

shrivelled creature who now sat at home all day cramped in on her own miseries.

He put her out of his mind and kept the thought of Emily there, blurred in with a picture of the Meredith bitch. Not that he needed a picture of that one. She was there in front of him all the time, nowadays. When she wasn't asking questions about the mess her father was getting himself into with that emigrants' reception centre, it was her latest fad— the new Bostock ship. Under Hesketh's feet all the time, and promising no good in the end.

Who had ever heard of cabins such as she was dreaming up; or of one completely furnished before the hull even took to the water?

Playing at dolls' houses, that was all it was. And holding up progress even further.

The vessel on the stocks of Reith's Birkenhead shipyard was destined to take to the seas in late spring. Jesse Bostock was growing impatient. Construction was running less than a week behind the agreed timetable, but that was enough for Bostock to be repeatedly demanding latest details and explanations, greater speed, and news of each slightest delay. He cursed Hesketh and cursed Reith's workmen. Hesketh was used to that. But he would never get used to Nell Meredith's interference. Didn't her grandfather realise what delays *she* was likely to cause? Her orders for the installation of one complete stateroom as the model for the rest at fitting-out and a basis for ordering leather, linen, and fabrics and engaging seamstresses and upholsterers, went against anything the contractors had ever been used to.

All so that those with money could embark in hitherto unknown comfort, wining and dining in a rosewood saloon and sleeping in luxurious bunks with fashionably patterned curtains.

So that Nell Meredith could inherit the earth—and the ocean.

It was not until a week after his visit to the washhouse that Hesketh all at once saw what advantage might be taken of that prototype stateroom. It wasn't for the likes of him to travel in; but all the same he was damned well going to be the first to use it. He laughed out loud. The more he thought of it, the better it seemed. Yes: he had known the opportunity would come, and here it was.

Each morning the ferry-boats from the far bank brought businessmen from their residential hotels and Rock Ferry estates to the landing-stage, and younger men and girls who rushed up the sloping gangways towards the offices of Water Street and Dale Street. Each evening they bustled down the gangways again and were carried home. There was no great rush at the time Fred Hesketh chose for his excursion. It was mid-morning, and the boat was two-thirds empty. He watched it struggle in against the tide and then swing with it. Black smoke gushed, there was the rising thunder of reversed engines, and the stage trembled once as the boat settled against it. The gangway rattled down.

Hesketh caught up with the girl as she hurried aboard.

"Taking a day off, Emily?"

"Ooh, Mr. Hesketh. You did give me a turn."

Her eyes widened with a hint of alarm, but the twitch of her shoulders said something else.

She went on hurriedly, "Just off to spend a night with me mam in Wallasey."

"Tommy away again, then?"

She pouted. "No sooner home than he's off again."

Two men squatted on the deck, set a cloth cap before them as a collecting bowl, and started to squeak out a fiddle and clarinet duet. Hesketh took Emily's arm, feeling her flinch and then force herself to relax, and led her to the starboard bulwark. Side by side they leaned over the rail watching the water foam as the paddles plunged and churned and thrust the ferry away from the stage.

"You been on board the new Bostock ship?"

"Not me, Mr. Hesketh, no."

"Like to have a look over her?"

"I wouldn't be let."

"I'm inviting you," said Hesketh importantly. "I got some work to do there. To check that things are going the way they should. You're welcome to come and have a look."

"Well . . . "

"What time's your mother expecting you?"

"Oh, any time. Sort of late in the day. I didn't settle nothing definite."

"Nothing to worry about, then."

"I don't know. I mean, I don't know if I ought to, like."

But she was going to come with him. He knew it and she knew it.

Nobody bothered to look round when they went aboard. Carpenters were working aft, and from within the bowels of the hull came a steady hammering. Hesketh, brisk and strutting, led the way without once looking back at Emily, down a companionway in the waist of the ship. Past the end of an uncompleted bulkhead he indicated with a masterful wave of his hand the gleaming limbs of the paddle machinery, at rest and waiting their time. They went in semidarkness between walls smelling of new wood, with only a pale milky light filtering down from bullseyes in the deck, and an occasional porthole or gap through the outer cradle of

66

scaffolding. He opened a door and, for the first time, did not lead the way but stood aside to let her pass.

Emily faltered an instant on the threshold, then went into the cabin. She gasped.

Although the stateroom was small, it had been devised to make the most of the available space. Instead of cramped bunks against the wall it had two single brass bedsteads, a dumpy sofa, and neatly fitted washstand. Under the sofa were three drawers, fitted with turnbuckles so that they would not slide open if the ship rolled. Curtains ran along rails the length of the cabin, cutting the beds off from the rest of the room if required; and there were trimly looped curtains shading the daylight through the scuttle.

Hesketh closed the door and turned the key in the lock.

Emily started at the sound but kept looking away until he put his hands on her shoulders, turned her to face him, and pushed her hard against one of the beds so that it caught her behind the knees and she sprawled backwards onto the counterpane.

"Mr. Hesketh, you don't have to get so rough."

It was too much to hope that Nell Meredith would one day travel in this cabin. Too much to hope that he would catch her here on her own one day, unawares. Catch her, take her . . . like this.

Emily gasped again. "You don't have to . . . "

He dragged her skirt up, and was surprised by the swelling tightness of her skinny body.

"You expecting?"

"Yes."

"But you haven't been married that long."

She wrenched her head away and laughed harshly. "Yes, well, that's why, isn't it?"

Another of them. Like the drab his mother had forced him to marry. Poor Tommy Connor, trapped, just the same. But anyway they couldn't blame Fred Hesketh, not this time.

He climbed over her.

"Another contribution'll do no harm, then."

Her eyes in the midday twilight were greedy and frightened at the same time. Just the way he liked them. Just the way he'd like to see those other detesting, detestable eyes.

Someone began to hammer more insistently in the depths of the hull. Hesketh laughed, and took up the steady, pounding rhythm.

"Mr. Hesketh." She was really frightened now. "You don't have to be such a . . . I'm not going to . . . " He knocked the breath out of her before she could finish. Now she was trying to fight him off, and that made it even better. He hit her, and she struggled, and every moan was a goad to his back, and he plunged and reared and the hammering drove him on.

"You bastard," she managed faintly.

At last he pushed himself away. She lay where she was, her legs wide and exhausted, her face grey in the greyness.

"You didn't have to." She could scarcely get the words out. Her right hand clawed at the pain. "I wasn't stopping you, you didn't have to be so . . . didn't have to go on like *that*."

One day it would be the Meredith girl's turn to sob in just that way.

Hours before the launch the streets approaching the shipyard had become the setting for an impromptu carnival. Workers given a holiday for the occasion had chosen the best vantage points early in the morning, many inside the yard itself, on walls and roofs and scaffolding. They sang chorus after chorus of old songs and new songs, shouting one another down and drowning the soloists who came plying their poor entertainments. Near the gates a one-legged man pumped a concertina, while beside him two ragged children rattled tambourines, at intervals jerking one upside-down and holding it out for coppers. A ballad chanter strolled up and down, croaking out rough and ready verses about a recent grog shop murder.

The sun shone. The surge of voices was sometimes a murmuring breeze, sometimes a gale.

As the time for the ceremony drew nearer, a band clambered on to a platform set back from the main dais. Some of its members had earlier been playing in a public house and were now inaccurate on some notes and gratingly out of tune on others. It mattered little. As the tension built up, people sang and whistled along with the band, many of them yelling improvised words of their own.

Keel blocks were lifted away, so that the ship was held in place only by wooden dog shores.

The music stopped. A burst of clapping and a jumble of jokes and cheers whispered away into silence. The band played a ragged fanfare. The Mayor of Liverpool made a quite inaudible speech, ultimately submerged by shuffling and renewed mumbling from the crowd.

Nell took a deep breath and stepped forward.

The faces peering up at her made a pale, rippling carpet flecked with bright feathers and the intermittent dark blots of hats and best Sunday jackets. She felt lost and tiny, dwarfed by the cradle timbers and the high, long hull poised on the launching way.

Her father stood well back as if to disassociate himself from the proceedings. In fact he had, this once, actually played one significant part in them. Sailing ships in the Bostock Transatlantic service had for some years been named after early queens of England. The idea had been Owen Meredith's when cataloguing Jesse Bostock's library; and by the time he eloped with Jesse's daughter a number had been commissioned and it would have been too obvious and too petty to have made a change. So the sailing ships were followed by two paddle steamers, the *Matilda* and *Isabella*, and now there was to be this third paddler.

Nell lifted the magnum of champagne at the end of its white ribbon and held it aloft for a moment.

"I name this ship . . . " She hesitated, absurdly unsure of being able to say the word, scared by the suddenly strange, mystical responsibility. Then, as loudly as possible into the bright air, she cried, "*Eleanor*. May God bless her and all who sail in her."

The bottle splintered across the bows. The wine fizzed and gushed out. Dog shores were kicked away. For an instant the hull seemed stuck in its place, reluctant to leave its womb. Then, at first slowly but with gathering speed, it began to slide down the ways. A groundswell of cheering rose to a roar. There was the smack and rush of water as the stern plunged into the rising tide. Cables ran out and tightened when the hull was waterborne, slowing it and keeping it riding gently on the small tumult of waves.

Cheering broke and rippled. The band struck up again. A group of children began throwing flowers and streamers.

Watching the ship settle into the water, Nell felt a lump in her throat. She gulped it away. Immediately below her an elderly, frock-coated gentleman was wiping his eyes and pretending that dust on the wind had stung him. But it was a mild wind, and he was not the only one with tears in his eyes. Nell surrendered, as they were all doing, to the sentimental joy of watching a new vessel slide into her natural element.

She forced her gaze away, only to meet her grandfather's moist but proud eyes. He put out his hand and painfully gripped her wrist.

"Eleanor," he said. "Eleanor." It sounded so loving—towards her and towards the ship.

Before the final fitting-out began there was a party on board. The saloon between decks, immediately aft of the paddle machinery cutting athwartships, was provided with several long tables. Passenger cabins installed along each side would later narrow the saloon area, but for the time being there was a wide promenade, encouraging guests to stroll and talk while they helped themselves to the huge cold buffet. There were cold meats and game pie, Benares brass bowls heaped with fruit, an array of cheeses, and a constant supply of champagne, Rhenish wine and claret. Shallower bowls of flowers hung from the ceiling, swinging with the gentle sway of the hull. Looped between the scuttles were strings of flags, with Union Jacks and the Stars and Stripes predominating.

"The pantry will serve the main cabin from here." Jesse Bostock flourished his glass dangerously to demonstrate a point. "And the staterooms . . . " He, too, had fallen under the spell of the American word. "Staterooms. No more cramped cabins and narrow bunks and washstands that slop all over the place. No more hard seats. We're sparing nothing to fit them out. Bostock Navigation aims to make travel itself a pleasure instead of an ordeal. We . . ." He caught Nell's gaze on him, tried to avoid it, then grimaced. "My granddaughter," he proclaimed, "has badgered me into ordering special curtain material, special upholstery, special carpets and God knows what. Even the steerage will live like lords, if she has her way. And," he said more gently but so that everyone could still hear, "she *will* have her way."

"You're still relying on paddles, sir." Paul Whitlaw, at his elbow, was sober in tone yet swaying slightly as if the vessel were already on the high seas. "They do tell me the future for comfortable travel is with the screw propeller."

"Can't rely on it. Drive it too hard, and the screw snaps. And there you are, having to hoist sail and rely on the wind again."

"Your navy and ours, sir"—Paul's wineglass slipped from side to side between his fingers—"have both been turning towards screw propulsion for quite some time. If fighting ships find it preferable, then I'd say—"

"Men-of-war are used to discomfort. And they don't have to show a profit."

"The future," slurred Paul, "the future's with the screw."

"There's not the stability. Paddles hold a craft steady."

"Not in heavy seas they don't. No, sir. Roll right out of the water. And at the best times only the submerged blades give any thrust. The rest are wasted. Right? With a screw, it's immersed all the time and working all the time."

"For a banker, Mr. Whitlaw, you've been taking a great interest in maritime affairs."

"Interest it is, sir. Always a banker's concern. Interest on investment, and profit ratios between different methods of conveyance. What's international trade about if it's not about that?"

A phrase here and there caught the attention of other men, who began to edge towards Bostock. They scented the chance of happy argument. They could talk for hours for and against steam, for and against sail, for and against paddles, and for and against wood or iron hulls.

Whitlaw, edging aside, looked vaguely at his empty glass and then at Nell. His smile was vague, too, but filled with the warmth of an old friend—although in fact she had seen him only twice, and then fleetingly, since the ball last year.

He hiccuped gently. "Have you ever considered crossing the Atlantic on a visit to my side of the world, Miss Meredith?"

"I've thought about it, yes. Who hasn't? And wondered about it."

"You just stop wondering and come see for yourself." His hand fell on her arm and began, almost imperceptibly, to stroke it. "My family would be honoured to offer you hospitality, that I'll promise."

"You're very kind, Mr. Whitlaw."

She took a step back. His hand groped vainly, and he made an effort to steady himself. "There's a cousin of mine liable to visit some months from now. When she's finished her holiday in England, maybe you'd fancy going over with her. . . "

Across Nell's vision walked her mother and Lord Speke.

Her father was away in Lowestoft, summoned at short notice to conclude the sale of the bookshop. "Thank goodness," Julia had said. "If someone's fool enough to make an offer, accept it, whatever it is. Let's be done with all that nonsense." Now, in his absence, her face was turned eagerly up to Speke's; and Speke's limp hand covered hers. They halted before a steward with a tray of brimming glasses. "Adrian," Julia was breathlessly cooing, "do you remember what you said once, long ago, before I went away . . . "

Speke eyed the steward's tightly buttoned jacket and tight uniform trousers.

Nell felt a twing of sickness that had nothing to do with the faint, lulling motion of the ship. Paul Whitlaw's arm came unexpectedly around her as if to steady her; though he was the one in need of steadying. To her astonishment he tried a hasty peck behind her ear.

"Mr. Whitlaw, really!"

"Oh, now, Miss Meredith, it's a very special occasion. And I was told young ladies over here are much freer than in New York. Or," said Paul with owlish gravity, "in Philadelphia."

"Were you, indeed?"

She pulled away. But his flushed face was endearing rather than offensive. She had to smile. He took this as encouragement and made another attempt to encircle her waist.

Suddenly beside them, and then smoothly and decorously between them, was Edmund Gresham. His nod at Paul was courteous but dismissive. When he turned to Nell his handshake offered a reassurance for which she had not asked.

"Congratulations on the grace with which you performed the launching ceremony, Miss Meredith."

"Thank you, Mr. Gresham. You're most kind."

"I was only *very* kind," protested Paul blearily, at Edmund's shoulder. "You call him *most* kind."

Nell looked up into the taller, older man's face. He was neither sentimental as so many had been at the launch, nor damp-eyed as an equal number now were on Jesse Bostock's lavish hospitality. Now, as then, he was dry-eyed: perhaps with that sober gaze estimating her present value and its possible increase, and the investment and dividends involved in a bid for partnership?

Her grandfather was waving to her, demanding her company. As she joined him, the persevering Mr. Whitlaw fell in again beside her.

And she surprised herself as much as any of them when she said, "Grandfather, don't you think I ought to travel in my namesake—on her maiden voyage?"

He stared, then slapped one of his older companions on the back. "You hear that? Not satisfied with redesigning every bed and bolster on board, she wants to go and find out what's wrong with all the fancy notions she's made me pay for! Namesake, indeed—the *Eleanor* is all Eleanor's!"

Paul Whitlaw beamed even more radiantly. "So you do fancy a trip to the United States, Miss Meredith?" He held out his glass to be refilled, and spilt a good third of it over his hand. "I've really tempted you?"

She wondered whether on his home ground he would blossom without the need of drink to give him courage. The fact that Mr. Whitlaw was destined for a banking career and usually wore his manners as high and tight as his collar did not mean that a warmer, livelier Whitlaw was not lurking beneath the starched surface—a Whitlaw in danger of breaking out this very evening. Conscious of being a young American in a foreign land, he admirably played a very correct role before the English. In himself he was probably capable of something quite different.

She was in a mood for change; for surprises.

But when she turned to smile at him, he was blinking. Not now at her, but past her.

Sauntering closer came Poppy between Malcolm and Edmund Gre-

73

sham. But the older brother paused, nodded stiffly again to Nell, and then moved off at a tangent.

Malcolm Gresham said, "Miss Meredith. Haven't had the pleasure of seeing you since we trod the lancers together at the ball. And of course from a respectful distance at the launching. You remember Miss Rivers?"

"Miss Rivers . . ."

"From the Yangtze to the Mersey. An appropriate surname, don't you think?"

So this was what he had dubbed her in his characteristically flippant way. Nell had heard that for many months she had simply been Poppy, deserving no more than that one name he had bestowed as one might bestow a pet name on a cat or dog. Was he now lightheartedly nudging her towards a semblance of respectability?

The two women stood face to face.

When men's heads turned, Nell felt a prickle of antagonism towards all of them. The picture was so obvious: the beauty they all coveted, set against the fledgling businesswoman whose prospects might offer the better catch.

All Poppy's movements seemed a fraction slower than those of ordinary people. When she held out her hand, the fingers drooped like curling petals at the ends; and Nell was not even sure she was intending to shake hands. Then the fingers touched hers. It was a cool, limp touch until Poppy tightened her grip and turned Nell's right palm upwards. Her drowsy eyelashes lowered and she stood lost in contemplation.

"I'm sure it's a bad omen," said Malcolm brightly.

"Reading palms aboard ship?" Nell was embarrassed by the long pause and the other woman's stillness. "Is there some superstition connected with it?"

"I haven't heard of one before. But if Poppy can put the evil eye on it, you may rely on her to do so."

Poppy looked up. "No need your hand." In speech, too, she was slow, enunciating each syllable with the faintest sing-song intonation so that one could not be sure whether she understood what she was saying or was merely practising words for the sheer sound of them. "I see best in your face. What is there."

"Getting quite talkative, aren't we?" Malcolm glanced curiously from one to the other of them.

"You will lead. This ship, only the first. You lead, yes? But"—the dark hair gleamed as her head tilted—"I am afraid."

"Afraid?"

"I do not know. . . . where you lead." The ghost of a shiver ran down

74

the slender reed of her body. She was staring at Nell as if truly seeing her for the first time. "You are . . . dangerous. That is the word, yes?"

"I doubt it." Malcolm made a joke of it. "Oh, I doubt it. And yet . . . mm, yes, Miss Meredith, perhaps you are, perhaps you're very dangerous?"

"I," said Poppy, "I also, I am dangerous."

She might have been reciting a lesson she had somewhere learned by rote. But if there was no real assurance behind the words, her eyes as they looked into Nell's were smouldering; and then they narrowed and misted and almost closed, like those of a languidly contemptuous yet ever-wakeful cat.

THE CROWD had started as a number of separate groups at eight o'clock in the morning, but by nine o'clock began to melt together. It was impossible to tell whether the mob formed purposefully or was built up by forces beyond the comprehension of the original scattered agitators.

Last year's food riots had taught the police a lesson or two. This time a strong force moved swiftly into position across one end of Scotland Road, while another contingent raced to cut off further recruits. But there were too many alleys linking the back streets, cutting through the warren of courtyards. The police knew the back lanes, but their inhabitants knew them even better. The crowd dissolved into a dozen rivulets, streaming away under low arches and across foul open drains to emerge in another road, reforming and advancing from a fresh direction.

There was the crash of breaking glass. Twenty or thirty men lunged onward through a baker's shattered window, grabbing buns and loaves, passing them back or greedily holding on to an armful and turning to run.

Once it had started there was no stopping it. Hunger, gnawing away inside for so long, had bitten its way out. Even those most weakened by that hunger had the strength to smash windows and burst through shop doors. A grocer trying to put up his shutters was knocked into the gutter and trampled on. A butcher and his assistant stemmed an assault only by snatching up meat cleavers and blocking the doorway.

One constabulary charge broke through the main body of rioters, but they leaked away through their conduits and came together once more in a street nearer the docks. Word was sent to call out the militia. But in the time it would take to bring them to the scene there was still food to be stolen and eaten or hidden away against the hard days to come.

"Bloody Irish loose again!"

Shopkeepers seized brooms, walking sticks, rakes, awning poles, anything that came to hand.

"Off my step, you pox-ridden Paddy . . ."

Herrings laid out for sale on slats along a pavement were swept up. A coal cart was overturned, and lumps of coal hurled at windows. Some, instead of breaking the glass, crumbled to thin slivers, and a black dust blew across the street and silted up the gutters.

It was unfortunate that a consignment of West Indian rum was being transferred to a bonded warehouse. The ragged army fell upon the casks, broaching them and rolling them wildly about so that fiery spirit spilled over the quay. Howling with laughter, a score of men sank to their knees and lapped at the setts. Others steadied casks and got their mouths to the bung.

Horse-drawn lorries were halted on the slopes, their cargoes dragged down to be shared out or fought over.

Edmund Gresham heard the distant threat of the storm from his counting-house. It approached and then seemed to recede. The distant chime of a bell on George's landing-stage announced the sailing of a packet. Then the ugly storm of voices broke into neighbouring streets.

Three people halted below the Greshams' window. They were Jesse Bostock, his son-in-law, and his granddaughter. With his back to the main door, Owen Meredith was indicating something high up on a building at the end of the street. Bostock nodded impatiently before coming with the girl into the counting-house, up the half-flight of stairs made necessary by the abrupt slope of the hill at this point.

Nell Meredith was wearing a perky bonnet with a dip in the centre of its wide brim, trimmed with a tight cluster of feathers. Her buttoned jacket narrowed to a slim waist and then billowed out above the flounces of her skirt. She looked trim and very appealing. Had the whole turn-out been contrived to impress the man they were calling on? Edmund thought not: Miss Meredith's barely concealed reluctance to be here in his office at all contradicted the charm of her dress.

She sat stiffly in the only comfortable chair in the room while her grandfather, leaning forward on his stick as if he might at any moment topple on to Edmund's desk, said bluntly, "Thought I'd call in on my way past. See what ideas you have on this railway nuisance. I suppose you've been having troubles, same as the rest of us."

Edmund opened the drawer at his right hand and took out the list he had been working on only the previous afternoon. "Differential rates." He nodded. "It's making it difficult to know what prices to quote to a customer when the railways add on unpredictable amounts—"

"And the Manchester mill-owners encourage them. We're going to have a fight on our hands."

"The Dock Committee—"

"Is refusing to commit itself. It's simply marking time until everything's handed over to the new Harbour Board. And while it waits, the Corporation lets Manchester and the railway companies beyond Manchester squeeze us dry. At the next owners' meeting I thought you and I might stand together." His glance strayed briefly to Nell, inviting her into the team. "And when we get round to forming a separate Steamship Owners' Association, which is long overdue . . . "

The noise from outside was no longer a background noise but a tumult. Nell Meredith rose from her chair and went to the window. The two men followed.

At the corner of the street the iron grille of a public house clanged protectively into place. Deflected, the mob turned uphill, darkening the far pavement.

"Rats," said Bostock vehemently. "Irish rats. Swarming in, infesting the town—chase them out of one sewer and they breed in another."

"Papist bastards." Faintly the cry drifted downhill.

It was no longer a food riot, a scatter of brief skirmishes. The looting provided an excuse for another of the fatal Liverpool confrontations: Catholic versus Protestant. The original mob closed its ranks. A rival faction, stumbling downhill to meet it, quickened and came on at a rush.

Nell let out a cry.

Her father, bemused and unsure, had emerged from the building for which, Edmund had heard, negotiations had been opened a week ago. His head might have been full of schemes for its conversion to another reception centre or lodging-house: there were some ironic rumours going round the town about Meredith and the muddles in which Jesse still indulged him. Certainly, lost in reverie, he had not been anticipating the battle into which he was sucked the moment he reached the open air.

Jesse Bostock swore, and began swinging himself towards the stairs in a crab-like shuffle.

"No, sir—don't go down there!"

Edmund tried to seize the older man's arm, but Nell was between them. Bostock clattered down to the outer door. When he opened it, the pavement was already blocked. A couple of men fell inwards, kicking and punching and yelling the same obscenities over and over again. Bostock kicked one in the ribs and jabbed his stick into the other's thigh.

Owen Meredith, crushed between the two factions, was lifted off his feet so that for a grotesque moment it seemed he was about to be carried triumphantly on someone's shoulders. He tried to say something—something pathetically reasonable, no doubt. Then out of nowhere young Malcolm Gresham was fighting a way towards him. Struck by a flailing fist, he reeled aside, but plunged back as Owen was dropped and lost in the heart of the struggle.

Edmund got his arm round Bostock's shoulders and tried to drag him back.

"Let me get at them."

"You can't do any good out there. If we don't block this door they're likely to—"

"I'll not be scared by scum like that."

With a desperate heave Edmund hauled him back into the narrow passage and urged him towards the short flight of steps.

Nell could not force herself away from the window and the sickening sight of boots kicking, fists smashing into men's faces—a senseless frenzy, and in the middle of it somewhere her father . . .

Two men seemed to be looking for him. Or descending on him. One raised his arm and hammered down, again and again, with the stroke of a brutal mallet. A gang of sailmakers from some establishment behind a nearby court hurried to join in, brandishing the tools of their trade. Blood spurted.

Malcolm Gresham's head rose from the confusion. He was tugging at something or someone.

Even through the closed window the snatches of abuse came clear and raucous.

"Outer the way, you."

"Bastards, see how you like *that*."

"Come on, *at* 'em . . ."

With his shoulder braced against the door, ready to close it if the aimless rage of the mob turned this way, Edmund saw his brother fight suddenly clear, with Owen Meredith leaning dazedly against him. There was an open space. They tottered across it. Edmund pushed the door wide and stepped out to meet them.

Another space opened, a corridor in one flank of the crowd. Down it a sailmaker ran as if released from a trap. He was carrying a reamer, its hollowed-out blade jutting before him like a lance. Whether he was blind with anger or drink, or whether he had lost his balance when the gap

79

unexpectedly opened, it was impossible to say. A few seconds, a scramble of feet, and he had run hard against Owen. The reamer drove straight in. Owen stood there, still propped against Malcolm Gresham. Then when the man stood back, staring stupidly at his empty hand, Owen began to slump.

Nell was at the foot of the stairs, sobbing, trying to force her way past Edmund. He put his arm round her, as he had put it round her grandfather. She tried to fight him off and run out. He tightened his grip. All of a sudden her father was upon them. His voice was making a hideous, strangled sound in his throat; and as he tried to reach for her there was a bubbling of blood along his lips, thickening and beginning to flow down his chin and on to his lapels. Edmund pulled Nell's head forcibly round so that her face was driven into his shoulder. Even through the braid of her jacket he felt her heart beating; and her breath was a hot, shuddering pulsation against his throat.

Malcolm had half-lifted Owen Meredith inside, kicking the door shut behind him. In the restricted space Edmund reached past to shoot the upper bolt.

"Please, Miss Meredith. Give us room to move your father."

They helped him up into the office. The rusty stain dripped its way up each step and across the carpet. Edmund turned the armchair so that his brother could lower the stricken man gently into it. The shaft of the reamer stuck out from his side like a hideous, unnatural bolt holding him together. They did not dare to touch it or drag it out.

Nell crumpled to her knees beside her father, oblivious to the blood pumping, spurting in little rhythmic spouts that dotted the light blue of her jacket.

"Marshall." Edmund shouted through to the clerk in the back office. "Get Dr. Sandison. Go out the back entry."

"Yes, Mr. Edmund."

"As quickly as you can."

But it would be no quick matter to get a doctor here on a day like this, through these bloody streets. And even if he were miraculously here within a few minutes, it was doubtful if he could be of any use.

Owen Meredith tried to speak and choked on a moan.

Easing him into a new position, Malcolm said tersely, "Two of them—in the thick of it—weren't there by accident. A couple of runners. Taking the chance of smashing him because of the reception centre. One of them I've seen—"

"Told you." It was Jesse Bostock, hunched against the desk. His voice was slurred, unlike his usual boom. "Told you it wouldn't . . . told you . . ."

Owen's head slumped forward.

Nell patted his hand helplessly, trying to lean forward and look up into his face.

There was a heavy thump behind them. Edmund looked round.

Jesse Bostock had slid to the floor. His stick fell away from limp fingers. His eyes were wide open and he was trying to say something—perhaps to deride Owen again for his hopeless idealistic notions. But no words would come.

OWEN MEREDITH was dead and Jesse Bostock all but speechless after his stroke. Meredith would dabble no longer in his silly schemes. His daughter would not sail in the *Eleanor* on her maiden voyage. Those were two things to please Fred Hesketh. There were other things not so pleasing. Within a few weeks, in fact, Hesketh began to wish that Nell Meredith had gone to New York after all, and that she had stayed there a long, long time.

Old Jesse could scarcely communicate with anyone now. He could not drag himself from chair to chair without help. The left side of his face drooped, his left arm was paralysed, and the sounds he made did not add up to words—or none that Hesketh could interpret. If such a blow had fallen in the past, Hesketh would have been the one taken into Bostock's confidence: made to listen, to learn, to work out some way of working together, made to suffer hell . . . but the one on whom the old man would have depended. Now his chosen messenger was the Meredith girl.

She was worse than ever. Not that she was impolite. When she approached Hesketh with some new order from her grandfather she did not hide her dislike, but very correctly assumed they were working together in the same cause: the Bostock cause. He did as he was told, hating every minute of it. Did these instructions really come from old Jesse or was the girl twisting them to suit herself?

Jesse's last public appearance was at the departure of the *Eleanor* on her first run to Queenstown and New York. He was unable to speak to the *Mercury* reporter or to his own captain save through Nell. He grunted and growled at her, and she made out that she understood.

A week after the new steamer's sailing, Fred Hesketh jibbed. On the return of a Bostock barque from delivering iron and tinplate to Boston, one crew member lodged a complaint with the magistrates that he had been overpowered by Liverpool crimps, beaten insensible, and sold into the crew of the ship. Crimping was no crime on the other side of the Atlantic; but on English shores it was. Hesketh set out to deal summarily with the complaint. Precious few who had been snatched away dared to protest, counting themselves lucky to get home again and be paid off. Those who did whine could usually expect a fresh beating in an alley, plenty of gin forced into them, and a stupefied despatch on some other ship: no complainant, no evidence, no case to answer.

Yet Bostock, who knew the rough code of the waterfront as well as anyone, had sent a message down by his granddaughter that the company must itself investigate the complaint and lodge the man comfortably until the truth was established. Was he going soft? Hesketh could not credit it. Any more than he could credit Nell Meredith's assurance that her grandfather still intended, in spite of her father's death, to let her go ahead with the emigration centre and maybe a second one.

He took the horse-bus to the top of the brow and made his way to Bostock's gates. The gatekeeper came out of his cottage and touched the peak of his cap—more casually than if Hesketh had been a shipping magnate or insurance broker; but then, such would roll up in their own carriages. At least he offered a token of respect.

"Hello, Watson. Mr. Bostock at home?"

"Never anywhere else nowadays, Mr. Hesketh."

"Just a few points I'd like to tidy up with him."

Hesketh tried to walk jauntily on, as he had done many a time in the past. He was Jesse Bostock's manager: who better to handle each and every problem as it arose?

"Sorry, Mr. Hesketh, but if there's a message you'd better let me take it." Watson was blocking his path.

"You know me."

"Yes, Mr. Hesketh, but orders are that Miss Eleanor deals with everything for Mr. Bostock while he's . . . not himself."

"He might be dead for all the rest of us know."

"Oh, he's not dead, Mr. Hesketh."

Watson stood aside, without relaxing his vigilance, and pointed across the lawn. At the side of the house Jesse Bostock was limping along, a painful step at a time. One foot dragged. He looked as if his arms were doing all the work, magically balancing him on top of his stick. Standing a few yards ahead, arms slightly spread to catch him—or embrace him—Nell Meredith waited. He managed a nod, seeming to ask what she thought of his progress.

"I've got to talk to him," growled Hesketh. "I'm not happy about the instructions that get down to me."

"If you want me to ask Miss Eleanor—"

"No, I don't damn well want you to ask Miss Eleanor any damn thing. I want Mr. Bostock himself."

"You wouldn't understand what he says, Mr. Hesketh. Only Miss Eleanor understands."

Only Miss Eleanor. Miss blasted cunning Nell.

Hesketh turned on his heel.

"I'll tell her you called," said Watson after him.

Hesketh walked the entire way back. He would not have trusted his face or voice, sitting opposite people who might know him in the omnibus. So many people knew Fred Hesketh. He looked down on the roofs and nests from the hillside. To his right he picked out the contours of Jesse Bostock's empire. He was a part of it. He had made quite a lot of it for Bostock. It was a world that girl would never understand. He stalked on down, and that world opened up to receive him. An old woman on a corner bobbed her head to him. Another scowled and dodged away. The tang of Mersey mud at low tide seeped along the alleys. Flotillas of long, wide lorries creaked over setts and cobbles, drawn by great white and dun horses.

Tommy Connor crossed the street and stopped in front of him.

"You. Mr. Hesketh."

"Connor. A few days at home, hey?"

"*Mister* Hesketh."

The threat in the tone was shaky but real. Hesketh braced himself, the glib friendliness draining away from his own manner. "Something wrong . . . Tommy?"

"I think you know what."

"Haven't an idea, son."

"Look." Connor was not used to throwing a challenge into anyone's face like this. Not anyone as important as Fred Hesketh, anyway. "Look, was it *you* . . . ?"

"Was it me *what?*"

"She was expecting. My wife. Now it's all gone wrong."

Hesketh felt a momentary chill. He forced a brusque nod. "Sorry to hear that."

"She's not well. Not well at all. She's . . . in a mess."

"Sorry to hear it," Hesketh repeated. "But what's it got to do with me?"

"That's what I'd like to know. After what I've been hearing."

"And what have you been hearing?"

Connor was trying to stare him out. But Connor's eyes were the first to wander. A whisper of a sob in his throat, then he turned and blundered away. He wasn't going to risk it, not with Fred Hesketh. And that was just as well for him.

Hesketh walked on. It wasn't his fault. Whatever had happened, it was nothing to do with him. Could just as well be Tommy Connor's fault, coming home from Dublin and getting a bit too rough for a wife in that condition. Could have been any one of a dozen things. Working in the warehouse, twisting herself, playing the fool, not looking after herself properly. Girls in the Devil's Acre dropped their kids by the score. Good riddance, most of the time.

The air along Salthouse Dock was sharp with the smell of soda being loaded into a three-master. Hesketh had crossed the street and was on the corner before he realised someone was waiting for him.

Mrs. McCreedy, aging but still one of the brawniest of the washer-women, stood in the doorway with her great red arms folded across her bosom.

"So you've come back, Mr. Hesketh."

"Often come along here." Hesketh tried a broad, matey wink. "No view like it, so far as I'm concerned."

"Haven't seen much of you lately, though."

"Been a bit busy."

"Yeh. Done a bit of damage, too."

"Damage?"

"That girl."

"I don't know what—"

"Tommy Connor mayn't open his mouth to you, don't suppose he'll dare, but that doesn't stop the rest of us."

He ought to have ignored her and walked past. But he wasn't going to stand that sort of talk from an old bag of that kind. He approached and looked her menacingly up and down.

"That's no way to talk to me, Mrs. McCreedy."

"Isn't it, then? You think you can get away with treating a girl like that—tearing her to bloody bits?"

"I don't have to listen to—"

"Maybe you're right. Talk's not much use, is it?"

She was heavy and her arms were thick; she looked a slow old cow; but when she struck, she struck fast. A meaty hand grabbed Hesketh's shoulder, and he was flung past her into the washhouse. Quivering with rage he turned, to find her planted firmly in the doorway.

"Get out of my way. By God, you're going to hear about this."

Mrs. McCreedy did not say another word. She stood there until he flung himself at her, smacking against those arms and that awful sagging bosom. She laughed.

The laugh was taken up behind him. But very quietly.

He felt rather than heard the other women slopping across the floor and clustering behind him. When he jerked away from the spongy bulk of Mrs. McCreedy it was to be caught by other hands—one on his shoulder again, tugging him to one side, another tangling in his jacket and pulling him further into the room, another gripping his neck as if getting the measure of it before choking the life out of him.

"Get your hands off me or I'll—"

A reeking wet cloth was thrust into his mouth. He gagged on the strands twisted around his teeth. A hard edge struck into his buttocks, and willing hands knocked his legs up so that he was tipped on his back on to a cold stone slab. It couldn't happen to him, it wasn't possible. He kicked out and tried to yell, but water dripped down his throat from the cloth. Then—no, it couldn't be, oh God it couldn't be—eager fingers were tearing at his trousers. He tried to fight an arm free. It was captured and pinioned back. His trousers tore. Gleefully he was being raised from the slab while they were dragged away down his legs.

"Doesn't look so proud today."

"Wouldn't have thought it could *do* that much damage."

Laughter broke off abruptly. Savagely one of the women said, "But it did, didn't it?"

Hesketh tried to explain, or threaten, or just shout for the sheer need to shout. But the gag was pushed more firmly into his mouth.

His jacket was wrestled away. Shirt, vest, socks. His whole back was chilled now, his whole body naked, flesh sticking to the bitter stone.

Three greedy faces loomed above him. Their grins had no humour in them. Even before he knew what was coming he was terrified.

Then one of them held it out before his eyes.

Her scrubbing-brush with its harsh bristles was poised for an eternity. The smell of alkaline soap was the smell of cargoes along Salthouse Dock. It stung. But nothing like the sting when the brush descended.

Fred Hesketh screamed soundlessly in his head. The woman stooping over him and relentlessly scrubbing could not have heard the sound, yet knew. Her eyes met his in ravenous joy. Bristles tore down his chest and over his belly, digging and scraping, working up to a frenzy. Then a second one scoured its way over his left shoulder; and one over his right shoulder; and when all three collided on his navel, the hags screamed with laughter and leaned harder on the brushes.

He felt his flesh being lifted from his body, stripped away and laid out in shreds around him. It couldn't go on. There was nothing left, they couldn't go on gouging down through blood and veins and keep going on, on and on. Couldn't .

"We'll get you clean, Mr. Hesketh." Who was it said that, which one of them? "Clean you up like you've never been cleaned before."

There was a woman still waiting in the background. Even as he threshed to and fro, trying to escape the hands which held him like clamps, he had a hazy picture of her, getting hazier as his eyes watered with pain and then he was openly, helplessly weeping with it all.

He had been flayed. Every square inch of him burned and shrieked. The yellowed ceiling above swam, beginning to spin like a merry-go-round.

"Stop!"

A scrubbing-brush was lifted before his eyes, every spine of it red and sticky.

It was over. They were tired, they had given in.

Cold air was like the blast of a furnace on what they had laid open.

The patiently waiting woman stepped forward. The bristles on the brush she held were clean and hard and golden. You'd have said it was newly bought and newly brought here from the shop.

"All right, then, Mrs. Clarke."

Clarke? It wasn't a name that meant anything to him. He tried to focus through the mist as her face swam closer to his. Very distinctly she said:

"I'm Emily's mam."

The hush might have been described as holy. Mrs. Clarke, erect, lifted her shining new scrubbing-brush like an offering. And drove it down. Down into his groin. And began to twist it. Then to lash it to and fro. Impossible agony scorched into him. Down it went and up, this way and that, circling and scouring and scalding the wet horror between his legs.

A door slammed. The gag was whipped from his mouth, leaving shreds stuck to his gums.

"Let's hear him."

The scrubbing-brush was a sizzling iron. If he screamed he did not know his own voice.

Everywhere was blood. How could it have spat that high? His eyes were clouded with red, the ceiling was red, the world was red and raw and then deeper red as he slid down into black torment . . .

When he awoke everything was unbelievably still. He felt something soft under his right hand as he tried to move. Yet the softness became

87

torture when he drew that hand an inch or so across the sheet. His eyes opened, and he was gazing up into a pale green vaulted ceiling.

He turned over. And howled out loud.

A middle-aged woman with starched cap and apron and an expression that might just as well have been starched hove into view and looked down at him.

"Doctor, he's awake."

There was a young man there, too, with high collar and haughty nose and godalmighty expression.

Fred Hesketh whimpered. He was burning all over: burning, stuck by flames to everything he touched.

Yet they were grinning. Trying to look serious and attentive, but grinning. The nurse had to turn away and put a hand to her mouth.

As he came back to full consciousness—the searing heat all over his body, the blaze through that pulp in his groin—when he could stop weeping and begging them to do something, he saw the shift of expression in all of them: not just the doctor and nurses, but the other patients when he could force himself round to inspect them. In other beds in that long ward of the infirmary lay men without limbs, a man without a jaw, a man with his testicles shot away—"But not," Hesketh heard the sniggering after the gas lamps had been dimmed, "not *scrubbed* away." Injured men shipped home in the last batch from the Crimea could lie there and laugh at Fred Hesketh. In the middle of the night when everyone else was asleep he still heard the chuckling in his head, keeping time with surges of pain from his raw flesh.

Ointments were rubbed on with the assurance that they would soothe. They burned. The doctor made soothing noises, and could hardly keep a straight face as he spoke.

When at last Hesketh could put on his clothes and hobble out into the fresh air, it was no better. Everyone knew. Everyone who had worked with him, respected him, feared him, or tried to outdo him was informed of every shameful detail. And not one of them feared him any longer.

"Had a good clean-up, Mr. Hesketh?"

And a brash young shipyard foreman from across the water could forget who he was supposed to take orders from and say, "Had your bottom scraped, Fred?"

It reverberated from one end of dockland to the other. Such a large town, such a world, and him such a big figure in that world: but when it came to trouble like this, how like a village it was. The waterfront communities knew one another, and gossip spread as it would have done through the pettiest country hamlet.

For years he had thumped the weaklings whenever he wanted to. Now the weaklings knew what a band of women had done to him, and they laughed. They remained weaklings, they would never have the courage to hit him too boldly. But they could live on their laughter: nothing would stop them laughing now, on and on and on. Day and night, the gale of laughter, drowning out everything else.

"Got a clean bill of health, I hear, Mr. Hesketh?"

And Jesse Bostock died.

"Died?" Hesketh got the news not, for once, from Nell Meredith but from the Bostock counting-house clerk. Still stooped against the aftermath of pain pulling at his vitals, Hesketh said, "Another stroke?"

"I suppose you could call it that. Took him unawares, you see." The clerk, wearing a black tie and black armband, endeavoured to look solemn. But his face cracked where it ought not to, and the grin that everyone else was wearing took over. Jesse Bostock was dead, but there was still a joke to be had. "He died when he heard. About you and the washhouse, you know. Died of laughing."

11

"WELL, GIRL, it's up to you now." Nell could hear her grandfather's voice so clearly. It was impossible that he should be lying silent in the box with brass handles in that black hearse. Unthinkable that he should have given up. She listened still for his next painfully shaped syllables. "Up to you now." Was that really what he was saying, or had she misheard it this time?

The black plumes on the horses' heads bobbed and pranced towards St. Nicholas' church. Silk mourning ribbons streamed from silk bands on tall black hats. As the funeral procession made its way beside the churchyard wall, overlooking the dockside road that Jesse Bostock had trodden so many times in his life, men from the quays lined up to doff hats and caps in flickering succession. At the church gates a platoon of lads from the Seamen's Orphanage sprang raggedly to attention.

The exchanges of Brunswick Street and Dale Street, the counting-houses of James Street and insurance offices of Castle Street were closed. No Liverpool gentleman of any consequence was absent from the procession, and there was no vacant seat in the old church.

Nell half-heard the solemnities about death in the midst of life, about resurrection, about the virtues of the deceased and his reward in heaven; listened to promises of the life to come, and could think of her grandfather only in this life.

He had been so bearish, domineering, dictatorial. She had never got

90

over that assumption of his that she and her parents existed only as his courtiers. Yet they had so often laughed together and struck sparks. Testy or not, he had so often let her have her own way—even if only, as she sometimes suspected, to see what sort of fool she would make of herself. His decisions might often appal her, but it was the sheer ability to make decisions and bluster them through that had made him and kept him what he was. Nothing daunted Jesse Bostock.

Yet he had allowed himself occasional bursts of disturbing self-revelation in her presence. She knew without being told that he had never in his career been so frank with anyone else. It put a heavy responsibility on her, which was perhaps what the cunning old schemer intended.

"When I was a lad I used to get cross because I wasn't allowed to get my hands on things. Too young to take the big decisions, I was told. You know, Nell, for half your life you're the wrong age—too inexperienced to command respect. Then when you've got the experience, you're getting too old and just an infernal nuisance, always in other folks' way."

"There must be a period," Nell had protested, "when you're in your prime and everything's absolutely right."

"I seem to have been blown round that. Missed it."

"Nonsense, grandfather."

The face that was dead came into her mind's eye again, lit by its seamed, ancient, wicked grin. "Nothing so disgusting as self-pity, eh? Anyway, one thing I can tell you: even when you're old, if you cling hard enough to the helm they'll all be too respectful—or a sight too scared—to notice you could be steering quite the wrong course."

In those last days, when he could no longer harangue her, he had clung to his stick as if it were indeed the helm. Forcing himself to hold the weakening vessel of his body on course, forcing himself to live, striving to give commands in words that refused to obey him, he asked her daily with his eyes and a sequence of grunts and mumbles if she didn't think he was doing a little better than yesterday. Nell had never consciously put words into that failing mouth. She had tried to interpret accurately and to put his wishes into action. But could she be sure she had not sometimes nudged him in one direction or another?

If so, he must have known—and secretly approved.

She had been sure he would defeat the paralysis just as he had defeated every other opponent. Until at last he succumbed to that gale of helpless laughter, leaving Bostock Navigation without its navigator.

Nell was alone. The emptiness was so vast after the massive presence and power of Jesse. And so silent. *Grandpa, come back. Just for an hour. Please, just for ten minutes. All those things we never had a chance to talk about, because somehow there was never time, and I didn't realise.*

I never told you I loved you, because I didn't know.

She had seen her father dead and tranquil in his coffin; but had never seen anything so dead and drained, so obviously discarded, as her grandfather's corpse. Within that husk lingered no rustle of dry breath, not one last croak.

"Not you." He had laboured to wrench words into shape after her father's funeral. "Not your fault." She had longed to believe him. But without her intervention would Owen ever have been saddled with the emigrant centre and its dangerous problems?

"Well, girl, it's up to you now."

She looked sidelong at pews across the aisle, filled with bulky, well-fed men, and wives decorously in their shadow: self-confident men who ruled the town, their businesses, their homes, their families.

At the end of one pew Edmund Gresham's profile was as solemn and strong as any of the others.

They kneeled. Rose. Sang a hymn. At last were beside the damp hole in the ground.

"Earth to earth, ashes to ashes, dust to dust . . ."

In the dining-room of Bostock's Brow, those invited to share the funeral meats talked sombrely for a while as they picked at cold ham, a galantine of veal, turkey, and spiced cakes. Then someone risked a careful joke, it was capped by one more boisterous, and the chatter of the living grew louder to blot out echoes of the dead.

Nell herself had drawn up the list of guests, choosing the names she was sure her grandfather would have expected. His head clerk deferentially approved her selection.

Julia insisted on adding one name of her own choice.

"Lord Speke and your grandfather were very close towards the end. Father had a great respect for Adrian."

It was, thought Nell, regrettably true, though respect was not quite the right description: reluctant awe was more like it. Jesse Bostock had half-despised anyone as effete as Speke, living on the family name and the inherited monies of the family estate. But for all his pride in being a self-made man, and by Liverpool standards a gentleman, he could not entirely repress a sneaking snobbery. Aristocratic blood somehow empowered a man to offer advice which from any other source would have been spurned. Speke's strange attentiveness in recent months had made Jesse uneasy; yet he had been flattered, and allowed Speke to visit him after the stroke, when others had been kept at bay.

Nell had fractionally hesitated before including the Gresham brothers. She wanted no speculation in offices and cocoa rooms and counting-houses. But there would have been greater comment if she had excluded them.

Edmund Gresham spoke first to Julia and then came to Nell to express ritual condolences with an uneffusive courtesy. His manner reinforced her earlier impression of someone steady, secure . . . likeable.

So she would like him. There was no harm in that: she had no need of anything more than liking him.

Malcolm Gresham stood for a moment beside his brother and expressed similar sentiments, then excused himself and walked away. Deliberately leaving them alone together?

Edmund said, "Miss Meredith, if ever I . . . that is, if ever we can be of any practical assistance, please don't hesitate to call on us."

"I'm most obliged to you, Mr. Gresham."

"I wouldn't wish you to regard it as an obligation. We'd be the ones to consider ourselves favoured."

His diffidence sounded sincere, in an odd way adding to his strength. But Nell was conscious that from every corner of the room people were sizing the two of them up, perhaps snickering behind their hands that Edmund Gresham was losing no time in staking his claim, taking it for granted that there would soon be a mutual understanding needing only a nod and the flick of a hand as in some transaction on Exchange Flags.

After the reading of the will she would know better what her position was. And so, when its terms were published in the *Mercury,* would all Liverpool.

The will was read in the presence of herself, her mother and Lord Speke. Nell was on the verge of querying this intrusion of a stranger, supposing it to be another of her mother's tasteless indiscretions, when the Bostock solicitor made it plain that Speke was joining them in the library on his specific invitation.

Nell felt a tremor of apprehension. Something had been going on, or was about to start, of which she had had no inkling.

Mr. Embery settled himself at the library table, glancing half-apologetically at Nell and venturing a melancholy smile. She had often carried messages from her grandfather to Mr. Embery. Now the position was reversed. Mr. Embery was bringing her the old man's last message.

Jesse Bostock left ten thousand pounds to his daughter Julia Meredith. All else of which he died possessed, including the fleet and assets of Bostock Navigation and all related warehouses and wharf leases, went to his beloved granddaughter Eleanor Meredith.

The legacy was accompanied by the wish—it was expressed no more strongly than that, but the four in the room could hear Jesse's voice resonating with greater emphasis—that she should without delay enter into some suitable partnership according to her own best judgement. By which he implicitly meant, of course, his own best judgement.

Lord Speke was appointed her guardian until her twenty-fifth birthday or until she married.

Nell caught her breath.

Mr. Embery turned to Speke. "I understand you had already expressed to the late Mr. Bostock your willingness to act in this capacity."

"I was honoured to accept."

There was a silence. Mr. Embery tapped the will abstractedly into neat alignment with a large legal envelope.

"So, Nell." Julia's brittle laugh made them all start. "Isn't that wonderful? I don't know how father could have entrusted *quite* so much to you, but I'm sure that with Adrian's guidance you'll make the right decisions."

Speke leaned towards Nell so that he could put his flaccid hand on hers. The yellow pouches below his eyes drooped like those of an ingratiatingly mournful dog. "I trust this hasn't come as too great a shock to you, Eleanor. I'm flattered, really deeply moved, by your grandfather's trust in me. I'll serve you as well as I can." He risked a smile. "Your obedient servant."

She sought for words and found them as difficult to frame as the ailing Jesse had done.

"I . . . there's so much to think over."

"Of course." His fingers patted her gently. "Of course. We'll have plenty of time to talk. In the meantime, just leave everything to me."

Julia's voice rose more shrilly than ever. "There is just one small point, Mr. Embery."

"Yes, Mrs. Meredith?"

"Well, actually that *is* the point. About my name." She gulped, glanced at Speke, and rushed on: "It's given in the will as Julia Meredith but I'm not really Julia Meredith any more and . . . but it won't make any difference to the bequest, will it?"

"I don't follow you, Mrs. . . . er . . . "

Julia drew herself up. "I am Lady Speke."

Mr. Embery's jaw dropped.

"It makes no legal difference, does it?"

"Purely a technicality," said Mr. Embery with some effort. "But I had no idea, none at all. If it is in order to offer congratulations, I . . . "

Speke said smoothly, "I knew Julia, Miss Bostock as she then was, many years ago. It was a very dear friendship. And now a most happy outcome."

"A friendship," said Julia, "which ought never to have been . . . interrupted." She trembled an appealing smile at Nell. "My darling, you won't think too harshly of me, will you? I was loyal to your poor dear fa-

94

ther, you of all people can't deny that. But you also know, don't you, what a wretched existence I had to endure? Punishment for my own folly, I'm not denying it. If only I had known then what I know now."

You could have been an Honourable . . .

Nell fought off another twinge of the sickness she had felt that day aboard the *Eleanor,* watching the two of them together.

"But now!" breathed her mother. "Now! I still can't believe life has given us a second chance like this. To think of Adrian waiting all this time, like one of those novels you used to . . ." She had been about to draw Nell into a remembered picture, but turned abruptly away. It was a picture to be forgotten. The days when her daughter worked in a circulating library were to be dismissed as summarily as her dead husband and all else that had happened in Lowestoft.

The next day Nell was taken to her new stepfather's home, where he obviously felt more confident of handling the necessary explanations.

Orrell Manor stood in unkempt parkland on the northeast outskirts of the town. When it was built in the time of Queen Anne it must have stood virtually alone in its marshy setting; but now houses were encroaching, and the western rim of the wasteland was broken by mounds of earth and stone heaped around excavations for yet another dock. The house had a faded grandeur utterly unlike the heavy flamboyance of Bostock's Brow; but faded that grandeur undoubtedly was. A musty smell met one in the gracefully proportioned hall, and a fine pall of dust seemed to drape most of the furniture like a protective covering. Tapestries above the dark oak staircase looked heavy with grime. It was a relief to pass into a brighter, small parlour looking out over a ragged plantation. Even here there were signs of neglect in the sun-bleached curtains, the rubbed fabric of chair arms and fraying ottoman cushions.

Lord Speke rang for tea and indicated that Nell should sit between himself and her mother—his wife, Nell had to keep telling herself in dazed disbelief.

Before he could speak, Julia gushed, "My darling one, you must think we're terribly naughty to have kept you in the dark about our little secret."

"Why did it have to be a secret?"

"It was for your sake more than anyone's, so you wouldn't be too upset. And of course one has to think of other people, such silly people—"

"We felt," Speke interrupted in a thin voice almost as hurried as her own, "that to many unsympathetic people it would seem improper that we should marry so soon after your father's unfortunate death. Not knowing all the circumstances, ordinary people do have very limited ideas."

"What circumstances?" asked Nell stonily.

"My dear"—her mother took up the refrain—"I was so lonely, I did need someone to lean on, and Adrian was so wonderful, there just wasn't any doubt in *our* minds—"

"Did grandfather know about this?"

Speke cleared his throat. "Well . . . "

Of course they would not have risked telling him. Speke, whose dilapidated house and grounds displayed all too patently his need for money, had foreseen the likely future of the company after Jesse Bostock's death and played his cards accordingly: played on Jesse's snobbery, wormed his way into the old man's good graces by promising to stand by Nell, and secretly secured himself into the heart of the family by marrying her mother. But that final move had had to be concealed: old Jesse, however deluded by Speke's pedigree, would have interpreted *that* mating too shrewdly.

"And now all that nonsense is over and done with." Julia toyed with the ringlets which Nell had half-noticed accumulating but only now saw in their full prodigality. "We can all move in here and be ourselves, and the whole world can know I'm Lady Speke."

"But grandfather's house—"

"Oh, that dreary mausoleum." Once so gloriously preferable to the rooms behind the Lowestoft shop, Bostock's Brow was in turn being relegated to limbo. "There's an awful lot to be done here, that goes without saying. It needs a woman's touch." Julia smiled rouishly at Adrian Speke. "The dining-room will have to be redecorated before we can receive anyone. And we must do something special for Eleanor. Such a nice room I've picked out for you, dear, but I won't deny it needs lightening a bit."

"All in good time," said Speke dubiously.

"But the good time for that sort of thing is now. We do have to liven up the place before—"

"I shall live at Bostock's Brow," said Nell levelly.

"That might be a sound idea for a few days, until we've decided exactly what has to be done here. But I've had a bed made up for you tonight, so you can decide what alterations *you* want, get the feeling of the place—"

"I think I must get back now."

"I can send a message for your maid to bring your clothes," said Speke, "and anything else you need."

"I shall live at Bostock's Brow," said Nell again. "And I must get back there to go through grandfather's papers. There are several matters waiting for a decision. He wouldn't have wanted them to wait too long."

"Carter can manage," said her mother. "That's what chief clerks are for. Adrian will see him and—"

"Naturally I shall bring Carter in. We'll go through everything together."

When Nell left, cooly brushing aside her mother's continued protests, her head was in a whirl. Instinctively she had shouldered a burden without asking herself whether she could carry the weight. Speke, seeing her to the door, had warily suggested that he should be with her, should take some of the strain, should discuss matters with her before she immersed herself in the complexities of commerce. For a frozen, endless instant she had been tempted. Had she not always told herself that she wanted someone else to make decisions, someone else to settle disputes—someone more powerful to take the blame and disguise her own blunders?

Now she could have Speke to rely on, or some man she might choose to marry.

Or herself.

Mr. Carter, when summoned to her house, made it plain that he too had been considering these various aspects. He showed mild surprise at finding Nell alone. "As Lord Speke has been appointed your guardian, miss, I thought that perhaps he'd—"

"He is a guardian," said Nell, "not a regent. Control of this firm has been vested in me. With your help, Mr. Carter, I'll discover how best to exercise it."

They drew up their chairs and began to go through files and loose papers left by Jesse Bostock. Glimpsing a name on one scribbled memorandum, Nell said, "Hesketh. I'd like to be rid of him. After all that's happened, I couldn't work with Hesketh."

"Well," said Carter with the hint of a stutter. "Mm, yes . . well. I think . . . well . . . mm, I think one may say he has virtually—um—dismissed himself. His authority along the docks has been considerably undermined by . . . um . . . " He went pink.

Nell came to his rescue. "He has been made a laughing stock. I trust you're right. If he elects to disappear of his own accord, far from Liverpool, that will save us a great deal of unpleasantness."

They turned their attention to a number of unanswered letters. Among them was an invitation to a meeting the following day. Shipowners were urged to attend a conference on the formation of a Steamship Owners' Association and its representation on the Dock and Harbour Board, which, in spite of all opposition, was to replace the declining Dock Committee. At the same time a public statement would be formulated on the Corporation's eleventh-hour attempts to block the Parliamentary Bill for the Board's formation.

97

"You think the Bill will in fact get through?" In spite of her grandfather's more aggressive harangues, Nell was vague about some of the provisions of the new system.

"In one form or another it'll have to be passed. The town's prosperity depends entirely on the river, yet the docks and the shippers have to pay dues and poor rates and any other number of exactions into Corporation coffers—out of all proportion to what's offered in return. There's got to be a self-governing body, and an end to town dues. And it has to have the power to negotiate on equal terms with the railway companies, stop them chivvying the shippers, juggling rates and playing off one merchant against another."

"But surely we're all in the same business? Without railways, how would we shift our landed goods? Without *us*, how could they get anything into or out of the country?"

"Well, yes, that's about the size of it, miss. Only it never works out quite as simple as that. There's a lot of bargaining has to go on."

"It's important, then, that I should attend the meeting."

"You, Miss Bostock? I mean, I'm sorry . . . Miss Meredith. I wasn't thinking. Just for a minute I thought of you as—"

"I'll take it as a compliment, Mr. Carter." She looked at the invitation again. "Ten o'clock tomorrow morning."

"But you can't go, miss. It's at the Beckwith Club."

"Why should I not go?"

"It's a gentleman's club."

"Then they should hold the meeting elsewhere. Or for once let a lady in. Which I shall insist on their doing."

"Only once a year, miss, on Ladies' Night. No use in your going there tomorrow."

"I'm a steamship owner. And lessee of a considerable stretch of wharfage."

"You'll have to appoint someone to speak for you."

"I shall speak," said Nell, "for myself."

In defiance of Carter's warnings Nell arrived at ten minutes to ten the next morning on the steps of the Beckwith Club. The doorman bowed politely, but the politeness became icy when she made a move to enter.

"Sorry, ma'am, but I'm afraid you can't go in there."

"I am attending a meeting."

"Not here, I'm afraid, ma'am. It's for gentlemen only."

"I am Eleanor Meredith of Bostock Navigation."

"That's as may be." The man grew sterner. "This club's for gentlemen only, and I've heard nothing about altering the rules today."

She wondered whether to flout convention and force her way past him. As she hesitated, poised to make a move he was anticipating with dawning horror, a man came up beside her. Below, pausing on a lower step, another was taking his leave of a young woman.

Edmund Gresham raised his hat to Nell.

His brother put his head closer to Poppy's and murmured something in her ear.

Edmund said, "A spot of difficulty, Miss Meredith?"

"I'm having great difficulty, yes, in gaining admission to the meeting to which the head of Bostock Navigation has been invited."

"Ah, I see." Obviously Edmund did see. He glanced at the doorman, who puffed out his bemedalled chest and made it clear he was not going to budge.

99

"This meeting," said Nell, "is for those of us with steamships and an interest in reorganising dock administration."

"Just so."

"I am the controller of Bostock Navigation."

"There has never been a lady at such gatherings before."

"Then today will mark the beginning of a new era."

"I fear not, Miss Meredith," said Edmund with unwavering affability. "You would have done better to send a proxy."

His brother and Poppy came up the steps to join them; or, rather, Malcolm joined them, his eyes twinkling at Nell, while Poppy stood passively to one side.

"It's absurd," said Nell indignantly. "I believe I'm right, Mr. Gresham, in saying that your company so far has only two steamships, and those only coastal paddlers. The Bostock line has four ocean-going vessels, each of them four times as large as yours. Which of us has more right to speak in there?"

"Good for you, Miss Meredith." Malcolm slapped his hip. Poppy, clad in deep orange, responded to his appreciative tone by a slow turn of her head and a long, unblinking stare at Nell.

Two new arrivals passed, raising their hats to the ladies and covertly studying them. A third did not pass but joined the group. The doorman's heels clicked to attention.

"Good morning, m'Lord."

Adrian Speke put a patronising hand on Nell's arm. It made her flinch, as all his touches and gestures did. "Your mother was most upset, my dear, when we heard you had set out here on your own. Most distressed."

"There's a meeting," said Nell stubbornly, "at which I have the right—"

"The right to have your views represented. No question about it." When the Greshams had retreated a pace, Speke went on, "But for the present that's my task, to represent you at such gatherings. You know the town and its customs well enough by now. It's a man's world, Eleanor. That is why your grandfather appointed me—until you marry." His smile was as patronising as his touch had been. "You need not fear that I'll urge you to marry in haste, my dear, merely to further your grandfather's somewhat arbitrary plans for an amalgamation of Bostock's with . . . " He glanced to one side. Edmund Gresham was disappearing within the doors of the club, while young Malcolm still talked assiduously to his young woman. "With other elements," Speke concluded. "There's no hurry, Eleanor. None at all. If there's to be a man speaking on your behalf during the next few years, I shall do that speaking."

If it was meant as a reassurance, Nell was not reassured. She tried to summon her grandfather back, to put it to him and listen to what he could say. But there was silence.

Adrian patted her once more and then was bowed into the club by the insufferably triumphant doorman.

Nell swung angrily away. Poppy—Miss Rivers, indeed!—had just reached the foot of the steps and was meditatively walking past shop windows down the gentle slope. Men, like dogs detecting a provocative scent, turned to sniff as she dawdled outside a milliner's. Was there, to a man's senses, something animal about her—something alien, to do with her different colouring and the way she walked, making her more savage and desirable? Savage and yet tautly controlled: untouchable, unattainable, provoking strange fancies without changing her expression by the tiniest flicker. If she spoke English really fluently, men might soon find her as empty-headed as any archly flirtatious girl of their own kind. Nell, consoling herself with this thought, was about to go down the steps herself when she realised that Poppy's escort had not, at her departure, continued on his way into the club. He stood a few feet away, studying Nell with a sort of waggish sympathy.

"It's an unreasonable world, Miss Meredith."

"I'll not detain you, Mr. Gresham. You'll want to be in there with your friends, settling our future."

She went down two steps. Malcolm hurried down four and insinuated himself in front of her.

"I've already decided, like you, to leave all decisions to my elders. Then nobody can blame me when things go wrong, ha? Will you not join us"—he looked down the street after the slow, contemplative Poppy— "for a morning interlude in one of the cocoa rooms?"

"I shall drive home, thank you."

He did not move aside. "Then may I see you safely there, Miss Meredith? Our own carriage will wait for my brother, but if your coachman could drive us to Bostock's Brow—you're still in residence there, I hear?—I'll happily come back on the omnibus. Better than sitting in that stuffy room in there."

"Mr. Gresham, I'm sure you should be attending to your business."

"My brother's much better at it than I am. Complete confidence in him."

Poppy had halted and was looking back at them. From this distance it was impossible to tell whether her face was puzzled or whether she was indifferent to whatever Malcolm chose to do.

Nell found that she was pacing down the steps with young Gresham beside her.

"Good," he said. "It'll give you a companion to scourge."

"You think I'm prone to scourge my companions?"

"It's remarkable how a young lady of such charm can look so like her grandfather."

By the time they reached the carriage she was already regretting his presence. His capture of her had been easy only because a large part of her mind was still railing against that smug building and its smug doorman and all the complacent club members within.

She sat back, silent, as they toiled up the hill.

"It must be exasperating," said Malcolm pleasantly, "to know that you're better qualified to speak than most of the old pirates attending that meeting."

"Better qualified only by inheritance at the moment."

"Oh, no, Miss Meredith, I won't have that. You haven't been wasting your time since you've been in Liverpool. My brother was saying, only yesterday—"

"I can't think your brother knows enough about me to express any opinion."

"The two of you together would make a formidable team."

"I'd be obliged if you would not make such bold assumptions."

They reached a fork in the road, the right-hand branch of which led towards Bostock's Brow.

Nell said abruptly, "It's kind of you to have kept me company this far. If you'd care to be set down here—"

"I have a better idea." Before she could stop him he was leaning forward to slide open the pane behind the driver's seat. "Higson, isn't it?"

"It is, sir."

"Well, Higson, we'd be obliged if you could take the left fork and set us down outside the Zoological Gardens."

"Right you are, sir."

As Malcolm plumped back against the tan-coloured leather, Nell protested, "But this is no time to visit the Zoological Gardens."

"I'm sure it will do you good. Certainly it'll do no good for you to go home fuming. Who is there at home to fume *at*?"

"I wasn't aware I'd been fuming at you."

"No, but I'm prepared to offer my services."

He was impossible. The lightness of his eyes was deceptive. Their shifting brown hue could sparkle with any number of different reflections as he narrowed them, widened them, laughed at her with them, invited her response.

Nell let out a sigh that was close to a laugh.

"Splendid," he said.

"I shall not stay long."

"Long enough," he said, "to throw a bun to the bear and watch him climb his pole—and teach the parrots a few new phrases about shipowners and shipbuilders and their wickedness."

Higson watched ruminatively as the two of them walked away into the grounds.

There were few visitors at this time of day. The bear was delighted to see them and went through his paces. The shady walks under arching trees, beside velvety turf, were almost deserted. The sun came out, and the leaves and grass glowed.

"What a delightful day," said Malcolm. "Isn't this better than sitting indoors squabbling with a lot of opinionated old profiteers?"

Despite herself she nodded. They strolled past the lake with its swans and waterfowl, and laughed in unison at a gangling stork that kept in step with them along the bank. Under the trees again, round a corner of shrubbery, they were startled by the squawk of macaws from a cage skilfully positioned to take visitors by surprise at a junction of paths.

Nell said, "You were right. It would have been silly to go home in such a childish temper."

"I wouldn't have called it childish."

"I'm too impatient. Liverpool menfolk won't be changed by rational argument in a matter of minutes."

"If ever." He glanced at her more seriously. "You do understand it'll always be the same? You'll never run Bostock's entirely on your own. There are doors that won't open to you, men who won't do business with you direct because you can't meet them where they expect to be met—on 'Change, in a club, a tavern. There'll always have to be a man to negotiate for you."

"There will come a time," said Nell resolutely, "when I'll do all the negotiating myself."

As if he had not heard her, he said, "I trust Lord Speke's qualified to handle your interests successfully."

"Have you any reason to suppose otherwise?"

"I'm sure he'll do what he can. That he'll do everything for . . . for what he considers the best."

"You had better speak out, Mr. Gresham, or say nothing at all."

"I merely wondered if he had quite the resilience to take on the rough and tumble of Liverpool commerce and come out a winner. A winner on your behalf, that is." Malcolm was not looking at Nell but out over the ripples of the lake. "And I'm wondering," he said, "if there couldn't be someone younger and stronger. Younger—but with plenty of experience."

A cloud darkened the grass and trailed its shadow over the water. Jolted, Nell said sharply, "If your brother wishes to plead his cause, Mr. Gresham, shouldn't he be man enough to do it himself?"

"And would you listen to him?"

"I have no wish whatsoever to listen to him."

"Then," smiled Malcolm, "there's little point in wasting his time or yours, is there?"

A cockatoo from another half-hidden cage screeched derision and hopped up and down, then from side to side. Nell felt her own feathers ruffled. Malcolm Gresham strutted beside her like one of those birds over by the lake. It came to him so naturally yet meant so little. Perhaps it was his way of entertaining that Poppy of his, herself an exotic bird even when sporting the most simple, single-coloured plumage.

The sun came out as they made their way back to the carriage.

Nell's mother was waiting at Bostock's Brow. The door was barely open before she came fluttering across the hall, one arm waving distractedly.

"I thought you would never get back. I've been here for ages. You have no consideration, Eleanor, none at all."

The refrain awoke sad old echoes. Nell said, "Mother, I simply went out to—"

"To make an exhibition of yourself. I hope Adrian arrived in time to save you from disgracing yourself entirely? We do have a position to keep up now, you know."

"If that's all you've come here to say—"

"No, Eleanor, that is not all. You have another visitor. I accompanied the poor man here in the hope of finding you at home. I have done my best to entertain him in your absence, though what he must be thinking—"

"A visitor?"

Julia made an effort, and as she drew Nell with her into the drawing-room became a gracious mother, long-suffering and sweetly forbearing.

Paul Whitlaw rose to his feet and thrust out a hand, smiling straight and frankly at Nell with undisguised pleasure.

"Miss Meredith. How good to see you again, how very good to see you."

"Mr. Whitlaw. You've been away quite a time."

"Visiting my folks in Philadelphia."

"We've missed you," cried Julia ecstatically. "Haven't we, Eleanor?"

"Yes." Seeing him again, unprepared for him, Nell found it was true. "Yes, indeed we've missed you."

"Mr. Whitlaw has something to ask."

Julia edged aside but did not slacken her eager, watchful grip on them. Her tongue dabbed at her lips. She might almost have been framing a message, urging the young man to hurry and pick up his cue.

Paul straightened his already rigid back another fraction of an inch. "First, Miss Meredith, I do apologise for that little contretemps when we last met, at the launching party."

"Eleanor, were you rude to Mr. Whitlaw?"

"No, no," he hastened to assure Julia. "It was very much the other way round. My fault entirely."

"I don't believe it, Mr. Whitlaw. My daughter has so few of the social graces that sometimes I doubt whether—"

"Mother! You told me Mr. Whitlaw has something to ask."

But Julia could not contain herself. "Oh, it couldn't have come at a better time. Eleanor, we were already making plans. Adrian and I, we knew how upset you were when you couldn't go on the maiden voyage of your ship—the *Eleanor*. You gave it up to stand by your grandfather in his hour of need. It was more of a strain than you may have realised, and now that's over you need a rest. A real holiday. We think that *now* is the time for you to make that trip to America."

The floor seemed to be sliding away from beneath Nell's feet. If her mother was right about nothing else in the world, she was right about the strain—the tiredness, the accumulated worry and irritation and sadness which now, at last, welled up to engulf her.

"My cousin," Paul Whitlaw was saying, "is in London right now. She'll be coming to Liverpool—and you'll both be going to New York together. Just the way I put it to you, remember?"

To board ship, thought Nell. To commit herself and let someone else take charge of her destiny, someone else take over the steering, someone else establish the rhythm of the hours and days. To set out at last over that horizon which had always tempted her.

MISS EUGENIA COYTE was a thin young woman with fresh blue eyes and a smile that skipped between uncertainty and unalloyed pleasure. She had spent six weeks in England and was as open about her bewilderments as about her enjoyment. Nell warmed to her at their first meeting. In such company the voyage would be an agreeable experience.

"I shall be asking you to straighten out all my impressions of England," warned Miss Coyte.

"In exchange for your instructing me on what to expect in New York."

Paul Whitlaw, travelling again to New York—this time on business—a week after his cousin's appearance in Liverpool, had promised a suitable welcome when they got there. The thoroughness of his programme was in fact a trifle alarming. Ungratefully Nell felt worried about the whole enterprise being spoilt: this busy organising of lunches, dinners, visits, transport and introductions threatened to reduce the ocean to the proportions of an everyday suburban street between one everyday household and another.

On the afternoon before the Bostock steamer *Eleanor* was due to depart, the two young women went to inspect their accommodation and see if any last-minute additions to their luggage might be advisable. The ship had discharged its eastbound passengers the previous day. Decks were being scrubbed down, food containers and containers of waste were hoisted ashore, and cabins cleaned ready for the westbound voyage. Casual visitors were unwelcome, trespassers were unceremoniously jostled back down the gangplanks. But Nell was Jesse Bostock's granddaughter and, as they all knew by now, his successor. It was still too early for her to be accepted as his equal, but she was important enough for the captain to be in personal attendance when she set foot on deck.

They each had a tiny cabin with a single curtained bed, wardrobe, easy chair, and a wash-basin over which folded a maple table top. Walls and ceiling were panelled in walnut. Between the two cabins was a compact sitting-room with sofa, table, and two easy chairs. The damask hangings had been one of Nell's more inspired choices. She looked around with a certain creative pride.

"We must be sure not to quarrel." Eugenia Coyte spoke seriously but with a sparkle in her eyes. "Sharing such a room if we were not on speaking terms—oh, my goodness, it doesn't bear thinking about!"

When they went ashore she excused herself. So many people had been so hospitable, she simply had to go and make a round of farewells.

Nell lingered awhile on the landing-stage. It was a gusty autumn day with water slapping threateningly against pontoons and chains. She thought of the warm intimacy of that little cabin, and of wearing the new dresses she had bought and packed. Until the last minute she would honour Liverpool decorum by wearing mourning for her grandfather, but once afloat she intended to do as her mother suggested: forget sadness, forget the weight of responsibility that Adrian would shoulder in her absence, and enjoy herself.

Waves from a passing tug smacked against the stage. With a first tremor of unease she wondered what that snug little cabin would be like in high seas.

A smaller paddle-steamer, the *Tenacity*, lay within the dock walls. Casks, crates and hutches were being loaded while a lengthening queue of men, women and children shuffled along the quayside, carrying battered cases and bags of sacking or sailcloth, edging submissively past emigration officers and raising their eyes in hope and disbelief at the two slender funnels between towering masts. The line snaked in and out of a hut known as the Doctor's Shop in which two world-weary physicians took it in turn to make cursory inspections of tongues, faces and occasionally the skin of the hands. There was no appreciable slackening in the pace of the procession: a man or woman went in, and came out of the other door as if nothing had occurred within the hut. Only by the barrier near the waiting ship did the queue come to a halt. Heads bowed against the wind. A dozen swarthy-featured men and women from some part of Europe surely too remote to belong to the same planet as this grey-boned city were herded forward by two men spitting orders in a Liverpool dialect so thick as to be incomprehensible to any other Englishman, let alone a foreigner.

They waited. Nobody was allowed into the emigrants' steerage until the last minute, after all cargo and cabin passengers and a lowing, cackling, bleating consignment of animals had been safely taken aboard.

There was a wail from the shuffling line of people. A woman stumbling out of the hut had been rejected by one of the doctors. She set up a wild keening until her husband came out to join her, shaking his head in despair. The shawl she had been clutching about her face fell open; and the blotches on her skin were as black as the shawl itself. Those closest in the queue edged away. When the two tried to push back into line, to make another attempt at going in and out of those vital doors, a buzz of antagonism ran along the queue. Weeping, husband and wife slumped down against a bollard, not believing the repudiation could be final.

People were still reinforcing the end of the queue. Some walked with sacks of belongings and bedding over their shoulders; others were hustled into position by carters who dumped loads of boxes and bags on to the cobbles so that they could hasten back to quote extortionate prices to other victims in need of guidance.

A hundred yards behind the last straggler a carrier had halted his cart beside a horse trough. The horse was drinking, but that was not the main reason for the stop. As Nell crossed the street she saw a woman collapsed against the stone trough with two small girls clinging to her. A boy stooped over her, with no idea what to do.

"If you can't stir yourself," the carter was bellowing, "you'll have to be left. I haven't got all day."

Any answer was inaudible. The woman's face was as mottled as the stone. She coughed, doubled up, and clapped a crumpled rag to her mouth.

Nell stood above her. "This lady's ill."

"She a friend o' yours?"

"Anyone can see—"

"Anyone can see she's not going to get to America, the way she's carrying on. If she can't get no further'n this, how d'you suppose she'll stand up to the rest of it?"

"If you've brought her this far—"

"Half the length of a street, from Mother Widgery's place. And if this is the best she can manage . . ."

He dragged a sacking bundle and a heavy case to one edge of the cart, ready to pitch them on to the road. Nell put an arm round the woman and tried to lift her. There was another convulsive cough, and blood seeped through the cloth.

108

"To the ship . . . their father . . . they've got to . . "

"Your husband's on the *Tenacity*?"

"Waiting for us. New York. Be . . . waiting." The woman clawed at the side of her dress. "I've got the letter . . . letter he sent . . . show it's all right . . . got to meet him."

"She'll not find her way to the end of the queue," said the carrier, "let alone through the Doctor's Shop."

"We've got to get her back to her lodging-house," said Nell. "Come along, give me a hand."

"Mother Widgery won't want her back there."

"Mother Widgery's going to get her back there. And if I don't have your assistance I might have some words with the emigration authorities and with the constabulary. I imagine they have some information on your activities, and might well welcome more."

Whatever the carrier was muttering under his breath did not prevent him from coming round the trough and taking some of the woman's weight from Nell. One of the girls whimpered as she saw her mother being lifted and rolled on to the cart.

Mother Widgery certainly did not look pleased at the return of her lodger. Birds of passage, satisfactorily plucked, were supposed to migrate and not return to a nest already made available to some fresh voyager.

"I insist," said Nell before objections could become too vehement, "that this lady is allowed to rest while I send for a doctor."

"What'll folk think if they see a doctor coming in here?"

"They might think you were a reputable landlady showing compassion to an unfortunate guest."

Nell and the carrier eased the almost unconscious woman into a twilit parlour beside the front door. It had peeling dun plaster, and a window whose shredded curtain looked out on to a side yard and crumbling brick scullery.

"That ship . . ." The urgent whisper struggled for wakefulness. "We've got the tickets, got his letter, he's expecting us, it's all all *right*. But if we're not on that one . . . it *has* to be that one, or he'll not know . . . be there and not know . . ."

"When the doctor has decided how long you need to get well," said Nell soothingly, "we'll find somewhere for you and the children, and send a message by another ship."

"It has to be that ship. He'll be waiting for us. Has to come down the . . . the Hudson, that's it, isn't it? . . . meet us and take us back where he's working. If we're not on it, how'll he know . . .?"

She was racked by coughing again.

Nell said: "Someone must go for a doctor. Now."

"Not me," said the carrier. "Enough to do."

With gruff, grudging pity Mrs. Widgery said, "I can send our Gladys."

The children plucked beseechingly at their mother. She was drifting away from them and they were frightened. Nell, on her knees beside the wheezing wreck of a woman, said gently, "The papers. Give me the tickets, the papers, your husband's letter. I'll see the children get there—somehow."

"Got to be on that ship, like it was worked out."

A feeble hand groped papers from a belt satchel, scattering them on the floor. Nell gathered them up. Dora Fenwick and her children George, Mary and Charlotte were booked for New York aboard the steamship *Tenacity* with a guarantee of support from Thomas Fenwick, attested by his employers in Albany.

"And who d'you think'll take 'em off your hands, miss?" asked Mrs. Widgery sceptically.

"Once I'm aboard I'll have a word with the captain."

"Will you, now? But kids'll still not be allowed to travel unaccompanied, take my word on that, love."

Nell looked about the drab, depressing room. Frightened yet calm, she knew what she must do. "Have you any writing paper?"

The carrier sniggered at the mere idea.

Nell took out her engagement diary and tore off two sheets. Quickly she pencilled a note to Mr. Carter.

"Take this to the Bostock Navigation office—"

"Not me," said the carrier again. "Lost enough time and money already."

Nell dropped two silver shillings in his palm. "And there'll be half a sovereign when the message is safely delivered. But only then. You understand?"

Blackened nails and knuckles closed over the coins. "Tell you what, miss . . . ma'am"—he brightened momentarily—"before you take 'em aboard I could get you some nice bacon and cheese. Cheap. Otherwise they'll be short of vittles on that journey, take my word for it."

"Under the Passenger Acts the captain is compelled to provide a sufficient quantity of wholesome food. There's no longer any need for dockside chandlers and their trickery."

The carrier raised his gaze to heaven.

"And before you leave," said Nell, "you'll move the baggage back to the quayside. Then be on your way, and quick about it." To the children she tried to be both brisk and comforting: "Now, then, kiss your mother, and come with me."

The boy, the oldest of the three, mutely shook his head.

"Go with the lady." There was only a whisper left. "I . . . I'll be coming later. Tell your father, give him my . . . my . . ."

Still the three hesitated. Nell put out her hand to the youngest, and after a moment the little girl took it.

"I'll make sure they're safe aboard and well treated." Nell spoke with more confidence than she felt. "Then we'll see how soon we can arrange for you to catch them up."

Never, said Mrs. Widgery's pursed, unmoving lips. *Never, and you know it.*

"God bless you." The woman knew it, too.

Nell hurried the children out, with the grumbling carrier behind. They made their way back to where the queue had almost completed its progress through the Doctor's Shop. As the carrier dumped the baggage, Nell said, "You'll deliver that message if you expect one penny more."

"Half a sovereign you said."

"So it will be. But on your way—now!"

Nell smiled down into the three wan faces. The little girl had tears in her eyes but was trying not to let them escape.

"You're going to see your daddy."

They nodded, neither believing nor doubting: just too stunned to grasp anything.

In the medical hut, daylight was uncertain and the hissing gas jet only added more confusing shadows. Nell was glad now that she still wore mourning. Anything else might have made her too conspicuous in this line—though a German couple ahead were wearing an obviously local costume, defiantly bearing a last cherished memory into the New World.

"Hold out your hand." The doctor inspected her fingers without touching them, and indicated that she should turn up her palm. It was in such contrast to the work-worn hands of her predecessors that now he glanced up into her face. Fortunately he was a newcomer, not one of those who might have seen the well-known Miss Meredith on the dockside before. "You're not travelling alone?"

"With three . . . with my children here. My husband's waiting for us in New York."

"Hope he can afford you." The doctor snorted as he stamped her ticket. "Right. Next."

From outside came a cry of exultation made discordant by panic. The emigrants were being allowed aboard. An emigration officer went through a pantomime of supervising the rush, then backed away. A mate by the gangplank was bellowing at the top of his voice. Two other seamen appeared on either side of the queue, urging folk along like cattle. Nell tried to protest as the children were caught up in the stampede, trying to grab the arm of one of the seamen. He waved as if to beat her across the rump and keep her moving in the right direction.

An elderly man escaped plunging into the water between ship and dockside only by clutching a rope and hauling himself painfully up over the bulwark. A box dropped and sank. There was pandemonium. After coming so far and waiting so long, the emigrants were terrified of missing the sailing. From the passenger deck a group of more comfortable travellers leaned over the stanchions and marvelled and laughed and pointed, laughing even louder when there was a near-accident to an Irish couple who had been drinking too assiduously while awaiting the signal to embark.

Little Charlotte was weeping without pretence now. Nell kept an arm round her while lugging the sacking bundle along. The boy, George, gallantly humped the case up while murmuring reassurance to his other sister.

Somehow they were safely aboard and, in a surge like that through a broken dam, pouring down a steep companionway, bruising shoulders and keeping their feet only because there was not an inch of space into which to fall. Two sailors on the lower deck were snapping orders, pointing, pushing. "On your own, mister? Right up for'ard, then. Come on, look lively—single men the other side of that bulkhead." Married couples and families were directed into compartments with flimsy partitions and two-tiered berths end on to the central aisle. There was no room in the cramped sleeping quarters for baggage, which by the time Nell and the children reached the lower deck was already heaped along the available space, so that they had to clamber their way to a narrow cubicle with four rickety bunks. It was dark, the only light coming from three bullseyes in the planking above and from hanging lanterns at each end of the aisle.

Mary and Charlotte huddled together on one of the lower bunks. Nell tried to squeeze into the opposite one, half-sitting and half-leaning forward with a slat of the upper berth digging into her shoulder. She thought of the cabin set aside for her on the *Eleanor*; and leaned over to comfort the two little girls.

From above came the clangour of a bell. What had been a slow and steady heartbeat amidships began to pound more fervently. Woodwork trembled and creaked and protested. One droning note thrummed through every fibre of the vessel and its passengers. A jolt like the first clumsy jolt of a cart when the horse takes the strain was followed by a jar and dip of paddle blades. Someone cheered. In the men's quarters a dozen voices took up a maudlin chorus. There was an infinite second of seeming weightlessness, then they were drawn into a slow circle as one paddle raced and a new note vibrated from the engines.

"I'm thirsty," said Mary in a small voice.

"When we're properly under way," Nell soothed, "we'll see where everything is."

George was still manfully on his feet. "Are you coming all the way with us, miss? And up the river with us, and father?"

She knew so little about them, and as little about what was in store as they did themselves. Before she could speak, Charlotte said, "I don't remember him. I can't hardly remember him at all."

Nell had no intention of travelling further than she had to. There would be a way out soon. By the time they had crossed the Irish Sea she would have found someone to take care of the children, someone would surely be waiting for her at Queenstown, and it would all somehow be tidied up.

The boat juddered, and she felt herself lifted and cradled on the waters of the Mersey. For the first time in many a month she thought of the novels she had passed across Mr. Trigg's counter. The right romantic ending to this adventure would surely be that she reached New York after all, fell immediately in love with the widower Thomas Fenwick (of course he would by then be a widower), and courageously went with him and his children off to the new frontiers.

She rubbed her stinging eyes. It had been a mad day, and was now a madder dream. If she closed her eyes and opened them again quickly wouldn't she find herself in her bedroom at Bostock's Brow—or even, gently rocking, in her cabin on the *Eleanor*?

The engines seemed to miss a beat and pause, so that the ship drifted for a few seconds. Into the hush sang the hollow note of a Rock Channel buoy, ringing its mournful farewell.

14

THE SEA was beginning to punish the *Tenacity*. Packed in their hundreds into the bows, the steerage passengers took the impact of each wave, punching down, sideways, upwards, like a mighty swinging fist. The ship rolled and reeled, shuddered its whole length, nosed on to meet the crash of the next blow.

A woman the other side of the partition from Nell began to moan. A faint, shouted order from aloft was drowned by a lash of spray scouring the decks.

"Hold on tight." Nell heard the children rustle into fresh positions, each clutching a single thin blanket taken from their mother's bundle, at the same time trying to brace leg and hip against the insecure wooden edges of their berths.

"I'm thirsty," lamented Mary again.

Nell ventured out into the aisle. A sudden lurch tossed her back. She steadied herself and set off again, a step at a time, picking her way over bundles and boxes. Once she kicked the ankle of someone sprawled over an improvised mattress, and got an oath in response.

The lamp at the foot of the companionway was swinging wildly to and fro, chasing shadows along the creaking beams. Nell got a grip on the stair rail, held on as the ship reared and dipped, and began to climb. As she reached the fifth step a growl came from above.

"And where d'you think you're going?"

A man in a peaked cap stood in the doorway at the top, legs straddled to ride each pitch and toss.

Nell said, "When are we going to be provided with food and drink?"

"Tomorrow morning."

"But you're supposed to provide an evening ration."

"You should have eaten before you came aboard."

"I've got three children with me, and one of them wants—"

"Should have eaten before you came aboard," he repeated.

"They're thirsty."

"Should have brought something with you. We don't give anything out till morning. And the way we're going, I'd be surprised if many was in the mood for eating, anyway."

Nell's hand tightened on the rail. "I wish to see the captain."

"Do you, now. What for?"

"I . . ." She thought of the three wretched little shapes in that darkness between decks. "I wish to transfer to a cabin. I'll pay for it."

"Why didn't you, then, when you had the chance?"

"I . . . had to make some last-minute decisions. I'd like to tell my story to the captain."

"Every trip there's plenty as'd like to do that. He's not much of a man for stories, though, not Captain Egan."

Nell continued to climb. The man said, "Look, missus, steerage passengers aren't allowed on the upper decks."

"I insist—"

"We'll have none of your diseases brought up to the rest of us. Cabin passengers get very awkward if they're quarantined because of mixing with the steerage."

"I'm not suffering from any disease." Nell's voice and eyes blazed.

The man's expression changed as he took a longer look at her. "Mm, well now. Maybe you ought to see the captain, at that. He likes a bit of company on the voyage, and he hasn't taken his pick yet."

At first Nell did not grasp his meaning. Then she cried, "How dare you? If you imagine I would trade—"

"If you want a cosy trip, missus, it's your best chance. You don't look at all bad to me. Come to think of it, I quite fancy you meself." He took a step down to meet her; then his face hardened again. "But just a minute. Didn't you say something about children?"

"I have three children with me. It's for their sakes that I want a proper cabin."

"Oh, no. Not three kids. You'll have to stay where you are." He was turning away.

"I insist on explaining to the captain. A purely business transaction. My credentials—"

"Unless you want to be put ashore at Queenstown, you and your kids, you'll keep your fussing to yourself. He likes a quiet cargo, does Captain Egan."

The door closed, and even through the turmoil of wind and engine noise Nell heard the crack of a bolt slamming home.

She eased her way down the steps and leaned against the rail to get her breath back.

A soft Irish voice said, "You'll not be getting anywhere with the likes o' him, missis."

"But it's disgraceful."

"Wait till you've had ten or twelve days of it."

"There should be a water ration, an evening meal, we ought to have—"

"Not on this kind of ship."

"It's subject to the Passenger Acts like any other."

"No, that it's not."

"But it's a British ship, flying the Red Ensign, with—"

"No." The man had been crouched in a corner with his arms round his knees, rocking with each roll of the ship. Now he pushed himself upright, and in the swaying light she saw a seamed, middle-aged face with the smile of a rueful old man. "American-owned, this one. Built on the Mersey and registered in Liverpool—and it's after flying the Red Ensign because Congress don't allow ships built outside the United States to fly the Stars and Stripes."

"But the Americans have Passenger Acts as well."

"Which don't apply to mail steamers."

"This is a passenger steamer, not a packet-boat."

The ship heeled again and threw both of them halfway across its breadth. There was a clatter of tin plates and mugs. Baggage slithered from one side to the other, then back again. A child began to scream.

"And weren't you noticing, then, the sack of mail we took aboard?" The Irishman clutched the rail close to Nell. "That makes it a mail-boat, so it's exempt from any regulations about passenger accommodation or food or the care they're after giving you—or not giving you. One bag of mail, that's all it takes."

"You seem to know a lot about it."

"Worked the Dublin shore for years, so I did. Get to know all the tricks that way."

"If you knew that much, why choose a ship like this?"

"Not a matter of choice, me darlin'." He was resigned but humorous.

116

"The cheapest one. I'll be needing every last penny I've got, the other side."

Nell clawed and crawled her way back to the children. Once she stepped in something slimy, and the stench of vomit followed her. By some miracle Charlotte, in spite of the rearing of the ship, was asleep, George having wedged her into the back of a lower bunk and set his shoulder against her.

The night was a nightmare. The thump of striving engines, creak of timber and resonance of iron were deafening. Wood screeched and groaned, and from every quarter came sudden, irregular, explosive snapping sounds. Planks fell from the shoddily made bunks. One woman hiccuped with seasickness hour after hour, until exhaustion at last silenced her convulsions. The *Tenacity* fought its slow way on. Every now and then, following a deceptive lull, a particularly vicious wave would smite out of nowhere and heel the ship over so that one paddle came clear of the water, thrashing impotently in midair.

Wait till you've had ten or twelve days of it.

By morning the gale was slackening but there was still a continual bumping and jarring along the hull. A muffled lowing and bleating came from the animals somewhere aft.

A blast of cold but welcome air lashed without warning between decks. Doors had been opened on to one outside space in the bows. There was a rush to escape, to breathe clean air for a few minutes. The area was cluttered with winches and cable, a length of chain, the hump of a hatchway. Water streamed across the deck and gurgled through the scuppers. Spray stung lips and cheeks. But after the foul smell and oppressiveness of the steerage, the cramped promenade came as a blessed relief.

The Irish coast sketched a dark line to the west. The *Tenacity* churned southwards through grey morning and drizzling afternoon, already running late for the coaling stop at Queenstown.

At last food had been served: a breakfast of thick cold porridge, a dinner of soup and potatoes. The soup was ladled into the emigrants' tin mugs along a sort of bucket chain from the hatch of a small galley, some of it slopping on the deck. A few families, less trusting than Nell, had bought extra provisions from the crooked dealers of Liverpool and were cooking over a stove in the centre of the aisle, its fumes adding to the smell between the bunks.

One of the stewards, sleeves rolled up above greasy elbows, caught Nell's eye as he passed a mug to Charlotte.

"Like some fruit? Ham and eggs?"

"I'm glad to find someone's prepared to—"

"Buy some for you at Queenstown, if you've got the money."

117

"But . . ." His gaze was still on her, but ready to wander and seek pickings elsewhere if she didn't at once make up her mind. She thought of what the children's fare was going to be, day in and day out, if she did not submit to his extortion. "Yes," she said, "I think I can afford a few things."

"Good thing to have a supply, missis." He handed along another two mugs. "Wouldn't have a drop of whisky with you?" When she shook her head he shrugged. "That's a pity. It'll have to be a sovereign, then."

"For how much food?"

"For what we can get you."

She handed it over.

It was dusk as they approached Queenstown. The thought of firm ground so close in the gathering darkness was a dreadful temptation: to set foot on it, leave the children to someone else's mercy, be done with this insane, impulsive adventure . . .

A few cabin passengers came aboard, but there was no way of seeing if anyone she knew was among them. Surely there must be somebody?

Unless that carrier had bungled his mission.

A few score of emigrants came tumbling down from above. Nell felt another protest rising within her—there were too many, the ship was carrying more than its legal complement—but who should she protest to? She contemplated another attempt to see the captain. And tell him what? That she was travelling on somebody else's papers, that she wanted a comfortable cabin for herself and the children but would have to promise payment later?

Thomas Fenwick would be waiting in New York for this ship and no other.

Until the last minute, when the engines quickened into life again and the paddles bit into the water, she clung to the cowardly hope that someone must have come aboard and would smooth out all the problems. Her message to the Bostock office must have been passed on, Adrian Speke must have acted, a fast cutter must have pursued the *Tenacity* and would arrive in the nick of time. There would be explanations and readjustments, the children would travel on in comfort, and she could turn for home.

The *Tenacity* steered out towards the Atlantic.

Nell felt a twist of griping pain in her stomach. Or was it simply a little knot of determination tightening? She had promised to ensure the children safe passage across the ocean. Nobody else could fulfil that promise.

So, no whining. She had made her impulsive decision and would abide

118

by it. Nothing must jeopardise the children's attainment of journey's end.

She wondered if her grandfather would have laughed or raged at her conduct. It made little difference now. He had been left far behind in time and space.

That night she prayed, and asked the children to pray especially hard, though without alarming them.

"It's so dark."

Two men crouched over the flickering stove were adding yet another smell to the thickening mixture. They had saved fat from the gristly meat at supper and were rendering it down into tins. A twist of cotton-wool, and they had a glowing, sputtering candle.

At breakfast, when the same thick porridge was ladled out, the hunk of bread slapped on to the tin plate, and a ration of water poured into a mug, she said to the steward, "I paid for fresh food to be bought for us in Queenstown."

It was not the same man. He looked around indifferently. "Who did you pay?"

"I don't know his name. He . . ." She was at a loss to describe him.

"Whoever he is, he'll be along in good time. If he didn't fall asleep in a bar and get left behind."

Time hung heavy; and still there was so far to go. Some of the European families had their own little songs, and one man played dexterously on a concertina. The children grew interested, and as the *Tenacity* settled on to a more even keel Mary tried to dance in the confined space. Later, Nell told them all a story. She was thankful for all the novels it had once been her task to read. Now she could adapt the themes to childish tastes, and improvise where necessary to fill awkward gaps.

The midday meal brought no steward she recognised and no fresh fruit or anything else.

It did bring an officer who brazenly inspected every one of the younger women and bent over to mutter invitations to three of them. Two sent him packing. The third, after apprehensive glances around, picked up her case and went off with him.

At supper Nell complained again. The man looked grumpy at first, then more sympathetic. "Must have been Bill. He's laid up a couple of days. Twisted his ankle. But he'd have handed over any stuff like that to one of his mates. I'll ask for you."

A woman keened a wistful song in the shifting light. Two children, hand in hand, stumbled their way towards the stinking lavatory: there was one at each end of the deck, each serving some two hundred people.

119

The ship rolled gently, almost somnolently. Nell told the children another story.

"Along there." A man's voice came from the end of the row of cubicles. "Halfway along, with those three little 'uns."

Another man edged his way through, grunting to himself and kicking any hummock of baggage that got in his way. He swung a small bag of rough hemp from one hand.

"Someone order these vittles from Queenstown?"

Nell leaned out and signalled to him. He came closer and propped himself against the partition, looking down at her.

It was Fred Hesketh.

"WELL, THEN, if it isn't Miss Meredith. Running away from Liverpool already?"

It was so like that first time he had found her, back in Lowestoft. Squat and sure of himself, he gloated over the situation. Perhaps more so now than before.

Nell was about to snap back at him, to be a Bostock and remind him of the fact, when she realised what the facts of her own situation were. Steadily she managed to say, "My name's Fenwick. Mrs. Thomas Fenwick."

"*Mrs.* Fenwick? Well, now, who'd have believed it. I didn't see any announcements in the *Mercury* about Miss Meredith marrying any Mr. Fenwick."

"You're making a mistake."

"Somebody's made a mistake, yes. Wouldn't be at all surprised."

"I paid for some supplies. I believe you have them with you."

"A few little luxuries, yes, that I have. Surprised you didn't think of buying 'em before setting out, you being such a sharp one."

People from the next cubicle leaned out to peer at them. A couple of men sauntered with growing boldness from the single men's quarters and perched on a heap of someone else's luggage, watching. Hesketh had an aura about him. It had carried him through many a trouble; and whatever might have driven him to take a position as steward on this

121

ship, Nell saw he would assert himself again, when and how it suited him.

He leaned forward to drop the bag of food in her lap.

"If any of the rest of you fancy doing me any favours," he said with a suggestive wink, "then I'll see about some favours in return."

Nell said, "Do you think they'd be entertained by a story of what happens to those too ready to bestow their favours, Mr. Hesketh?"

"So it's Mr. Hesketh, is it? And how would Mrs. Thomas Fenwick know my name, then?" He began to lower himself towards her, his eyes greedy. In an undertone he said, "After what you let me in for, you fancy little bitch—"

"*I* let you in for it?"

"Drove me to it, right enough. If it hadn't been for you and your fancy ways . . . But we haven't reached the end of the road yet. Or the end of this voyage. Not by a long way we haven't."

His hand was reaching for her when a voice rang along the aisle. "Fred! You there, Fred? Mr. Hammond wants you."

Hesketh straightened up. "I'll come and see you again, when I'm good and ready. It's not only the officers who help themselves, you know."

The children nuzzled closer as he went away.

"Who was that? He wasn't very nice."

"He was horrid."

"You think he's going to bring us presents again?" Mary's gaze was fixed on an apple that had rolled out of the bag into Nell's lap.

The next day Nell waited for Hesketh to reappear, sure he would have devised some cunning humiliation. Her only weapon against him was her knowledge of his reason for fleeing Liverpool. Only that one thing could account for his presence on this ship. He had been finally laughed out of the port. Travelling as steward, perhaps working his passage to a new world where the story was not known, he would hardly run the risk of the truth coming out—ribaldry accompanying him on the voyage and bellowing out ahead of him across plains and valleys and cities where he was hoping to set up in some new kind of enterprise, whatever it might be.

The weather was not too unkind, so she took the children for a few minutes on to the patch of open deck, setting their backs against the hatch cover so that they would not be tripping and falling over the ropes and chains.

A banana fell at George's feet. He stared at it, incredulous. By the time he was beginning to stoop, an older boy darted in and snatched it away.

They all scanned the heavens from which this manna had fallen.

Two thick slices of navy bread followed.

The scramble and chatter of young voices were those of quarrelling cage-birds—treating it half as a game, half as a real conflict.

Men and women leaned over the rail above, pointing out a boy who was scuttling off with a torn half of one of the pieces of bread. "I'll wager on . . ." Heavily gusting wind tore away the end of the sentence. A few coins fell on the deck, some lodging in the hatch coaming, one bouncing off a winch into an old woman's apron.

A sterner voice asserted itself. "Ladies and gentlemen, please. It's against regulations to throw money or eatables into the steerage."

Mary and Charlotte continued to stare hopefully upwards until Nell led them, protesting, back between decks. She tingled with indignation. *To be treated as a spectacle, patronised, fed scraps like animals in a zoo* . . .

That night she was unable to sleep. The sea was still calm and the children, growing used to cramped conditions and the plodding rhythm of the days and the engines, slept soundly. Little Charlotte clutched Nell's hand so tightly, even after her eyes had shut, that Nell was forced to sit for an uncomfortable time on the edge of the bunk. Finally the grip slackened and she was able to tuck Charlotte's hand under the blanket.

Stretched out in her own bunk, she winced at the memory of Hesketh. Stoicism in the face of dirt and discomfort was one thing; in the face of a personal, vicious danger, quite another. There were so many days and nights ahead, so many things he might do.

For the children's sake she must make another attempt to reach the captain in the morning.

In spite of their smooth progress the timbers creaked as penetratingly as ever. She felt shut in; the straining and groaning grew louder; to it all was added the rasp of snoring from a nearby bunk. In the cold stuffiness Nell was convinced she was about to suffocate. She swung her feet cautiously out. Edging between sleeping families and their bundles, she reached the space at the foot of the companionway and rested her brow on the rail. Hoarse breath from the surrounding darkness kept time with the shafts and pistons of the machinery. Some man from for'ard had come adventuring and found a woman who, by the sound of her, was not unwilling.

Nell put a hand on the rail. At once another hand pinned it down. Sour breath blew across her nostrils. A mouth sought hers. She struck out, scratched a jaw.

Hesketh growled, "Come on now, Mrs. Fenwick. A married woman like you, you musta been missing it. So . . ."

His arm dragged her closer.

"If you don't let me go at once, I'll have you—"

"You'll have me, all right. I been promising myself that a long time since."

She twisted her head away. Physically he was more than a match for her. She struck out with all she possessed. "I hope you won't hurt yourself. The strain, after what . . ." A hand clamped over her mouth. She tried to bite, but he was ramming her cruelly back against the woodwork, his full weight holding her so that his other hand was free to snatch at her skirt. His head, wedged against hers so that she could not pull away, held her in place. Wet breath fouled her ear. "You'll get nowhere by complaining, Mrs. Fenwick. Or Miss Meredith. Illegal, that's what you are. Illegal immigrant, travelling on papers that don't belong to you, with kids that don't belong to you. How d'you think the kids'll get along if I was to tell what I know?"

Her innermost being cringed away from him, but her body was held immobile.

"Be quiet and it'll be the better for you."

He tore at her waistband and she felt it give way.

Light spilled over them as if a shutter had been suddenly opened. The door at the top of the companionway was open, a storm lantern was held high. Hesketh pushed back a few inches to shout a curse at the intruder.

"Get back, and take your bloody lantern with you."

Malcolm Gresham said, "So it's Hesketh, is it? Not the most potent star in the Bostock firmament, as I recall."

Hesketh, caught off balance, retreated from Nell. Malcolm bounded down the stairs, two and three at a time. He hardly paused to hand the lantern to Nell, who narrowly escaped dropping it. Shadows raced up the bulkhead and pounced. Malcolm Gresham's arm was swollen and distorted in the light as he swung at Hesketh's jaw. The man went down. But the impact was enough to arouse him. Hesketh had been too long a dock fighter not to move savagely when the need arose. He was on his feet, adjusting to the sway of the ship and letting it give him added impetus. He smashed into Gresham and drove him back full force against the side. They were propped there in a parody of affection until the ship reared again and Gresham was able to push himself outward. He fell into Hesketh's hard right fist.

But Malcolm Gresham must have learned more in the ports of the Orient and on the high seas than one would have guessed from his young, madcap face. He showed how to enjoy the blow and how to cushion himself against it as he swung in twice, three times, and a fourth devastating time to chop Hesketh's head from right to left, left to right, sending him skidding across the deck. One hand stayed raised, to beat him down again.

Hesketh rolled over and moaned.

Gresham prodded him with his foot. "Are you getting up?"

"I'll . . . by Christ, I'll see you . . . I'll . . ." But the threat choked in his throat, and when he tried to get up it was only as far as his knees.

"We shall see in the morning," said Gresham, "just what report to submit to the captain."

Hesketh was crouching, now, like a dog regaining its will to leap and bite. "If there's any reporting to be done, I'll have a few things to say about *this* one and those kids with her." He groped to his feet, then swayed and slunk away into the gloom.

"Mr. Gresham." It was all Nell could utter. She was stupefied, first by Hesketh's assault and now by this incredible arrival of a saviour. "Mr. Gresham."

Gravely—but didn't his eyes have that old impudent glint in the flicker of the lantern?—he offered her his arm and led her to a bench on which, during daytime, several of the older women sat patching clothes or talking, already, of the old country.

Nell was glad to sit down. Malcolm Gresham stood above her, balancing against an upright of metal piping.

"Mr. Gresham." Nell tried again. "How long have you been aboard?"

"Long enough."

"It's too much of a coincidence—on this same ship all the way from Liverpool."

He kept her waiting for a moment, then said, "Not all the way from Liverpool, Miss Meredith. The only coincidence was that of my being in the Bostock office talking with your Mr. Carter when your message arrived. Naturally I was intrigued."

"You followed me—"

"Overtook you, rather. I took a screw packet for Queenstown, and somewhere on the Irish Sea we must have passed you."

"A screw steamer! I was always telling grandfather—"

"And now you're in a position to tell your own contractors. Have your own way all the time." As the ship veered a few degrees to starboard, Malcolm shifted his arm and stooped closer. Nell caught a faint tang of cigar smoke from his jacket. "But you must learn not to be *too* impulsive, Miss Meredith. It was a gallant gesture to take charge of those three children, but what about your other responsibilities—to your own family? Your poor worried mother, for instance." There was a tinge of mockery in the reproof. "What about your guardian?"

125

"He doesn't seem to have acted as swiftly as you did," Nell observed.

"No. No, that's true. But he could hardly have spared the time to come himself. He's so busy looking after your business interests that he may well have felt you couldn't both be spared at the same time. Very sensible of him. We can't *all* be creatures of impulse, can we?"

"You're hardly in a position to lecture me, Mr. Gresham. What about your own responsibilities?" She remembered his carefree abandonment of the Beckwith Club meeting so that they could walk in the Zoological Gardens. And now there was this. "What about Gresham Brothers?"

"Ah, but there we are. There's another brother. Much worthier than I, as I've told you once before."

She got up. "I must get back to the children."

"For what's left of the night, yes. We can't cause an upheaval at this hour. But in the morning I'll make more suitable arrangements."

"I'm sure I'm quite capable of—"

"Are you?"

She was weakened by the palpitations of relief through her. To cover her willingness to surrender, to be dependent on him, she said sharply, "You took your time in making your presence known."

"I . . ." He grimaced. "Oh, dear, I must confess I wanted to see what you would make of it."

"Amusing yourself at my expense!"

"Admiring you," he said so quietly that it was almost lost in the thrum of the engines. "It was only when I saw Hesketh and guessed who his prey would be, once he had spotted you, that I decided to intervene."

She thought of patronising eyes watching from the upper deck, of the gratuities offhandedly scattered. "Otherwise," she challenged, "you'd have left us to ourselves for the entire voyage?"

"It was your choice, setting out on the journey."

She could hardly deny that.

Back in her bunk, Nell lay awake for another hour. Her head was in a whirl. The sudden violence, the equally sudden rescue, the whole new tenor of things . . . She was not sure how much she ought to accept from Malcolm Gresham, who had so lightheadedly raced after her—a splendid joke to him, no more than that—or what might still have to be faced with Hesketh.

Tiredness drew her down at last in a long descending spiral into a rocking sea of sleep.

She and the children had been awake less than an hour in the morning when Malcolm Gresham came for them.

Unlike most of the men in the steerage he was washed, trimly shaven, and smart. Questioning, envious eyes followed his progress. He did not belong. When he put out his hand to Nell she pretended not to notice but busied herself tugging at Mary's and Charlotte's crumpled dresses.

The boy looked stolidly at the newcomer.

Malcolm said, "Which are your belongings?"

He had brought a steward with him. Together they carried the insubstantial luggage to the companionway. Nell and the children were led up to that forbidden deck, through a saloon with a long polished central table, and on along a passage lined with cabins. A door was opened. They bunched together on the threshold.

It was a family cabin with four curtained bunks and a narrow sofa. Just inside the door was a washstand, plain and unornamental, but clean. Facing them, the deadlights were back from the scuttle, letting in a cold morning light which to the four of them was brighter than the sunniest summer day.

"Now." Malcolm took charge, resting one hand encouragingly on George's shoulder. "Let's see what else you'll require."

The two girls edged towards the porthole and craned to look out at the unstable mountain ridges rearing up before them and then falling away, one moment steeped in steely light and the next shot through with deep green shadow. Dream faces appeared: a white forelock blown over the vanishing eyes of an old man, a wildly leering monster. Caves opened in watery cliffs and at once were inundated.

Nell said, "Mr. Gresham, we must reach an agreement on payment for these improved quarters."

"We shall reach an agreement on many things, I trust."

She looked away from him at the panels of rosewood and bird's-eye maple, with gilded cornices and a repeated inlay based on the fleur-de-lys. Sunlight struck from a wave crest and glimmered off the brass rim of the deadlight.

Nell had to draw closer to Malcolm Gresham to whisper. "Their mother. Before you left, did you hear any word?"

"Before I left," he whispered back, "she had already died."

"God preserve them."

There was a rap at the cabin door. Gresham turned away and opened it.

"Ah, Captain Egan. How thoughtful of you."

The captain was a lean American with cracked lips and sourly sceptical eyes. He bowed to Nell but contrived at the same time to declare she was here only on sufferance.

"You've got all you'll be requiring?" He was daring them to criticise.

"I'll have a word with the steward about anything lacking," said Malcolm.

127

"I'm still none too happy about this whole notion. What the owners are going to say about it all—"

"It'll be a fine advertisement for them. Looking after three helpless children and—"

"And everyone else expecting the same treatment."

"A fine story it'll make, you taking the owner of the Bostock line on her first voyage—aboard a rival ship!"

"He'll need a fine story," interrupted Nell unforgivingly, "to counteract the complaints I'll register with the American consul in Liverpool about treatment of steerage passengers."

"Now, hold you hard, ma'am . . ."

Malcolm Gresham had him by the arm, steering him out of the door with a muttered joke. As they walked away, Nell heard a guffaw. When the young man returned she said, "I'm sorry you chose to remove him before I'd finished."

"He's captain of this craft, Miss Meredith. We don't need to be too obsequious; but antagonising him might do you and your charges no good."

"We never settled the matter of Hesketh."

"I settled it," he said. "Take my word for it, Hesketh won't trouble you again."

The children knelt on the sofa so that they could peer out incessantly at the sea. Daylight was as physical and immediate as water pouring over their shoulders.

That evening the two girls and their brother were fed in the cabin. Afterwards they lay back in their bunks cosy but subdued. "Is this really all right, miss?" Charlotte voiced their doubts. The interlude surely could not last: they expected at any moment to be bustled back into the smell and noise and darkness.

When she was sure they were settled, Nell went along to the saloon to dine with Mr. Gresham. She recognised one of the stewards and saw how he compensated one part of his work with the other: deferential here, bullying and scornful when doling out rations from the poky galley in the steerage.

She said, "Mr. Gresham, we really must settle here and now how you're to be recompensed for your help, and when."

"Let's not bother our heads at the moment. Some arrangement with discounted bills later, hey?" He tried to dismiss it all with a flippant wave of his hand.

"I insist you keep full records."

"The motion of this vessel would have a terrible effect on my handwriting."

"Please—"

"We'll have a reckoning," he promised, "before we're too much older."

She was tempted to remark that he sounded as menacing as Hesketh. But whereas the mere presence of Hesketh had nauseated her, in this man's company she felt a quickening of the pulse. He was not just different from his earnest brother, but different from his own self as she had encountered it in Liverpool. At sea he was in his element. She sensed that the rougher the conditions, the remoter the ocean, the more he would revel in it.

Next day conditions did indeed roughen. A fierce wind turned into a gale. The paddle blades tilted again from the water, waves smashed down on the bows and foredeck, a hideous rolling motion was interrupted by buffets along the port quarter like wayward kicks from a heavy boot. Lying in a bunk with feet braced against the end of fingers clutching the inner handgrip was safer than attempting the daily promenade.

Malcolm Gresham staggered from his cabin to Nell's, swinging in on the door as the ship heeled and letting the return motion close the door. He propped himself between two bunks, let himself sink to the sofa with one arm curved over its high end, and began to tell the children stories. They were inconsequential, often starting in mid-air—or mid-ocean—but enthralling in the colour of their background. Skilfully he wove incidents in with the plunges and shudders of the *Tenacity* so that they came instantly alive, the ship itself seeming merely to obey his orders as stage manager. Three rapt faces turned towards him. When waves crashed against the deadlight the children did not even jump. They listened; and watched sometimes Gresham's eyes, sometimes his mouth.

Nell, too, found herself watching his mouth: the mobile lips, the little twist in one corner when he told a story against himself, and the slight, excited pout when he remembered something particularly dramatic. The Bay of Biscay, the Cape, the pirate-infested waters of the East, the bustling ports of India . . .

She longed to ask about his eastern woman, not so far mentioned in any of his anecdotes.

After the first pleasure of their new accommodation had worn off, Nell noticed shabbinesses here and there. The gilt cracked, some panelling was split, there were cheap veneers and rough-and-ready joints. Cabins had been hastily smartened up to attract passengers in this expanding trade, but the gloss was a surface one only. As with the steerage, the company was after quick money for as little expenditure as possible. Nell was sure that more money, and a steadier flow of it in future, could be won by offering something better; and offering it consistently.

The steerage. . . . Recollection of conditions down there drove her to

129

the rail, to look down on the cluttered patch of open deck that was all they were granted—not looking down in derision, but suffused with memories, brief as they were.

A sudden squall drove the emigrants below under cover.

Nell turned towards the companionway, taken by the desire to go below and gather opinions and frame the account she would give when she got back to Liverpool. Her hand was on the knob when the second mate came up beside her.

"Sorry, ma'am. You mustn't go down there."

"I see no reason why I should not."

"Orders, ma'am. No communication between saloon and steerage class. Saves a lot of health and quarantine questions on the other side."

"I have a lot of questions of my own to ask."

Nell turned the knob. The door was locked. Before she could demand that he open it for her, a hand on her shoulder turned her gently but firmly round.

Malcolm said, "You'll be clapped in irons, the way you're going on."

"I see no reason why passengers of any kind should be confined like—"

"If you want to improve conditions afloat"—he was guiding her away from the mate—"you can set about it when you're back in England. Play with your own steamers to your heart's content."

"I don't regard it as play," she said hotly. "It's work of the first importance. I promise you that after these experiences I'll inspect every berth, every dormitory, every cranny in every ship under the Bostock flag."

"You'll be a hard task-mistress. Do you also promise to allow time for enjoyment? For living?"

Imperceptibly he had linked his arm with hers, and they were strolling the promenade deck like an affectionate brother and sister. Or a married couple. Laughing as they reeled against a stanchion, they came face to face with Hesketh, on his way on some errand. He stopped short and looked at their linked arms, glared, and plodded round them.

"I'm sorry for the United States of America," said Malcolm, "when that one's let loose there." They stayed against the rail for a few minutes, gauging each oncoming wave and bracing themselves against the impact. "If you devote your life entirely to figures and ledgers," he resumed, "and account books, or even to good works in the town, will that be enough?"

"I doubt if you'd have been able to afford this escapade," she retorted, "if there hadn't been someone reliable at home to keep the balance sheets."

"Ah, back to Edmund. Good old Edmund."

"There has to be someone to make the decisions, keep the business alive, while you . . ."

"While I what? You really must finish your sentences tidily, Miss Meredith. Nell."

"Malcolm . . ." Again she faltered, and this time he was delighted. His name had come unbidden to her tongue. She could not have echoed his brother's name, could not have referred to Edmund. Yet already it was fatally easy to smile at this man who held her arm, and call him Malcolm.

"You and I. *We* are the ones who should be partners, Nell," he said. "On great voyages, great explorations. To the ends of the earth and back again."

"I thought you'd already been to the ends of the earth."

"Then beyond."

"Beyond? In what kind of craft?" She was forcing herself to be deliberately prosaic.

"That you would have to leave to me. I'd want to surprise you. People ought always to surprise one another, not bore one another, don't you think?"

His fingers curled gently about her wrist.

"You're already too full of surprises, Mr. Gresham."

"Oh, that won't do. I don't want to go back to being Mr. Gresham again."

His mouth was rueful, the lower lip thrust out as if to disown his exaggerations, yet savouring them. When he lowered his gaze she could tell that he was guessing at what lay beneath her severe black jacket and comparing it with that Poppy of his. Shamefully Nell wondered how she fared in such a comparison.

He said, "Mourning becomes you. It heightens your colouring. Such beautiful colouring. But don't mourn too long, Nell."

He escorted her back to her cabin door. As she reached for the knob he was all at once tipping her chin up, his lips dancing to meet hers.

Nell jerked her head away.

"Such voyages," he said quietly. "Such explorations."

Inside, she leaned back against the door. The children looked up, their faces filled with an anticipation that faded.

"Thought we heard Mr. Gresham."

"Thought we might get another story."

That night Nell threshed to and fro in her bunk, fighting a weakness that had a strength of its own. She longed for Malcolm Gresham to be here with her, so that this time she could let him advance, this time not avert her mouth. It was wrong, perverse, all out of character. But then this whole voyage was out of character, out of the normal world. She was stirred by him, she told herself, only because he was her only link with a world she knew. They were so far from land, irresponsible because aboard ship they could be responsible for nothing.

She remembered his hand on her arm and wrist—and tried not to remember it.

Burying her face in her pillow she thought outrageously of his hands moving, seeking and possessing all of her until the final enfolding and possessing, which she scarcely understood, was afraid of but longed for—a violence as ravenous as Hesketh's, but ecstatic where his had been bestial, a fury she could answer with her own.

She wondered if Malcolm lay awake in his bunk reaching out for her, too, with mind and flesh.

Or if he was thinking of reunion with that inscrutable, beautiful creature he had left behind.

There was no appreciable gap between the pounding in her breast and the pounding on the cabin door that awoke her and the three children. As she slipped from her bunk, steadying herself as much against her own waking daze as against the motion of the ship, she heard Malcolm calling through the dissolving mists of her dream.

"Land! Landfall! Don't you want your first sight of the New World?"

THE THREE children clung to the rail between Nell and Malcolm. The *Tenacity* buzzed with an anticipation as powerful as the paddle machinery thrusting the ship on to that near, attainable land. The battle was over. Safe haven was in sight.

The smudge of coastline became an inlet. The land grew—a patchy grass, which sprouted into a palisade, which in its turn separated with intolerable slowness into trees and buildings, the spires of churches, smoking chimneys, fenced in by masts and funnels.

Rising from the water like a vast circular ornamental buoy, moored to the curving stern of Manhattan Island by a covered gangway, was a building that Nell recognised from engravings she had seen. One of them had been incorporated in a Bostock Navigation pamphlet. It was Castle Garden, the lavishly equipped entertainment hall converted into an immigrant depot, which, for all her poor dead father's urgings and her own thwarted efforts, still had no equivalent on the departure quays the other side of the Atlantic.

"She's in before us," said Malcolm over the heads of the children.

He nodded towards the meditatively smoking funnel of a vessel moored in the East River: the *Eleanor*.

"Doubtless having borne that companion," he added, "who was unlucky enough not to be your companion after all."

She tried not to smile too conspiratorially at him.

Clusters of men were forming into gangs along the waterfront, jeering and whistling. Even from a distance Nell could see one group setting off in a rowing-boat towards the artificial island of Castle Garden, only to be waved off by guards. Here, as in Liverpool, the runners and crooked salesmen were eager to snare the unwary traveller; but here were held back by a high wall, that well-policed passageway and the water around the depot itself.

Watched from above by a still dubious captain, Nell and the children returned to the steerage for the last few hundred yards of the journey. With twelve days of boredom, discomfort and sickness behind them, the immigrants were all filled with wild impatience to set foot on land, to be off to New England by railroad or on to a steamboat up the Hudson, off into far territories to meet other challenges. Some glared suspiciously as Nell rejoined them. But although Malcolm had urged other ways of putting her ashore and explaining to the authorities, Nell was convinced that in the long run the straightforward immigration procedure would prove safest. It was the only way she could be sure of meeting the children's father.

Medical inspection was as perfunctory as at Liverpool. The queue was nodded on with only an occasional check, a man or woman chosen at random rather than because of any obvious defect. In the great rotunda of Castle Garden an array of bumptious but knowledgeable clerks inspected baggage, money and documents, directing streams of arrivals to canal and railroad booking offices in the building. In the centre of the main hall a fountain was playing, where children sailed paper boats while waiting for their parents to conclude the formalities. An open doorway showed a broad-beamed riverboat nudging in, proclaiming itself in large letters the transfer vessel for the Erie Eisenbahn, with connections for Cleveland, Cincinnati, Louisville and St. Paul.

Mrs. Thomas Fenwick and her children went through without mishap. Nell could not believe they were free to leave. Right at this last moment she felt a constriction in her throat, was sure there would be some question she was unable to answer, and that the bewildered children would be turned back towards England.

When a clerk was momentarily free from inspecting baggage, she asked timidly, "Can you tell me where people are met? My . . . my husband should be waiting for us."

She held out the letter that had crossed the Atlantic west to east and was now returning east to west.

"Outside, lady. Depends where he's from. Fall River steamboat landing, or the railroad: there's collection points all along the Battery."

"Won't he be looking for me in here?"

The man groaned. "Let one in, and you let in the baggage smashers all pretending to be friends and relatives. And you watch they don't get *you* once you're outside."

Out in the open and on to land, she learned what the warning had meant. A runner waving a sheaf of tickets bore down on her. Another man tried to wrest the bag from George's hand.

"Get you a billet in the best boarding-house this end of Manhattan. Fix your ferry tickets . . . "

Two men shouldered the touts aside.

Malcolm said, "This gentleman has been looking for you."

Nell was confronted by a man little more than thirty who had seen enough to make him middle-aged before his time: bronzed, but paling now as he looked down at the children and then back at her.

"George—it is George, isn't it?"

The boy took an awkward step forward. Fenwick clutched him and tried to beckon the little girls closer. Charlotte, wide-eyed, held back and sought Nell's hand.

Nell said, "Mr. Gresham has told you the sad news?"

He shook his head, not in denial but in disbelief. There were no words for what he was trying to comprehend.

"I think we all deserve a good lunch," said Malcolm. "If you'd do me the pleasure of being my guests—"

"That's kind of you, sir." Fenwick had a deep, musical voice that began to gain strength. "But we'd best not be beholden to you any further. Got to make our way back."

He stared at Nell as if willing her features to change into those of his wife, so that they could walk away with their children.

All at once Charlotte let go of Nell's hand and reached for her father's. She began to chatter about the voyage. Mary joined in; it all came out in a flood, and without being conscious of it Fenwick allowed himself to be shepherded by Malcolm and Nell towards a restaurant that clearly relied for custom on happily reunited friends and relatives.

When they were seated, and the girls' eager tales about what the kind lady had done for them and the wonderful stories the gentleman had told them faltered before the sight of plates heaped with food, Fenwick recovered himself.

"Miss Meredith—and you, sir—I owe you a debt I can never repay. If I'd waited and there'd been no one to bring the children to me, how would I have known . . . how would we ever have met up, ever . . . ?"

"And what will you do now, Mr. Fenwick?" Malcolm made it sound comradely and cheerful.

"I shall . . . manage."

Nell tried to imagine the conditions under which the children would exist, the hours of loneliness while their father worked, what schooling they might hope for, what would fill the aching need for the woman left forever in an old, discarded world.

Malcolm was saying, "I think it might be advisable for you to rest here a few days while you make plans. If there's any way in which I might help—"

"You've helped enough, sir."

Again Fenwick risked a glance at Nell. Her face would not obey him: she would not become his lost Dora. He turned his gaze out of the window on the the busy street.

"It will be difficult for the children," Nell ventured. "And for you."

"I'll find somebody."

She was surprised by his abrupt, bitter confidence. He could not possibly mean, so soon and so brutally, what she was thinking. Yet what else could he mean: what else was there? Young women were arriving every day, daughters of immigrant families, who could be married almost as soon as they set foot on the quay if they so chose. It was not conventional, let alone romantic: but then, neither was the life of toil that lay ahead for most of them.

"I shall manage." Fenwick was quite firm this time.

When they parted, the girls were crying. George's lip trembled but he stood beside his father with a pride that brought tears to Nell's own eyes. There was a wrench of pain and loss inside her as she and Malcolm left.

"Damn," said Malcolm softly. "Oh, damnation."

He was swearing, as she was inside, at fate and cruelty and everything that went wrong for people who had done no wrong.

She had achieved her mission. Now she was ready to let someone else take over. She was in Malcolm's hands, and had no will to protest. He booked them into a large hotel of white marble on Broadway, choosing for her a room four storeys up, overlooking a thoroughfare turbulent with hackney carriages, white-topped omnibuses, shays and carts and strolling shoppers. Before she could adjust to these new surroundings—and before the room had ceased to rock to and fro, the motion of the ship still tilting the floorboards under her feet—he was insisting that he accompany her to a store where she would select new clothes.

"Here you'll not be expected to remain in mourning. You planned a holiday: it's high time it began."

He talked gaily, inconsequentially, incessantly. One of his motives was to drive out of her mind the memory of the three children to whom she had been so close for those days which in retrospect seemed months. She tried to halt the flow of words, to assure him she was all right and, like

136

the sturdy Thomas Fenwick, would manage; but there was no checking the sheer exuberance of his conversation.

They promenaded, as hundreds of others were doing, along broad sidewalks, comparing the Broadway windows with those of Bold Street and Lord Street. Four-horse carriages rumbled magnificently up to the kerb. A bulletin wagon stopped at a crossing, giving them time to read mysterious advertisements for patent medicines and unheard-of plays at local theatres.

As dusk crept over the city, gaslight invited from bars and restaurants, and the windows of their hotel made a chequerboard pattern high into the sky.

Dining together, they fell companionably silent. Nell had found this day more exhausting than all the days before it. She was glad Malcolm no longer felt the need to distract her. He shared her silence without effort or constraint.

When he saw her to the door of her room she thought he was about to kiss her. She did not want the touch of his lips tonight, but after all he had done for her she felt she must not turn away.

He smiled, keeping his distance. "Goodnight, Nell. Tomorrow we'll have a great deal to talk about."

"Gracious me. More than today?"

"Much more." He bowed over her hand. "Goodnight."

In the morning a message was brought by a pert little uniformed page to say that a Mr. Whitlaw and a Miss Coyte were downstairs asking to see her.

Nell gulped. She ought to have been feeling guilty about the two of them and about the havoc her disappearance must have wrought in all their generous plans. But until this moment they had not been numbered among the things that troubled her. She examined herself in the glass, trying to see her hair and new violet jacket bodice and organ-pleated skirt through a critical eye, and assured herself that she was perfectly calm and in control of any situation that might arise.

She went down to meet her visitors.

Eugenia Coyte was seated in an alcove to one side of the main lounge, near the warm breath of a central heating pipe. There were two unoccupied chairs close by, but Paul Whitlaw had chosen to stand, unbending, beside her.

"Mr. Whitlaw. Dear Eugenia."

"Miss Meredith," said Miss Coyte, "we have searched absolutely everywhere for you. We have been beside ourselves, literally beside ourselves."

"I'm sorry. I'm truly so sorry."

"If only you could have let us *know*. Simply dashing away like that!"

"It was most inconsiderate," agreed Nell. "All I ask is that you take my word that in the circumstances I had no alternative. There were three motherless children, it was an emergency, I had to act."

Paul Whitlaw, erect with one hand on the back of his cousin's chair, made a grudging move to bring another chair closer. Nell sat down.

"It has all been most unfortunate," said Paul above her head.

"I've said I'm sorry. And I'll say it again. Please believe me."

"Hm. Added to which, the rumours about Mr. Gresham—"

"Rumours?"

"A broker who handles contracts for my family reports that you were much in Mr. Gresham's company aboard ship."

"Because he most generously helped to make the children comfortable."

"And you are staying," said Eugenia Coyte, "at the same hotel."

"It's a very large hotel," said Nell heatedly. "There are no grounds for rumours of any kind. No grounds whatsoever."

"Oh, I wouldn't really suppose it for a moment. But you do see our position? We had made such plans for your reception, people knew about you, it has turned out most embarrassingly. But let's have no more reproaches. We'll make the best of it, I'm sure. We will dismiss any hint of scandal—"

"Especially as there is no cause for scandal." Malcolm Gresham stood at the edge of the alcove, leaning on a fluted column that cut off the view of the entrance and reception desk.

"I'm sure neither of us doubts your word, Mr. Gresham," said Paul Whitlaw hurriedly. "Or Miss Meredith's."

Eugenia summoned up a welcoming smile. "And *I* was just saying to Eleanor—"

"After all," Malcolm went brightly on, "Miss Meredith is going to marry me."

Nell half-rose from her chair but doubted the ability of her legs to sustain her.

Eugenia Coyte was staring. "Can this be true? You mean . . . really, I . . . it's not . . . "

"It's true," said Malcolm. "Isn't it, Eleanor? Nell?"

"I—"

"Naturally we wished to break the news more formally, at an appropriate time, but in the circumstances I felt I ought to dispel all misinterpretations."

Paul Whitlaw stepped between the two chairs, scarlet with some undefinable emotion. "But what about your . . . you already have

138

. . . " He stopped and seemed to draw himself up on tip-toe. "Really, sir. Miss Meredith. I trust this *will* all be made clearer. I think you owe us an explanation. Really I do. And if after sober consideration Miss Meredith feels she needs the advice of . . . Miss Meredith, if you will turn to someone who has so far thought highly of you and been anxious to be of service . . . " He went an even deeper hue.

Eugenia Coyte stood up with a peremptory toss of her head. Paul took her arm, and without another word the two of them walked in stately indignation towards the doors and were gone.

mark, Mr. Gresham."

"Sober consideration." He echoed Paul Whitlaw. "And unforgivable— is that what sober consideration has already made you decide? *Mr.* Gresham. And presumptuous!" He was so close, so overwhelming. "Was I really presuming so much?"

"There are ways of asking these things, I believe."

"And ways of answering. What kind of answer may I expect, Nell?"

She knew the question that had been burning on the end of Paul Whitlaw's tongue. Before she could venture one word of what Malcolm waited to hear, that same question was torn from her:

"And pray what will you do about that . . . that woman of yours?"

FALKNER SQUARE was quiet in the early evening save for the rustle of dried leaves twitching in the gutters. Behind drawn curtains the lights came on in fits and starts. As Edmund Gresham walked the length of the square for the fourth time he heard someone begin to play slowly and cautiously a sentimental little melody on a piano. It faded as he reached the end of the square; strengthened again as he retraced his steps.

In the Gresham house a light was on in the front drawing-room. He wondered what she was doing: reading to increase her English vocabulary, sewing or embroidering; or simply sitting placidly impervious to boredom or to any sense of the outside world? Somehow the picture of Poppy devoting herself to the domestic quietude of embroidery was unconvincing. Yet she had a flair for design: he knew from Malcolm's offhanded boasts that her most striking dresses were of her own creation.

That talent, at least, would be of use to her when she was alone—as she soon would be.

He made himself walk up the steps to the front door. Four times already he had done this, and four times faltered and walked away.

It was his own home. He had every right to put his key in the lock and open the door whenever he chose.

Across the square the pianist played a wrong note, fumbled, struck an even more wayward discord, and stopped.

Edmund put his key in the lock.

Then he withdrew it and reached for the bell-pull.

McGrath opened the door. "Mr. Edmund! Nice to see you home, sir." He stood back, and Edmund stepped into the hall.

"Is Miss . . . Miss Rivers in?"

"The lady is in the drawing-room, sir."

"Will you let her know I'm here, please?"

In stony disapproval of such diffidence on the part of one who was owner rather than visitor, McGrath went to the door on his left, tapped, and went in. When he turned back he was holding the door open for Edmund.

Poppy got to her feet as it closed again. She was clad in emerald green taffeta, with bare forearms and a jade pendant as smooth as her throat.

"Mr. Gresham." She spoke with a slurred accent but without as much effort as she had once needed to shape English syllables. "Why must you be announced? You come in, please, it is yours to come in." She waved him towards a chair: his father's chair.

He would have preferred to stand, but that would have made the whole scene look sterner and more dismissive than he wished it to be. He sat down. If anything in his manner worried or warned her, she did not show it. Hands folded in her lap, she waited for him to speak.

He said, "Poppy." The name was silly, but Malcolm's invention of Miss Rivers was even less manageable in her actual presence. "I've had a message. From Malcolm."

"How fortunate you are. I have no word, none."

"He's never been good at writing letters."

"But you have a letter."

"Yes."

She leaned forward an inch or two. "There is no bad news?"

"You may find it so." He steeled himself. "Malcolm has married. In New York."

Not a muscle quivered in that exquisite face, and there was no expression in her voice when at last she said, "So soon?"

"I gather that laws in the United States governing—"

"I mean he finds a wife in America so soon."

"He found Eleanor Meredith."

It was all so slow, as if she still needed time to translate such sentences in her head and then painfully phrase an answer in this alien tongue. "But I tell . . . hear . . . I am told other plans. Other plans for Miss Meredith, no?"

Was she angrier than she appeared—angry enough to be deriding him, hating him for having brought such news?

141

"No plans that I know of," he said.

"So. But still she becomes a Mrs. Gresham."

"It must be a shock. I wish there were some kinder way of breaking the news, but I'm glad it comes from me and not from somewhere else. If there's anything I can do—"

"He does not write. He sends you to tell me."

"Oh, it's not quite as bad as that."

Yet was it not as bad as that? The letter in Malcolm's large scrawl with its boisterous loops and underlinings had been ingenuously persuasive. He and Nell were married, they would be back within ten or twelve days of Edmund's receipt of the letter, and naturally it would be better for all concerned if Poppy were not there on their return. He wasn't asking Edmund to do his dirty work for him. Once he was home he would face Poppy himself and make sure she was well provided for. She was a gifted designer, knew a lot about silks, they could place her in a good situation with friends at Durnley Mills in Macclesfield. Unless Edmund had any other ideas?

"Malcolm will want to talk to you himself when he gets back," he said.

"I think not." The deadness of her tone made it frightening.

"Of course he does. But he wanted the news broken before he got back, to give you time to think things over."

"He writes to you. Not to me."

"Well . . . Perhaps," Edmund improvised, "he thought you would have difficulty reading English. Stupid of him, I grant you. I mean, your English"—flattery, which Malcolm would have found so easy, sounded false on his own lips—"is so fluent now. You've done wonders."

"He gives me money. For myself. I spend—I have spent—for private lessons. He does not know. Lessons in English, in case he gets bored, and I must become someone else to please him. I have left it too late, yes? He finds someone else already."

"I'm sorry. If I knew exactly why it all happened—"

"It happens. So I leave."

"You don't have to start packing this very night."

"But tomorrow morning, I think. And how far away do you wish I go, Mr. Gresham?"

"*I* don't want you to go far away." He shocked himself with the force of his outburst.

She stared. He tried to probe in behind those opaque eyes and win some direct response. But he had no right to demand any response from her.

Poppy got up. "I think I start tonight."

"I'll find you somewhere to stay. Until Malcolm can come and explain. If there's anything I can do . . . " He stood a few feet away from her, yet the gap was vast. The thought of any man being able to hold her in his arms was incredible. Even more incredible, the thought of wantonly discarding her. "Anything at all," he said. "Perhaps if you and I were to meet from time to time, so that you don't feel entirely cut off . . . "

She held out her hand, as cool and lifeless as her gaze. "I think I do not wish to be . . . *passed on*, Mr. Gresham."

He was dripping with sweat as he walked back to his rooms above the counting-house.

He found her a room in a small private hotel with a view of the pleasant paths and conservatory of the Botanic Garden, and felt sick when he let himself consider her isolation: the days of lonely waiting for Malcolm to arrive and make his excuses. But after what she had said he could not let himself risk calling on her.

The next task was a thorough cleaning of the Falkner Square house ready for the married couple's return. Mrs. Earnshaw clucked disapproval over the unseemly haste of it all, but was really delighted with the upheaval and drove the staff into an orgy of dusting, washing, polishing and ironing, while she herself went repeatedly from floor to floor in search of any last lingering traces of Poppy that needed rooting out.

Their first two nights back in Liverpool were spent by Malcolm and Nell with the bride's mother and Lord Speke at Orrell Manor. On the third evening they dined at Falkner Square. Edmund had invited no other guest. The three of them would have too much to talk about.

McGrath, Mrs. Earnshaw and the rest of the staff assembled in the hall to offer congratulations. Mrs. Earnshaw wiped away a tear. The maids curtsied and giggled happily.

And Nell was nappy. Her eyes were radiant as she turned to consult her husband or share a smile, a phrase, a joking memory. He had brought her blazingly to life. And Malcolm himself was more ebullient than ever; though from past experience Edmund suspected that some of his exuberant talk was meant to bluster through inconvenient questions, laughing things away rather than justifying them. But they brought a new brightness into the house, the two of them, with their accounts of New York and their honeymoon voyage home and the odd people and nice people they had met. McGrath came in with another bottle of wine and beamed at the joyfulness of the scene.

"And what," asked Edmund, "do your mother and Lord Speke think of this surprise you've sprung on them?"

Nell and Malcolm exchanged glances and became more serious. Nell left it to Malcolm to speak.

143

"From what we can make out," he said, "they've been thinking up a few surprises of their own in our absence."

"It's little wonder they were in no great haste to track me down," added Nell.

"Have you heard any whisper of land dealings north of the new timber dock site, Teddy?"

Edmund frowned into the purple depths of his wine. A fleeting recollection bubbled in his mind like a glint in the cut of the glass. He had indeed been aware of a Speke hireling moving busily between Exchange and the Dock Committee offices, and had overheard one remark on the possible significance of a private luncheon in the back room of the Beckwith Club. But comment had been too sketchy to interpret; and in any case it had been none of his concern.

He tried to fit the fragments together. "I did hear of a parcel of Speke land being offered in the new graving dock area. It seems logical enough to tidy up the loose ends there."

Again Nell silently consulted Malcolm; and Malcolm began to explain; and Edmund began to see how it all fitted.

Manchester manufacturers and the railway companies, already in constant strife with Liverpool dock interests over dues, fares and differential freight rates, had for some time been expressing alarm over the impending formation of a unifying Docks and Harbour Board. In autocratic control of the whole system, such a body was even less likely than its predecessors to make concessions to inland manufacturers or railway directors. Manchester believed in free trade; Liverpool in a profitable monopoly.

Lord Speke was planning to play off one against the other. A stretch of his land running down from the sandstone ridge into a shallow peat moss had for generations been worthless. Now, as dock extensions moved inexorably along the river, this swathe of wasteland would have to be incorporated in any comprehensive plan. There was a lull in construction while the last haggling took place over transfer of assets from the old Dock Trustees to the new Mersey Docks and Harbour Board. In that lull, Speke as Nell's guardian had pledged Bostock resources to buy the adjacent waterfront and amalgamate it with his own land; and now was offering it to a consortium of Manchester businessmen and railway shareholders as a self-contained river terminal, to which a spur could be taken from the existing railway.

"But having done so," Malcolm summed up, "he has let details leak out to the Liverpool Parliamentary Office. They'll at once apply pressure to get new clauses into the Bill forbidding outside groups to split the wa-

144

terfront. And Manchester and the railway interests will retaliate by sending *their* Parliamentary advocates into the fray."

"At which point," mused Edmund, "Lord Speke will presumably offer his property, and the property he has bought in the Bostock name, to the highest bidder."

Malcolm nodded. Where Edmund felt distaste for such manipulations, it was clear that his brother admired the strategy. "But the Dock Trustees will win, of course. At the last minute Speke will announce a change of mind, and let local patriotism prevail."

"Provided the price is high enough."

"But my guardian"—Nell intervened for the first time—"has to have my signature on the Bostock purchase. Because when he made it, he was legally no longer my guardian. I'm married, and now I'm the one who decides how Bostock assets are to be used."

"You'll sign, of course." Edmund took it for granted. "You'll back him up."

"No."

"But there can't fail to be a handsome profit for Bostock Navigation, without you having to lift another finger."

"That's what I've been telling her," said Malcolm fondly. "We let the scheme go through, collect our share, and travel round the world on the proceeds. Speke may have been up to no good, but he can do *us* a power of good."

Nell looked at him affectionately but with a tinge of wistfulness. To Edmund's amazement she turned abruptly and challenged him: "You and I are going to have to handle this, aren't we?"

"Are we?"

Malcolm dreamily sipped his wine, pushing his chair back a few inches to detach himself from all further responsibility.

Nell went on: "We must hold on to that land, right down to the waterfront. Not sell it off. My stepfather has been using Bostock resources: from now on they'll be used for Bostock's benefit. We build our own properly equipped passenger terminus—only it'll not be a terminus but a junction. We reach agreement with the Lancashire railway, on our terms and not theirs, to take a spur from their line so that passengers can be delivered direct to the quay. It'll be good business for the railway company and good business for us. There'll be co-ordinated timetables, cheaper fares because we'll commit ourselves to faster and more efficient screw steamers across the Atlantic, and once word gets around the Continental collection points and the more reputable brokers, we'll offer a through service at the lowest possible price."

Edmund was dazed. His brother gave him a sympathetic wink.

"It's too big," said Edmund. "Too big for one company. Look at the Harrington Dock Company—a fine mess they got into, trying to do the whole thing privately! Had to sell out to the Corporation in the end."

"This is different. The Gresham-Bostock team—"

"So it's all settled?" said Edmund ironically. "Gresham-Bostock . . . two marriages all at one go?"

"We *have* to amalgamate. By putting our joint capital in, putting the full weight of both companies behind it, we can carry the scheme through. It means committing everything, I agree. But that's where the future is. Your eastern cargo trade can't make the profits we'll make on the Atlantic. We amalgamate—and concentrate."

"If such a partnership were contemplated, it would be wiser policy to spread the risks. A slump in one trading area could then be compensated for by profits in another."

"Half-measures in different directions don't add up to full measure in any."

"Gresham's have always been known in the China trade. We're building new clippers—"

"Sell them off. Concentrate!" said Nell again, fiercely. "We mustn't make the mistakes the Americans made, not a decade ago: building clippers for the gold rush, dabbling here and there, neglecting the Atlantic—and neglecting steam until it was nearly too late. Look what it cost the Collins Line to take on the Atlantic run! Too late, too expensive. And then losing one of their steamers, paying out again for a replacement— and now on top of all that they've had their mail subsidy cut to less than a half. Did you know that? We learned a lot in New York."

"So I see."

"Collins have never yet paid a dividend, and they're not likely to now. They're near collapse. The farmers and railroad interests are jealous of their subsidies and *want* them to collapse. Now's the time for us to take over what they're abandoning. *Now!*"

Edmund felt a rueful amusement. It was such a short time since Nell Meredith had shown a ladylike unwillingness to discuss shipping and the port. Now here she was, forcing the subject upon them at the dinner table: a forceful Miss Meredith who had become, though not quite as the gossips had predicted it, Mrs. Gresham.

He looked at his brother. They had to act together. Gresham family interests were indivisible. But Malcolm was still leaning back, indifferent. Nell had been right. It was obvious who would have to make the decisions.

146

"Well, one thing I'll say." Edmund set his glass down. "You're certainly going to make this house hum with life again."

"But we shan't be living here," said Nell.

"Not live here? But where, then?"

"Bostock's Brow, naturally."

Naturally.

Nell was smiling at her husband for confirmation. He shrugged and said, "Best thing, when you come to think of it. You can move back in here, Teddy, and do a bit of livening up on your own account. Come to think of that, too, it's high time *you* got married, old lad."

Bostock's Brow . . . Edmund was on the verge of saying, if only to himself, something about Nell continuing to live under the shadow of her grandfather. But her declarations this evening made nonsense of that. She was a young woman who had made up her own mind and was under nobody's shadow.

Not even her husband's.

IN THE mirror of her dressing-table Nell could see Malcolm at a slightly tilted angle across the bedroom, undressing with that desultory untidiness she found so exasperating—and so endearing. He had ambled through from his dressing-room to complain about the state of the Bostock's Brow window-frames and the draughts they admitted, lost interest in the subject, and now, without bothering to go back, was dropping his shirt on a chair and his socks on the floor.

Light glistened in the fine stripe of sandy hair down his naked back. Nell contemplated the reflection and longed to run her fingers down between those shoulder blades. Instead, her hand shaking slightly, she loosened the muslin fichu at her neck.

His eyes intercepted hers in the glass.

"You know," he appealed, "I'm dashed if I see why we shouldn't go on a voyage. You've kept saying how you loved being on the water and going over unknown horizons. But the moment you're back in Liverpool, you're back in . . . "

The wave of his hand accused the room of corrupting her judgment.

Back in Liverpool. She would have found it humbling to describe to him—or attempt to describe—the emotions that had possessed her as the steamer churned up foam and swung its bows towards the Mersey landing. She had not expected the rush of affection, like tears of happiness in her nose and throat, choking her at the sight of that smoking, scarred, aggressive skyline of a city. Malcolm had been away so often and come

148

home so often. How could he have understood that for her, too, this had suddenly and heartrendingly become home?

"We didn't know what we'd have to face when we returned," she said. "Now that we do know, we can't just turn our backs on it and leave the problems to someone else."

"I don't see why not. Old Edmund knows what's going on. We talk it over with him, agree what he has to do on our behalf, and then go off and see the world. Nobody'll be a penny the worse in the end. And Edmund'll love it. It's just the sort of thing he's good at."

He came and kissed the back of her neck. Even in stooping over her he tantalised her with the smell of him, but she kept staring straight ahead—only to see his bare arm reach over her shoulder, his hand searching out her breast.

"Another honeymoon," he coaxed.

"We can have that here at home," she said, "any night of the week."

"It would be so much more amusing somewhere else."

"Amusing?" Beside his face in the glass she saw her own face, peremptory and goading. "I can prove otherwise."

"You're a forward young madam."

"Yes."

He kissed her again, nuzzling her shoulder with his lips, then stepped back to kick the rest of his clothes into a heap.

Nell forced herself to look away from his lean-limbed reflection. But the picture was stored in the memory of her eyes, just as the smell and touch of him reverberated in her nostrils and flesh and bone. Memories of exquisite hurt—the first exultant shock of a wedding night loud with pain and all he had said to her and all she had shamelessly sobbed back—creating the only sadness: after days and nights aboard ship, on their bed, against the reeling wall of their cabin, this way and that until she was an ache of his own lust and her own joy, she ached all the more with the knowledge that she could never again have quite that tearing anguish of ravishment. But she could be what the heroines of those circulating library novels were never allowed by their authors (and certainly never by poor old Mr. Trigg) to be: a young woman with resilient hips and a gaping hunger, luring him into herself and tasting him and letting herself be mastered by him.

She had so wanted him to be master—to take charge of everything just as he had taken possession of her body. To arrange their travels, their home, their comings and goings; to take over the business chores she had inherited. Rather Malcolm than Adrian Speke. Above all that he should dismiss, or take on his own shoulders, the powerful shade of her grandfather.

It had taken so little time, so very little time, for her to sense what she would not let herself even hint aloud: that he was not strong enough. Lord of their flesh, but not of their livelihood.

Well, girl, it's up to you now.

As her petticoat slipped from her she glanced fondly at Malcolm. She would let her self suffer no disillusionment. His physical presence and sheer animal vigour and appetite filled such a large part of her life already: the rest could be filled with other things, other responsibilities, which need not prevent their being happy. Need not—must not.

"I see quite a different picture of you in that side of the glass." Malcolm had propped himself meditatively against the wall. "Quite a different woman."

"Would you prefer a different woman?"

Am I good enough? Whatever weaknesses she might suspect in him, they were as nothing compared to worries about her own inadequacy in this one thing, this all-important thing. She longed to ask the one question she dared not ask.

"Young women aren't supposed to enquire about other women," he said. "They're not supposed to know other women have ever existed."

There was a perilous silence. Both might have tripped over an upturned corner of rug and, catching breath, taken a few seconds to find their feet again.

"I'm not very good at pretending," Nell said.

"No." The hiss of breath between his teeth tried to convert it into a joke. She could almost have predicted that. "No, you're not, are you?"

"Why did you get bored with . . . with *her* . . . and choose me instead?"

"Nell, we can't possibly—"

"Will you get bored with me, too, in the end?"

He pushed himself away from the wall. "A fine thing for a wife to ask, I must say."

"But she meant something to you. She must have. I can't believe you're going to obliterate her entirely. Obliterate her memory, I mean. You're not going to deny that for a long while she . . . gave you pleasure?"

In the glass she saw that he was not even looking at her. And whatever or whoever it was he dreamily contemplated in space was taking on flesh: *his* flesh, rising and hardening in response.

Nell turned on him. If it was Poppy he saw, Poppy shouldn't have him. His wife and not Poppy should drain the heat from him tonight and every other night. As Nell seized him, his head snapped round and now he was forced to see her and nobody else. She murmured a word he had taught her. And if in the past he had taught Poppy the same word . . .

150

no, that was dead. Nell squeezed Poppy out of existence with a grip that made him moan.

"It's a good thing I've got you, isn't it?" he said with agonised intensity.

"I hope you think so. I hope . . . " But his mouth smothered all doubts and questions.

He bore her up and drove her down again, down with the thrust of a plunging bowsprit. Through her own wetness she felt the seeking figurehead streaming with spray, rearing above the waves and cleaving back into them. But she was not that avid figure stretched along unyielding hardness: she was wide and sprawling, buffeted by waves, smashed down by gale force and then speared, lifted on the sprit and stabbed down again, soaked until her loins streamed and she tried to pull away from his cruelty and then, gasping, to rise and clutch herself around him again.

The storm roared and she heard her own voice scream through it, scream and whimper and whisper away into silence as they were tossed at last on a warm and sleepy shore: a sleep and silence lasting until, at dawn, the storm raged over them with renewed fury.

Nine months later she bore twin sons, and they were named Jesse and Alan.

It was almost another three years before Nell discovered that Poppy had never left Liverpool but was discreetly, one might even say decorously, installed in a smart little house on the edge of Prince's Park, where Malcolm visited her regularly.

Two

Storm Centre

THE HURDY-GURDY usually toured the streets below Bostock's Brow on Wednesday and Saturday afternoons, luring children out of the terraced houses on the slope. When it stopped they sang and danced round it, fitting new skipping rhymes and nonsense words to old tunes. When it moved on they followed uphill and down again. Jesse and Alan Gresham could hear it clearly if they ran to the end of the garden and stationed themselves by the hedge. They were not allowed to go out and join the ragged audience: there was no gap in the hedge, and their mother and nurse both said it was too far round by road, and too dangerous. So they stood on the grass and listened. Jesse was always the first to grow bored and run back to the house. Alan would not return until he was called, or until the music had gone away. He liked the different echoes you got as the sound approached, or turned along a street, or drifted off downhill. One of his earliest memories was the sad yet enchanting whisper of it fading utterly away round some distant corner.

Another was of his grandmother playing the piano in her big house, and sometimes playing the one here when she came visiting. From the very first time he heard her he knew she was somehow not playing things properly. Even when the tune was right, there were notes underneath that didn't belong. He could not have explained what was wrong or why it was wrong; but he knew.

When he himself began to practise at the piano, his grandmother

155

made a great fuss of him. She was so glad her talent had been passed down. When he visited her or when she was here for a party she would insist on his playing to her or to friends, sighing, telling everyone: "Of course he gets it from me, if only I'd had time to develop my fingering . . . such a waste . . . "

Later, much later, when Alan looked back he found it hard to remember a time when music had not been in his head and in the air about him. He could not remember actually studying musical notation. Had it really been so easy to assimilate?

Yet there were other, often trivial, things he recalled quite clearly: things that his mother would say he couldn't possibly have remembered, he was too young, he wasn't really remembering but making it up from things one of them said. In spite of that he did retain some pictures and sounds as vividly as if they belonged to this same day, even this same hour. Often it was difficult to get them in the right order. Events standing out with equal sharpness might be separated by several years. Others were misted over, and when he tried to see them in their true perspective they shuffled themselves out of sequence and became larger than life or else vanished altogether. Some overlapped or were chopped off like the pictures on the scrap screen in the nursery. Alan's panel of the screen was a mosaic of country scenes cut from old calendars and magazines, two pretty ladies from a box of soap, and items from a furnishing catalogue thrown aside by his mother. Jesse preferred pictures of ships and machinery, in defiance of Alan's complaint that a lot of them were out of proportion and spoiled the whole look of the screen.

He remembered snow all over their second Christmas. It had been wonderful, the snow when they were little. Looking out across the river from an upstairs window he could see windjammers picked out by a white lining to their yards and bulwarks, stark and clear against shimmering mist along the Wirral shore. And sounds were as brittle as the frost: a peal of church bells tingled in the air, and then there was the unexpected chord of a clock striking the hour and the clang of the packet bell from the landing-stage.

He remembered Uncle Adrian—not grandfather, because grandmother for some reason said he didn't want to be called that and so became a sort of uncle—watching him when he first picked out tunes and chords on the piano, smiling vague encouragement with those funny watery eyes yet not truly hearing the music itself. You could tell he didn't know how to listen or what to listen for.

And often, when later Alan plucked out memories at random and found in them an adult significance which had then been as far from his grasp as music had been from Uncle Adrian's, he was reminded of grandmother in some of those odd clothes of hers. With her hair cut un-fashionably short, she dressed in what looked almost like hunting cos-tume, tightly nipped in at the waist and around her behind, severely masculine in appearance. "That's how Uncle Adrian likes me to look," she said when once young Jesse boldly asked why she adopted such a style.

Jesse was from the start bolder and more forceful than his younger twin—younger by ten minutes. The gap was small, but large enough to make Jesse instinctively an older brother. Obviously he was destined to take over the Gresham-Bostock business. After ten minutes of music he walked away, even when he was little; but when it came to talk of ships, or a trip on the ferry, or visits to ships and docks, Alan was the one to grow quickly bored.

Yet even there, memory played its own tricks. Alan never forgot the sight of the greatest vessel any of them had ever seen, when the *Great Eastern* steamed up the Mersey and moored in the Sloyne. Thousands of people lined the shore, and a flotilla of ferry-boats and dinghies was crowded with onlookers.

"You see"—he would never forget the excitement in his mother's voice, almost singing as she let go of his hand and clutched his father's arm—"it can be done. An iron ship of that size, carrying all the coal it needs to get to Australia and back. It *can* be done. Think of how it might be adapted for the Atlantic trade! But the paddles are a mistake."

"Paddles and screw," said Uncle Edmund. Edmund was a real uncle, not just called one, like Uncle Adrian. "Taking no chances."

"He should have gone all out for a more powerful screw. Or more than one."

"It won't work as a passenger liner, whatever you do to it. Brunel him-self said so before he died."

"But if it had been designed for that from the start . . . if . . . "

It was the sort of talk Alan grew up with: the sort in which Jesse loved to join, even when his squeaky childish contributions made the grown-ups laugh. All the time there was talk about cutting the Atlantic passage by another half-day, a full day, two and three days; the need for the new horizontal engines; strange phrases about return connecting rods, nomi-nal horsepower, lifting screws and hull stresses—first parroted and then knowledgeably appropriated by Jesse. Then there would be abrupt switches to argument about Dock Board contributions to the poor rate, and how they must stand out against the Corporation. In Alan's mind all the different occasions and different arguments tended to run together.

Out of nowhere he remembered the smell of the bowl of pot-pourri his grandmother kept on the hall table of Orrell Manor. How he had

157

loved to scamper up to it, pretending to be winded, and puff so that flakes scattered like coloured snow, leaving a faintly musty fragrance drifting across the hall.

His father had never seemed to throw himself into the business like Uncle Edmund. Or even like Alan's mother. She and Uncle Edmund were the ones always talking together and poring over plans together, inviting Jesse and Alan to join them if they wanted to, but shrugging and smiling faintly at each other when Alan hinted that he would like to slip away and play the piano.

Father was often missing altogether. On one occasion Alan was sure, while out with their nurse for an afternoon walk, that he had seen his father walking briskly along the path to the far side of Prince's Park when he surely ought to have been at work. But Mrs. Dinsdale had seen nothing and said he must have been dreaming, and when he asked his father about it that evening all he got was a quick laugh and a vigorous shake of the head. His mother had looked puzzled for a moment; but a few minutes later, when the boys were on their way up to bed, Alan heard her laughing in the way she did when his father was teasing her or bringing her a present or telling some outrageously high-flown story.

Father was good at telling stories. Seated between their two beds he would contemplate the scrap screen and keep them waiting until it suited him to point at one of the pictures and say, "That reminds me." Then he would close his eyes and pretend to grope back through the years, though you knew he already had it all worked out in his mind. When he was ready to start he did so in a shy way as if unsure that you'd like what he had to tell. It was always wonderful. Maybe only half its facts were true facts, but still it was all wonderful. When he reminisced about far seas there was no dull stuff about engines and engineering, freight charges, stowage ratios, passenger fares and turn-round times. Shanghai and Bombay were not merely wharves manipulated by English traders calculating profits from afar. New York was no mere extension of the North Eastern Railway or the London and North Western. Places came alive, even if it were only the life of a poetic, twopenny-coloured fairytale. Better that hectic colouring than the sober black and red of a balance sheet.

Their mother rarely came to the nursery to tell stories. When she did, she could be fascinating; but all too often, halfway through a tale her mind would wander and she would obviously be anxious to get away and attend to something else, and all the excitement and poetry would be lost. Most evenings she contented herself with a quick kiss, asking if they were all right and then asking Mrs. Dinsdale if she was quite sure they were all right. She was warm and sweet and sweet-smelling—he would never forget that very special smell just in the shadow of her throat—and whenever she left their room he would lie awake hoping against hope that she would decide to come back and talk just to him, while Jesse was asleep. But so many things claimed her attention. Every now and then she would make a big fuss of them at bedtime, talking too loudly and apologising for not having spent much time in the nursery lately. Alan could tell from the way she hugged him how much she loved him. And Jesse too. But they were only one part of what mattered to her: part of the complicated world of Bostock's Brow, the river, the docks and warehouses, the routes laid across the ocean by two great-grandfathers dead before he was born. Her love had to be shared out, allocated.

She was easier and readier to smile when their father was there. Nothing pleased her more than his arrival after she had been on her own with the boys for ten minutes or so. Occasionally she would sit on the end of a bed, Jesse's or Alan's, while he told one of his stories. One evening she smiled beautifully and lovingly at him, saying, "I remember you telling that one on that dreadful ship," and Alan felt surrounded by warmth and happiness and the assurance of safety for ever and ever, amen.

But other nights, if the nursery door was left ajar or had creaked open as it often did of its own accord, he would overhear her more usual tone of voice, brisk and assertive. It worried him. It rarely sounded right: the notes were wrong, the harmonies did not match, she was forcing the pitch to disguise her own uncertainty about that pitch.

He remembered grandmother, very shrill in the hall: "I'm sure that's not what your grandfather would have wanted."

"It's no longer a matter of what grandfather would have wanted. It's what the firm wants. What *we* want—Malcolm and I."

"Malcolm and you? Hm. More likely Edmund and you. Or just you."

And once there had been that terrible row. So different, their voices: his mother's and his father's. This definitely belonged to those first couple of years of his life, and he did remember it. It was in fact the clearest of his recurring memories, perhaps because it was the first time he had heard his own parents shouting at each other like the sort of men and women who yelled at each other in the streets below or along the docks. It was all about someone called Poppy, who for some reason ought not to have been in Liverpool and wasn't going to be allowed to stay in Liverpool any longer. The ugliness of the sound had hurt his ears.

Yet another memory, not all that much later, conflicted with this. A beautiful lady called Poppy, with slanting eyes and a soft voice as musical as a cat's purr, dined at Bostock's Brow with some other guests, and everyone seemed perfectly happy about it. And Uncle Edmund was there, and there was an American gentleman, and a lot of champagne was

159

poured and there was laughter in the garden and lots of congratulations about something or other, and mother and father didn't seem to mind Poppy being there after all. And later there was news of Poppy's daughter, and of course there was the time when Poppy's daughter appeared in Liverpool and . . .

But that was later, much later than the original puzzle and distinct from it. The clash between those early fragmentary memories was such a nagging perplexity that it was one of the first things he made Poppy explain when, at the age of eighteen, he was first taken into her bed.

"Of course," said Poppy expressionlessly, "it was your mother's doing. Of course she was cheerful when it had worked out to her satisfaction. She arranged it, just as she has arranged so many things."

THE DOOR of the lodge was closed and remained closed as Nell went up the drive in a hired cab. With so many things on her mind after the frustrations of the afternoon, she was only half-aware of this in passing; but when she stood on the step, paying off the driver and watching him go back towards the gates, the fact was another irritation to add to her store. Yesterday she had agreed readily enough to let Mrs. Watson go to Morecambe for a week to visit her married daughter. Now Watson, with his wife out of the way and his employer supposedly off the premises for the entire afternoon, was apparently stealing an hour's snooze.

Nell went indoors and straight upstairs to her bedroom. Trying to unknot the ribbon bow of her bonnet, she succeeded in drawing it tighter. In a mood to be incensed by any triviality now, she rang for Kitty, her maid.

There was was no response.

Of course Kitty had not expected her back so soon. The girl could be anywhere in the house. Nell rang again, and waited. Still nobody came. It was not Kitty's afternoon off. She ought to be somewhere within hearing.

As soon as they thought their mistress's back was turned for any length of time, they were all asleep or absent.

Nell wrenched her bonnet free and began to loosen the hooks of her bodice.

Such a disgraceful waste of time. With urgent decisions to make of the final refurbishing of the Liverpool Sailors' Home, the trustees had spent the first ten minutes talking as usual about their pockets: about the American Civil War and its repercussions on Liverpool profits and losses. New routes and new hazards to their ships were more important than the welfare of the men who worked those ships. Financed by local merchants and owners to provide clean and cheap accommodation for seamen, the original Home had deterred as many as it attracted, with cast-iron galleries like those of a prison around a bleak inner courtyard. After its gutting by fire, Nell's reputation for planning crew and travellers' lodgings in Liverpool, and shipboard accommodation, led to her appointment to the reconstruction committee. But after all the work she had put in, all the plans she had taken to this crucial meeting today, and the carriage sent home with instructions not to return for another two and a half hours, here she was delivered home in a hansom. All because three of the most important committee members, notified of the arrival of a blockade runner with a valuable cargo from Charleston, had abandoned all pretence of interest in rebuilding the Sailors' Home and rushed off.

She wanted to vent her annoyance on someone, get rid of this surplus energy. Her time, of course, was no concern of those men: invited on to the committee because part of it could be regarded as woman's work, she could as easily be abandoned and left sitting there with the merest sketch of an apology.

Half-laughing at her own resentment, she crossed the bedroom to the door of Malcolm's dressing-room and turned the knob. It was unlikely that he would be in at this time of day, but she must find *someone* to wrangle with.

The door would not open.

He could surely not have locked it from the inside—unless for some ludicrous reason he were secreted in there himself?

"Malcolm." She could hardly bring herself to say it aloud.

She tried the knob again, and pushed harder. The door sprang open. It had merely been stuck. Of course there was nobody inside. Why should she have half-expected it: what should she have expected? There had been a moment of doubt. She was ashamed of it, ashamed of herself. But the picture had appeared unbidden. Kitty was now a buxom and bold-eyed nineteen, too bold-eyed to be utterly innocent, though so far there had been no mention of any regular follower.

Nell went a few steps into the room. She was facing the window. Through it she saw her maid edging along in the shadow of the hedge, heading for a spot where she could make a quick break across the gar-

162

den towards the yard and the servants' entrance. There could be little doubt where she had been, in spite of the wide detour she was making. The lodge door had been closed. From within, the two of them must have heard the hansom arriving: had perhaps peeped through the curtains and seen that their mistress was back.

Nell stormed from the room, out and along the corridor to the back stairs. She had reached the bottom tread as the side door opened. Kitty bustled in, pushed the door shut behind her, and leaned against it for a moment. She let out a sigh of relief. Then she saw Nell.

It was not just the hastily half-tidied dishevelment that gave her away. In that narrow space at the foot of the stairs there was no mistaking the smell of her and what she had been up to.

"Well, young woman. And what have you got to say for yourself?"

Young woman! Nell heard in herself the tone of a starchy old matron.

"Mum, I was just taking a turn round the grounds. Haven't been gone a minute."

"No, not a minute. Enjoying yourself in Mrs. Watson's absence?"

A defiant grin tweaked at the girl's full lips. "What a thing to say about Mr. Watson, mum!"

"I'll not have that sort of thing going on in my house."

"Wasn't actually in the house, mum. Not this one, I mean."

"Don't be insolent. You can pack your bags and go."

Now Kitty's lips trembled, but she remained defiant. "What, just 'cos of that?"

"Yes, just because of that."

"But what about *him*? He was the one who led me on, and me not the first neither. What about *him* packing his bags?"

"I shall speak to Watson in good time."

"And tell him not to do it again, and let him and his missis stay on? Oh, yes, he'll get away with it. They always do, those sort."

"I told you, don't be insolent."

"And you'd better watch out for yours as well," Kitty screeched suddenly.

"You'll go to your room before I lose my temper."

"Lose a lot more besides, the way he's going on. But I suppose he'll get away with it too. *He* gets away with *anything*, doesn't he?"

"What are you trying to suggest?"

"Me, mum?"

"If you're daring to suggest that you've been carrying on with . . . " Nell could not let herself utter it.

"Oh, no, not me, mum. I'm not saying he hasn't pinched me bum now and again, but it didn't go no further than that. More's the pity."

163

"I won't listen to any more."

"No, you'd best not."

Scarlet-cheeked but unrepentant, Kitty made to go up the stairs. Nell barred the way.

"You did tell me to go to my room, Mrs. Gresham."

"What exactly were you trying to tell me, just then?"

"None of my business to tell you anything, is it?"

"If you want any kind of a reference from me, my girl . . . "

This did at last bring the girl up short. "But you couldn't not . . . I mean, I've worked hard for you, you can't say I haven't done what I was supposed to. For *you*, I mean. Just because me and Mr. Watson—"

"I can't have you on my staff exposing him to further temptation. But I'll give you an accurate reference if you will tell me precisely what you meant."

"I won't say no more. It's not fair."

"Kitty!"

"No more than . . . well, you want to ask where he goes those late afternoons when he's not back at his usual time. Playing whist at the club, eh? And what he's been at while you've been doing all those plans and pictures for your meetings."

"Where?"

"You could try round Prince's Park, for a start. Must cost a pretty penny to keep her there in that sort of place."

Nell stepped down to Kitty's level, not sure whether she was going to seize her or slap her face or throw her bodily out of the door. Kitty did not wait for her to make up her mind. Sliding past, she ran upstairs and up the next flight on to the linoleum outside her attic bedroom.

Nell would not, could not go back the way she had come. She went out into the yard and round the corner of the house. The door of the lodge was open. Watson's shadow was in the doorway and she was sure his face was turned expectantly, fatalistically towards her. She took a step in his direction, then another, and was quickening her pace so that she should not falter, when Malcolm rode in through the open gates. He saw her and slid from the saddle, smiling surprise and happiness.

"I thought you wouldn't be back for ages."

She felt a leap of answering happiness. Of course he hadn't expected her back, yet he himself was back—back to his own home—and everything else was wicked slander. What better opportunity could he have had than this afternoon for deceiving her? But he hadn't.

His arm was round her. He whistled piercingly for the groom to take his horse, and led his wife into the house.

"How did your meeting go?"

She told him, at the same time half-attentive for some betrayal on his part of what he had kept so secret all this time. When she explained how the committee had dispersed, she knew from the repetitive little gulp in his throat that he was longing to interrupt with some item of news or comment of his own. It was so funny and familiar a habit that she was disarmed, her suspicions fading. As soon as she had finished, he said, "Yes, I heard about the Charleston cargo. But there's more to the story than that. Did you know the ship was boarded and taken over by a prize crew from a Northern warship?"

"But they wouldn't have brought it all the way here."

"They were supposed to take it to Philadelphia. But after the warship had gone, the captain and three of his men overpowered the prize crew and clapped them in irons. And then steamed for home." Malcolm beamed. It was just the sort of exploit to delight his heart.

"There'll be trouble," she said, "with the American government."

"Depending on who finishes up as *the* American government. In the meantime, there's already talk of a commemorative dinner for the captain, and he'll probably be presented with a gold chronometer or some such token of the Liverpool brokers' esteem."

The thought of those Liverpool brokers, of the cotton men and tobacco men and shipping men and their preoccupations, reawakened Nell's ire.

"Esteem! What's the esteem of men like that worth? We condemn slavery, but do underhand deals with the states that want to preserve it—support legitimate government with one hand while holding out the other palm to the South, offering them gunboats and pushing up prices so that everyone not in the cabal pays in blood and starvation . . . . "

Malcolm held up his hands in mock horror and backed away. "Don't blame me! I wasn't one of those at your meeting. And we're not in the freight business any longer. But you've got to admit it, running the blockade and getting caught and then turning the tables like that—it's pretty good, oh, it's pretty good."

How he would have loved being on board and taking part!

Nell said, "We'll dine early, if you've no objections. Then I can fit in a couple of hours' work."

"You're not shutting yourself away with diagrams and specifications again? Not after the meeting collapsed the way it did?"

"All the more reason. So that when we reassemble, argument is cut to a minimum. They'll find that all the loose ends they left are tied up the way *I* want them."

"You never stop, do you?" He pinched her ear. She thought of Kitty, whose bottom he had pinched; and again found herself listening, gauging his motives and reactions. "Another lonely evening for me, then?" he said lightly.

"We'll have to find you a spare lady friend."

"What an obliging wife you are!" He laughed too loudly, then said, "I suppose I could nip down to the club for an hour or so."

"Why not?"

"A few hands of whist. Unless you want me on hand, in case you finish early."

"I'd be poor company."

"You're never that."

How sincere, or insincere, or caring or uncaring was he?

After dinner he made a show of lingering, then said, "If you're quite sure . . . ?" and began to hum to himself as he left the house.

Nell was alone, wondering what she had hoped to prove. Or hoped not to prove. When she had offered him the excuse for going out she had harboured some vague notion of following him, tracking him across Prince's Park, unmasking him as a villain. It was unthinkable. At least, impractical. How could she follow him unobserved, how keep close enough to spy on him without his just once turning and recognising her?

Now that he was absent, could she go through his desk, his wardrobe, the chest-of-drawers, every pocket?

Nell groaned.

If she had not taken Kitty by surprise, the truth—if truth it was—might not have come out for many more years; perhaps never; or might in time have ceased to be truth.

She had still to speak her mind to Watson.

Malcolm's arrival had deflected her this afternoon. He was not here to deflect her now. She slipped a light cape over her shoulders and walked down the drive. At this time of the evening the gates were closed and it was reasonable that the door of the lodge should also be closed. The spring evening still shone like fine steel along the western horizon, but the trees cast a shadow across the lodge, and behind drawn curtains there was a light in the front room. It was only after she had let the knocker fall twice that Nell wondered if Kitty might have risked a visit for a tearful farewell—or an equally tearful denunciation.

Watson opened the door. His shoulders slumped when he saw her, then he braced himself. Waiting for her to appear or send for him must have been something of an ordeal.

"Come in, mum."

"Thank you, Watson. I'll not come in. What I have to say won't take long."

"No. No, I s'pose it won't."

166

She had not rehearsed what she would say to him. The situation was so crude and obvious that no premeditated address had seemed necessary. But now, facing him as he tried to guess what kind of blow she was about to deal him, she found she had no idea whether she was going to berate him, dismiss him, or deliver a long moral lecture.

A smell of burnt toast drifted along the passage from the kitchen at the back.

"You've left something on the stove?"

"No, mum. That was my tea. Let something fall in the grate."

Twilight made pallid pewter of his brow.

Nell said, "You know what I've come to see you about."

He nodded. Her tinge of uncertainty made him less abject than when he opened the door to her.

"I think your behaviour has been despicable."

"Yes, mum."

"I'm sending the girl away."

"I'm sorry about that. If you could see your way to—"

"No."

"No, mum."

"For a man of your age . . . " She wanted the words to flail him, but saw that he was carefully regaining confidence. "I ought to send you packing, too."

He nodded, cautious, waiting.

"But you served my grandfather well. Your wife is a good woman."

"Oh, she's that all right, mum. None better."

"You've both served us well. I'm disgusted by your conduct. It dirties everything that's gone before. But I don't want Mrs. Watson to suffer."

"You sound just like your grandfather, Miss Eleanor," he wheedled.

"You mean he had cause to reprimand you for the same sort of behaviour?"

"Oh, no, miss . . . mum . . . no, not that, that's not what I was meaning." He smiled in crooked ingratiation. "If there's anything I can do to make up—anything at all, honest. You've only got to ask."

Was this an offer of betrayal? He must know what there was to be known of Malcolm. If Kitty knew, then Watson must know: had perhaps been the one to tell Kitty in the first place. A great masculine joke it must have been. But he would abandon the master to stay in the mistress's good books. For a dizzy instant Nell was tempted to take him at his word and ask outright; and if he faltered, or pretended she had misunderstood him, she would trade his revelations against a threat of instant dismissal.

167

No. She would not demean herself by making him her servile accomplice.

She said, "From now on you'll behave yourself. This girl goes, and you'll keep your hands off any others."

"I will, honest I will."

"She must go. And I'll have no gossip. About this or anything else. You understand?"

"You don't have to worry about me, Miss Eleanor. Mrs. Gresham." He was already inching thankfully back into the lodge. "From now on you don't have to give it another thought."

The door was closed almost before she had turned and started to walk away.

Back in the house she paced aimlessly from room to room. There was no question of settling to more work on the decoration and furnishing plans for the Sailors' Home. She was plagued by other questions. Which put her on a level, she thought wryly, with those committee members whose other obsessions she so much deplored.

Ought she to have asked Malcolm outright, the moment they met this afternoon—and been righteously condemned for listening to evil gossip? To have asked him outright—and given him time to cover his tracks?

Or should she establish the facts beyond mere hearsay, by going through his desk, his pockets . . . She had thought of it earlier, dismissed it, and now here it was again to torment her.

She went into the library. She had made many alterations within the house, but some rooms she would not touch. This was one of them. It remained as it had been in her grandfather's day.

What would Jesse have said about her marrying the wrong Gresham? She was sure he would have thought Malcolm the wrong one. The Gresham-Bostock partnership had come into being as he had wished, but not in the form he had wished. Nell had long since ceased to hear the echoes of his voice, so it must be her own voice that challenged her within her head: it's always Edmund you turn to in business matters, isn't it, always the two of you who make the final decisions, always you or Edmund who cover up for Malcolm's fits of carelessness and extravagance, isn't it? You know that for the firm Malcolm was the wrong one.

But the right one for me.

The certainty of it stiffened her resolve. In this there was no Edmund to turn to. Even if he had not been on a visit to New York, negotiating for adequate protection of Gresham-Bostock interests there during the war, this was not something she could discuss with him. What dry, carefully calculated advice could she expect from him?

168

Perhaps, even, he had known all along about his brother's inconstancy.

How many did know: how many laughed at her or pitied her, or took it for granted?

A pretty penny it must cost, according to Kitty.

Nell had never openly queried Malcolm's expenditure, his share in the firm's profits, his contributions or withdrawals. But she could, if put to it, have estimated them fairly closely. From his own pocket he could unobtrusively have paid for the upkeep of another establishment: but only just. To have bought a place outright would have been to make too large a withdrawal for it to pass unnoticed. A regular rent was within his means, but with all the other expenses of keeping a woman could even that be kept a secret? So far nothing had leaked out. But somewhere, surely, it must show if one looked—once one had been given reason to look.

It took Nell four days. During part of that time she assured herself that she was not seriously spying on her husband. During the rest of it she devised plans and then abandoned them, sometimes in a mood of revulsion, sometimes because they were downright nonsensical. On the second afternoon she absurdly skulked near the office to watch him leave, and then acknowledged what she had already thought earlier: pursuit was impractical without either attracting Malcolm's attention or arousing the curiosity of a cab driver, passers-by, and chance acquaintances.

On the fourth day, knowing Malcolm would be at the dry dock where a Gresham-Bostock paddler was in for repairs, she went resolutely to the accounts office and summoned young Mr. Carter. The father who had served so many years with Jesse Bostock was now retired, but his son would remain young Mr. Carter for some indefinite time in spite of being almost forty years of age. He was sallow and looked permanently ill, but was a tireless worker, brought up reverently in the Bostock tradition and going in worshipful awe of Nell.

"Mr. Carter, may I see our property ledger?"

"It was audited only a month ago, Mrs. Gresham. Nothing amiss, is there?"

"I'm sure there's not. I just wanted to make a few notes of our resources."

She had been studying the rents, outgoings and capital values for less than five minutes when the address leapt off a page at her. Why did Gresham-Bostock have a house at 5 Albert Crescent, Prince's Park, on their books? Not wanting to ask too direct a question too soon, she scribbled meaningless notes for a few more minutes, then leaned forward to look out of the window by the desk.

Below was the sturdy brick building of their new passenger centre. At one end a shining gangway bore the G-B emblem—a happily patriotic coincidence that had been Malcolm's doing, insisting on the registration of the company as Gresham-Bostock rather than Bostock-Gresham. Rival companies and foreign travellers, even knowing what the initials stood for, could not help carrying with them an implication that somehow the authority of Great Britain stood behind the shipping line. The wharf was busy today. It was rare for it not to be. And the day after tomorrow, or at worst within two days, there would be a ship in from New York—with a profitable number of passengers, or half-empty because of the war? Soon after, Edmund must be back with reassuring or alarming news.

All of it so impressive and of such great import; yet today of less consequence than a house in Albert Crescent.

Young Mr. Carter was behind her. "Everything in order, Mrs. Gresham?"

She made a show of looking down her list, nodded, and pointed out two irrelevant items, which he explained without trouble. Then she tapped a finger on the one that most concerned her.

"I don't recall our investing in this kind of property."

"Oh, yes. That came from the Gresham assets, not from the Bostock side. When they started work on Prince's Park in 1844, old Mr. Gresham . . . I never had the privilege of knowing him personally, you understand, but my father said he had a shrewd eye for every kind of investment . . . "

"My husband says the same."

"I'm sure he does, Mrs. Gresham. Well, old Mr. Gresham bought one of the new houses there for his family, but then changed his mind and decided on Falkner Square instead. But the house was kept in the family. Or in the business, rather. I think I'm right in saying it was rented for some years to Captain Quine, master of the old Gresham flagship, after he retired."

"And he's still alive?"

"I wouldn't think so, ma'am." Carter turned away and took down another ledger. His eyes went down the page, over to another page. "Well, no." He looked mildly puzzled. "I'm sure Captain Quine passed on some years ago. But it's still listed under his name. The payments seem to be coming through regularly. The entry's always initialled and passed by Mr. Malcolm. Do you want me to ask him?"

There was no hint of complicity, nothing but innocent helpfulness in his face.

"I think I can manage that myself, Mr. Carter." Nell smiled, scribbled another cypher on her sheet of paper, and left in no apparent hurry.

Hudson was waiting stolidly on the carriage in the railway yard. For a moment Nell debated whether or not to summon a hansom. But she was in a mood for a frontal attack. If Hudson already knew anything, just let him dare to give himself away—to her or anyone else!

He did not show by the faintest twitch of an eyebrow that 5 Albert Crescent meant anything to him.

The house was in a polite curve of red brick and white lintels, set behind smug little shrubs and green railings. The trees of Prince's Park concealed streets on the far side, topped only by a distant church tower.

"Drive round the park," said Nell as she descended, "and come back in twenty minutes."

Hudson touched his whip to the brim of his hat, and moved steadily off. Nell looked up at the neat little porch of the neat little house, walked up the three white steps, and tugged at the polished brass bell-pull.

If the woman had heard the carriage arrive, and looked out between the heavy folds of lace curtain, she might decide not to answer the door.

Footsteps came along the passage. The door opened.

Until this moment Nell had been trying to pretend that it would be somebody else, some meaningless creature, one among several successive playthings who could be frightened, paid off, and forgotten. But of course she had really known all along who it had to be.

"Good afternoon, Miss Rivers. May I come in?"

Poppy was wearing a red merino shirt and slim black skirt with a red and gold Greek fringe. Her hair was wound tightly into a serpentine coil. She had a look of classical remoteness, so remote that she might not have taken in what was said to her, for she made no move to stand aside and let Nell enter.

Nell said, "This is a Gresham-Bostock property, Miss Rivers. The directors have the right to inspect it at such intervals as they may choose, to make sure it is being respectably maintained."

"It has been inspected recently." The parted lips barely moved.

"I don't doubt it. Along with all the . . . the contents. I would still like to be admitted."

They went into a prim little parlour. It was just possible to see into the crescent through the lace curtains, as Nell had guessed, but no passer-by would catch more than the faintest hint of movement within. Filtered afternoon light glimmered in the silk cover of an ottoman. The seats of two high-backed chairs were covered in Berlin wool-work: an occupation which doubtless helped Poppy while away the long hours of solitude. Nell would have admired the skill and the attractive domestic interior if it had not been for the sour tang in her throat.

171

"You will sit down, Mrs. Gresham?"

"You do remember from time to time, then, that there is a Mrs. Gresham?"

"I have little choice."

Nell seated herself close to a firescreen embroidered in peacock hues. As Poppy perched on the edge of the ottoman, a blue Persian cat sauntered from a corner of the room and sprang up beside her, turning a deep amber gaze on the visitor and swishing its bushy tail slowly along the whispering silk.

"I won't ask," said Nell, "how long you have been entertaining my husband on these premises. Obviously it has never ceased during the whole time we've been married."

Poppy's fingers dug into the luxuriant fur of the cat's neck as if to strangle it; but the cat purred sonorously, opening and shutting its eyes with a laziness as heavy and complacent as her own.

"It has done you no harm."

"No harm? You can sit there and tell me my husband had been deceiving me with you, keeping you all these years, frittering away his time and money—"

"Ah, yes. I think in Liverpool the money is most important. That is what hurts most, yes?"

"No!"

Nell managed not to raise her voice, but something in its timbre made the cat's back arch. The silky blue head twisted away from Poppy, whose fingers were left momentarily in mid-air and then found the animal's head again, stroking it hard, forcing the two of them back into evil-eyed companionship. Poppy's skirt folded inwards, into her lap, to form a shadowy cleft. Nell tried not to stare into the dark crease, knowing how deeply Malcolm had driven beyond it and knowing what sounds he would have made and just how he would have poised and fallen, risen and fallen. As steadily as possible she went on, "I'm not interested in money but in my marriage. I won't have that made a mockery."

"It has not been mocked here. And never will be, by me or by your husband."

"Or by others who know?"

"Who told you I was here?" asked Poppy.

"It seems to be known to half Liverpool."

"That I do not believe."

"To enough people for me to be able to find you."

"Only after three and more years."

"But I've found you. And now it's out in the open, it must stop."

172

The steady stroking of the cat's head stopped. "When?"

"This very day, of course."

"Your husband agrees?"

"He will."

"So you have not yet told him of your discovery?"

"I came to see you first."

"How strange."

"I didn't want to make any accusations until I was absolutely sure."

"And now you are sure."

"Yes," said Nell, "sure it mustn't go on one day longer."

Poppy stared ahead with no hint of any plea for a reprieve in her face. Rather she seemed to be trying to mesmerise Nell and implant something in her mind that would never again be dislodged.

"You should count yourself fortunate," she said. "There has been no trouble, no scandal."

"And there'll be no risk of any once you've gone."

"Gone." The dying fall was lost in the cat's purr. "Gone where?"

"Now I know the truth, I'll decide that."

"You are being very foolish."

Nell was glad that she could no longer contain her seething anger. "Foolish?" she shouted. "To want my husband to myself—for myself and our family. I bear his children, look after them, look after him and his home and a large part of his business—and I'm expected to share him with a kept plaything, who offers nothing, suffers nothing . . . "

"Suffers nothing?"

"A daydream doll," said Nell.

Poppy was quite still. The cat turned an enquiring face up, and yawned. Poppy said, "He has his diversion, and it is good for him. And he does not neglect *you*. Does he?"

"How dare you ask such a question?"

"We both belong to him, we can talk about him together."

"I certainly do not *belong* to him."

"No. No, perhaps that is true. You are too much yourself. You speak of your home and your children but you are so much away from them, there is so much time for your accounts and your schemes and your ships and your docks and—"

"Is that what he tells you?"

"I do not need to be told. It is only your pride that suffers today. If you wished him content, you would be content with us as we are. You have all you desire. You have him when you want him. But I, I have him only when it pleases him to call."

"What about your own pride, then?" Nell flung back. "Sitting here all the time, not allowing yourself to be seen in public, shut away like a caged wild animal."

"A tame animal, Mrs. Gresham."

"But what sort of life is that for you? What about *your* pride?"

"I have none."

"It's disgusting."

"Only to you. But now"—Poppy sat erect—"since you will not allow us to go on as we have done, just what are we to do?"

"I've told you, I shall decide."

"When you talk to . . . to him . . . " She had not once called him Malcolm.

"*I* shall decide. And I'll let you know."

"Yes." For the first time there was a stab of sheer malevolence through Poppy's voice, her eyes, her whole taut body. "I always knew that in the end you would be the one to decide. But it is dangerous, to be always the one who gives the orders."

Nell got up. The cat blinked and slid to the floor, its tail threshing more violently. Poppy moved more slowly, uncoiling herself and gliding across the room to show her visitor out.

At the front door Nell said, "Until you hear from me you'll make no attempt to get in touch with my husband."

"I never do. He does not allow it. But if he chooses to come here to-morrow, or the next day—"

"He won't," Nell promised. "I'll make sure of that."

NOVA SCOTIA had been left a full day's steaming back in the west when the watch on the *Eleanor* reported a vessel heading in from the starboard quarter. As she overhauled them her lines became clearly those of a warship: a wooden sloop with a telescopic funnel that could be lowered, and the screw raised, when sailing under canvas. The Stars and Stripes fluttered from the mizzen mast.

Edmund came on deck just as the stranger drew abreast, narrowing the gap between them.

Above the steady beat of engines a shout came across the water. "Heave to!"

"What the blazes do they think they're playing at?" The second mate, a few feet from Edmund, gaped as a rank of ugly snouts thrust out of the open gun ports.

The *Eleanor* did not slacken speed. There was another shout from the sloop, though it appeared to be changing course a couple of degrees and veering off. As Edmund hurried to the bridge, the reason for this became plain. The crump of an eight-inch gun was followed by the whistle of a shell obliquely across the paddler's bows. It splashed into the sea and coughed up a gout of steam and spray. Then the bows swung back into line, and again the gap contracted.

"Captain Ferguson." Edmund reached the bridge. "What d'you suppose this is all about?"

"Search me, sir. But they seem set on making us heave to."

"By what right?"

"That's a Union warship, Mr. Gresham."

"I can see that. And we're neutral."

"Full steam ahead, then, sir?"

Edmund looked across at those menacing muzzles. "You're in command, Captain Ferguson. But I confess I'm none too keen on losing one of our ships."

"Or the passengers, sir? Bad for our reputation."

The engine bells clanged, and the *Eleanor* began to lose way. The sloop matched its pace to theirs, and as the churning hiss of the paddles slackened the voice bawled again. "I'm sending a boarding party."

"Is he, by damn?" Captain and owner looked at each other. Then Captain Ferguson shrugged. "We'd best let 'em aboard, sir, and see what they want."

"And register a strong protest to the American consul when we reach Liverpool."

"Aye, sir."

The swell took first the nose of the sloop and then of the *Eleanor*, so that they rose and fell a few seconds apart, performing a slow dance like the horses of a slowing merry-go-round. A whaler swung out from the warship's davits. Some passengers on the paddle-steamer crowded to the rail to watch the sailors rowing over the choppy water. Others backed away into half-concealment behind the main deckhouse, hoping to be out of the line of any possible fire.

Edmund and Captain Ferguson left the bridge to await the arrival of the boarding party. As they stood at the rail they were joined by Paul Whitlaw. Edmund turned on him.

"Well, Mr. Whitlaw, is this the way your Navy treats the unarmed craft of a friendly nation?"

"I don't understand it." Whitlaw shook his head. Then he drew himself up with an almost military stiffness of bearing. "But as to a friendly nation, I tell you, Mr. Gresham, I'd not be on my way to England now if we didn't have some reservations about what that friendship of yours amounts to. Nor would you have had to unravel so many problems in New York, right?"

The boat drew closer, and the ladder was there to meet it.

Edmund leaned thoughtfully over the rail.

Within a week of the flare-up at Fort Sumter, President Lincoln's

Secretary of State had proclaimed a blockade of all ports along the coasts of the secessionist States. No goods would be allowed in to the rebels; and no cotton, sugar or tobacco would be allowed out to the markets of the world. A British ship caught within Southern waters made a run for it before the watchdogs were in position, and reached Liverpool with a cargo whose price was already soaring. Outraged, Liverpool shippers and merchants demanded immediate action by Parliament against the United States Government. When this took the form only of diplomatic messages and legal discussions, they took the matter into their own hands.

Governments of Europe pointed out that technically the American Secretary of State was at fault. A nation dealing with a civil insurrection should close its rebel ports where feasible; but in international terminology could use the word "blockade" only with regard to ports of an enemy nation. Which meant that the North, in spite of all protestations to the contrary, was virtually acknowledging the separate identity of the South and its separate rights under international law.

"And," a member of the Steamship Owner's Association had thundered at a meeting just before Edmund set out to New York, "a neutral nation with trade in the South is entitled to continue that trading without harassment. Ram that down their throats when you get there."

The choice of wording was, thought Edmund, almost as unfortunate as that of the blockade. Having anything rammed at them was the last thing Federal authorities wished at this stage of the war.

In less than a year, Atlantic trade had been taken over almost exlusively by Britain. Most American commercial vessels had been taken over by the military; and those that tried to maintain an import trade—including arms and supplies from Europe—became the prey of Southern raiders. Britain made its neutrality clear by running its regular services to and from the North . . . and building fast blockade runners to smuggle goods out of the South.

"And," Paul Whitlaw had raged to Edmund, meeting him aboard the *Eleanor* as they left New York, "your Merseyside yards aren't simply building blockade runners for your own profit, but commerce raiders for the rebels—ships to attack *us*. And before you've finished you may find them attacking your own merchantmen, and how funny will you find that? You support the rebels and still hope to continue doing business with us."

"That's why I've been in New York," Edmund quietly pointed out, "to ensure that we do continue doing sensible business. The war won't last for ever."

"But while it does your country will profit—from both sides."

"That's not Gresham-Bostock policy, as you know well enough. We don't deal with the Confederates. But it's not our concern to blame those who do. We believe the North will win because we believe it *has* to. Until then, we want only to maintain an uninterrupted passenger service, which your own people are no longer able to provide."

"Not everyone in your country is of like mind."

That was hard to deny. Edmund had left Liverpool in a ferment and knew that Manchester was in a far worse condition. Loss of raw cotton supplies had not hurt at first. Stocks in the Lancashire warehouses were plentiful. But as the war went on they dwindled: fresh supplies were unpredictable and insufficient, and thousands of mill hands were out of work. Public meetings were held to raise funds for relief, but without a renewed flow of raw materials there was no prospect of regular employment or a living wage. Starvation spread a dark shadow. At the same time the sun shone upon speculators around Liverpool Exchange who were raising prices, cornering markets, gambling, making fortunes; and risking losing them overnight. A few daring ventures to Savannah and Charleston could make a man rich. A captured ship could ruin him.

At least the Merseyside shipyards were kept busy building slim, fast blockade runners for British traders, and iron rams for the South to attack Northern shipping.

Edmund had to admit it was a somewhat ambiguous neutrality. He shared Paul Whitlaw's stern doubts about the morality of battening on the misfortunes of a country torn by civil war.

But as the boarding party began to scale the *Eleanor*'s ladder, he had equally grave doubts about the Federal interpretation of neutrality.

"This," he observed to Whitlaw, "won't do your cause much good in European eyes."

"They wouldn't have stopped this ship without good reason."

"The reasons will need to be good."

First on to the deck was a young man with a short tuft of light brown beard on his chin. A double row of highly polished buttons led down his blue uniform coat, clamping it squarely below a tight collar and dark blue stock. His peaked cap was squashed straight and hard above his ears. Seamen springing aboard behind him looked almost leisurely with their flat tam-o'-shanter bonnets and open-necked jerseys.

The young man carried a pistol in his left hand.

Captain Ferguson gave him no time to introduce himself. "No man carries arms aboard my ship, sir. Not without my permission."

The visitor transferred the pistol to his right hand; then, with two bright pink spots burning high in his cheeks, hastily switched it back again so that he could salute.

"Lieutenant Harland of the United States Navy, sir."

"An unexpected visitation, lieutenant." Edmund positioned himself beside Ferguson.

"I am acting on behalf of the legitimate government of the United States. Captain Irvine of the U.S.S. *Elkhorn* presents his compliments and will be grateful for your cooperation in transhipping two traitors from your vessel to ours."

"Traitors?"

"You called at Halifax on your way from New York."

"To pick up mail," growled Ferguson, "and a number of passengers."

"From British territory," Edmund added.

"Quite so, sir." The young man looked at the faces of those passengers who still lined the rails. "But those who came aboard were not all British subjects."

"Nor were those who came aboard at New York," said Edmund. "We have the privilege of offering hospitality to many of your countrymen."

"Including two traitors."

Captain Ferguson's jaw jutted a challenge, but he glanced at Edmund before venturing an opinion. Edmund said severely:

"Lieutenant Harland, you're labouring under a serious misapprehension. You can tell your Captain Irvine that Britain is a neutral nation in this war of yours. We have accorded the Confederacy belligerent rights, and we do not recognise the citizens of one side or the other as traitors."

"Regrettably that's so, sir—whoever you are."

"I'm one of the owners of this ship, and we are in international waters."

Now Ferguson spoke. "So you'll kindly take yourself off now, if that's all you have to say."

"No, captain, that is not all. Two Confederate agents made their way to Halifax in order to board this ship and operate illegally in Britain."

"In what way will their behaviour be illegal?"

"International rules of war, sir, allow a neutral country to trade with belligerents of either persuasion. But this is no war between nations. It is a rebellion that we are entitled to suppress. And in no circumstances should neutral nations build or equip ships as men-of-war for sale to one side in the dispute."

In the background Paul Whitlaw nodded staunch agreement.

Captain Ferguson said: "I don't know about that—"

"I do," said Edmund. "You're quite right, of course, lieutenant. If any

179

agent of either side should try to commission such craft, it would be up to our authorities to prevent them."

"Then you'll allow us to remove the rebels, sir?"

"No, we will not. For you've no proof of their intentions, and even if their intentions were what you claim them to be, that would be a matter for the British Government on British soil. At this moment we are well outside your territorial waters, and our passengers sail under the British flag. There is no more to be said."

The young officer checked that his men were still at his back. His lips set firm. The pistol came up to point at Captain Ferguson's chest.

"How dare you, you young puppy!"

"Do you realise the damage you'll have done your country when this becomes known?" said Edmund.

"Nowhere near the damage those rogues'll do if they're let loose in *your* country." The pistol did not waver. "I'm sorry, but I must insist on being allowed to search this ship and drag them out."

Edmund felt the deck lift and tilt gently beneath his feet, and at the same time something shifted and turned cold in his stomach. Without even glancing at them again he was overpoweringly conscious of those guns such a short distance away, capable of blowing them out of the water. The commander wouldn't dare. You could say that in a fine wrath of self-righteousness: but when it came to it, out here on the limitless ocean, could you be sure of it? He was angry, and afraid. But as the cold knot hardened and swelled inside him, anger predominated over fear.

"You having any trouble, Harland?" The shout was loud in the near silence between the *Elkhorn* and the *Eleanor*.

"No, sir."

"Then be quick about it."

Lieutenant Harland drew himself up and looked again, with reinforced arrogance, along the faces of those passengers within range. Then he motioned his men to head for the companionway leading to the main saloon. One who had been standing at the back of the group till now slid a rifle through the crook of his arm and took up post at the top as the others clattered down the stairs.

Ferguson shouted, "I gave nobody permission . . ."

Edmund touched his arm, cautioning him to stay where he was. Only when the search party had disappeared below did Edmund detach himself and casually cross the deck. The sentry kept an eye on him. Edmund, whistling with a deliberately false nonchalance, strolled along the port side so that the man had to slew round to keep him in sight, then take an uncertain step after him.

180

Captain Ferguson followed without any tell-tale suddenness. Past the open doorway he caught the sentry from behind, tipping him neatly into the shade of the deckhouse. Edmund turned back and was at once on his knees, pinning the rifle down while Ferguson bent the man's arm behind his hip and stuffed a kerchief into his mouth before he could cry out.

A seaman wriggled along to sit on the sentry's back and keep his face pressed to the planking. Then Edmund and Captain Ferguson edged close to the companionway door, crouching below eye level of anyone on the sloop.

They waited.

Edmund was amazed by his own speed and his own calm. At any moment there was the possibility of a blast of grapeshot scouring the superstructure, yet his heart did not beat a whit the faster. Malcolm of course would have revelled in such a situation; he would not have thought himself capable of deriving such enjoyment from it. He was aware of the smell of pitch and varnish, of drifting coal smoke and steam, and of the salt air. How furious his sister-in-law would be if they brought her namesake home riddled with shot—or failed to bring her home at all!

Footsteps clumped slowly back up the stairs. Two men appeared: passengers, emerging into daylight and turning a resigned gaze on the gently simmering smokestack of the sloop. They blocked the view of Lieutenant Harland as, with pistol cocked, he stooped to come out behind them.

In an instant Ferguson was diving for his ankle and jerking it from under. Harland struck the coaming with a thud that winded him. The pistol dropped under Edmund's swiftly planted foot. The second mate scurried in from an angle, bent double, and helped his captain manhandle Harland round under cover. Edmund reached out to slam the companionway door shut and drop the outer storm bolt.

The two men who so few seconds ago had been in Federal custody stared round, bewildered.

"What's going on over there? Ahoy, there! You there, Lieutenant Harland?"

Captain Ferguson straightened up and ambled to the starboard rail. It was emptying of passengers. Even from the *Elkhorn* the commander must be able to sense the mounting tension.

"Your youngster's busy. Too busy for his own good." Ferguson had the stentorian bellow of a foghorn. "If you want him and your boarding party back, you can start by closing those gun ports."

"If you've laid a finger on my men—"

"What about the fingers laid on my passengers, hey?"

"I'll blow you to kingdom come."

181

"And your men with us."

One of the two who had been driven up from below stepped to Ferguson's side.

"Captain, we're not aiming to be responsible for the shedding of innocent blood."

"If anyone's responsible, it's going to be that madman over there."

"You're being mighty civil, sir, but we'll not allow it. We'd sooner give ourselves up than let those Yankees fire as much as one shot at you and your passengers."

There was a hush. Captain Irvine of the *Elkhorn* could not have heard this quiet exchange, but guessed something significant was happening and awaited the outcome. Edmund waited for Ferguson to turn to him in mute consultation, so that he could shake his head: there was no question of handing anyone over to these attackers. No matter what the consequences.

Paul Whitlaw was at Captain Ferguson's other elbow.

"No, sir," he said very distinctly. "You'll not hand them over."

"Now just a minute, sir." The Southerner cocked his head, peering past Ferguson. "From what I heard no more'n an hour ago when you were talkin' down below to a friend, I figure you're a Union man."

"I am, and proud to be."

"Then what's the trick?"

They stared at each other. Edmund felt his mouth twist into a sad grin. The two Confederates were older than Paul Whitlaw or the young lieutenant still pinioned near the deckhouse. Yet the features of all four could have been those of not too distant relatives. Their clothes were not unalike. They had the same stark, dedicated expressions. Yet they belonged to opposing sides within their land, sworn to fight and kill. Only the Southern spokesman's voice suggested a difference, and that none too great: just an older, more knowledgeable and more languid drawl, with an amused undertone that seemed to agree with Edmund that capture, imprisonment and possible death were all rather grotesque when you came to contemplate them.

"I'll be no party to a breach of international procedures," said Paul Whitlaw. "Whatever dirty stratagems you and your kind get up to, we still have no right to lower *our* standards. Captain Ferguson, I'll be obliged if you'll have me rowed across to the warship."

Ferguson gulped. "So that they take a couple of my men hostage to trade against their own?"

"When the commander has listened to me—"

"If you get a chance to speak," said Ferguson sceptically.

182

"We know one another's language. You'll see."

Edmund said, "You're sure you know what you're doing, Mr. Whitlaw?"

"Yes, Mr. Gresham, I do have a pretty sound idea."

"Then to be on the safe side we can send the *Elkhorn*'s whaler back with you. Release two men to row you over—and bring you back."

"If he comes back," grunted Ferguson. "Look, sir, how do we know this gentleman's not—"

"Getting to safety before they sink you?" Whitlaw turned balefully on him.

"I fancy you'll want to apologise for that, captain," said Edmund, "when Mr. Whitlaw returns."

Ferguson faced out across the water and cupped his hands about his mouth. When he had bellowed his request, there was a pause. Then from the sloop came an answering boom:

"Very well. Send him over. But you'll be covered all the way, mister."

Two of the warship's crew were released from below, and set off with Paul Whitlaw, incongruously tidy and civilian, in the whaler. A few passengers crept timidly back to the rail to watch it go.

Ferguson did not budge until he saw the boat set out on its return journey, with the young man once more on a thwart. Then he stepped back, folded his arms, and said to no one in particular, "Well, whatever it is he's done, he's done it."

Paul climbed awkwardly aboard.

"It's all right. You can let Harland and the rest of his men go. There'll be no further attempt to take the rebels."

"Or to sink us or cripple us?"

"Or to sink you or cripple you."

Edmund said, "Let them go, captain."

Ferguson watched dubiously as Lieutenant Harland was helped to his feet and handed his pistol. The young officer tugged his cap back to its correct angle and curtly saluted.

As the whaler once more drew away from the *Eleanor,* Edmund was alarmed to find that his knees were shaking. He seemed to be staring straight into the muzzle of a blackly menacing cannon, first lifting to point above his head and then settling to a direct aim again.

He said, "And what are they proposing to do now?"

"They'll go their way," said Whitlaw, "and we'll go ours."

"What on earth did you threaten them with?"

"Their conscience. The conscience of the Federal cause. I told Captain Irvine of the difficulties I already face, trying to convince England of the

183

harm the rebels can and will do. It's tough enough without one of our own ships turning pirate and getting us a bad name."

"You didn't actually call one of your own naval commanders a pirate?"

"As good as that, yes," said Whitlaw stiffly.

Captain Ferguson said, "I owe you an apology, sir."

"Accepted." The acceptance was icy.

"You must have been very persuasive," Edmund observed.

"I had to be. Somebody's patience was nigh to running out. But I made him see it. Johnny Rebs or no, those two men"—he nodded condemnation at the two still standing nearby—"did, as you say, come aboard a British ship at a British port. They're spies, sure enough. They mean harm, sure enough. But it's up to the likes of me to find legitimate ways of stopping them, not for some over-anxious sailor to blast his way through every rule in the book. Even if," he concluded with a ferocity of which Edmund would not have thought him capable, "you Britishers flout the rules any time it suits you."

The sloop's whistle let out a shriek that might have been of polite farewell or derision. Then smoke poured from the stack, water boiled above the screw, and the *Elkhorn* began to describe a long arc, swinging away into the distance.

As the paddles of the *Eleanor* began to churn again, the two Confederates approached Paul Whitlaw. One held out his hand.

"You're a gentleman, sir."

Whitlaw stared at the outstretched hand and shook his head. "I've stood by my principles, but that doesn't mean I condone your behaviour now or in the future. And I don't shake hands with my country's enemies."

He strode away.

For the remainder of the journey the two Southerners kept tactfully but proudly to themselves. Paul Whitlaw was at first hailed effusively as a hero, but then, after a day or so, adulation diminished and opinion split into two more critical camps. A number of American travellers of Northern origin said that maybe he ought to have let the sloop have the Rebs instead of allowing them to roam free, while some British hinted that after all he was a Northern man himself and it was the Northerners who had flouted the laws of the high seas and were capable of doing so again.

Captain Ferguson drove his ship hard to make up for lost time, and had reason to look pleased as they passed Point Lynas on the Isle of Anglesey. Now the telegraph message would speed on its way from one signal station to the next, and the Gresham-Bostock organisation would be ready for the *Eleanor* when she reached their quay.

Edmund stood beside Paul Whitlaw as they rounded Rock Lighthouse and the familiar markers lay ahead. Smoke belched from an ironworks chimney. Windmills were silhouetted against the sky; noisier, darker mills and forges shook and strained and breathed up their fumes from below. Masts bristled from docks on the Liverpool shore. New, naked masts thrust up from the Birkenhead shipyards. And there was a scattering of newly painted funnels; and along one stretch a new, high wall.

The two Confederates came on deck, glanced at the shipyard and its wall and then at one another, and smiled and looked away.

Whitlaw said, "Well, Mr. Gresham? And what succour are you preparing for our enemies behind that barrier?"

"I'm not in the confidence of the builders."

"But you're not incapable of hazarding a shrewd guess."

"No," said Edmund unhappily. "We can all make our own guesses. That doesn't mean we'd be accurate."

Whitlaw continued to glare at the sheltering wall as if longing to summon a Federal gunboat to the Mersey so that it could smash its shells through the bricks and reveal what secrets lay behind. Before Edmund had left for New York there had been a plague of rumours. So far as he knew, the main craft being built in that yard was an innocuous wooden screw steamer listed simply as "Number 290." But gossip had it that the number, certainly not that of the two-hundred-and-ninetieth ship produced by the company, represented the number of Liverpool merchants who had subscribed towards its laying down. And since when had it been the custom for rival merchants to collaborate in the construction of one shared trader? Which of them, in the end, would be responsible for running it—or selling it off to an already committed buyer?

"You were all very high and mighty about the conduct of that United States warship," Whitlaw said. "But you've got very different standards in your own waters, by the look of it."

The justice of this comment made Edmund answer more sharply than he would have wished. "So you've been sent here to spy on what our craftsmen are engaged on?"

"No, Mr. Gresham. Openly and without subterfuge to represent my country's lawful interests where all men may see me—and them."

"Of course. I'm sorry."

They were slowing into the mainstream of Liverpool traffic. A Cunarder heading for the bay whistled a courteous welcome. Tugs rocked perilously beneath their bows, and a ferry came bobbing out in its long, precisely executed arc from Woodside. As the *Eleanor* turned towards her moorings, the G-B pennant broke from the mast above the passenger office.

185

"Your sister-in-law," said Paul Whitlaw with strained politeness, "she's well and happy?"

"I have that impression, yes."

"I doubt she'll want to renew my acquaintanceship."

But within two days of their berthing an invitation came. Mr. Whitlaw was not, and would hardly have expected to be, invited to the Chamber of Commerce's celebratory dinner and presentation in honour of the Liverpool skipper who had thrown a Northern prize crew in irons. Instead, he was requested to dine at Bostock's Brow with Mr. and Mrs. Malcolm Gresham.

4

"I'VE HAD enough of this sort of thing. A bellyful." Malcolm strode into the drawing-room and tossed a batch of invoices on the table at Nell's elbow. "They won't pass a single one until you authorise them."

"That's our usual procedure."

"So it is, so it is. And I'm getting sick and tired of your usual procedure."

"In Edmund's absence—"

"In Edmund's absence why shouldn't my signature be good enough, without you having to countersign every last little item? I'm no better than an errand boy. That's how they're coming to look on me down at the office. I fetch and carry for you, and that's all I'm supposed to be fit for."

"It keeps you out of mischief."

"Mischief?" He tried to look domineering, then attempted a smile, sidled closer and stood above her and slid his right hand along the back of her neck. It would take only a thrust of her neck against those fingers to cure him of his sulks. Instead, Nell felt a prickle of gooseflesh and sat motionless. Mimicking a thick Irish brogue Malcolm said, "Sure an' where would I be after gettin' up to any mischief, an' all?"

"At 5 Albert Crescent, possibly?"

It was unfair, like striking a child without immediate provocation and without warning. He went white and still and silent. Then he tried to summon up a cheeky smile, to pull himself together and push trouble away as a small boy would, seeking a fib that would serve, an endearing grin that would melt mother's heart.

"Well," he managed. "Well, now."

"You needn't lie," said Nell. "I know all about it."

"That's more than I do. Would you mind telling me what this mystery means?"

"Don't make it worse. I've told you, I know. The house, your Miss Rivers, the way you *do* look after that account yourself. Everything."

He gauged his chance of bluffing it out, then fell back into a chair. "For how long?"

"Four or five days. Confirmed yesterday. While you . . . you've had over three years. How many years did you hope to go on deceiving me?"

"I don't much care for that. Deceiving you—it makes it sound so . . . well . . . so shabby. And it's not, it never has been."

Nell had thought she could remain cool and critical. But his refusal to consider himself as a deceiver, his genuine indignation—again like a child caught out, in the wrong circumstances and at the wrong time, in some petty dishonesty—enraged her.

"Not shabby?" she blazed. "You don't think that after three years of lies and infidelity and—"

"I won't be shouted at."

"Won't you?" Fiercely she choked back tears which threatened to blur her words. "You think I should sit here and nod and accept it and say it doesn't matter, it's gone on all this time, it can keep on going on, and nobody should raise their voice?"

"It wasn't serious."

"All these years and it's not serious?"

Malcolm kicked the toe of his right shoe against the sole of his left. "I've played whist at the club for longer than that, and that's not serious. Or—"

"Why do you still need her? Why? Am I so useless," Nell cried, "so uninteresting, so stale, so—"

"You know what I feel for you."

"No, I don't. I don't know anything at all."

"Nell—"

"I thought I knew, but now I see it has all been a fraud, all this time."

Now he was the one to shout. "A fraud? You think a man can keep up a fraud like that ? Force his body on to a woman who doesn't interest him? You think I get hard for you as a matter of *duty?*"

"How do I know it's me you hold in your arms? How do I know you're not thinking of that woman all the time, forcing yourself, pretending it's not me but her?"

There was an appalled silence. Malcolm began slowly, dazedly, to shake his head. "But it's not in the least like that."

"Then why have you kept her all this time? Why do you still need to go and see her? What can she do for you that I can't?"

His answer, when it came, was nothing she could ever have predicted. "She's very soothing," he said. "That's the main thing."

"The main thing?"

"Yes."

"Soothing?" She could not take it in.

"Very restful."

It was the last thing she could have visualised in her fantasies about that sinuous, alluring creature. "And I'm not?"

"Can't we leave it—"

"No, we can't."

"It can only hurt, and it doesn't have to hurt."

"You think we can brush it aside, and you'll go on seeing her, and indulging in whatever soothing activities you may devise between you?"

"Nell, please, we mustn't quarrel."

"She never quarrels?"

"Or tries to pull the strings." His attempt at an impish smile was pathetic.

"You'd have preferred a demure wife with a proper sense of humility."

"I have the wife I prefer."

"Restful," Nell persisted. "You hoped for someone restful and soothing. I'm sorry, truly I'm sorry. I didn't know."

"I've told you—"

"But you're not telling me you merely sit and talk? And she listens respectfully, and strokes your brow, and waits on you, and that's as far as it goes? You're not telling me you never . . . never use her bed . . . dig your fingers into her, bite her neck, shove your . . . your . . . "

"That will do."

"You're not going to tell me—"

"No," he said, "I'm not going to tell you any such thing. But all that isn't . . . well, it isn't as important as it was. Not since I met you."

"She's got to go." Nell was on her feet, could sit still in judgement no longer. She tripped, kicked at an edge of carpet, howled, "Your Miss Rivers, your Poppy—oh, what a name, what a . . . " Malcolm put out a

189

futile hand, but she was past caring whether the whole household heard or not. Didn't they all know, anyway? Hadn't they all been laughing, all this time, behind her back? "She ought never to have been shipped into Liverpool. A disease, that's what she's been—a disease. And she's not staying in Liverpool any longer."

"No." Malcolm's hand fell back on his knee. "I don't suppose she can. I'll go and see her. Find a way of ending it."

"You'll not go near her."

"But I can't just leave her without a word. Something will have to be done for her."

Nell steadied herself against the mantelpiece. "I'll see to that." She managed to make it quiet and final.

"No, I can't let you. It wouldn't be right. It's my responsibility."

"It was your responsibility to get rid of her before we were married. You didn't take it seriously then, and I doubt if you would now."

"You don't trust me."

"No."

"That doesn't promise much of a future for us."

"I said I didn't trust you. I didn't say I didn't need you."

He looked up wonderingly, but with a tinge of cowardly relief. "If I leave it to you . . . it makes me look such a swine."

"If she's such a wonderfully understanding person, her hopes of you won't be too high."

"Her opinion of me isn't as low as yours."

"If you so much as attempt to see her again," said Nell, "I'll institute proceedings for dissolution of the whole partnership."

"Our marriage? But—"

"The firm."

"Nell, you know you wouldn't dream of it."

"I'll withdraw the Bostock holdings. We can both start all over again. Perhaps your brother will be more sympathetic, and not treat you as an office boy."

"You couldn't. I know you. You couldn't bear to pull it all apart."

"If you pull our married life apart, I can do the same with the business."

She didn't mean it, of course she didn't mean it, the whole idea was preposterous. But she was in a mood to hit out, to destroy, or at least to speak destruction. And it wasn't whether she meant it or not: it was whether Malcolm would be convinced or not, or even half-convinced.

She had only to look at him to see that he was afraid. Poor Malcolm— how readily he could be made to believe! How readily she could despise him. But she could not live without him.

Dejectedly he said, "You still put everything into business terms, don't you?"

"They're so much clearer than your emotions."

"I'll have to think about all this. Then we'll talk."

But he knew the talking was ended.

For all his impetuousness and bubbling vitality, in some ways he was so like her father.

And as for herself, was she so like her grandfather?

A dozen times that evening Malcolm looked up at the gilt clock on the mantel, a wedding present from Gresham employees, or surreptitiously consulted his half-hunter. But he made no effort to argue further or to take matters into his own hands and storm out of the house.

The next day, with news of Edmund's impending arrival telegraphed from Point Lynas, he announced that he would go down and make sure the reception procedures were in order, the unloaders and baggage men standing by, and the Custom Office notified.

"I'll follow you down," said Nell.

"There's no need. I'm perfectly capable of administering the—"

"I'll come nevertheless."

"You're not proposing to let me out of your sight, are you?"

She did not reply. He set out with his right finger and thumb snapping compulsively, his face white and vengeful.

Nell reached the Gresham-Bostock building forty minutes before the *Eleanor* was due. Malcolm was nowhere in the main office.

"Oh, Mrs. Gresham, one thing Mr. Gresham forgot before he went. Reservation of two coaches on the train over there. I'm sure we promised two special coaches for that Canadian party booked on to Scotland."

"Indeed we did. See to it, will you?" Nell slapped her gloves against the counter. "Leave them to scramble for their seats this time, and next time they or their friends'll book direct and put that Glasgow run back in business."

Before he went.

She said, "Did my husband leave any word where he would be?"

"Said something about going to the old counting-house, ma'am. You know, Mr. Edmund's place."

Nell went out to her carriage and urged the driver along the Goree and Strand Street. It was maybe pointless to hurry, for she did not expect to find Malcolm there. But she wanted to know the worst as soon as possible. And then continue the pursuit?

The old Gresham counting-house remained Edmund's favourite spot. He had insisted on keeping it on as a personal indulgence, but at the same time, with one faithful clerk in the outer office, got through more work there than most did in the newer building.

"Wait here. I don't suppose I shall be long."

Nell looked up at the windows. The curtains were drawn, as if all activity had ceased in Edmund's absence abroad. She tried the door, and was surprised when it opened. She went up the half-landing to the inner door.

And Malcolm said, "You didn't think I'd be here, did you?"

He stood in the curtained twilight by the old, lumpy leather couch, his fingertips resting on its arm. In the foggily yellow light that oozed through the curtains he looked less tense than when he had left Bostock's Brow, more relaxed and, in some way, ready.

"Whatever brought you here, anyway? What have you been doing?"

"Waiting for you."

He waved towards the desk. In the centre of the large pad of blotting paper stood a chipped vase, sprouting a flourish of red and yellow tulips.

"Flowers—for Edmund?"

"No. For you."

He left the couch and strolled behind her to slip the bolt on the door. The sudden gasp of his breath on her cheek told her what he intended.

"Malcolm, don't be ridiculous."

"I'm very tired of being told how ridiculous I am, one way and another."

"Don't touch me."

"It's all right, Edmund won't come straight here. Plenty to occupy him at the quay. And I've sent old Potts off for a long lunch."

"It's hateful. I won't . . . "

His hands on her shoulders were forcing her back and bending her over the arm of the couch. He pulled expertly at her skirt.

"If you keep resisting, Edmund *may* get here too soon. Come on, let's see how quick we can be."

Outside, the horse shifted a fretful hoof. The sound seemed to spur Malcolm on. He pressed Nell further back and his face descended on hers.

"It's filthy, foul, it's . . . I won't . . . it's . . . "

"Going to scream? Bring poor old Hudson dashing to the rescue?"

She was sprawled across the arm and against the pitted back of the couch. And he was climbing on her like some thief cocking a leg over the wall of a back alley, straddling her as he might have straddled the crumbling mortar along the top of the wall, seeking a crack in which to steady himself with his hand or a burglar's jemmy. Only it was no hand and no iron shaft, though iron was what it suddenly, piercingly felt like.

192

She tightened, cold and rigid. The pain was worse because she hated him and wasn't going to let herself yield.

Leather squeaked and creaked.

"Now, Nell. Now, my girl."

She would not move. Would refuse to take pleasure or give it. Pretend it was happening to somebody else, and let him know it. He was striving, stabbing, demanding her response. She would not answer.

"Nell." It grated out of him.

She would not even whimper under the assault.

Outside the horse pawed the street again and whinnied a wild laugh. Malcolm took it up, shaking with it, and all at once it was no use: Nell couldn't resist. He felt the change in her at once and went on laughing, and she tried not to but was panting and clinging to him. The leather bolster in the arm of the couch thrust up behind her, and when she clutched his buttocks and dragged them imploringly closer they, too, were the texture of leather. And inside her the piston moved faster and faster but smoothly now.

When at last he climbed off, hopping awkwardly on one leg to regain his balance, he said, "Did that feel as if I was thinking of somebody else?"

"You're loathsome," she said weakly.

"You're a liar."

Oh, yes, that impudent slut Kitty had been right. Malcolm was indeed one of those who would get away with anything. Already he was confident that he had pleased her and so smoothed over any real trouble between them. And all would go on as before.

It will not, she said to herself. Aloud she complained, pulling her dress straight, "I've lost a button."

"Leave it for the charwoman to find. It may put Edmund up in her estimation."

They left arm in arm, Nell with the spray of tulips in the crook of her free arm.

And when she laughed again, the evening of that day when he told her that Paul Whitlaw had reached Liverpool on the *Eleanor* along with Edmund, he thought in some obscure way that she must be still complimenting his masculinity and that the storm had well and truly blown over. He would not have understood her smile as she wrote her invitation to Mr. Whitlaw and ensured that it was despatched without delay.

The dinner party was small and informal. Julia, first to arrive, apologised for her husband's absence in such a way as to make it plain that the fault was Nell's rather than Lord Speke's.

"He has so many committee meetings these days. He's on absolutely *everything*. One most important one at the club this evening, and you couldn't expect him to alter it at such short notice."

"No, mother. It's perfectly all right. We'll be even numbers this way, so really it's worked out quite nicely."

"Such a pity you couldn't give reasonable notice. These sudden fads of yours, Eleanor—will you never settle down?"

Malcolm was pouring his mother-in-law a sherry as Edmund arrived, with Paul Whitlaw close on his heels. Paul shook Nell's hand with a vigour that might stem from his embarrassment at meeting her again. It was a long time since that abrupt announcement in New York, her wedding to Malcolm and their return home. Yet with Paul's earnest, slightly reproachful face before her again, it might have been only a matter of weeks. He had altered so little. And he was even more himself when the reproachfulness evaporated and he thanked her with such unfeigned sincerity—thanked her for inviting him to dine so soon after his arrival, when it was obvious that many elements in the town would not care to invite him at all.

She heard the sound of wheels on the drive, as the carriage she had sent for their last guest drew up.

Julia heard it too and looked inquiringly at her daughter.

Nell said, "I did promise even numbers."

She was waiting in the open doorway as Poppy crossed the hall; and rested one hand on Poppy's arm as they entered the room.

"You all know Miss Rivers, I think?"

CONVERSATION AT the dinner table would have been slow to start if Julia, confused by the reappearance of this woman whose part in her son-in-law's life she had never quite fathomed, had not considered it her duty to show how a lady of rank could cover other people's gaffes. She set out to charm Paul Whitlaw, was glad to see him in such splendid health, asked if he were married yet and, when he said no, commiserated with him on living in a strange country where eligible young women were so few.

"And I'm sorry," she said, "so sorry Lord Speke could not be here to renew your acquaintance."

"The loss is mine, your ladyship."

"There, isn't he charming?" said Julia to the glowering, speechless Malcolm. "It's wonderful how the right people can keep up civilised standards in the most unpromising surroundings. And with this dreadful war we hear so much about, Mr. Whitworth—"

"Mr. Whitlaw," Nell corrected.

"My husband is much involved in good works, Mr. Whitlaw, to alleviate some of the suffering in this war of yours."

"That's most gracious of him."

"These callous attempts to starve those poor black folk in the South. And our own mill workers. Not to mention those very gallant gentlemen who—"

"Mother, Mr. Whitlaw represents the—"

"I wish you would learn not to interrupt, Eleanor. As I was saying, Mr. Whitlaw, my husband has been used to dealing with gentlemen all his life, and he intends to go on doing so. And as a gentleman, he stands by those he respects and who have shown us a proper respect."

"You mean, Lady Speke"—Paul somehow preserved an attentive smile—"he is one of those who subsidise the building of commerce raiders to destroy Northern shipping and murder Northern crews?"

Julia blinked. She picked fussily at a couple of crumbs on the table beside her plate, but still did not quite grasp the implications of what he had said. "Oh, but those Northern vandals!"

"Mother, please—"

"Sinking all those old whalers across the harbours so that our friends can't get out! Hulks full of stones. Is *that* how honourable men fight a war? As my husband says, our sturdy Liverpool workmen have spent centuries trying to clear channels into the river and keep them clear—while those terrible people over there, with no motive other than sheer dreadful spite, set out to ruin ports not just now but for ever. It's barbaric."

Edmund said, "Lady Speke, Mr. Whitlaw represents the Union cause."

"The Union—what Union?"

"The North."

Julia laid her knife down with a clatter. "Then what are you doing here, my good man?"

"The wanton destruction wrought by these Southern gentlemen, as you like to think of them, is crippling our normal maritime trade."

"Lord Speke and his friends would not grieve to hear that."

"Lord Speke and his friends may sooner or later be responsible for having supported privateers who won't scruple to attack ships sailing from their own home port—*this* port, madam—under their own colours. Making a profit from blockade running, *and* from building ships for the rebels, *and* from chartering and insurance for . . . "

Paul had been carried away. Edmund raised a warning head just in time.

"Insurance?" said Julia.

"There's profit everywhere, Lady Speke."

The generalisation misted the battle lines. Nell asked if anyone would care for another slice of capon, indicated that Malcolm should offer Poppy a vegetable dish, looked around for more wine, and set up a mild clamour of distraction. Paul Whitlaw dabbed at his brow and carefully avoided Julia's still querulous gaze. He looked at Poppy, slim and silent and uncontentious in emerald and brown striped satin, smiled, and went on looking.

196

It was by no means a rigourously guarded secret that he was here to discuss insurance problems with British brokers. Losses to Northern shipping had been so enormous that premiums had risen astronomically, and it was hard to find any firm in the United States to cover trading vessels. At the same time Paul would be privately making enquiries, on behalf of nameless and supposedly unofficial interests, into the chartering and insuring of British ships under the British flag. Not to carry military supplies, of course. Similar negotiations had been afoot over the last few months, and nobody on Exchange could be unaware of this. But Nell was anxious to avert the risk of her mother gushing her own inflated version of such matters to Adrian Speke, distorting and magnifying the whole thing and provoking new disputes along Merseyside.

She turned towards Edmund, waiting for the confirmatory wink he often gave her during tricky business conferences. But Edmund was looking not at her but at Poppy.

"I never heard anything like it." Julia glared at her daughter, adding this offence to an accumulation of so many others.

Unexpectedly Edmund and Paul began to argue. Not too loudly or too acrimoniously, or in a fashion too discourteous to their hostess. Nell assessed the group she had assembled for this deliberately informal dinner, wondered if she had cause to worry about the skirmishes that had broken out during the main course and seemed likely to spread during the dessert, and decided it would suit her to let all the courses run their course: the deliberation was still paying better dividends than the informality.

Let Paul Whitlaw say what he might. It had nothing to do with what anyone had discussed before or was likely to discuss now. He was mounted, prancing, vaunting himself in the lists with bobs and coxcomb shakes of the plume on his casque. And his opponent, Edmund, was settled into a secure saddle, not attacking and not retreating, balanced for the jab of a lance that would never unseat him.

"I think you'll agree, Mr. Gresham, that those who make sordid profit now from both sides will insure for themselves no love from either victor."

"And those who speak of neutrality as something which quietly favours one side only will be wounded by any number of ricochets."

They bared their teeth in hostile appreciation, while Poppy remained heavy-lidded and imperturbable through the jousting.

Nell sat back. She was fairly sure that Malcolm and Poppy had not exchanged a single glance. And as for the other two men, she had already decided who must win the contest.

When the port decanter had been set on the table and the ladies withdrew, Malcolm pushed back his chair and, with a muttered apology, followed her out of the door. While Julia led Poppy into the small drawing-room, he said in a fierce undertone, "How dare you bring her here like this?"

"I thought you enjoyed her company."

"What are you playing at?"

"Malcolm, dear, I think we should each go and look after our guests."

She swept on in the track of the other two women.

Julia was already setting herself assiduously to entertain Poppy, to make up for her daughter's remissness. Moving past them and looking down at the exquisite dark lines of Poppy's head, Nell felt herself quite in control of the situation. Of course Malcolm was hers and would never make any real effort to escape. So why could she not have allowed him his Poppy—his one insignificant, irrelevant diversion?

Because she loved him with a single-minded need that tolerated no other appetites or indulgences, no matter how trifling.

Julia condescended, "And what are you doing nowadays, Miss Rivers?"

"I have a position in the Prince's Park neighbourhood."

"A position?"

"I suppose you could say"—Poppy neither courted nor avoided Nell's gaze—"I am a companion."

"Ah, indeed."

Coffee cups were set before them. When the maid had gone, Nell said, "Mother, it occurred to me at dinner. Wouldn't you say Miss Rivers and Mr. Whitlaw would make an admirable match?"

Poppy did not stir. Julia made up for it with a wild agitation of her hands, plucking at the severe brown bow at her throat.

"Eleanor, how you can be so forward . . ."

"Miss Rivers would be a wonderful asset to the right man. Especially in North America, where there has so far been so little infusion of ladies from good families."

"Good families?"

"Didn't you know Miss Rivers comes from a distinguished Sino-French family?"

Julia made a quick appraisal, then nodded. "Of course. One knows these things at once, doesn't one?"

"Thank you." Poppy's fingers sinuously interlaced. "But I think Mrs. Gresham is too ambitious on my behalf."

"Oh, please pay no attention, my dear. She's always wanting to get her hands on people's lives and twist them to her own fancy."

"Or straighten them," said Nell.

After a pause during which Poppy assimilated this, Julia let out an

198

affected little cry. "But I haven't been up to the nursery to see my little darlings."

"Mother, they were tucked up long ago. They'll be asleep by now."

"I won't wake them. Just take a little peep."

When Julia had left the room, Nell waited for Poppy to speak. No comment was forthcoming. Nell said, "Don't you think I'm offering you a very interesting future?"

"I think it is not for you to make the offer."

"You must know how little arranging it would take."

"So I am to be arranged."

"For your own advantage. Liverpool has nothing further to offer."

"No?"

"Nothing," said Nell firmly.

"Mr. Whitlaw's family—perhaps they do not approve of someone who looks like me."

"I've already suggested that you're the descendant of a mysterious but noble Sino-French family. They're great ones for a mingling of the races, the Northerners. Emancipation and equality and so on. Mr. Whitlaw will persuade himself and everyone else that he's putting high principles into practice. I assure you he's very anxious to persuade himself of anything if only he may possess you."

Poppy nodded as slowly and rhythmically as a porcelain figure with delicately sprung head. "But I do not wish to go to America."

"It will offer you more than Liverpool can."

"But why must I go so far?" The nodding stopped with Poppy's head raised and steady. "Mr. Whitlaw is not the only gentleman this evening who shows interest."

"If you mean Edmund—"

"You will not say he is not interested? I think if I show myself willing, he—"

"Out of the question. Not with Malcolm and myself here. Not with the three of us partners in the same company."

"Ah, yes. The company. We must not disturb the smooth work of the company."

"If you attempt anything so stupid," Nell said, "I'll see you're driven out of Liverpool. In disgrace."

"Taking Edmund with me?"

"He wouldn't go. Not when it came down to it."

"It is true." Poppy submitted without humility. "For him also it is the company first, as with you. Only Malcolm thinks of other things."

"Malcolm will think no more of you."

"You will arrange that."

199

"I'm suggesting," said Nell, "that you set your sights on Paul Whitlaw. If you do, I'll do all in my power to help you. If you don't . . ."

Julia returned, explaining how dear little Alan had woken up, but it hadn't been her fault, he was such a light sleeper, and anyway he was so delighted to see her he would sleep the more soundly for it. And Jesse, bless him, hadn't even stirred.

When the men rejoined the ladies it was obvious that the duel had been growing more vigourous. Malcolm, Nell suspected, had sat silent and brooding and made no attempt to intervene.

"Two days," Paul was declaiming as he entered the room. "A mere two days here and already I know the kind of double-dealing that's going on. That ship over in the yard, it's going to be sent out nice and innocent, isn't it, with a crew of dockside scum—"

"No Liverpool shipowner's in the habit of letting dockside scum run a brand new vessel."

"It's not a question of Liverpool owners, is it? Or of that skeleton crew running it for long. I *know* what the game is, I tell you. That ship's clearing the Mersey as fast as they can get her away. And heading where? I'd bet on the Azores. Where there'll be guns and ammunition, and a Southern skipper waiting with picked men to take it over and turn it loose on *our* shipping. And I'd like to know when your Government is going to stop turning a blind eye to this kind of jobbery."

"Your own boarding of two neutral ships this last fortnight leaves you in no position to condemn—"

"Neutral, you call it?"

They strutted and crowed before Poppy. Nell was struck by the basic absurdity of it. Paul and Edmund were basically on the same side: Gresham-Bostock trade was, and would continue to be, with the North, and Paul knew it and by tomorrow would be requesting their help in tactful introductions. But in front of that woman they had to play out their cockfight.

"Neutral?" Paul raged on. "When Prioleau sits there in Abercromby Square, flagrantly representing the rebels and openly doing business with anyone willing to sell his soul. And there are plenty of those in this town."

"This sort of thing does give me such a headache," Julia said.

Nell moved between the two men. "Mr. Whitlaw, it's a most agreeable night. Why don't you take Miss Rivers for a stroll in the garden? I'm afraid mother and I have been boring her, talking business."

"Eleanor, I haven't said a single word about—"

"You've already had a taste of what it's like when Greshams and Bostocks get together. We're abominably poor hosts, I fear."

As Whitlaw diffidently escorted Poppy out on to the terrace and down to the lawn, both Gresham brothers turned outraged faces on Nell. Without hesitation she lured her mother into a conversation about the boys, about Jesse's sturdiness and Alan's dreaminess, and what they ate and how much weight they were putting on.

When goodnights were exchanged, Julia held out her hand in gracious forgiveness to Paul.

"How long do you expect to stay in England, Mr. Whitlaw?"

"Another two weeks should be sufficient. I reckon I can get through all I need to do in that time."

"I'm sure you can," said Nell.

When the door had closed behind their guests, she found Malcolm at her elbow.

It was the same question, gnawing away at him throughout the evening: "What are you playing at?"

"We don't usually send a ship to the breaker's yard if we can sell her off somewhere else, do we?"

"If you imagine for one moment—"

"You can help conclude the deal by tempting Mr. Whitlaw with descriptions of the delights in store for him. Especially if he favours someone soothing and restful."

For a frightening instant she was not sure whether he would laugh or strike her. Then he turned away. The slam of the drawing-room door struck the faintest chime from the grandfather clock.

Nell made her way more slowly along the passage, stopping at the mirror into which her mother had, as usual, peeped on the way out. Her own face was aging and hardening, surely? Setting into a certainty that would petrify it for the rest of her life? Nell was aghast at her own ruthlessness. And surprised that behind her in the glass was no clear background of the old slave market, with a woman slave being stripped and put up for auction—and plenty of prospective buyers. A woman soon to be shipped off across the Atlantic.

Her face stared back at her, revealing no tremor of the fears inside.

Who am I? She marvelled at herself. Who *else* am I?

6

On a warm autumn Saturday in 1866 a photographer set up his tripod on an untrodden gravel path between virginal grass patches and newly planted flowerbeds. With a deferential semaphore he marshalled members of the family group into position and then, stooping below his black cloth, studied them upside-down with professional detachment. His right arm emerged to wave the little boy at the right just a fraction closer to his brother. Then he ducked, took a last sighting, and squeezed the bulb.

The picture would appear in tomorrow's newspaper along with one of certain Liverpool dignitaries, and would also be enlarged and framed for a long career on the library desk of Bostock's Brow. Mother and father and sons, together with the boys' uncle, would smile on, ageless and unforgettable for so long as there was some descendant to inherit and remember. And between them would be the imperishable bronze glower of their greatest predecessor.

Yes, look at them: old Nell had always had that piercing look that kept trying to catch you on the wrong foot; and Edmund Gresham had never got rid of that serious stare, not so much at you as beyond you; and Mr. Nell—what was his name, yes, Malcolm, that was it—well, you only thought of his name coupled with hers; and kneeling in front of them was that young Alan, who was never anything but pale and odd and a bit adrift from the rest of them—oh, and matching him below their father's knees young Jesse, all keen so that you'd say he was just about to jump out of the picture at you.

Faces trapped and frozen as they peered out and on and into the future. Faces as they had been long before that awful disaster, which left the whole group gouged and broken and never the same again.

And because Mr. and Mrs. Malcolm Gresham in the centre had been coaxed by the photographer into leaning a few inches apart, the reason for the photograph made the centrepiece of the picture

On what would have been old Jesse Bostock's eightieth birthday, Bostock Gardens had been formally opened by his granddaughter in the presence of her family, the Mayor of Liverpool, the Chairman of the Docks and Harbour Board, and a number of long-serving employees in their Sunday best. The departed Jesse was immortalised in bronze and a glass negative: a bronze bust atop a marble plinth, still as solid and real as any of them, making up a managerial quartet with Nell, Malcolm and Edmund Gresham. Newly varnished and rising at an angle from the foot of the plinth was the bowsprit salvaged from the Greshams' old sailing ship, the *Naomi*, before she went for breaking up. The slim, striving arms rose in supplication or in sad worship of the departed but still dominating Bostock.

"And now, your Worship . . . Mrs. Gresham . . . if we could just have another one, looking this way—over *this* way, if you please—and . . . oh, yes, admirable. That will do admirably."

It was over. The assembly split up into little groups, some choosing to be first to use the new green-painted iron seats, some strolling round the central monument and down one of the paths that made spokes from this hub. Edmund stood beside his brother where they could have an uninterrupted view of the memorial.

Malcolm looked at the naked wooden figure in its polished subservience below Jesse Bostock.

"I'm surprised Nell allowed you that little indulgence," said Edmund.

"She didn't indulge me. The idea was her own. I knew nothing of it until she produced the final plans."

"I'd have thought she preferred you to forget."

"After all this time? I wouldn't have thought it mattered."

"Wouldn't you?" said Edmund curiously.

"Well, if it means anything I suppose it could be a symbol—of magnanimity or victory, if you see what I mean."

"Yes, I see what you mean."

They had been fixedly regarding all that was left, after these years, of Poppy. Now both had to force themselves to look away and join everyone else in studying the small enclosed garden. There was a shelter against one wall, a trellis for roses against another. Inquisitive faces were pressed against the ornamental iron gates leading in from the main road. Flowerbeds formed converging crescents towards a drinking fountain. Exploring this new hunting ground, a wasp zoomed and snarled past Jesse Bostock's head.

Bostock Gardens had been Nell's inspiration and to some extent her salvation. Just under four years ago, less than a year after her dismissal of Poppy into the arms of Paul Whitlaw, she had been delivered of a stillborn daughter. It had been a dangerous time. She was warned against hoping too soon for more children. They might come, they might not, but certainly she should be careful for some time into the future.

Within a few days they heard from New York that Poppy, too, had produced a daughter. The girl lived and was christened Rosalind.

Refusing to stay at home convalescing, Nell took on more responsibilities, sat on more and more committees; and bought a small tract of land near the centre of the town where she could busy herself laying out a green space in the stone and brick desert for people to sit and breathe and remember the name of Jesse Bostock.

Edmund looked at the bronze, broad head, and then down at the figurehead in its humble surrender. When Nell stood beside him, inviting his approval, he said,

"You had to make it clear who was the victor and who the vanquished?"

"Good gracious, is that how it strikes you?"

"Malcolm obviously got over it long ago. Did you really have to remind him?"

"It just seemed so . . . oh, I don't know . . . appropriate. A Bostock symbol, and a Gresham one." Nell inclined her head to an alderman who, touring the paths, was raising his hat admiringly to her. She said, "Edmund, something I never asked you at the time—did you know all along that Malcolm was keeping her on in Liverpool?"

Edmund scuffed his foot against the grass verge. He had put it all behind him, he had not shown then what he felt and he did not propose to betray it now.

"Oh, it doesn't matter," said Nell. "I just wondered, that's all."

She just wondered. And it didn't matter. Who was she to decide what mattered or didn't matter, and to whom? No, he would not let himself even think about it.

"What a good thing," Nell went on airily, "that she didn't set her cap at *you.*"

"That was never likely."

"Oh, but it was. At one point there was a distinct danger she might have done."

If I'd thought for one moment that there was the faintest chance . . .
He almost cried it aloud.

"But we didn't particularly want to keep her in the family, did we?"
Nell was smiling past him as the Mayor approached to congratulate her.

Various groups coalesced into one, encircling her and offering thanks
and compliments, and then breaking up again and straggling towards
the gates, outside which the carriages waited. A park attendant touched
the glossy peak of his new cap and smartly pulled back the nearer gate.
As the carriages were driven away, Edmund glanced back to see passers-
by hurrying to sample the delights of the new oasis in these crowded
streets. A labourer who had been taking oysters from his pocket as he
waited, flicking them open with a knife and swallowing them, was first in.
He opened another oyster and was about to toss the shell on the grass.
Then he looked sheepishly around, grinned at nobody in particular, and
made his way to a bin against the side of the shelter.

At Bostock's Brow a sideboard had been laden with a baron of beef, a
spiced cold roast, pheasant galantine, and two mounds of grapes and
crystallised fruits shaped as ornamentally as any skilfully clipped hedge.

Jesse and Alan marched earnestly from one guest to another, offering
bread rolls and plates of nuts.

The Mayor bowed over his ample stomach so that the mayoral chain
swung and caught Jesse beside the ear. "Well, young fellow, you've got a
great name to live up to. Another Jesse Bostock keeping us on our toes,
eh? Splendid thought. Or should I say an alarming one?"

Through the laughter Julia bustled across the room. She caught
Alan's arm and led him forward to take his brother's place. "Alan must
play for us. He has so much talent, it's inherited of course, you *must* listen."

"Oh, grandma, not now."

"Mother, I'm sure this isn't the time or the —"

"Nonsense. In the great old days it was all the fashion. In the best
places, when people had taste. Everyone had music, of course they did,
to accompany dinner or conversation, or . . . Oh, do sit down, dear.
You must play for everyone. They're longing to hear you."

As Alan was led reluctantly to the grand piano in the bay of the window, the mayor moved back a few paces. A major subscriber to the Philharmonic Hall and the series of Philharmonic Concerts, he preferred to
keep the results of his philanthropy out of earshot save for unavoidable
public occasions. Malcolm grinned awkward encouragement at his son,
but then started talking boisterously to a councillor's wife; a man cleared
his throat noisily; and Julia cried, "Hush, everybody, let him get started."

Edmund contemplated the faces of the twins, so alike and yet related
only in the sense that they were two sides of the same coin. Where Jesse's

205

chin jutted and his mouth pushed resolutely forward, Alan's nearly identical features lacked that razor edge. His lips pulled slightly back in; his weir-grey eyes were as intent as Jesse's but reflective where Jesse's were demanding.

The formal harmonies and stately tempo of a Mozart minuet paced through the room. Alan looked at his thin, probing fingers for a few measures, shutting himself off from his audience; then raised his head and played with less concern but still quite remote from everyone else in the room.

Two maritime engineers near the door began to talk quietly. A gentle swell of conversation buoyed up the music and then gradually lapped over its edges and inundated it.

Alan played on, imperturbable now. The music dominated the discord of reality.

"I've told my daughter she must nurture such talent." Julia, propped decoratively against the end of the piano, confided in Mr. Astbury of the Docks and Harbour Board, who would happily have followed the retreating Mayor but was too courteous to do so. "He simply must go to the Royal Academy. Of Music, I mean."

The Mayor was close to the door when it opened and the parlourmaid came in. She handed an envelope to Nell, who glanced at it and then passed it on to the Mayor.

"Ladies and gentlemen!" Alan was stopped in the middle of a bar. "This"—the Mayor waved it above his head—"is a copy of a telegraph message just received . Greetings from the Mayor of New York!"

"The telegraph—they've got the line working?"

"The *Great Eastern* has not merely laid an Atlantic cable, but has recovered and connected the one lost last year. A fraternal greeting from the New World. I must go and send a reply."

There was a spattering of applause. Glasses were raised.

Edmund noticed that Adrian Speke had no intention of moving far from the wine table. His shaky hand held out a goblet that the butler must surely have refilled six or seven times within the last half-hour. Speke was haggard, fidgeting, looking fitfully over his shoulder but attempting conversation with no one. Draining his glass once more, he edged towards the sideboard and began helping himself from a full brandy decanter that had been set there.

In the chatter of jubilation as the Mayor was taking his leave, Astbury moved closer to Nell. He began talking persuasively to her; she shook her head but was smiling and, Edmund realised, blushing with pleasure; then she beckoned him to join them.

"Mr. Astbury has just been paying me a wonderful compliment."

"I've been asking Mrs. Gresham," said Astbury, "if she would allow her name to go forward as one of the dock ratepayers' representatives on the Harbour Board."

"And I've said they ought to be asking you rather than me."

But she was aglow, waiting to be persuaded.

"What about Malcolm?" asked Edmund.

"Oh, yes, Malcolm." Nell looked vaguely around. Astbury pursed his lips and smiled unenthusiastically.

"Someone taking my name in vain?"

"We thought you ought to be present," said Edmund discreetly, "while one of our partners is asked to serve on the Docks and Harbour Board."

"One of us?"

"Mrs. Gresham," said Astbury. "We're hoping she'll consent to being nominated."

It was Malcolm's turn to go pink. "Nell—a woman on the Board?"

"And why not? It's about time." But with an effort Nell said, "But perhaps it ought really to be Edmund."

Of course, thought Edmund, *she was going to accept.* It was the sort of thing she had been working towards for years. She would not be able to deny herself the chance of making up for that incident on the Beckwith Club steps.

He said, "Mr. Astbury is asking if *you* wish to stand for nomination. I think he's very wise."

Her eyes were grateful.

There was the crash of breaking glass. Lord Speke's glass had slipped through his fingers and shattered on the floor. He stared down at the fragments, swaying, not daring to stoop.

"Adrian, whatever's come over you?" Julia fussed towards him.

Astbury said, "I may put your name forward, then?"

"I'm honoured," said Nell.

Guests began to leave. Adrian Speke was led into a quieter room to sit down. Astbury shook Nell's hand, patted Edmund amiably on the shoulder, and contented himself with a nod to Malcolm as he went.

By Monday the sun that had blessed the opening ceremony of Bostock Gardens was shrouded. The air remained warm and even sticky, but a dark mist impregnated with coal smoke drifted up from the river and swirled along every side street like a tide seeking out fresh inlets and channels.

Edmund rode to the office by a more circuitous route than usual. It was safer to stay off the main roads, with carts and coaches and other riders looming without warning out of the haze.

In one back street alone, half the front doorsteps were occupied by men slumped with their elbows on their knees, chin in hand. One took a last swig from an ale bottle. Another was playing a desultory game of marbles with two children; then snarled at them for no apparent reason, got to his feet, and shambled indoors. Several looked up with glum hostility as Edmund rode past.

Next month there might be work for them. Or the month after. There would be new prosperity on the Atlantic as trade picked up: new ships going into service on British passenger routes before the war-crippled United States could rebuild its own merchant fleet.

Next month or the month after: such promises were little comfort to men who needed to feed themselves and their families this week and next week. Their wives went out as washerwomen, market stall keepers, workers in the nail or match factories, barmaids; but when the men had no money to spend, there was little call for extra barmaids.

A year after the end of the Civil War, Liverpool was still suffering. Blockade runners were abandoned on the mud. The cotton warehouses were three-quarters empty. Men who had made quick money had lost it just as quickly. And although the shipyards were growing busy again, they were putting all their efforts into steamships—which left a lot of skilled men sitting on their doorsteps or leaning at street corners, unemployed and unemployable.

"They say the wind's free," Nell had observed six months ago. "But too free for our tastes. We want ships that can run to a dependable timetable. We want four new steamers with new compound engines, and a fifth when we can afford it. To run an absolutely reliable Transatlantic service we can't manage with less than five."

Of the handful of remaining sailing ships on the Gresham-Bostock books, the *Naomi* and another had been scrapped, and the others sold off to Far East traders in search of a bargain. If a few new clippers were still under construction for the tea trade and the opening up of an alternative cotton trade with India and Egypt, there were too few to provide work for the men who, like their fathers and grandfathers before them, had plied their skills as sailmakers, ropemakers and carpenters in the courts and alleys and walks of the riverside.

Generations of inherited craftsmanship trickling away, thought Edmund, swamped by more powerful currents and the backwash of new engines and new needs.

The capital investment demanded by Nell's plans had alarmed the Gresham brothers. But Nell was right, as usual. Such American companies as wished to renew operations on the Atlantic had no modern ships, and few seaworthy old ones to enter the race. They had to charter foreign ships with makeshift crew—"Or," said Nell, "they can charter a number of our ships with fully qualified crews and run a service combined with our own. That way we can cover a good part of our initial costs and half our running costs."

Edmund came out beside the theatre in Williamson Square, with a recent advertisement peeling away from its wall. It billed the American Slave Serenaders: "Nigger Minstrels, the only combination of Genuine Darkies in the World." A slave troupe entertaining the public of the greatest slave exporting town of all!

Late in the afternoon, with the sooty haze casting an early dusk over the quays, Lord Speke was announced in Edmund's office.

He came in with hunched shoulders and his right arm shaking forward as if to feel his way or ward off a blow that might knock him over. His handshake was limp and cold. Sitting down, he raised pink-rimmed eyes to Edmund, twice started to speak, then hummed and coughed.

"You don't look too well, sir. May I offer you a brandy?"

"Oh, no, I . . ." Speke tried to wave the offer away, but those eyes betrayed his craving.

Edmund opened the corner cabinet and filled a glass, allowing himself only a small tot to keep his guest company. Speke sipped, and summoned up courage to speak.

"I come to you in the strictest confidence."

"Nobody will disturb us."

"I have a favour to ask. Or advice. I suppose you'll feel I ought to have talked it over privately with my daughter, but I . . . she . . . she's a very formidable young woman." He essayed a smirk of complicity. "I felt it would be better man to man."

"Yes?"

Speke drained his glass. Edmund did not offer to refill it. "Mr. Gresham, I'm in some financial difficulty. There may already have been talk, and soon there'll be much more."

"Nothing has reached my ears so far."

"Oh, it will, it will. I'll be frank with you. I put money into one of the cotton houses during the war. And then raised more money. It was an excellent investment at the time."

"In the short term," said Edmund dryly.

"Quite so. I fear none of us foresaw the outcome. We needed blockade runners, we had to pay high premiums, and the cost of premises around Brunswick Street soared, you'll remember."

Edmund well remembered: even during the profitable years he had seen expenses eroding the inflated incomes.

"I was forced to mortgage my estate."

"But there were profits. Did you put them all back into the business—not bank any?"

"I banked with Barnard's."

209

Edmund could hardly bear to look into the man's despondent face. The story was too drear and familiar. The artificially stimulated cotton trade had slumped catastrophically with the return of peace to the United States. It was not just working men in the back streets who felt a cold wind off the sea: many a strutting merchant prince had been exposed as living in borrowed clothes on expensively borrowed money. Losses to the town's commerce within a few months were estimated at twelve million pounds. Barnard's and the Royal were two Liverpool banks which, along with any number of commercial enterprises, had collapsed.

"What's the extent of your commitment?"

"I owe seventy-five thousand pounds. Orrell Manor is mortgaged to the hilt, and my creditors are pressing for payment."

"Why have you come to me?" asked Edmund, though he guessed the answer.

"I helped Eleanor with the business after her grandfather's death."

"And made a reasonable profit on the land deal for our terminus."

"As you say yourself, a reasonable one. But have I ever tried to claim anything from your later expansion? I haven't even asked for my wife to receive some appropriate dividend from the firm that her father did so much to establish."

"Lady Speke was left a legacy that Mr. Bostock presumably considered adequate. Is it still intact?"

Speke leaned forward to set the empty glass on the edge of the desk.

"It was invested with my other assets. My wife shared my belief in what we were doing, she knew all about the committees I sat on and the financial groups I belonged to. She was glad to leave the necessary decisions to me."

"But you haven't told her of the present situation?"

"I don't know why you should assume that."

"Have you told her?"

"No."

"And you've come to me—"

"There must be a way you could intervene. Given guarantees by Gresham-Bostock, my creditors will wait. And we can work out some way of paying them off."

"With what?"

"The debt and the whole estate could be transferred to the Gresham-Bostock books. Set off the liabilities against the property assets."

"But the estate's of no value to a shipping company. It wouldn't be a balance against your liabilities—it would just be an additional liability."

"I'm sure you could think of something," said Speke wretchedly.

What Edmund was thinking of was the investment to which they were already committed: new ships for their twice-weekly Transatlantic service, the cost of more highly paid crews, the installation of new comforts to attract new passengers.

Speke shifted on his chair. "Now, if *you* were to put it to Eleanor, as her partner, as a strictly business proposition . . ."

If Edmund were to put it to her, first there would be an almighty outburst against this incompetent creature who had let his greed run away with him—and who now had the impertinence to expect the salvage of his wrecked schemes to be carried out by a firm that he knew had unwaveringly set itself against any discreditable dealings with the Confederates. But after her denunciations Nell might weaken. For family reasons, under hysterical pressure from her mother, she might reluctantly give way. Which could do nothing but damage to the Gresham-Bostock operations.

It was unfair to put the onus on her.

"I'd prefer to take the blame for any decisions myself, Lord Speke," he said, "and frankly I don't see how we could justify intervention in your misfortunes. It would place an unfair burden on our own organisation."

"I'd be prepared to work for the company at a nominal salary. For a pittance. You could use my name wherever it suited you—it still carries some weight, you know."

It was pitiful. The man had no case, no right even to plead a case. Yet to kick him out of the office was too brutal. He was waiting—and Edmund, wanting to be done with this distasteful affair, could not strike. Was he, in any event, being too puritanical? All commerce was a dangerous, risky game: tomorrow someone might condemn him for mistakes just as he was condemning the crushed Speke.

He knew what his father's blustering verdict would have been. Or old Jesse Bostock's. And their memory deserved his support more than this man did.

But could he let him sink altogether?

He stood up. "It's a very grave situation. I shall need to consider all the aspects."

"Will you, old chap? I'm sure that in the end you'll see your way to something—ah—mutually satisfactory. Not a good thing to have too many financial crashes, you know. Saps the confidence of the public. I'd like to keep my head above water—and Gresham-Bostock are pretty good at keeping things afloat, hey? Mm . . . Edmund?"

Edmund saw him off the premises.

It would have been more honest to reiterate the reasons for letting the man sink. Left alone, Edmund occupied the better part—or worse part—of two hours not with evolving impractical ideas for saving Speke

211

but with justifications for telling him that there could be no such salvation. Better to have told him brutally on the spot, and not let him go away with false hopes.

As he was about to leave the office, young Mr. Carter came back from the Custom House. "I'm glad I caught you, Mr. Edmund. Lord Speke was here earlier, wasn't he?"

"He was."

"Looked a bit downcast to me, sir."

"He has certain matters on his mind. Not our concern."

"Just passed him, sir. Looked as though he had . . . well, begging your pardon, Mr. Edmund, but I'd . . . well, I'd say he'd been partaking of a bit more than was good for him."

"It's not up to us to regulate Lord Speke's habits."

"Some could lead him into trouble. He's not in a fit state, sir, truly he's not. Staggering about that pub on Canning Dock corner—you know, where you get those lads hanging about waiting for fellers like him."

"Like him?"

Carter glanced prudishly away. "Ah, well, *you* know, Mr. Edmund."

Edmund hesitated, then took a heavy walking-stick from the umbrella stand. "I don't suppose I'll find him in that warren. But I'd best go and see."

"And I'd best come with you."

Edmund did not argue. The courts and cellars and old slave keeps behind Canning Dock were no place for a man to venture alone after darkness had fallen.

There had been no rain, but the clinging mist had left damp smears on the pavements. Street gas lamps struck a septic green iridescence from the cold sweat on the cobbles, flooded by yellow puddles near the door and windows of the public house. Masts in the dock, lowering on the outgoing tide, made a sketchy palisade above the quayside.

Carter said, "If he's anywhere about by now . . ."

They found him in the yard behind the pub. Looped across the unevenly paved squares was a thick rope, strung between wall and wall so that the worst drunks could sag over it and spew on the flagstones rather than on the floor of the bar. The rope had another use. Hanging from it at this moment with his breeches down, sniggering, was an urchin of eleven or twelve years old. "A florin, then." It was Lord Speke's voice, hoarse in the moist gloom; and Speke was lurching out from the farther wall. "Half a crown," came the tormenting, adenoidal answer, "or there's nothin' doin'." Speke grunted, and folded himself like a flapping bird of prey over the boy.

Edmund heard Carter's moan of disgust, and took a step forward.

212

The ferrule of his stick rang a metallic note from the paving. The boy ducked his head under the rope and squinted back.

"Christ, it's the coppers!"

He slid nimbly to one side and was off across the yard, dragging up his breeches as he went.

"No," squealed Lord Speke. "Come back, it's all right, I promise you . . ."

They were running, the boy tugging open the gate to the alley with Speke lumbering after him, jarring a shoulder against the gatepost but panting on.

Edmund reached the quayside twenty yards or so behind them. The boy, small and shadowy in the haze, glanced back once and quickened his pace, darting along beside a row of bollards and then vanishing: down a flight of steps, a rope ladder, or under the lee of a warehouse, it was impossible to tell.

"Come *back.* Half a crown . . . five shillings, damn you." Speke reached the edge of the quay and rocked to and fro, looking down into the shrouded undergrowth of masts and spars. "You down there?"

Edmund tensed, touching Carter's arm to keep him back. Holding his stick high so that it would not rattle on the ground, he walked as quietly as possible towards Speke.

"Please." It was a whimper as screechy and brief as the rasp of a rowlock in the night. "Come on up, *please.*"

Speke leaned forward. And went on leaning forward, slowly, his arms beginning to spread in the slowest and most despairing of entreaties. He hovered for a few seconds; then, before Edmund could reach him, toppled without another sound off the quay.

They heard him smack hard on to a deck below. Then there was the silence of death, save for one scrape of a fender against the dock wall and the gurgle of the turning tide.

ALAN GRESHAM was eighteen years old when he gave his first public recital in his home town, and when Poppy Whitlaw came back to that town for the first time since her marriage.

Mr. and Mrs. Whitlaw were in the audience. So were Mr. and Mrs. Gresham, Alan's uncle, and his widowed grandmother; but not his brother. Expressing regret at not being able to attend because of his marine engineering studies and an imminent examination, Jesse was relieved to have a genuine excuse for avoiding what interested him as little as marine engineering interested Alan.

The Philharmonic Hall was not full, but the audience was by no means a meagre one. Alan suspected his mother of drumming up attendance. She was on so many committees, a subscriber of such regularity to the concert season, and donor to so many charities, that she knew where to apply pressure. There were those who would have considered it impolite to stay away: and others, no doubt, who hoped the performer would play poorly and make glaring mistakes so that they could have a little gloat over Gresham pretentiousness. He had played a number of times in London before a more knowledgeable audience than this. Nobody here was qualified to be as critically scathing as his fellow pupils at the Academy, or the professionals who came to their special concerts. But here he felt more exposed than ever before. A musician had to work doubly hard to win honour in his own birthplace.

Alan began with two small pieces by Mendelssohn, a Schumann Romance, and then plunged into Beethoven's *Appassionata* Sonata. Within two or three minutes of starting on the first movement of this he had lost all consciousness of the audience and was thinking himself into and through the music, emerging at last defiant and then reeling under the unexpected broadside of applause.

After the interval he threw himself into his favourite kind of music— the dance rhythms of Chopin's polonaises and mazurkas, and then pieces that were as strange to his listeners as they had been to him until early this year: unpublished Bohemian polkas and furiants, brought back from Prague by a friend at the Academy, full of strange accents and sudden leaps of the left hand. He had been entranced, and remained under their spell. The hall rang with the exhilaration of their rhythms, with strange voices from distant hills and plains and forests.

Often he had been reproved by his professor: "Kindly do not tap your foot when you're playing, Mr. Gresham. The feet are for the pedals when needed. You should be able to keep time without such aids."

It was not a question of keeping time, but of the time itself driving through Alan's muscles. He felt the pulse not only in his feet but in the back of his neck. And there were tunes, like the Bohemian dances and like the waltzes coming into London from Vienna, which once heard could never be banished: away from the Academy, he unashamedly beat time with his right hand or swayed his shoulders in rhythm, whistling as often and compulsively as any errand boy.

There was a difference in the applause at the end of his recital. From various parts of the auditorium came the enthusiastic clapping of those who had enjoyed the surface lightness of the music, and found the evening had passed less solemnly than they had anticipated. But here and there were patches of disapproval, of groups feeling that somehow the whole thing had turned slightly frivolous after the interval.

In his dressing-room Alan listened to the congratulations of his family, the Whitlaws, and a few friends who had come to pay their respects; and found, to his dismay, that all the compliments were meaningless. He had been headily alive while he played, with the music thrumming through him like an invigourating breeze through an Aeolian harp; and alive to the audience's response at the end. But now it was over, the keyboard was no longer beneath his fingers, he was drained and indifferent.

215

It was a good thing they were all talking at once, saying the right things to him and then turning away on to more familiar ground.

"A very sweet little tune, that last one . . ."

"A most enjoyable evening, Alan." Uncle Edmund was serious and sincere, even though he had understood nothing.

And his mother was already talking earnestly to Paul Whitlaw. It could have had nothing to do with music. None of it was real to them—not compared with the rhythm of the waterfront, the throb of engines, the fugue of figures in a ledger. His mother had been generous, arranging this concert not with any boastful intent but because at this time, in her eyes, it was the right thing for him. She had given it as much of her time as was necessary to ensure its smooth presentation, and now would be on to something else. Because she had so much to give, and not enough time in the world to spend on each gift.

He was grateful. But in this lull, when he was with the people in this room yet no part of them, he wished—for her own sake, for her own pleasure—she could slow down her own tempo and listen to what he had to say, to interpret, through his playing.

She would think that either conceited, or funny, or both. And wouldn't she be right?

He shook hands with a burly man and a shy, narrow-shouldered girl urged towards him by his grandmother.

"Mr. Cubbin is so anxious to meet you, Alan. He was so impressed by your lovely touch, weren't you, Mr. Cubbin?"

"It was a treat. Oh, yes, you can play, young man, I must say you can play." Cubbin stood helpless for a minute, then said, "Our Catherine plays the violin."

"Oh, dad, honest, only as an amateur. You know that."

"I know it sounds all right to me. Good enough for all you're likely to need it for, anyway."

The girl smiled timorously at Alan.

He tried to bring himself back to the present. "You go to a lot of concerts?"

"Well, we don't have that many, you know. But I love it. Like tonight."

"Richter has been conducting in London. I can't say I'm fond of Wagner, but he does work wonders with the orchestra."

"Oh. Does he?"

"No," Nell was saying in the background, "no reason why he shouldn't make a part-time occupation of it. Not a complete career, I don't think we'd want that. Give him some insight into the way we allocate our donations and subscriptions and that kind of thing. He'll meet the important people and be able to talk their language—a great deal better than I do, I'm sure."

"Oh, come now, Mrs. Gresham."

A sly voice added, "It'll be your Jesse who's the real power behind the company, when he's trained?"

"We think so, don't we, Malcolm?"

But Alan's father had moved closer to Alan. "I thought you sounded marvellous," he said warmly.

"Thanks, father."

"Don't know much about it. Can't pretend I do. But I wasn't bored for one minute—if that means anything to you."

"Yes, father, it does."

They smiled awkwardly, almost secretly, at each other.

Mrs. Whitlaw joined them. And at once, without conscious effort on his part, Alan was fully awake and alive, restored to the present. Like a sudden crescendo the sounds of the room broke through the muffling curtain of his tiredness. He felt the gentle drift of the woman's hand into his; saw with frightening clarity, as if under a magnifying glass, a little bead of moisture on her lower lip; and heard the quiet, precise music of her level contralto.

"For me it was not piano pieces," she said. "It was . . . was feeling. Knowing. Knowing something for—how shall I say it—for the first time."

Her husband was shepherding them all to the door. "You gave us a great evening, Alan," he said benevolently. "A great talent you have there." Then he was nodding to Nell, respectfully taking Julia's arm, and waiting for the others to follow him. "You're all having supper with the newest patron of the arts—me!"

Alan thought of his bedroom at home, of lying in bed thinking back over what he had done wrong, overplayed or underplayed, letting the themes run sleepily down through his toes and finally escape.

"It's very kind of you, but—"

"It's my privilege. Your mother has enough on her mind tonight."

"And not only on her mind." Malcolm put his arm round his wife and kissed her extravagantly.

"Malcolm, have you no discretion? At your age I'd have thought, and with guests here . . ." Julia did not complete the tale of what she would have thought, but her glance at her daughter's thickening waistline made it plain that she disapproved of such goings-on at Malcolm's and Nell's age.

217

Alan, startled, supposed he ought to have noticed sooner. The swelling contour was skilfully disguised by a quilted jacket and the apron-front of her full skirt, but undeniably she had filled out. And undeniably she was blooming, as much under the warmth of his father's attentiveness as from the new life within her.

Another child, after so long: the whole idea seemed not so much distasteful as impractical, nothing to do with her present way of life.

Paul Whitlaw had reserved a table in one deep recess of the Lord Street supper rooms. He made a fuss of Nell, mollified Julia with jokes about their past differences over American policy, which he deftly turned to her advantage, and said in Alan's direction that after the earlier part of the evening anything would be anticlimax, but that he would do his best.

Alan was seated facing Mrs. Whitlaw. Close to her again, he was wakeful again, and glad—glad that he could marvel at her across the table, attracting less attention than if he had had to lean forward and peer past a neighbour. He had never seen anyone so strange or so beautiful. Her eyes seemed gently provoking, though there was nothing provocative in her slim serenity. No smile touched her lips, yet he was sure one waited not a fraction of an inch away, ready to be flicked forward on the tip of her tongue.

"It's a market we can't neglect." His mother started on Paul Whitlaw as soon as the turtle soup had been set before them. "I've always tried to keep us in the forefront with just this sort of development in mind."

"Holidays in America are still not a great draw. Most of the traffic's the other way."

"That may be reversed before you realise it. Now, if between us we could put before your investors a policy . . ."

Poppy said across the table, "My daughter Rosalind is only a few years younger than you."

"She's not with you?"

"We left her with her grandparents. But one day she must see Europe. She's fond of art galleries, and concerts. She would have enjoyed this evening."

"She plays?"

"Like most of her friends, she has lessons, but I don't think they'll amount to much."

"I don't suppose mine will either, in the end."

She held her soup spoon poised without a tremor, and there was no tremor in her voice. "It is you who decides, yes? It must be nobody else."

218

Nell must have caught a few snatches of the exchange. She stared down the table, then shifted into a more comfortable position.

A daughter. Having lost that one, years ago, she must be hoping for another. Alan wondered what it would be like to have a very much younger sister. Would a girl now soften his mother, coax her away from business and bring a new, feminine gentleness into Bostock's Brow?

Towards the end of the meal, when Alan was trying to make cheerful conversation with his grandmother, Poppy turned to his father and said, "It's so long since I was in Liverpool. I must visit some of the places I knew."

"You'll find a great many alterations."

"Exploring them will fill in time while the rest of you talk about prices and percentages and horsepower."

Quickly Nell said, "But that's why Paul is here, to talk about just such things. We shall all be busy with him, every one of us."

Poppy continued to study Malcolm, but for some reason he had turned his attention to a slice of apple left on his plate. "Every one of you," she said regretfully.

Malcolm looked up again, on the verge of speaking. Before he could utter a word, Nell said, "Except Alan, of course. He's not much interested in our calculations. And he's got time on his hands before he goes back to London for the new term."

The delicately lined face darkened under the eyes as if Poppy were tiring under the artificial light. Was she shadowed by the boring prospect of Alan, rejecting him before he had the opportunity to accept the suggestion?

He said, "I'd love to show you round."

"I think you wish to spend time at the piano. It is necessary to keep in practice."

"Please, I'd love to do it."

Everyone had stopped talking, as if this were the weightiest decision of the week.

"Then I shall be charmed. And we promise not to talk about ships. Promise?"

Yet next afternoon one of their first visits was to the figurehead from the dismembered *Naomi*. Automatically Alan had started their itinerary with Bostock Gardens, laid out some years after Poppy's departure and so quite new to her. It was only when he saw the wooden features through other eyes—through *her* eyes—and set them against her features, that he was gripped by alarm. What had he done, bringing her here?

She contemplated the figurehead for a long time. It had suffered recently: some of the varnish had weathered badly, and streaks of spongy wood showed beneath; in spite of the park-keeper's watchfulness, children had gouged a few slivers from the dwindling loins; and one nipple had been chipped off.

"Is that how she likes to picture me?"

Alan made no reply, for she was obviously not talking to him. But the fear persisted—fear of having done something without being given any warning of what that something might mean.

They walked on. Hurrying to quell his unease, he took her to the Walker Art Gallery, only recently opened, to the Zoological Gardens and, at her own request, for a stroll through Prince's Park. Here she fell into a reverie, and he was sure he had offended her. He was in danger of throwing himself down to his knees on the path and begging her forgiveness. And more than her forgiveness. Clinging to her, touching her, and so in some way restoring the pristine gloss of that reaching, yearning figurehead.

They went down into the city for tea, and there his confidence was restored. Wherever they walked, wherever they sat, men's heads turned. Men looked at her, and at him, and in their glances he read the greed that was already in his own mind. He grew more and more painfully aware of her every moment. And of her stillness—a willowy blade at rest in a sheath from which he longed to draw her.

His forehead was hot as they passed a group of young clerks in their usual afternoon hurry to catch the ferry—but not in such a hurry that they did not all slow and turn enviously.

"What are you thinking of?" asked Poppy.

"Oh, nothing special. I'm sorry, I was—"

"You're longing to get back to your piano."

"No," he said. "It's wonderful, being with you."

"You're so polite."

He caught her arm. Satin slid an inch upwards like a sleek extra skin. She slowed, then brought her other hand across and stroked his fingers with feathery lightness as if afraid of bruising them.

"If you would care to combine politeness with pleasure," she said, "you could perform at my musical matinee."

"I didn't know you were planning one."

"Neither did I, until now." Her elbow moved so that they were naturally arm in arm. "But there are several ladies to whom I owe hospitality. I think you would enliven it. The day after tomorrow, perhaps, so that I have time to select the right people?"

"I'm not sure your hotel will approve of it."

"We are not in a hotel. Some of my husband's friends from the Consulate happen to be away in Hamburg and we are renting their house for a month. It has worked out most conveniently."

The house was smart and new on the west of increasingly fashionable Sefton Park. Its drawing-room sported only an upright piano with singularly ugly candle-holders, but it had recently been tuned and provided sufficient volume for this confined space. The ladies numbered eight, ranging in age from seventeen to the middle sixties. Being wives or daughters of Paul Whitlaw's acquaintances in the Consulate and the American Chamber of Commerce, most of them were American. An ample girl in her twenties who announced that she could read music was set at Alan's left elbow to turn the pages for him. Each time she leaned forward she contrived to droop against him, then droop slowly and languorously back.

Alan played three Beethoven bagatelles and then, after a swift assessment of his audience, ten minutes of extemporised variations on a currently popular drawing-room ballad. This entranced the ladies and allowed him, as his fingers sought out trills and inversions and insidious key changes, to seek out in the polished rosewood front of the piano the ghostly reflection of Poppy with her head devoutly still, Poppy sliding towards a guest to pour a cup of tea, Poppy predatory and elongated because of the way she leaned first to one and then to the other. He left a dominant chord hanging in the air, resolved it, and then descended through a stairway of transpositions to a plaintive love song fleeing the original and telling that remote, ravishing reflection what he felt about her. At one cadence her eyes grew enormous in the dark panel; at another, she fled from him.

They were clapping. A large middle-aged lady bore down on him, beaming her appreciation, and explaining that she just happened to have brought with her the most exquisite little Italian soprano aria. Alan consented to accompany her. The girl at his left plucked irritably at the pages. To his right, Poppy swam ethereally beyond the top octave. The soprano sang a lyric printed inarguably in Italian but conveyed in an enunciation without language or meaning. But her friends applauded vociferously.

After two short dances by Schubert, Alan judged by the louder tinkling of teacups and the whisperings of his audience that it was time to bring the recital to a close. As he finished in a skittish six-eight time, he found that his heart was beating a conflicting rhythm. He wanted all of them off the premises so that he could be alone with Poppy. He was scared but ravenous.

221

Probably she would send him decorously away before the last of her lady guests had departed.

She did not.

When the thanks and compliments had faded off into the dying afternoon, she came back and smiled at him, inviting him to sigh and laugh with her, and without so much as a glance at the cups and cake plates and crumbs still on the tray and table she produced a bottle of champagne.

"You deserve it."

"To us," he said, exhausted and exhilarated.

She filled their glasses. Each took a sip, and she topped them up so that the bubbles frothed again.

"I imagine there are livelier ladies at your London matinees," she said. "And younger ones."

"Well . . . it's not quite like that."

"What is it like?"

He thought of the friend he lodged with, the son of a wine shipper who did business with Uncle Edmund. And of the music halls they had been to, the rollicking songs and solidly stamping rhythms; and the blowzy sluts who minced and postured behind the promenade rail or down the aisles. Twice he had been drunk enough to go along with Nick and Nick's notions; and for weeks had been terrified by the prospect of paternity or the pox.

"I haven't met anyone yet," he said.

"I do not believe that."

"No one," he said, "like you."

"You flatter too well to be a beginner."

"I love you." The way he threw it at her, it sounded an insult. "You'll think I'm mad. It's stupid, it makes no sense, none at all. Not in such a short time."

"Now you do not flatter. It is not nice to tell a lady you think it stupid to love her."

"Don't make fun of me."

He knocked his shin against the low table as he went to her, felt the pain of it and felt pain as he seized her and tried to kiss her and with the savagely swift pounce of a hawk she had dug her teeth through his jacket into his shoulder.

"Not here," she muttered against his throat.

She led him by the hand to the stairs and up to the landing with its opaque leaded window and a framed portrait of President Hayes. Alan tripped on the top step, and when her grip tightened he fell against the

222

bannister rail and tried to find his balance there—a balance he was losing in too many directions at once.

"Won't there be somebody, I mean someone about who . . ."

"My husband will not be back until very late, and there is nobody else in. I made sure of that."

"Made sure?"

She held him at the top of the stairs. "You wish to go back to your piano?"

He put his arms round her. She was motionless, but somehow gave out a reverberation of taut strings just losing their echo and waiting to be plucked again.

"Come," she said. He went with her to the door of a bedroom, and into the room, and there she released him. But only for a few seconds. "Come. Since there is nobody else, you must help me disrobe."

She was silently taunting him. As he fumbled, she lifted an arm, turned, put up one foot on a chair, and was solemn when he broke a fingernail and she ought to have been laughing. And when he had finished, she stood quite straight and calm, and let him feast his eyes and tremble. She was a cold and unapproachable goddess. He had wanted her to be revealed, and now she had let him unveil her he did not dare touch her.

"It is time for you to practise," she murmured. "As you practise the piano."

"I love you."

"It is too big a word."

"I swear to you—"

"You practise fingering of the piano, and so the feeling of the music grows real, yes?" She captured his hand and directed it. "There. Now you practise other fingering." Her mouth was no longer lax and slumbrous but shaping into a tight pout as if to inhale him. "Ah, yes, I think you make a talented pupil."

On the bed it was her stillness that stung him most cruelly. When she moved at all it was with the complacent laziness of a cat, but that slow twist of her belly was more inflammatory than all the bouncing and squealing of the London drabs he had known. He wanted to torture some response from her. She opened her lips and gasped twice, but somehow that was patronising him: her disparaging eyes demanded more, watched him and awarded him a few points, insisted that he prove something.

Afterwards, when her body had lost its chill and he could be proud that he was the one who had heated it, he longed for everything to go on

223

and on, so that next time he would make her close her eyes and surrender and demand no more proofs.

"Do you love me?"

"You know how to please," she said. "I like to be pleased."

"You won't go away?"

She propped herself up on one elbow. "When the time comes I go back to America. You know that. I have a home and a daughter, and my husband must make his living there."

"You can't want to go back. You can't love him. Not if . . ."

"If?"

"Not if you're here with me. Like this."

"Do not spoil this. Please."

Memories dripped into his mind, splashing and irregular, in no kind of order. He said, "Why did you go away?"

"I married. I have said, my husband works in America. It is simple."

"Once," said Alan, "I thought you and my parents weren't friends. When I was little I heard them shouting about something, about you having to leave Liverpool . . . I *did* hear them, I'm sure."

"How much did you hear?"

"Not enough to understand. What was there to be so cross about?"

"There was me."

"But why was mother so angry?"

"She had no reason for anger. I was the one who lost."

"Lost what?"

"Your father. I was foolish. I believed, once, that your father would marry me."

"But why didn't he? You're not saying—"

"She captured him," said Poppy, "while they were both away in America. And later she arranged for me to sell myself to an American."

"But if you hadn't wanted to give in, how could she have made you? After all, you all sounded cheerful enough later—not so long later. I remember that, too."

"Of course," said Poppy expressionlessly, "it was your mother's doing. Of course she was cheerful when it worked out to her satisfaction. She arranged it, just as she has arranged so many things. Like your concert. And your career—but not too much of a career, no? She will arrange your life if you do not take care. Your life, everything."

Desire was already stirring in him again. But he had to ask again, "So you didn't love him, you don't love him, you *don't*?"

"You waste time. And that is wasting life."

She thrust one leg further under him, to one side, and sprawled her arms wide on the pillow above her head.

224

At the instant when his body was convulsed and the sounds he made were hardly human, he heard through his own tumult her reflective, dispassionate voice burning him like ice: "I lost one. So perhaps I have the loan of another? Repay with interest, yes?"

He walked home so that he could sing out loud and beat time with his roll of music. Three boys in the gutter sniggered and began to imitate him, but ran off when he brandished the music at them. A dignified couple pausing halfway up their front steps looked down censoriously, debating whether or not to summon a constable.

At the gates of Bostock's Brow he tugged his collar straight and tried to adopt a more sober stride.

Beside the lodge stood a young couple with their backs to him, diffidently surveying the drive and the house. There was no sign of Debney, the gatekeeper and gardener who had taken over after Mr. and Mrs. Watson were pensioned off.

"May I help you?"

They started. The young man wheeled round.

"Would this be the Gresham residence?"

"It would."

"I'm aiming to renew the acquaintance of Mrs. Malcolm Gresham." Some of his syllables had a faint twang that reminded Alan of a Providence violinist who had studied at the Academy for two terms; others were oddly Yorkshire. "That's what she is now, I know. Though for a while"—he smiled an invitation to Alan to share some obscure joke—"she called herself Mrs. Fenwick."

"It must be my mother you're talking about. But I don't know that she was ever called Fenwick."

"Miss Bostock, then?"

"That was my mother's maiden name, yes."

His hand was vigorously shaken. "I'm pleased to meet you, Mr. Gresham. My name is Fenwick, anyway—George Fenwick. And this is my sister Louisa."

The girl could not have been in more complete contrast to the slim, worldly woman Alan had just left. Short and plump, perhaps Alan's age or a year or two older, she had a fresh face with a snub nose and a dimple in her chin, puckered in too deep for beauty. Her breasts were full and heavy beneath her sealskin jacket, emphasised by her jaunty stance and the tilt of her straw hat. George Fenwick, perhaps ten years older, had tried to age his face further by cultivating gingery, well-trimmed side whiskers. He wore a broad-brimmed hat, a cutaway jacket and waistcoat in subdued blue and green checks, and broad-banded trousers.

"Is my mother expecting you?"

"I'm afraid we've given her no warning, no. We're not long off the boat."

"From America?"

"From Philadelphia. Your mother got my sisters and me across to that side of the water, and I thought maybe she'd like to know how we've been getting along. If she could spare us just the time to present our compliments, and good wishes from my father . . ."

"I'll take you in."

The girl was a good twelve inches shorter than Alan. Her straw hat slanted even more coquettishly as she glanced up at him; but her smile was shy, and after that one glance she turned her attention to the hall as they went through it, and looked up in admiration at the moulded ceiling of the drawing-room.

So far she had not uttered a word.

Somewhere not long ago, yesterday or the day before or the day before that, he had wanted to be left alone to unravel the counterpoint of an evening and not have to be polite to anyone, not even a Mrs. Whitlaw. Here, now, he wanted to be alone so that he could pace up and down in his room with his skin burning harsh and dry and then sweating in memory of Poppy—Mrs. Whitlaw was nonexistent—but there were other formalities being thrust on him. He went in search of his mother, and found her in the library with Jesse, poring over sectional diagrams of tandem compound engines. She was reluctant to be distracted; and then began to crackle like a swift-burning fuse at the thought of the Fenwicks,

227

abandoned Jesse, and hurried ahead of Alan towards the drawing-room.

"Goodness, how you've grown!" About to shake hands with George, she could not restrain herself and threw her arms round him. The tear that sprang to her eye was reflected in his. "It seems only yesterday."

"This is my sister Louisa."

"But I remember the girls as Mary and Charlotte. And you, my dear, you don't look like . . . But of course. I did have a letter from your father telling me that he was remarrying. Louisa must be—"

"Actually, ma'am, my stepsister. Just a baby when my father married her mother."

· George smiled reassuringly at the girl. She wrinkled her nose, and the cleft in her chin deepened.

"And you're bringing her to visit your old homeland." Nell could spare no more than a nod for Louisa. She could hardly take her eyes off the young man. "It's so unexpected. So long since I heard from your father. We've all been so busy, haven't we? But sit down, do sit down. And you've got to tell me everything that's happened."

She rang for the sherry decanter to be brought, but both Fenwicks declined a glass. With the decanter came Alan's grandmother. Installed here since Speke's death and the loss of Orrell Manor and most of its contents, she was alert to any uncustomary sound or movement in the house. Unable to confine herself to her own small suite, she made a dozen forays a day into other rooms and corridors, sniffing out anything unusual and unwelcome.

"Mother, I've told you about George Fenwick and his sisters."

"No, dear, you haven't."

"The three children I took to New York all those years ago. When Malcolm followed me over. Oh, you must remember."

"Oh, that." Julia blinked condemnation at George and Louisa. "Yes, that was how it all started. Hm. Running off like that, I've never got over it. Never. And you're no better now, Eleanor. You didn't tell me anyone would be calling. Not a word." She looked from one to the other. "You said there were three. There are only two."

"Mother, George has brought his stepsister. The other two . . ."

Nell had to stop, not yet having been told how Mary and Charlotte were faring.

"I dare say," said Julia inconsequentially. "I dare say." And left the room.

"How *are* Mary and Charlotte?" asked Nell. "There's so much I want to know."

Alan settled himself on the fireside stool, apart from the others. He half-listened to George Fenwick's brisk, enthusiastic voice, but allowed

228

part of his mind to drift back over the afternoon, into bed and Poppy. Then he noticed that Louisa, though nodding confirmation every now and then of some point made by her stepbrother, was eyeing him and venturing an occasional little grin. She could not possbily know what he was thinking—could not possibly see Poppy sprawled across his mind like the slender figurehead restored to its original beauty—but somehow she was inviting him back, inviting his complicity. In what? He realised that, while she knew and approved of every word George was saying, she was gently amused by his fervour. She was quiet and demure, but no fool. Alan's mother seemed almost more dependent on George—as if she needed the security of knowing he was alive and well, and hearing of what he had been doing, and assuring herself it had all been worthwhile.

It appeared that some years after his speedy remarriage, Thomas Fenwick had worked in Albany, and as soon as his son was old enough had found him a job on the railroad. Then the family moved to Minnesota, which the railroad companies were virtually colonising as they pushed ever outwards. Even in England Alan had seen emigration newspapers and posters declaiming the virtues of these new paradises, waiting only for vigorous and ambitious men to open them up. Himself employed by the Pennsylvania Railroad, George earnestly explained how many a line had to create its own users: by encouraging settlement and the growth of towns along and ahead of its track, it guaranteed future freight and passengers. Men were coaxed from the eastern seaboard by promises of a richer and more spacious environment.

But George had not wanted to push his pioneering energy quite so far. He had found his way to Philadelphia, he was rising through the company ranks there, and stayed on to become an assistant superintendent.

During the Civil War his father had been injured, but had fought on, and in peacetime refused to let his wanderlust be crippled. Now, in George's world, another war had been going on: a war of conflicting companies and would-be monopolists, with Vanderbilt's New York Central granting concessions to some customers and reducing others to penury while Vanderbilt openly said, "The public be damned"; fly-by-night companies laying track in order to sell it off to existing operators; and the Pennsylvania Railroad giving battle to Rockefeller and Standard Oil, losing, and facing an internal battle when its own employees fomented a strike. But now the Pennsy was rebuilding and reorganising. And, George went on with an ardent loyalty that brought a glow to Nell's cheeks, Pennsy investment in the American Line was making the Philadelphia-to-Liverpool steamship service virtually an extension of the railroad—without any need of postal or other government subsidies.

"That's what Brunel tried to do with the Great Western," said Nell wistfully. "A man too far ahead of his time."

"And now Louisa's come back east and into the company." George's loud harangue mellowed. "She wasn't ever much content with Minnesota." Alan heard the different undertone, like a subtle but strengthening change of key. George's protectiveness towards his stepsister was heartwarming. "We always got on fine—I think I spoilt her, so she came running back. Right?"

Louisa cocked her head and chuckled. "Wrong." In just that one syllable she managed a perky little trill.

"She was such a baby"—George was sparring affectionately with her— "*someone* had to look after her. Mary and Charlotte were still so busy settling into a new way of life, and this poor little scrap . . ."

"I was a very big scrap," said Louisa. "They were always telling me what a lump I was."

They grinned a shared joke at each other.

As George went on to tell how Mary had married, but Charlotte had turned out not to be the marrying type and preferred to stay at home helping her stepmother, Alan wondered if his mother heard the same resonances as he did. George, loyal to his family as to his employers, did not in so many words say that his sisters Mary and Charlotte had not taken too kindly to the baby girl who was not even their own flesh and blood. But there was something veiled in his undertone as he described the crowded house that was their first taste of the New World, and when he talked of Charlotte's meticulous housekeeping.

"Very good at keeping us all in order, was our Charlotte."

"She's a cat." Louisa said it without viciousness, just as plain fact.

"It made better sense," said George easily, "for Louisa to come back east. We've got rooms in the same tenement, where I can keep an eye on her—"

"And me on you."

"She can find work to her taste, and not be got at all the time." He smiled to show that he was exaggerating, but you could tell he wasn't.

Nell said, "And what sort of work is to your taste?"

"I've just begun, ma'am, as a stewardess. This is my first voyage."

"On what line?"

"The American Line. George wouldn't think of no other." Her voice was fresh and light.

"But you should have let us know. I could have put in a word at the start and got you a good position on one of our own liners. It's not too late, if you'd like—"

"Thank you, Mrs. Gresham," said George firmly, "but my father wouldn't have wished that."

"He's had good reason to trust me."

"That he has, ma'am. And does. He's never stopped following the progress of Gresham-Bostock, that I can tell you. At home he keeps a book of cuttings, reads it all the time. Any reference in a newspaper, or some engraving or photograph, he'll clip it and keep it, and I regularly send him cuttings from the shipping news."

"Then why—"

"You did more than enough for us. We stand on our own feet now—all of us and each of us. But when we got to Liverpool I just had to bring Louisa to see you."

"So you're chaperoning her on her first voyage?"

"Just to see how she makes out this first time."

Nell waited for a contribution from Louisa, then prompted, "Was it too tiring, the first time?"

"Only avoiding the men's hands," said Louisa. "That's enough to tire any girl."

Alan laughed. His mother nodded, but the only smile she allowed herself was when she turned back to George.

"You'll both stay for supper, of course."

"Thank you, but we'll not keep you any longer."

"But my husband will want to see you again. You remember all those stories of his, George?"

"Never forgotten 'em, ma'am. None of us ever forgot."

"You must stay."

"They'll be angry if I'm not back," said Louisa, "and soon. I have to be aboard to tidy up and get ready for heading back west."

"They drive you hard?"

"We aim to be the best," said George.

Again Louisa shared a furtive smile with Alan, but there was no doubting her hero-worship of her stepbrother.

When they had gone, after many reassurances of calling again on another voyage, when there was more time to spare, Nell sat wiping her eyes and looking back into a world before Alan was born.

"He always was a sound lad," she said. "A brave one. A man before he'd had a chance of being a boy."

"He was very sweet with Louisa," Alan commented.

"Just like him, yes. Rather a saucy young woman, I thought. I can imagine her, rather than Charlotte, being the troublesome one at home. And I can imagine the other two girls guessing early on."

231

"Guessing what?"

"You'll notice George never said a word about his stepmother being a widow."

"Then what . . . oh, now, mother! You've no right to jump to such conclusions. I don't suppose for a minute—"

"It's none of our business and we mustn't go on about it," Nell decided belatedly. "And I don't suppose we shall ever see them again, either of them."

But George Fenwick had kindled a spark in Nell's mind that was fanned to a blaze when Edmund and the Whitlaws dined with them on the Saturday evening.

"It confirms what I've been telling all of you. The emigrant trade and the holiday trade—and the regular business trips—they all need longer range planning than anyone has yet attempted. All the big industries and communications in America are being drawn together in pools and trusts to monopolise the different sectors of the economy. The railroads and the oil business are already falling into a few grasping hands. Shipping will be next. Pennsylvania operate the American Line. There'll be others—and then a battle to control them under one overlord. What they're achieving on dry land, they can soon achieve on the ocean, unless we give battle before they leave port."

"In battle," commented Paul Whitlaw, "you need troops, and ammunition, and lines of communication."

"We have the troops—ourselves and our crews. The ammunition is the service we supply—competitive and in the long run superior to anyone else's. And lines of communication? We want to push those lines as far as they will go. Mr. Thomas Cook is doing very nicely, thank you, with his all-in holiday tours. But there's a lot of educational lecturing, and prayers at meals, and living in tents—very high-minded, but not what most travellers want. And why should we allow a middleman to cream off the profits? *We* make a contract with railway companies and hotels; *we* call the tune instead of letting the railroad men do it; and *we* offer new amenities on board so that the journey by ship is an integral part of the holiday, not just an uncomfortable way of getting from one place to another."

Edmund intervened, "Everybody else is advocating retrenchment at the moment. We've already had approaches from some of the other lines suggesting that we share our Transatlantic schedules and stand off half our men, so that we don't all go bankrupt."

"Retrench?" said Nell scornfully. "We expand, not cut down. We can build better ships, more cheaply, than the Americans. And keep the shipyards in work. And ourselves on the ocean. You know what that man Carnegie said."

"Don't be absurd, dear," said Julia from the far end of the table.

"He said you should put all your eggs in one basket—and watch the basket."

"There are far too many things that need watching," said Edmund. "The Germans—"

"The Germans are using the Channel route, and Liverpool still appeals to more travellers and businessmen than Southampton will ever do in *our* lifetime."

Alan felt he had been playing the same mute role, in the same situation, for days or weeks now. After his concert he had sat watching Poppy while his mother turned the conversation to business and sat exchanging amiable little grins with that girl Louisa while George Fenwick fired his mother's enthusiasm again. And now once more, against that same incidental music, he was trying to read in the ivory sculpture of Poppy's face some acknowledgment of her feelings.

His grandmother was protesting, "Eleanor, do we have to have this sort of conversation at mealtimes? I'm sure Mrs. Whitlaw is bored, and I can see Alan is. It's a pity we can't talk about music, or listen to it—you'll play for us later, dear?—something higher than this coarse marketplace haggling all the time."

Jesse, who had been absorbed in his mother's words, said, "The firm'll need someone in the marketplace if Alan's going to continue spending money without making any."

"What a cruel thing to say, Jesse."

Jesse winked at his twin. Alan knew the remark had been unmalicious—but sincere, all the same.

"It's so unwomanly, Eleanor," his grandmother continued. "And so dull. A lady should never be dull."

"I never find it dull. Nothing is ever the same two days running." Alan turned away from Poppy, realising how beautiful his mother was with her high colour, her eyes shining. "To see the successes and the failures, the things that work out and those that nearly work out and then offer a new challenge—can't you understand the pleasure of it?"

Malcolm leaned forward to pat her hand. Edmund nodded agreement.

Poppy said, with the deep richness of a viola carrying a theme out from a tangled counterpoint, "I could not feel so. Love or hate about business, no, I do not understand."

"No," said her husband, "you don't, do you?"

233

Malcolm laughed. "You don't know how lucky you are, Paul."

"For me," said Poppy, "I could apply such passion only to something personal."

The light in Nell's eyes grew steely. "Whereas I could never turn all my attention to a purely personal matter."

"No? But I am sure you have done, sometimes."

By the end of the meal it had been decided that Edmund should accompany the Whitlaws on their return to New York. "I'd love to go myself, but . . ." Nell pressed her hands to her stomach, and her mother frowned. Paul Whitlaw would, Nell decreed, make enquiries and introductions on Edmund's behalf. He was to be given first chance, for his company or himself, of investment in any subsequent partnership. A new joint organisation there would have to be: no wholly English-owned company would be allowed to make binding decisions on the use of American transport on American territory—use of railroads, highways, rivers and canals—any more than the Anchor Line in England had been prepared, a few years ago, to let the Pennsylvania Railroad take it over and then keep all books and decision-making in Philadelphia.

"If only I could go myself!"

Nell was to say this a dozen times in the next week. Alan unhappily echoed her wish. For the first time he was not looking forward to returning to London and the atmosphere where music was all, not merely a polite accomplishment for the leisured children of merchants. He would sooner have set out across the ocean with Poppy.

With her husband close at hand all the time?

He found it barely possible to look at Paul Whitlaw when they met, or to think of him with his wife.

There were interminable meetings now to draft plans and tentative costings. Nell had declared that Edmund must have a free hand to make all decisions on the spot; but before he left she was endeavouring to make as many decisions as possible in advance. At least this allowed Poppy plenty of free time. Time for Alan to visit her, hurrying off to Sefton Park and never knowing exactly how she would receive him: dressed as if for walking, or calmly reading and pretending surprise at his arrival; or leaving the door ajar and calling down so that he would climb the stairs to find her face down, naked, on the bed. Then there would be that little giggle of hers, and she would say into the pillow, "You will come in, yes?" as if, once upon a time, she had been taught the phrase like a parrot and found it easier than any other.

Three days before the party was due to leave for New York, Edmund slipped awkwardly from his horse on the cobbles near his old counting-house, tearing an ankle ligament. It was severe enough to make any longer journey inadvisable for some weeks.

"I shall have to go after all," declared Nell.

"You will not," said her husband. "We'll run no risks with *this* one."

"I'll be as careful as I can."

"I'll go," he said. "This time I'll take charge."

Alan sensed the tension between them. Then his mother brightened. "Take Jesse along. It's time he got a broader picture of our work. It'll be good for him."

"And wouldn't it be good for me, too?" Alan demanded.

His mother was taken aback. "Oh, but my dear, what do you suppose *you* would learn?" She reached out an affectionate hand. "Besides, you're going back to the Academy on Tuesday."

When Alan visited Poppy for the last time, hurriedly and savagely and with little time to savour her because Paul would be back within the hour, out of his general wretchedness he carped, "You'll not be getting fond of my father again, while the two of you are away?"

"I shall have a husband with me."

"Yes, but . . ." He rolled away from her and made a declamatory wave about the bedroom.

Her long musing silence frightened him. Achingly he realised that in loaning him her body she had yielded nothing of her true self. The time was coming for her to leave, and he could not be sure that she would give him one more thought once she was aboard ship.

"You did say"—he could not leave it alone—"that once my father might have married you."

"Once. Not now. And your mother is averting any danger by sending your brother as chaperon."

"If you had the opportunity, though . . ."

She reached out for him, as if to touch him for the last time and leave the memory of her flesh on his. "So you are jealous? Already you learn so much."

In the bustle of farewells at Bostock's Brow, Alan's father reserved a surprise for the last. With the cases in the hall, and Jesse chafing on the doorstep, he took a bulky parcel from the oak chest below the stairs and with a solemn bow presented it to Nell. He was chuckling and snapping his fingers as he usually did when concocting some impetuous treat, more eager than the recipient for it to be revealed and enjoyed. Alan re-membered occasions when he and Jesse had been gathered up with their mother and rushed off across the Mersey as if father had only recently discovered the joys of the ferry-boats and the existence of the Wirral sandhills and heaths. Repeatedly there had been his mother's protesting laughter, coaxed out of her grim preoccupation with weightier matters, and her wail of "Oh, Malcolm, you're impossible," which invariably led to a few hours of unexpected, uncomplicated joy for all of them.

His mother opened the box. Inside was a folding stereoscope and a set of stereographs.

"Views of New York," Malcolm announced gleefully. "The second one down, you'll find, is a picture of Broadway. Showing our hotel—remember? So if you get lonely while I'm away you can sit down and revisit old scenes. And remember."

She kissed him brusquely, almost chiding him, and they went out together on to the step where Jesse's impatience threatened to blow its safety valve.

"Do look after your father," she said.

IT HAD been a long time since he last set foot on the deck of an outward-bound vessel. Far too long, thought Malcolm as he leaned on the rail and watched Liverpool recede into a thin September drizzle. He had been on and off Gresham-Bostock steamers half-finished in the shipyards, had boarded them on arrival from New York or as they prepared to leave dock, checking and revising estimates or noting defects and repair needs; but not free as he had once been to cast off and head for the heavy swells of far oceans.

He was glad that Edmund had not seriously injured himself, but also glad it was Edmund who remained shorebound while he himself had been released on to the water.

In the years since he gave up his carefree voyaging, vast strides had been made in the construction of ships and their engines. He had known all the facts, supervised many a building programme and launching ceremony, watched the transition from paddle to screw and wood to iron, but until now had not actually felt under his feet a truly modern liner at full power. The *Philippa* was a 5000-ton iron screw steamer, still only two years in service, with four-cylinder compound engines that almost halved the coal consumption of earlier Gresham-Bostock craft. This had been every company's priority: competition on the Atlantic had trebled the price of coal, and to stay in business one had to find ways of pushing up speed and capacity while cutting down costs.

"Father, are we going to try for the Blue Riband on this trip?"

Jesse was beside him, pausing during what must be his third or fourth circuit of the ship. Allowed only once into the engine room along with Malcolm and the chief engineer, he was making up for it by inspecting the compact hospital bay, the ice house, the saloon and the dining-room over and over again, comparing details with sectional plans he had brought with him.

"We're not out to break any records," said his father.

"But we've got the power. We *might* just do it."

"Our motto has always been comfort and safety."

"But we can have that and speed as well, nowadays." Side by side they looked out at the rise and fall of the horizon, and the dark green plain that was beginning to undulate and break up into troughs and ridges. A few swooping gulls still followed in their wake, but would soon be turning back. "Wouldn't mother be pleased," said Jesse, "if we could bring that home for her?"

"Not if it shook the ship apart, she wouldn't."

"Dad, we're not fitting engines into old wooden bottoms any more, you know."

Yes, he knew. He knew, also, about stresses and strains and fuel consumption. But to Jesse, learning fast and showing so much promise, it was all fresh and challenging. He made a move to pat his son on the shoulder, but Jesse had stayed long enough and was heading for the saloon.

Part of a long central deckhouse with wide square windows on either side, the saloon bathed also in added light from a stained glass cupola in the roof, mellowing the dark crimson of padded benches and deep carpeting. A piano stood for'ard, secured against the roll of the ship. Malcolm followed Jesse in and around a mahogany rail guarding the stairwell that led to the first-class staterooms below.

"Everything shipshape, Mr. Gresham?"

Captain Wade had come in behind them, demanding rather than inviting praise of his vessel.

He was a man of some six feet in height, with a chest and shoulders which must have set tailors quite a task. Voluminous whiskers starting high on his cheeks were combed so that they streamed gracefully down across his lapels, framing a clean-shaven chin and genial lower lip. Wade had been lured away from the flourishing White Star Line after what he considered an unwarrantable reprimand for recklessness leading to an engine explosion. Edmund had gone carefully into the matter and formed his own opinion. Gresham-Bostock wanted no recklessness, but they did need commanders with determination and some style. Many regular passengers now chose between the various Transatlantic companies on the strength of their favourite captain—especially when the wives had the last say. The man's man of the windjammers had become the ladies' man of the liners.

"What sort of crossing do you think we'll have, sir?" Jesse stood virtually to attention in admiration of the imposing figure before him.

"Oh, we've got no worries, not at this time o' year. The glass is pretty steady at the moment. Should be an enjoyable voyage, I'd say." His gaze strayed to one of the windows. "Most enjoyable."

Poppy was strolling along the deck outside. There was no sign of her husband.

That evening at the captain's table, Poppy had been positioned beside Wade. He was an accomplished campaigner. Flatteringly attentive to the husband for several minutes on end, he then drew his prey towards his net with the most courteous, civilised observations, turned his attention suavely to other guests, but with a sly flanking movement was soon back where he had always meant to make the kill.

A piano in the dining-room provided unobtrusive accompaniment to the meal. After dinner, when well-fed travellers had adjourned to the saloon, the pianist was augmented there by two second stewards, one with a violin, the other with a cello. The trio would continue playing until the last passengers had retired to their cabins.

From time to time Captain Wade regulated a spattering of applause at soloist or trio, or nodded approval of a sentimental tune, most of his nods being directed at Poppy.

He had made his choice. Stewards, barmen and maids on the *Philippa* received tips, gratuities and the occasional condescension of a compliment. The commander's bonus was derived from the frills and scents and flirtatious admiration of the ladies under his care, from whom he selected the one whose company would prove most delectable for the forthcoming seven or eight days. He must not show himself too single-minded: scores of other ladies, married or otherwise, might not care to patronise his ship again. There had to be a fair rationing of smiles, jokes, glances and innuendoes. Young women on their first voyage liked a comforting arm round their waist from time to time, and the assurance that the juddering of the ship through a heavy swell did not mean that the keel was scraping over the rocks. Elderly widows liked him in earnest, stalwart mood—or, occasionally, proved to be women of the world with a taste for hard liquor and late-night drinking sessions, which the master had to steer between the twin hazards of quarrelsomeness and maudlin collapse. But always there would be the one belle, the truly feminine feather in his cap, the companion he most needed to impress, while her mere decorative presence at his side impressed everyone else.

Malcolm watched with nostalgic amusement. He felt some delightful twinges of memory, but not jealousy. In a way he was proud of Poppy: was she not to a large extent his creation?

At the ship's concert Captain Wade performed a rousing baritone solo, and while everyone else was clapping noisily he sought the approval of Poppy's eyes. Then Paul Whitlaw stepped forward, consulted the pianist, and hushed the audience with a finely articulated rendering of *Come Where My Love Lies Dreaming*. His clear tenor lacked the thunderous masculinity of Wade's baritone, but he made up for this with the unabashed fervour of his singing—almost as if Stephen Foster's plaintive little love song had, for a few minutes, attained the significance of the National Anthem. And he, too, sang directly and unashamedly at Poppy, but in a way that made Malcolm uneasy. There was an imperiousness in his look, not expressing tender sentiments to his wife but reminding her that she *was* his wife.

The following morning Malcolm encountered Poppy and Wade together. The captain offered her his telescope and his arm was around her, his fingers closed on her wrist as he guided the glass towards a faint, far speck of sail on the ocean. When they parted, Poppy sauntered along the boat deck near Malcolm.

"Paul will need to keep an eye on you," he said. "These skippers like to make a new conquest every voyage."

"Voyages are shorter than they used to be."

"Still long enough for a dashing commander like that."

"I was thinking," she said distantly, "of the *Naomi*. Things were better then, when we had all the time in the world."

"Yes, well." He had not expected this, and was still not used to her fluency, so different from those hesitant little phrases he had taught her for his private pleasure. "Good times, weren't they?"

"It was wrong they must end."

"Oh, but in the end it was all for the best. For both of us."

"Wicked," she said.

Heavier rollers were beginning to tax the ship's energy. The engines pounded more forcefully, and spray whipped in along the line of lifeboats as the *Philippa* dipped first to port, then to starboard. Malcolm turned his head to savour the wind whistling cold through his teeth. When Poppy spoke, the words were snatched away and he smiled cheerfully, spreading his arms to show that he had heard nothing.

She said it again, clearly: "I loved you."

"It was a wonderful interlude." He tried to dismiss it with a brotherly smile.

"An interlude?" To make themselves heard in the rising wind they had to move closer together in the lee of the deckhouse. Poppy clung to the deckhouse rail with white knuckles. "That is what you think, it was no more than that?"

"Poppy, you're happily settled with a prosperous husband, an interesting life—"

"I loved you." Her head was menacingly close to his. "I was your slave, I did all you asked, and also I loved you. You marry someone else, and still I love you. Yes, you marry—on the whim of a moment, or because you are too weak to resist her trap—"

"No, that's not true. I won't have you say that about Nell."

"I must not speak against your wife? You married her for love, then?"

"Why else should one marry?"

Poppy's eyes drooped shut, against the wind or against the pain of memory. "So for you it is happiness. You marry. And even then I accept. I accept the humiliation, shut away, a secret mistress. But still you betray me again. You let your wife dispose of me to that . . . to Paul Whitlaw."

"You didn't have to marry him if you didn't want to."

"What else could I do?"

"If you didn't love him—"

"I loved *you*. I told you so. Oh, so many times."

"I taught you to say it, yes."

"And you think I am only a parrot? I say it and do not mean or understand a word of it?"

"I'm sure," he said feebly, "that Paul's made you a better husband than I ever would have done."

"He marries me because it is a noble gesture. But now he is ashamed. When business goes wrong it is my fault because he married me, because his colleagues despise him. Oh, yes, they all want me for themselves, but they despise him for having me—for having had to *marry* me. He blames himself for that, and blames me even more."

"Oh, we all have rows of that kind. Whose fault this is, and whose fault that is. It clears the air."

"He is cold. And petty."

"Perhaps you're not going about things the right way. I mean, maybe he doesn't understand the way you have with you. If you could be a bit warmer yourself, a bit less . . . well, remote from us mortals . . . "

Her eyes opened. He regretted speaking to her, and letting it get this far. She said, "Malcolm. Tell me. What do you mean?"

"Well, you were always wonderful. Nobody like you. But . . . "

"Yes? But?"

"Oh, damn it." He was not going to be goaded like this. "You were compliant, all right, you did do anything, everything. But it was always cold. That was part of what was so special about you. Cool, and soothing. I once explained that to Nell."

"You once explained it to her?"

"She wouldn't believe me."

"But your wife is not cold? And not soothing? You must tell me what it is that makes her so much better than me."

"I didn't say better. But different. Right for a wife."

"Yes?"

"She's warm," he shouted, "and . . . and *cuddly*."

When he had said it he wanted to laugh, and thought Poppy would burst out laughing. But she did not. Here was a word she assuredly did not understand. Even if she had ever been taught it, the meaning escaped her.

"Look, my dear," he entreated, "let's not distort it all. Remember how good it was. I remember, I'll always remember you as a woman in a million. Or shall we say ten million?" Still she was not laughing, nor smiling. "There isn't a woman in the world," he said, "who couldn't take lessons from you."

"Your Nell," she said, "will have her lesson one day. I promise it. And if I could put a curse on each and every one of your family, so that indeed you would remember . . . "

Poppy's right hand came away from the rail. With slow deliberation she raised it and clawed long talons down his face, not in an immediate rage but seeming to calculate how she might best mark him for life. Then she moved past him, and even on this pitching deck she was not walking, or reeling and groping like most would do in such seas, but somehow making her own devious yet dedicated way back to her husband and their cabin and whatever that all meant.

Mopping the bloody streaks from his face, Malcolm pushed towards the bows and the antiseptic scour of the wind.

It roared in his mouth and in his mind. How true it had been, what he had said about Nell. How true their love. Even when they fought, when he was most incensed by her devotion to the business and her scant courtesy to himself, he loved the game they played, the knowledge of how he could weaken her and then love her all the more, of how she could surrender—in this battle if not for the entire conflict—and become all the more ravishing, and more willingly ravished. *Cuddly* . . . such an absurd word, but so right for her when she had been laughingly coaxed into his arms. That was how she had been the night this new child of theirs was conceived. Malcolm was sure he could identify the exact date: it had been such a warm, rich, loving, perfect night.

242

The sea wind struck cold, but he was conscious of only one chill: far away, unable to seize her and impetuously heap extravagances on her, he wondered if she really knew how much she meant to him. Had he told her loudly enough, directly enough, often enough?

It was ludicrous that he should have told Poppy so directly what he had perhaps never told Nell, perhaps never so clearly said to himself.

In the cabin, after he had washed his face and ruefully inspected the remaining damage, Jesse came in and said, "What have you been doing to yourself, dad? Looks as if you've been fighting off pirates. I didn't know they still carried cutlasses."

"That big roller ten minutes ago—threw me against a wire rope."

As if Poppy's summons had been obeyed, a gale was greedily hovering over the Gresham-Bostock liner. The heavens to the west were suffused with a darkness that appeared to rise like boiling ink from the sea itself. The line of the horizon was sucked into a thick bank of cloud, which, fed with the mounting blackness, began to pile higher and higher across the *Philippa's* course. Waves as mountainous as the clouds poured vicious avalanches over the bows and streamed away through bubbling scuppers. Incongruously the *Philippa* seemed to cram on speed.

"Malcolm," Paul Whitlaw said, "I think your captain is pushing this ship too hard."

"He knows what he's doing."

"Or else he's too mighty confident of himself to know what he's doing."

Venomous dark streamers of cloud curled out from the monstrous mass and stabbed forked tongues down on the mastheads, snapping like black serpents around the two funnels.

Jesse said, "Dad, you know Captain Wade's really got his heart set on the Blue Riband, come hell or high water?"

"Where did you pick up that sort of talk?"

"From . . ." Jesse faltered.

"From Captain Wade, no doubt," said Paul austerely.

A wave fell short, scooped under the bows, and lifted the ship so that cabin doors flew open and began to bang riotously, two sofas in the saloon broke loose, and a screaming woman was toppled down the staircase as she tried to claw her way up from the stateroom deck. The whole fabric of the hull shuddered. Striving on, the *Philippa* sheared across the crests of three wave ridges and then plunged down again into a wide-mouthed devourer. The screw seemed to lose its grip, dug, raced, spun and gripped again.

Captain Wade paced through the passenger quarters exuding confidence.

In the saloon he patted Jesse on the head and beamed. "Well, young man, getting a taste for the sea?"

Paul Whitlaw, his hip wedged against the stairwell rail, said, "Aren't you driving this ship too hard, captain?"

"We lose way now, sir, and this storm'll push us back to Liverpool."

"Even so—"

"The sooner we get to New York, the sooner those dear ladies will stop being seasick."

Again they sheared a series of crests, and the vibration struck ghostly resonances from the piano, reminding Malcolm of something Alan had played only a few evenings before departure: mournful yet captivating, full of longing.

Poppy appeared beside her husband, a slim statue against stormy light through the salt-caked ports.

"You think we might still win the Blue Riband, captain?" Jesse was asking.

"You'd like to take it home as a present, eh?"

Jesse looked eagerly at his father. Paul Whitlaw, over his head, said, "Malcolm, I'm of the opinion Mrs. Gresham wouldn't approve of this."

"My wife doesn't happen to be with us."

"If she were, don't you reckon she'd be ordering us to slow down?"

Poppy's head drifted into shadowy silhouette between Malcolm and Captain Wade. A lurch of the ship, and she stumbled, falling against Wade and steadying herself with one hand on his shoulder.

"Surely," she said, "we can't go *much* slower? It's taking an age."

The camber of the deck was to starboard now, but Poppy still clung to the captain. When her husband edged towards her she affected not to see him. Her lower lip stuck out a fraction — at Malcolm.

"Captain," he said, "I'm not one to question your judgment, but—"

"I'm obliged to you, sir, for not questioning my judgment."

"Mr. Gresham was quite a bold sea-dog when he was younger," said Poppy, "before he lost his sea-legs."

"Oh, a man never quite does that, ma'am." Wade tried a bluff, mollifying smile at Malcolm. "Besides, this is nothing like as rough as it used to be on the old barques, eh, Mr. Gresham?"

"Nothing like," said Poppy, still for Malcolm's benefit.

That night one of the electric cabin bells began to ring incessantly of its own accord. When it had been cut off, half the other bells ceased to work. Several more cabin doors sprang loose and set up an insomniac banging. Nervous passengers, escaping the confinement of their cabins and staterooms, congregated in the saloon. Two groups with feet and elbows rammed against the tables tried to play euchre. The gas jets sputtered and swayed, and there was a smell of scorching varnish where one had cracked its glass and was licking against the panelling.

Next morning offered no respite. Captain Wade was boisterous and cheerful as he paced and reeled from one unhappy cluster of passengers to another. But when Malcolm came upon him in the lee of the aft funnel, standing so that he sheltered Poppy Whitlaw from erratic gusts of the searching wind, his mask had crumpled into quite another, deeply creased mould.

"Captain, wouldn't you be better occupied on the bridge?"

Wade shuddered as Malcolm's words struck him like an unexpected cross sea. "I've got every confidence in Mr. Crampton up there. And you did say you weren't one to question my judgment."

"For the passengers' sake," shouted Malcolm, "and the ship's sake, I think we should reduce speed."

The door nearest to them in the deckhouse swung very slowly and heavily open, poised for a moment on the down-thrust of the ship. Poppy, a few inches from it, let herself slide through the gap. The two men followed, and Wade secured the door.

"It would be nice to reach dry land a bit faster," said Poppy. "*And* win that little ribbon of yours."

"Captain Wade, I must ask you again — "

"Mr. Gresham, sir. When you're ashore you or your good lady can take me on to run this ship, and when we're back ashore you can dismiss me and try to get my ticket taken from me if you're so minded." Wade drew himself up, staring at Malcolm but presenting his best profile to Poppy. "When we're at sea, I'm the master."

"I don't contest that, captain. But a good skipper listens to good advice."

"I've listened, sir. And I know what I'm doing."

Listened, thought Malcolm in an anger as white and seething as the wave caps, *to Poppy*. Her mild smile of defiance told it all. She would make him pay for his repudiation of her. *If I could put a curse on each and every one of your family*. . . .

All at once Malcolm was frightened—really frightened.

She must have seen it. "Don't worry, Malcolm. I'm sure Captain Wade won't let you down. An experienced man, a most experienced man. Isn't that why *Mrs.* Gresham took him on?"

Wade puffed his chest out. She would make him dance all the way to her tune, quickening his pulse rate and the revolutions of the engines.

But in the late, darkening afternoon, trying in his cabin to summon up interest in Jesse's interminable technical questions while they wedged themselves into opposite corners, Malcolm was summoned to the bridge.

245

Captain Wade was peering into the stygian tumult ahead. Against all nature there were several different shades of utter blackness wrestling with one another.

"It's blowing great guns and small arms."

"So I've noticed," said Malcolm stiffly.

"I have to report we're using too much coal, Mr. Gresham."

"So we'll have to slow down after all."

"Not as simple as that, sir." Wade stared on into the blackness rather than at Malcolm. "We don't have enough to make New York."

"Not enough?"

"That's how it is, sir. Sorry."

"But God Almighty, man, there's enough reserve fuel capacity in this ship to allow for three or four days' extra steaming time."

"True enough. But I didn't fill her up to capacity."

"You didn't . . . "

"Every ton saved made us a ton lighter and gave us a fraction of a knot more speed. We'd have been all right if we hadn't run into this weather."

"And we'd have been all right if you hadn't gone on overtaxing the ship just to show off to . . . to . . . " Malcolm was thrown against Wade. Pushing himself away, he thought how Poppy would have clung and entwined. "For your own conceit, your own selfish satisfaction . . . "

"What about the company's satisfaction? You'd all have been happy enough if I'd captured the Blue Riband, so everyone wanted to book every berth we've got for the next year and more. Oh, I'd have been a hero then, I'll be bound."

Malcolm stared at that dour, defensive face. "So we're not going to make New York."

"Not according to my engineer's reckoning, we won't. There's over three hundred and fifty miles to go."

"And we have fuel for how many miles?"

"At best, a hundred and fifty."

"After which we swim?"

"I've been working it out."

"A bit late in the day."

"All right, Mr. Gresham, all right. But we can make Halifax. Halifax is under a hundred."

There was no alternative. Arguments and recriminations could be saved for later. The *Philippa* turned north-east for Nova Scotia, for a while struggling broadside on to the tempest, then dipping her bows and ploughing on, angled against the buffeting from another quarter.

They fought on through the night. Few cared to go down to their cabins for more than a few minutes. Only steerage passengers had no choice. Cooped below, they were barred from using their low-lying promenade deck, rearing and lurching, lashed by the icy wind and by streamers of spindrift peeling away from the wave crests.

"We'll get there. Nowhere near as bad as it looks. I'll see this through, don't you fret."

Whom was Wade addressing?

In the upper saloon the pianist tried to play cheerful music but found difficulty staying on his stool or hitting the right notes.

Malcolm counted the hours. As dawn pitted its uncertain grey against the eastern reaches of the gale, he pored over Captain Wade's charts. If morning could only break through the dark masses piled above them, it ought soon to be possible to make out the Sambro Light.

"Breakers ahead!"

It was the first splash of brighter colour in the hellish murk. And breakers meant land.

They meant rock. Full steam at twelve knots, the *Philippa* bore down on jagged teeth foaming with a greedy saliva.

The first impact threw passengers along the saloon floor, into bulkheads, benches, sofas; against cabin doors and under splintering shelves and tables. Blood spurted from a seaman's cracked head. A stoker hurled and pinned against the maw of an open furnace door began to sizzle and char before the next jolt tossed him free. Two women in the steerage died instantly of broken necks.

The *Philippa* reared as if trying to climb over the savage fangs, but they tore gashes along her flank so that water poured in and she began listing heavily. The port lifeboats swung out, in, and then were caught by a titanic wave that tore them from their davits and threw them contemptuously over the reef. A terrible moan from the bowels of the stricken ship was drenched by a hiss of steam. Trapped steerage passengers were drowned into silence. The engine room was awash, icy cold to the knees and fogged above that with scalding, explosive gouts of steam.

Malcolm groped along the crazily tilted deck. Two ship's officers were helping women and children up at a perilous angle into one of the starboard boats. Lowering the boats down that slanting side of the hull would be a near-suicidal gamble. But what other gamble was there?

Jesse reeled towards him and clutched his arm.

Captain Wade was peering over the end of his twisted bridge, bellowing an order to a man with a coil of rope.

The lifeboat began to scrape its way down the seaward stretch of the ship. A breaker clawed up at it and fell back. Ropes jammed; one freed itself; the boat slithered stern first, then smacked on to the water. An ebbing wave pulled it clear. Then another gathered its strength to roar

247

in, pick the escapers up, and hurl them back against the iron hull. There was a crash; a bubble of screams. Once more the boat reeled away, and once more came back, this time lifted up a good twenty feet and thrown down against the mother ship. Planking snapped and tore. Twisted, fragile shapes went spinning out and down to extinction. The boat crumpled in on itself and slid into the water for the last time.

Malcolm and Jesse, salt-scorched and with raw throats, reached the bridge. Dawn was etching hard rocky edges and the shape of higher, heavier land no more than a hundred yards away. A mere hundred yards, but in such a maelstrom too far to swim. And even if the next few boats could be lowered more successfully than the first, it would be impossible to row them round the stricken liner's bows and into the boiling channel between reef and shore.

But above that cauldron a man was swinging down like a spider on its thread, swinging into position on the rock while Wade shouted and waved guidance from above.

It was the quartermaster, one end of rope lashed round his waist while the line was slowly paid out behind him. His arms were stretched to their limit through the slats of a hatch cover. When his feet touched one flat stretch of rock in the shallows he freed his arms and inched his way to the edge of deeper water, where the waves beat him about the head and shoulders. Stooping into their fury he set the makeshift raft on the water. Then, with knees rammed down and hands gripping the sides, he pushed away into the channel. The rope went taut. Three man braced against the tilting bulwark went on paying it out, fighting against the tug of currents dragging the raft from under the quartermaster. He was veiled in fountains of spray.

The ship groaned and shifted. Momentary slack in the rope let the raft shoot away before tightening again. In his own muscles Malcolm seemed to feel the wrench that must have racked the other man's arms.

But the quartermaster had reached land. Dawn light, intensifying over the bleak shore, showed him stumbling out of the water, doubled up, forcing himself towards a spur of rock round which he began to lash the line.

"Get them moving!"

The first woman brought to the rope wept hysterically and pushed her helper away. The third mate was urging her to climb out and swing her way, hand over hand, along that swaying lifeline. She could not, would not. Another woman clambered past her, desperate to get ashore, and set out. Halfway across she stopped, hung—and dropped. The next two groped painfully along and reached the far side. One more was lost.

Another succeeded. Three more reached safety, and then five in succession, their hands freezing on the salt sting of the rope, let go.

Silently counting, Captain Wade turned to Malcolm. "We'll be lucky to get even a quarter of them off that way."

"If we could stick it out till full daylight, when we've been seen and they're sending boats out to us . . . "

A huge wave scythed along the deck and cut down a man who was trying to help a weeping child on to the rope.

"Mr. Broderick!" Wade's hunted, haunted eyes watched human flotsam being swept overboard. "Pass word along that passengers should fasten themselves to the rail, or the lower rigging, till help comes out from Halifax."

They were so near to safety. Help must come. It had to.

Paul Whitlaw was dragging his wife behind him, his arm round her, offering her his puny protection against each stab of wind or rage of water. He guided her close in beside the deckhouse, heading for the rope's end.

Suddenly the wind snatched at her. The hem of her dress was flung grotesquely upwards, she was almost lifted from the deck, and shreds of material were hacked away as if by maniacal scissors. Beaten about the face by billowing cloth, Paul held on but was forced to one side. Pallid daylight fell on passengers trying to secure themselves or merely keep a foothold, or turning their faces up in prayer — offering icy-blue phosphorescent faces to the heavens. And fell on Poppy's bare throat and breast, thrown open by the jeering wind. For a moment wind and waves seemed to die down as if, after all, the old beliefs were the true ones and the tempest would subside if shown a naked woman.

In the lull there came another piteous moan from one length of the ship to the other. Lashed into fresh glee, a wave vaulted over the bows and drowned the deck. When it ran away, Paul Whitlaw was left sliding towards the scuppers, his neck twisted to an unnatural angle.

Malcolm jumped down from the bridge. Poppy was standing there, hardly bothering to protect herself against the shudders and lurches of the ship, shaking her head at nothing and no one. He reached her and yelled in her ear, "You must go. Get to land. Now, before it's too late."

She looked full at him, her brow and cheeks and mouth and breast soaking.

He gripped her arm and hurried her to the end of the rope. A woman and child were on it, the woman patting and urging the child with her hip, not daring to let go and comfort it with her arm. Again Poppy shook her head. Malcolm lifted her bodily and guided one hand towards the twitching, twanging rope. "Go!" Her fingers closed on it but with her other hand she was still clasping his arm. "Let go," Malcolm shouted. "You must let go."

She seemed to misunderstand and was letting herself slip away. He leaned over, fighting to stop her from falling; and still she clung to him. He leaned further, shouting, shaking her so she should wake up and reach with that locked hand for the rope.

Then he was too far over, and was gone . . . falling . . .

In the shallow gulf between life and the dark, Malcolm Gresham had no time to know or guess whether it was the lurch of the ship or the tug of Poppy's arm that threw him into the murdering surf.

THE TELEGRAPH brought the news with brutal speed and conciseness under the Atlantic. From a total of nine hundred passengers and crew, survivors of the *Philippa* numbered fewer than three hundred. Until the final roll-call was confirmed beyond all argument, Nell refused to believe in the names of three of the dead: Malcolm Gresham, Jesse Gresham, Paul Whitlaw. It could not be.

Confirmation was not long in coming.

Mrs. Paul Whitlaw was the only survivor of the four. She was in hospital and would rejoin her daughter in New York when completely recovered from the ordeal.

Poppy had survived.

Only Poppy.

"Oh, this on top of everything." Julia sobbed and tore at a lace handkerchief. "It's too cruel. For this to happen to me, it's too cruel."

"To *you*?" Nell's question was as numb as her heart.

"My life's been nothing but one long tragedy. What have I ever done to deserve this?"

Julia went off to look out a black veil.

Edmund, so white-faced that his skin seemed to have been bleached away to the bone, came to discuss plans with Nell for dealing with the aftermath of the disaster. There would be an official enquiry, there were scores of private enquiries to answer, insurance problems to settle, complaints from bereaved relatives to be investigated.

"I leave it to you," she said.

He talked about the cost of replacing the *Philippa*, of raising a loan or going even more swiftly than they had intended into partnership with an American company, using American craft as a stop-gap while building a new liner.

"We can't maintain a regular service with one ship missing."

She heard what he was saying but grasped none of it.

"I leave it to you."

Alan came home from London and sat with her. Once he began playing the piano, but after ten minutes the music struck through to her and she was horrified. "How can you bring yourself to sit there amusing yourself, now, at a time like this?"

"But mother, I thought you'd like—"

"Don't let me hear you again."

That same night she was racked by a nightmare in which all the garbled reports received from Halifax fused into a hideous chorus. There had been stories of boats which had arrived too late to save the drowning, but not too late for scavenging crews to tear the valuables from waterlogged corpses. Some bodies washed ashore had been mutilated by things other than the rocks: harpoons had dug into the flesh, dragging the corpse briefly aboard so that rings and jewelry could be snatched off, then been ripped out again and turned to other victims. Even in genuine attempts at rescue or reverent salvage of corpses, similar iron hooks had to be used to gaff them and drag them inboard. In Nell's dream she was fighting towards Malcolm while leering fishermen tried to hook her and claim her for themselves. Waves smashed repeatedly into her belly and left salt scorching in the wounds. Then she reached Malcolm and threw her arms round him and drew him from the cold sea into her warm bed and into her body, and he was loving and hurting her . . . until the hurt grew greater, like a barb dragging in slow agony through her flesh, until she screamed and woke up.

Awake, the pain was still there. Driving down, lacerating, tearing her apart.

She tried to find the bell-pull through a mist of terror. By the time her maid came, dragging a woollen dressing-gown about her, it was too late.

The child that had miscarried would have been a girl.

So that last, late joy that Malcolm might have left her was gone. But the nightmares would not go. By day as well as by night now she was tossed by their feverish waves. Even in moments when her eyes and mind cleared so that she could see her bedroom ceiling or reach out shakily for a glass of water, or see Alan's face and the pattern of the wallpaper and the flicker of a fire in the grate, ripples would soon race back across the floor and build up to a new stormy swell, breaking up and over her bed.

Somewhere in the middle of it was a doctor, coming and going. Like the others he could not stand firm but tottered then fell from the rocks on which there was no footing.

Alan talked to her, she was sure he did, but nothing he said penetrated the roaring and shrieking in her ears.

Edmund came back more than once, seeking lulls between her bouts of fever. On one occasion she saw him distinctly, seated at her bedside, and distinctly heard him say, "We can't put things off any longer. I must go to America."

If you had gone in the first place . . .

The tortured visions raged over her again.

By the time she had groped her way at last to dry land, Edmund had left for New York. Even then her feet tripped and stumbled and lost their way when she tried to walk back into the real world. Her bedroom carpet was a quicksand. She reached the library and tried to recall a dozen figures from the past, but saw only the lifeless book bindings and not her grandfather Jesse, her son Jesse, or her husband. Alan found her asleep at the library table. She had a vague sensation of his leading her away and telling her she must lie down, must sleep, must get better.

"No." Was that really her own crackling voice? "I must get up, I can't go on lying here, there's nobody else, I must get back and see what sort of mess they're all making of it."

That was a dream, too, in which the strangled sounds she produced were imitations of old Jesse Bostock's voice.

Again she fought her way out of a nightmare and on to the bedroom floor and the corridor floor and, when she had been persuaded to dress herself, on to the floor of the hall and on to the step outside.

"If Edmund's not there, then somebody must be there. Alan, you'll come with me."

She was dressed in black bombazine. Alan, with a dark grey suit, had a broad mourning band about his arm. When they reached the Gresham-Bostock quayside offices, they entered below a double loop of black crêpe to be greeted by a funereally deferential Mr. Carter—young Mr.

Carter, doing his best to look ancient and reliable. "I've got all the latest figures available for you, Mrs. Gresham." He also had to one side, a great leaning pyramid of letters of condolence that had been sent straight to the office rather than to Bostock's Brow. Mrs. Gresham had been shielded from them by her faithful servants. Now she was capable of accepting them, young Mr. Carter was capable of taking back some of the burden. "I suggest, Mrs. Gresham, that we prepare an appreciative letter of thanks—or a number of styles of letter, graded according to the people concerned. If you're prepared to leave that to me, I'll have them drafted and sent home to you for your personal signature." He nodded his respect to that accumulation of respects.

"I leave it to you," said Nell. "Alan can bring them up when they're ready."

The letters on one side, the graphs and charts and specifications and ledgers on the other, were all meaningless. Nell was frightened. Never before had she found it impossible to concentrate her attention on one aspect of this or one column in that account book. Now she had only to look at a signature or a total for it to blur and escape her.

Yet she was not unaware of Alan's tactful nudge of Mr. Carter's elbow, and their withdrawal to the outer office so that she might have time, alone, to decide what she did or did not want to do.

Alone, she could not even keep up the pretence of working. The sounds outside—shouts along the quay, a steamer's whistle, a bell on the landing-stage, the rumble of cart wheels—were the same as ever but muffled, as if straw had been spread in every street to await a funeral carriage, and every vessel on the river was being allowed to drift instead of forging ahead.

Then there came the clatter of footsteps. Outside a door burst open and there was a woman's cry, broken into by a male gruffness.

"Now come on out of there and don't go bothering—"

"Mrs. Gresham, I tell you I want Mrs. Gresham."

Nell heard Alan: "Just a minute, aren't you . . .?"

"Let me get her away, sir. There's three of 'em, like wildcats they are, and this one's the worst."

Nell went through to the outer office. A flushed girl was struggling in the grip of a beefy dock constable. She turned an imploring face towards Nell.

"Mrs. Gresham, you remember me."

"I can't say I do."

"There you are, you see. Trying to get away with a tale like that."

"But she does know me. Mrs. Gresham, you do remember."

Alan said, "Mother, it's the girl who came to see you. With her brother. Surely—it's . . . Louisa, isn't it?"

The girl beamed gratefully at him.

"Of course," said Nell. "Louisa Fenwick. I'm sorry, I didn't . . . wasn't concentrating."

"You're sure of this, ma'am?" said the policeman, disappointed.

"Quite sure. But what's the trouble?"

"Well, there she was flaunting herself along the parade there. Seemed obvious enough what her game was. There was three of 'em. Two regulars, and they didn't fancy this one shoving in."

"It's a lie," flared Louisa.

"I saw as plain as—"

"You're a liar. There was nothing to see, except me being attacked by those two hussies."

Louisa pulled free and raised her hand, but Alan came between her and the constable and eased her to one side.

"There's a lot of it, you know," said the policeman. "Girls who get to Liverpool and say they're off to join their husbands in America. Then they get robbed of their passage money, or never had it in the first place, and they set up as prostitutes. Begging your pardon, Mrs. Gresham."

"I think you've gone far enough, officer," Alan said. "This young lady works on an American ship—"

"Well, we get them off there as well." The man was still aggrieved. "We've got precious little control over the comings and goings of the Americans. But if you don't keep a weather eye on 'em, there's plenty of the women who go on the street for a few shillings—and some of them jump ship and stay on our streets."

When Alan slipped a florin into his palm and opened the door for him, the constable did not seem too reluctant to accept shillings for himself.

When he had gone, Louisa burst out, "I'm so sorry, Mrs. Gresham. We've heard about your loss, and I wouldn't for the world have broken in on you. But you were the only one I could turn to. The only name I knew."

"That's all right, my dear. Of course." Nell, dizzy, sat down. Young Mr. Carter fussed solicitously forward. "It must have been a trying experience. Too zealous, some of our watchdogs. Now, why don't you stay the night with us?"

"I ought to go back on board. And stay there."

For all her plump good health the girl looked small and lonely. Nell heard herself saying, "Alan will take you to collect your things. And real-

255

ly, why not stay over until the ship's next trip to Liverpool? Spend a few weeks with us."

"But I—"

"The house is so big," said Nell, "and so empty. It would be nice having you to talk to for a while. If you think you could put up with me."

"They'd be furious if I walked off just like that."

"Mr. Carter?"

"If the young lady's faced with any unpleasantness," said Carter readily, "we could provide a replacement stewardess from our hiring office. She does the double voyage and on her return Miss Fenwick takes over again."

"Then that's settled."

Louisa dazedly sought Alan's eyes. He smiled encouragement. She said, "Well, if I could actually help, if it meant something me staying on a while . . ."

"Alan, do go along with Louisa and see she's all right."

So awkward and diffident on her first appearance at Bostock's Brow, the girl now proved a cheerful little chatterbox, sharp and eager to please. Perhaps she tried too hard, but she was the right companion for Nell through those sombre weeks. Talk kept memories at bay. There was no need to listen to every single word, to every one of her tales or tart comments on life in Albany, in Minnesota, in New York with her brother, or aboard ship. A thread could be picked up and discarded at random. Hours went by, days went by, and Louisa became part of the household: even regarded as no more than a mechanical musical box, she had an agreeable gift of keeping silence at bay.

"I do have to write to George and let him know how it's going. And when I'll be getting back."

"Give him my regards," said Nell, "and tell him you're extending your holiday."

"But I can't do that. I can't stay for—"

"I'm asking you to stay," said Nell. "Please."

She showed Louisa the drawer of clothes she had prepared for her expected daughter. It was the first time anyone else had been allowed to see them. Louisa handled the tiny, beautifully stitched cottons and silks with awe. When she held up a satin-ribboned sock it was with a child's love for things tinier than itself—for dolls' clothing and dolls' proportions. And somehow that was right. It felt right for Nell; eased her own adult pain.

Louisa wrote to her stepbrother, while Alan took a message from Nell

256

to young Mr. Carter so that the right explanations and apologies should be conveyed to the Liverpool agents of the American Line.

"But of course I can't stay for ever," said Louisa.

Nell did not argue this, or anything else the girl might say. Most of the time she did not, even after insisting on her remaining, truly listen to her. But she would have felt the loss if Louisa had for some reason failed to be there.

Only at night, when Louisa was asleep far along another landing, did silence throb resonantly back. Nell longed unashamedly to dream of Malcolm, to hold him and feel him against her and in her until the dream resolved into reality. But he was not there. One night she woke to find her own fist thrust between her thighs, shiveringly clenched against the injustice of love and death. *Dead: Malcolm dead.* She made herself say it.

And did not believe it.

Her grandfather had disappeared utterly in such a short time. She had been disconcerted by the speed with which the dead could quit places they had so vigorously inhabited. But she could not yet believe that of Malcolm: he could not have gone so heartlessly, so soon.

Another night she got out of bed and walked in the faint light from the landing window. The floor seemed to sway beneath her. She was on board ship again. If she went on walking she would come to Hesketh, and then be rescued by Malcolm, and their life together would begin all over again.

There was no one in the shadows, no one waiting for her. She retraced her steps, past her own door and on to to the middle flight of the back stairs.

A hand fell on her arm. She gasped, half in fear and half in joy at what she had summoned up.

Louisa said, "Mrs. Gresham, are you awake?"

Nell stood quite still, urging herself back into her trance, so that she could start all over again and make it all come right this time.

"Mrs. Gresham, please—are you all right?"

"Where is he?" whispered Nell.

"You'll catch cold. You're shivering."

"He must be here somewhere. You're in my way. I can't see properly."

"You must go back to bed."

Nell drew away, along the corridor above the stairs and into the east wing. A smear of yellow light from the city cast fitful brightness on the wall and across a mirror at the far end. And there, in the glass, was the face she had been seeking. Nell broke into a run, fleeing from Louisa towards that face. Behind her she heard Louisa gasp with fright.

Alan said, "It's all right, Louisa. Mother. It's only me."

"I thought . . . I thought it was . . ." Then, as Alan struck a vesta and lit the jet beside the glass, Nell denied it. *I thought no such thing*, she assured herself. The shade in the glass was not the least like Malcolm. A caricature, no more. "Why did you have to trick me like that?"

"Mother, you're frightening Louisa."

"It's all right," said Louisa. "Truly. But Mrs. Gresham, do come along to bed."

Nell swayed, and now it was her turn to clutch the girl's arm. She let herself be turned away from Alan; was glad to go. But on her way back to bed she began really to wake up, and suddenly the flesh of Louisa's arm was too soft and young and new. She let go. "You've got so much before you, haven't you? You don't think you could ever become a miserable fool like me, you don't think anything terrible is ever going to happen to *you*. Stupid child."

"We can talk in the morning," said Louisa gently.

"How would you know what to talk about? Go away. Leave me alone." Then, in the chill draught along the landing, Nell cried, "No, I didn't mean that. Don't go."

But she was not sure what she had meant: that Louisa should not go now, or should not ever go from the house?

"I can't stay forever."

Hadn't the girl said that before? Was it just an echo that Nell was hearing, or was she saying it again?

Ten days later Nell sent Alan to the piano for the first time since her interdict. Settling herself on the far side of the room, she waved Louisa to the fireside chair. She must force herself back to life—or existence—again. Nothing would ever be altogether right again; but determination had made all things possible in the past, and must sustain her through the barren future. Trying to follow the limpid notes of the Chopin ballade Alan was playing, she contemplated through half-closed eyes the pretty domestic picture: Louisa comfortably sunk into what had been young Jesse's usual chair, absorbed in Alan's face and the dance of his fingers. It would do no great harm for her to transfer her mild hero-worship of her stepbrother to Alan for a little while. Nell saw them, in this setting, as virtually brother and sister themselves, tenuously yet indissolubly linked by the legacy of an Atlantic crossing all those years ago, by the three children who had travelled on that ship and the waiting father who had remarried, while she married Malcolm and came home to give birth to his sons. To this son, still with her. It was right that Louisa should be here.

She fought down the hopeless longing for Malcolm to come in now, through that door.

The door opened.

Julia swept in. "Really, Alan, do you think that sort of thing is suitable in a house still in mourning?"

Nell said, "I asked Alan to play for us."

"I might have guessed. I must say I envy you your indifference. When I think what I went through when poor dear Adrian died . . ." Julia turned a critical gaze on Louisa. "So you're still with us, Miss Fenwick."

Louisa's smile was polite and remote. She remained quite still, wistfully watching Alan's hands and waiting for the music to begin again.

Nell prepared herself for Edmund's return. When he was setting off she had felt no interest whatsoever in anything he might do, or what facts and figures and recommendations he might bring back. Now she felt things moving in her, as a child might move: a reawakened sense of old responsibilities and anticipation of new ones—all the living things that would not simply go away because she had half-died. *Work makes a callus against grief.* Where—in Mr. Trigg's Lowestoft library, or in the book-lined room at Bostock's Brow—had she read that?

She vowed she would be ready to cope with whatever Edmund had to put before her.

He must have lost at least a stone in weight, and his face was haggard and exhausted. But he was as concise and straightforward as ever in summarising the dry facts he had found.

Most of the insurance claims had been assessed, agreed and settled. There were two lawsuits outstanding, brought by families accusing the Gresham-Bostock directors of negligence. "Somebody has made a sworn statement that he overheard Malcolm ordering Captain Wade to go all out for the Blue Riband. But Mrs. Whitlaw put me on to a good lawyer Paul relied on, and I think we'll be able to settle without too much expense—or public disrepute." There was now the question of keeping the Gresham-Bostock fleet up to strength. Edmund had pursued the ideas that had been carried over by Malcolm and Paul Whitlaw but never delivered. Collaboration with any major railroad company was out of the question. The protracted war between the Pennsylvania and the New York Central occupied all the energies of their presidents and managers. On the sea the Pennsy had a heavy enough commitment to the American Line. Vanderbilt was more interested in driving rivals out of business on land than in extending the New York Central eastward across the ocean.

And although there had been a profession of keen interest from the Erie Railroad, its notorious habit of printing too many shares with too little cash backing had led to Edmund being warned off by two of the late Paul Whitlaw's partners—an introduction effected, again, by Poppy Whitlaw.

"But," said Edmund, "they put me on to a most interesting proposition. All this bickering between the different railroads does the public no good, and the public are beginning to notice. And visitors from Europe are beginning to speak their minds. They don't want to be changing trains half a dozen times a day, from one company and one lot of rolling stock to another. Which is where the Wylie Palace Car Company is making some impression. They've been building sleeping and dining cars in competition with Pullman—and setting higher standards. Now the influential travellers are insisting on through coaches all the way from east to west of the continent. Luxury cars handled by different railroads but routed straight through. And for the well-to-do European visitor landing at New York from a comfortable ship and wanting a comfortable rail car . . ."

He let the implications shape up without words.

"Yes," said Nell, "I can see it all. And this Wylie company, they want to invest in a through transportation agreement with us?"

"We can't go on any longer as a purely family concern. The world's getting too big, and the competition too fierce. It has been recommended to me, and it's a recommendation I accept, that we register under the Limited Liability Act and form a joint stock company." Edmund slid a foolscap sheet of figures across the library table to Nell. "In my view we should start with declared capital of a million pounds but issue only six hundred thousand. One hundred thousand shares will be offered to the public—but they'll be picked up at once by the Wylie company. The rest, meaning a controlling interest, to be taken up by you, myself, and some in Alan's name, as part payment for the Gresham-Bostock fleet, shore properties, and goodwill. We put in hand another liner—"

"Steel," said Nell. It came out spontaneously, but when Edmund stared she knew exactly what had been lying dormant in her mind. "Instead of an iron ship," she said, "we build in steel. With twin screws. Think about it."

He smiled a faint, comradely smile. "It's good to see you recovering, Nell. I'll think about it."

Then he fell strangely silent. She wondered if there were bad news he had not yet dared break to her. After a minute or two, when she was about to ask if he thought young Mr. Carter deserved a salary increase for shouldering so much extra work in recent weeks, he said, "I've had one or two things on my mind. Personal things."

"Edmund, you've met someone? Someone right for you?"

"I don't want you to feel sad if I mention Malcolm. Malcolm and you. I often watched you, and thought about you. How happy you were together, whatever happened—how obvious it was that you were happy. I need companionship of that kind in the years ahead."

He surely could not be suggesting the two of them should marry, as it had once been supposed they would? A man could not marry his brother's widow.

"Perhaps long ago," said Edmund, "we allowed things to drift, you and I."

"No, Edmund, I don't think so."

"If other people had not been so anxious to push us together we might have come together of our own accord. And the whole story would have been different."

Gently she shook her head. "I married Malcolm because—"

"Because you preferred him. For which I can hardly blame you. And certainly I don't blame him."

"We'll always be partners, you and I."

"Yes. But I need another kind of partner as well."

"And you think you've found one?"

Edmund got up from his chair and rested his fingertips on the table as if to address a public meeting. "I have brought Mrs. Whitlaw and her daughter back to England. She . . . they were not happy in America, and there was nothing to keep them there."

"Edmund, you're not telling me that you . . ."

"After a decent interval," he said, "Mrs. Whitlaw and I will be married. You'll wish us well, I know."

Nell could not speak. When it was far too late for her to frame some platitude, Edmund's face hardened and he said, "I would like to think you could be happy for us, Nell—for all our sakes."

When he had gone she walked up and down the library.

Poppy, just by being Poppy, had found a protector again.

Nell looked up at the bookshelves. Dull, lifeless, meaningless titles glinted or blurred behind the glass. She took three paces and stopped in front of the one she had half-consciously been seeking. It was a selection of *Tales from the Classics*—blandly summarised versions of Greek and Roman plays and legends. Taking it down and skimming the pages, she vaguely remembered that somewhere in it was the story of the widows of conquered Troy, their menfolk gone—husbands, lovers, sons slaughtered—while the woman whose inconstancy had led to the long war and the slavery now lying ahead for the rest of them was already weaving her enchantments again. Helen would not merely survive, but survive into a future as luxurious and self-indulgent as her past. Women such as Helen were saved without even having to try.

Nell found the right page. She drew her widow's cap on her head and sat down to read.

His Goal had been Vienna, but that dream city was receding ahead of him at increasing speed, dwindling away into a dream country which now he would never reach. When he sought to bring out the lyrical ecstasy of the *adagio* from the Moonlight Sonata his touch had lost conviction. Poring over the solo part of the Schumann piano concerto, he heard in his head a celestial orchestra moving towards that final ravishing shift into A major; and heard his own blunders which would bring conductor and orchestra to a shocked halt.

"Alan, you mustn't feel you have to give up your music." His mother was straight and sincere, yet uncaring. "You'll be needed in the firm now. But once you've mastered the work, you'll have all the spare time in the world for your playing."

There was no way of explaining that it was not a matter of spare time, of some tasteful little hobby to be indulged in the intervals between harsh commercial endeavour. And even if she had genuinely wanted to understand, this was no time to force explanations on her.

"Your mother needs you." Uncle Edmund was sympathetic but austere. "Set your mind to it, Alan, and you'll find what a fascinating business we run." He meant well. He was always ready to set aside time for explaining the ramifications of the company's operations, seriously awaiting the dawn of enthusiasm in Alan. And, like Nell, of course he conceded that the young man should continue with his hobby—later, when there was time for it.

Liverpool was not Vienna. The tinkle of money showering into the bank was not to be compared with the least of Bach's 48.

"Your father's will leaves you and Jesse a comfortable holding in the firm," Uncle Edmund explained as meticulously as he would have explained to an equal of his own age. "But Jesse's share will now come to you. And when we form our new joint stock company, your mother and I will see that the proportion is maintained. But you ought to regard it as a catapult, Alan—not as a cushion."

Despondently, when he was alone, Alan turned to his piano. And was cheated by it. His playing grew more and more sloppy, and he knew it and played all the more dreadfully for knowing it. There were times when, having vowed that he would insist on practising for a couple of hours without interruption, he found himself longing for an interruption. Playing a fistful of wrong chords, he waited for the door to burst open and Jesse's boisterous, chaffing voice to belabour him: "Even a Welsh fishmonger's got better scales than that." Or for Jesse to whistle deliberately and piercingly in the wrong key. Or to lean on the piano and say mockingly, but with the awkward affection both twins knew and never openly displayed: "All right, you make the music and I'll make the money."

Jesse ought to be still alive to shoulder the burden he was so well fitted for. Given time, they might between them have created something new, a balance nobody else would ever quite have understood.

Music was the only truth. Music must not fail him. Alan shut himself away and tried again. And was interrupted again, this time by another intruder from his own memories. He missed his father's easy-going grin, the slap on the back which seemed so casual yet was so full of shy generosity.

Closing the lid of the piano and going in search of his mother, he saw afresh what every empty hour of the day must mean to her. It was up to him to make up for all she had lost. He must try to be what she wanted him to be.

But did she really want anything he could give? Alan tried to reach through her grief but was unspokenly repudiated. Almost she was accusing him, numbly and without malice, of being still here when the others had been snatched away. He was of use to her in only one way.

Nell rarely went out of the house; was gradually cutting herself off from routine tasks with the company and from all the committees on which she had once been so busy. Like the Queen after the death of the Prince Consort, she had chosen to shut herself away and issue her dictates to her dominion through messengers and delegates. In Nell Gresham's case there was this one special messenger: Alan, reduced to little more than an errand boy.

At last he protested. "Do I have to be a go-between all the time? Half this running to and fro could be avoided if you and Uncle Edmund sat down at home and worked it all out between you."

"He doesn't care to come to my house."

"That's nonsense, mother. If you asked him—"

"He will not come unless I sometimes invite his wife. And that I'll not do."

"But why not?"

"You wouldn't understand." Even as he thought he might well understand, she went on, "No reason why you should. But I'll not have her in my house, and I won't set foot in theirs."

One afternoon when he had snatched a few minutes to play some light pieces—for he was ashamed to face up, now, to Beethoven or Schubert—he sensed that someone was standing just outside the slightly open door. He stopped in the middle of a bar, on an unresolved dominant, and said, "Yes, what is it?"

Louisa sidled nervously round the door, blushing.

"I'm sorry. I had to stop and listen."

Her plump, pretty moon face had acquired a pink dust of freckles on both sides of her nose, so that when her eyes crinkled into a smile they seemed to tighten and draw up the blush into two warm little pockets.

Alan said, "Come in. Don't stand out there. If you have a request, ask for it now, before I make my final bow."

She approached the piano timidly but with a bold, instinctive twitch of her hips that he had noticed often when they passed in a corridor or in the garden. When she spoke she gave the impression not so much of forcing something out as of holding something more powerful, more impulsive, back.

"There's a lovely little thing you often play." She tried to hum it. It was a warm little voice, but without much tune. It took several bars and a couple of spurts of giggling before he picked up the theme.

It was easy to play. Under her serious gaze he enjoyed playing it: Schumann's *Träumerei*, an idyllic accompaniment to the dream in which she was so quickly lost.

When he had finished she stood quite still where she was, and said, "I think I'll have to make arrangements to leave."

Time had slipped by and he had ceased to wonder, idly, when or whether she would go back to America. Attentive to his mother, fizzing off with a sudden burst of laughter in a corner or bending gravely over a

265

photograph album, frowning over a sewing basket and comparing her handiwork with that of two recently engaged workhouse girls, she had become one of the family—or one of the staff, or . . . He did not truly know how he had come to regard her.

But she was here, still here. It came as a jolt to realise that she might of her own free will decide not to be here much longer.

"My brother's been writing to me," said Louisa. "He wanted to come over and make sure I was all right, but I guess he had too much to do. And then there was the fare, and what might happen to his job while his back was turned. Things are like that, you know." She was staring at the keyboard as if to cling to what Alan had drawn from it, to deny that things had to be like that. "Now I get word he's going to be married."

"So there won't be much room for you anyway, if you do go back?"

"He thinks it's time I went, though. And he says he'll find me a place somewhere."

"Do you want to go?"

She reached out and risked pushing down a black key in the treble. It chinked a brittle C sharp and died.

"No," she whispered. "But I guess it's high time I did."

"Why?"

"I've got a feeling your mother'll be glad to be rid of me."

"But she was the one who—"

"She's rather turned against me. Or that's how it feels, anyway."

"She's turned against everyone," said Alan gloomily, "and everything." His right hand shaped a diminished seventh and resolved it mournfully down through a minor cadence.

"I don't want to leave," Louisa said. "I don't want to go at all."

"In spite of mother?"

"I just don't want to go away."

It dawned on him that she was flatteringly waiting for his verdict: his was the one that counted.

"We'll have to see what we can do," he said as confidently as if he had already thought of a plan.

It was Edmund who in fact came up with a solution. The Gresham-Bostock Hotel, as Owen Meredith's dreamed-of reception centre had become, was in need of an assistant manageress. Mr. Goffin, the manager, wanted an energetic young woman to look after the chambermaids, supervise bookings, and deal with all the troubles besetting women travellers. "Some ladies get very disturbed at that stage of the journey," said Edmund tolerantly, "or—according to Mr. Goffin—very difficult." He would interview Louisa personally, and then send her on for the manager's final approval, if she was interested.

Louisa was delighted. She flung her arms round Alan, kissed him im-

266

petuously, and then laughed and blushed and swung away so that her soft, full breast brushed his arm.

Nell was less pleased when Alan told her of the move.

"Who gave you authority to meddle behind my back?"

"One moment I'm supposed to devote myself to learning all about the Gresham-Bostock concern, the next I'm being accused of meddling."

Nell's eyes blazed with their old, beautiful fire. Then she nodded grumpily and looked down into her lap. "Oh, all right. Let her go."

"You were the one who was so anxious for her to stay. She saw you through some of the worst times."

"I'm sorry. I'm afraid I haven't been much pleasure to any of you, have I?"

"Mother, if you'd only let yourself—"

"It doesn't matter. None of it makes any difference now."

Alan drove Louisa and her luggage down to the hotel. She kept demurely away from him, keeping a gap between them as if afraid now of touching him. But when the manager came to greet them, there was a look in his eyes as he contemplated Louisa's dress and richly swelling contours that made Alan put his arm round the girl's shoulders. His hug, and the kiss he bestowed on her cheek, proclaimed that she was under the family's protection. Goffin clearly understood the message.

"You'll come and see me sometimes?" asked Louisa. "To see how I'm getting on?"

"Yes," he promised, "I'll come and see you, to make sure you're earning your salary."

When he was out in the street he felt an impulse to turn back and tell her to forget the job, to come back to Bostock's Brow where she belonged. He was so used to seeing her there, in that familiar setting. In the hall of the hotel he had felt a tingle of strangeness, of seeing someone he had not noticed before, and who was now slipping away before he could bring her into focus.

The next day his mother had another of her messages for Edmund: several sheets covered in her close, hurried handwriting. "It's urgent, make sure he gets it before he leaves." Alan went down to the office, to be told that Mr. Gresham had just ridden off to Falkner Square to pick up something before setting out on a visit to Manchester.

He hurried to Falkner Square.

The maid who answered the door was telling him that Mr. Gresham had already gone to catch the train, when a voice behind her said, "Who is it, Olwen?"

Alan recognised the husky slur that tied the notes of the words together. When the door was pulled further open, Poppy stood there.

"Alan. It's such a long time since we met. Do come in."

"I must catch up with Uncle Edmund before—"

"You'll never catch him now. Do come along in."

In the sitting-room she looked even more graceful and more assured than in those borrowed rooms where they had snatched their moments of love. Here she was in possession, mistress of the house, dressed to suit her own exacting tastes at no matter what cost, and clearly the arbiter of furnishings and ornaments, lights and colours. A deepening web of fine lines below the eyes made her look older, but none the less beautiful.

She seated herself in a chair facing him so that their knees almost touched.

"And how is your mother?"

"As well as may be expected," he said awkwardly.

"We never see her, of course."

"She keeps herself rather to herself. I wish she *would* come out more."

"But then, she would never come here. I'm glad *you've* come at last. I was afraid that you, too, were avoiding me."

She was trying to hold his gaze—to mock him, or tell him something? Alan's throat was dry. He said, "I thought you'd managed to find enough to occupy yourself. Without me."

"Oh, dear. Still the jealous boy?"

Jealous? Conscious of her nearness and the insinuation of her perfume, and remembering what she felt like under his hands and his loins and how she would feel if he reached out and laid his hands on her now, he was also conscious of disgust. That she should so easily and swiftly have married Uncle Edmund, should have come back to Liverpool so calmly and taken everything for granted . . . perhaps his mother was right not to let her in the house. In her presence he was aware of danger, of something slow and lasting and powerful, an untraceable echo that would not die away.

"Your uncle won't be back for two days," she said experimentally. "If you're in no hurry to get back to the mausoleum . . ."

"Why did you marry him? How could you marry him just like that?"

"You didn't want me ever to come back to England?"

"Do you love him? You didn't love Mr. Whitlaw. Do you love this one?"

"Still you ask so many questions. Just like before. It's a habit you must grow out of."

She was the one who leaned forward. Her nails scratched on the knee of his trouser leg, and crept forward, tapping, scraping, taunting. Just for the satisfaction of making him grovel—or because she was genuinely hungry for him?

He said, "It wouldn't really do, would it?"

268

"It is my house, it is simple, I arrange everything so it is simple for us."

"It wouldn't do," he insisted from his harsh throat. "I mean, after all, you're my Aunt Poppy now, aren't you? It would be . . . a bit silly. Can't you see it? Aunt Poppy."

Her fingers stopped, arched like a spider. Then she pulled herself back. The hiss of her indrawn breath was as dangerous as he could have predicted.

She said venomously, "You dreadful little weasel."

"Poppy—"

"*Aunt* Poppy, please! Isn't that it?"

He got up and moved away, sure she was on the verge of stabbing a claw at his throat.

From the side of the house came the clatter of hoofs on the cobbles. A horse was making its way down to the stables.

"You'd better go," said Poppy.

"If that's Uncle Edmund I ought to wait and—"

"It's not Edmund. It's my daughter."

In silence they went to the front door. In silence he opened it and turned. Poppy waved him out as if not trusting herself to speak. Behind her, the door to a side passage opened and a girl came out of its shadow into the daylight of the hall.

"Mama."

She stopped, looking a polite question at Alan. She had hair almost as dark as her mother's, but with a wide natural wave sweeping out behind her ears and turning smoothly back on itself under the bavolet frill of her riding hat. The mixture of French and Chinese in Poppy had been further fined down to produce a complexion like the palest peach, even with a soft down, lighter than her hair, beside her ears. Her smile was tentative and charming.

"Rosalind, my dear. This is your stepfather's nephew, Alan Gresham. Alan, my daughter Rosalind."

Slowly Rosalind took off her glove, and their hands met. He was sure in those first seconds that he had never seen anyone so beautiful, and never would again. And she was so sweetly unselfconscious. And not for a moment conscious, as he was, of the immediate anger pulsing its fierce rhythm through Poppy's mind and body.

SHOP GIRLS and factory girls danced on deck, sometimes with one part-
nering another, sometimes splitting up and straying invitingly near to
young men propped against the rails. Others had their regular followers
making the most of the day out, refusing to leave them, glaring at anyone rash enough to offer admiring glances in passing. It was Saturday,
and the excursion trains into Liverpool had brought mill hands and
shop workers for trips along the river to Rock Ferry. A small brass band
played amidships, at times marching up and down. When its music faded too far for'ard, or the breeze blew its sounds away, the dancers followed, tripping and swirling as if lured on by the pied piper of Hamelin.
Between pieces a bugler would tip the horn of his shining instrument up
and coax passengers to toss pennies in.

"You should see the ferries we have back home," said Rosalind. "And
the musicians on the riverboats!" She watched a gull dive for a corner of
crust thrown in the air by a little boy. "But I'm getting to like it here."

"And you'll be staying here?" said Alan apprehensively. "You won't
ever be going back?"

"Oh, I guess it would depend on who asked me."

"To stay—or to go?"

"Either."

When she teased there was no malice in it. Her eyes were wide and

270

frank, with none of her mother's dark undercurrents. Alan tried to catch in them some memory of Paul Whitlaw, but could not find it. Rosalind was Rosalind—and that was enough.

He had taken her to a concert, and although the programme included one of his favourites, the Mozart C Minor piano concerto, for once he heard little of the music: he was too busy trying to gauge her response, to tell from the turn of her head and the occasional restlessness of her hands whether she was absorbed in the music or bored by it, whether truly attentive or displaying her knowledge of polite procedure.

"I enjoyed my evening so much," she said afterwards. "Thank you, Alan."

Clearly she meant it, but it was not so clear whether she meant the music or just the sense of occasion.

A few days later she showed him a photograph of herself on a *carte-de-visite*. It was taken from what must originally have been a larger picture of a crocodile of young ladies out for a strictly supervised, strictly correct walk. "That was when I was at boarding school," said Rosalind nostalgically. "That's Emmeline, the one on the left. She was a very special friend. And Grace Farrinder—one of the Boston Farrinders—always the smartest of all of us. Of course, she could afford to be." Her own face in the foreground was as serious and exquisite in sepia tints as in real life, so alive and so close to Alan's. Riding the subdued waves of her hair in the picture was a pillbox cap trailing a silk streamer. She and the other girls wore muffs, their hands tucked in and elbows set at identical angles, each muff held as if obeying some school regulation as to its precise positioning before the stomach.

"Oh, and Gertrude Gilman." Rosalind took the photograph back from Alan and gave it one more glance before returning it to a slim card-case. "Her brother was the best-looking man you ever did see. And he was going to inherit a fortune. Gertrude got *so* many invitations because of him."

"Including invitations from you?"

"Oh, mother often had them over."

"But you won't be seeing any of them again, as things are."

"No, not as things are. Not for a long time, anyway."

He would have preferred her to sound indifferent rather than merely philosophical.

They went riding together in the park. All her words and gestures, her movements on horseback, were music. He wanted this hour to last forever; but when it ended was already offering her a dozen possibilities for their next meeting. Sometimes when they parted he realised that he

271

had talked too much, while she had been cool and friendly and unforcedly poised, and then he was horrified that she would not want to see him again, and he vowed to let her do all the talking next time, if there was a next time. But she seemed content to ride with him, walk with him, or sit with him and say little. When she did talk at any length it was usually about those distant schoolfriends, or about a new dress her mother was having made, or of some rare materials they had seen in a Lord Street shop window.

The days when he did not see her were intolerable. Now he used or misused his opportunities as his mother's errand-boy to catch at least a glimpse of Rosalind—on his way to the office, which became much more protracted so that he could take in the corner of Falkner Square, or through the doorway of a shop where she had hinted she might be spending some time one afternoon, or beside her mother in the barouche when they went out visiting.

Twice he made a deliberate error, pretending that he had thought Uncle Edmund would be at Falkner Square instead of at the office, and presenting himself there with messages from his mother. On the first occasion a maid had answered the door and told him that everybody was out. The second time he encountered Poppy, fumbled out his excuses, and fled. He was still wary of facing her alone, though no less wary when he had to go through the usual courtesies in calling for Rosalind or delivering her back to the house. Poppy's brooding expression worried him more and more. But only if they were alone together might she speak devastatingly out.

Somehow, soon, he knew there would have to be such a confrontation. There were things he knew he would have to ask her—after he had asked Rosalind.

Was Rosalind ready yet? If he spoke out too soon she might laugh and spoil everything. If he kept her waiting too long she might think him feeble and not worth her trouble.

To go on in this town, this dismal work that was no serious work at all, this emptiness, was impossible without her.

Even his mother noticed at last. "Alan, whatever is the matter with you?"

"Nothing at all, mother."

"Are you still sulking because you couldn't go to Vienna?"

"No, mother. I'm not expecting to go to Vienna."

"Perhaps one day . . . "

He knew he would never go. He would have to show how responsible he could be here at home, how capable of picking up the reins and eventually guiding the Gresham-Bostock destinies, how ready now to be given some real position in the firm. Nothing must hinder his marrying Rosalind Whitlaw.

"Mother, did you ever meet Miss Whitlaw?" he said.

For a moment it seemed not to register. Then she said, "You mean that girl—your uncle's stepdaughter?"

"Yes." Her name whispered in his head, and he risked it. "Rosalind."

"I think I met her a couple of times, briefly, when Edmund first brought them over." His mother was scrutinising him almost as suspiciously as Poppy had done. "Apparently *you've* met her more recently."

"We've . . . bumped into one another. When I've been taking your messages to Uncle Edmund."

"I see."

"She's interested in music."

"You must have a lot to talk about. I've wondered why it's been taking you so long to get through things, just lately."

"I thought we might invite her here one afternoon or evening. Just play a few pieces . . . have tea. And so on."

"And so on," said Nell dryly. But her smile was less disparaging. She hesitated, then added, "Will her mother let her come?"

"Will *you* let her come?"

"I . . . you know I'll not have her mother in the house."

"We're not talking about her mother, we're talking about Rosalind."

Nell hesitated. "I don't want to be a party to any young woman deceiving her parents." But curiosity was getting the better of her. "If it were just a brief call—a casual visit . . . "

Alan carefully arranged the casualness of it. One afternoon when he and Rosalind were strolling round the Botanic Gardens, she with her yellow parasol tilted to cloud the sun's glow on her face, he said, "We're only ten minutes from home. Come and have tea."

"But I thought your mother and mine didn't . . . weren't . . . "

"Don't be scared," he said, enjoying the masterful sound of his own words. "It'll be all right, I promise you."

"I'm not sure if I ought to."

He took her arm, and her parasol crackled faintly; then she adjusted its angle so that she and Alan could walk closely together.

"You're beautiful," he said, "so beautiful."

"Thank you, Alan. I'm glad you think so."

"Does it really matter to you what I think? Really?"

"Yes," she said, "it does."

The lustre of her shone beside him as they walked up the slope and along the ridge, shining untouched yet with the need to be touched. Or was it only his need to touch her that burned so fiercely?

His mother must have guessed that this was to be the afternoon. Or perhaps she had prepared herself two or three times, just in case they arrived. She had shed her black and was wearing a blue sateen teagown that made her look ten years younger. There was still, nevertheless, a regally withdrawn air about her, and when Rosalind came into the drawing-room it had the atmosphere of a formal reception, even if only for one guest.

Alan watched with doting admiration Rosalind rise to the unspoken challenge. To a polite question about her mother's health she answered with the necessary platitudes, and then hoped Mrs. Gresham herself was well, and admired the flounces on her dress. They talked about English fashion and American fashion: the contents of a New York emporium and of a Liverpool one. Tea was served, and Rosalind praised the Bostock's Brow cook. Once or twice she laughed deferentially, but not too readily: she and her hostess were waltzing to a very solemn tempo, which at intervals made Alan want to start conducting, quickening the pace and making it less formal. But he marvelled at Rosalind—and loved her—and did not mind at all if his mother saw how intent he was on every movement, every turn of Rosalind's neck, every courteous little nod.

At such a first meeting, as a matter of propriety, nothing of any great consequence was being said. But it was so amiable and unforced that he felt a rush of thankfulness. Everything was going so well. He played two Schumann novelettes, they had tea and he escorted Rosalind back to Falkner Square.

When he returned, his mother appeared not to have stirred from her chair. She smiled at him with a slow, thoughtful affection she rarely displayed nowadays, and again he felt a bound of optimism.

"Well?" He could not keep up the measured formalities of the afternoon. "What did you think of her?"

"She's an attractive young woman."

"She's beautiful."

"Yes," said his mother, "I suppose one must concede that she is."

"You liked her, didn't you? You did like her?"

"In other circumstances I wouldn't dislike her."

"Mother, what do you mean?" The parasol glow of the day clouded. "I thought you were getting on so well together."

"Naturally the girl has been taught how to behave. But"—Nell had been weighing it up in his absence—"she has no heart."

It took his breath away. "How can you say such a thing? When you've only met her a few times? She's—"

"I don't mean she's cruel, or selfish, or would do anything hurtful. But I tell you she has no heart. She'll always be correct, and pretty, and well turned out. If you want a well-dressed exhibition piece in your drawing-room and by your side at Corporation dinners, she'll perform with impeccable taste. But there's nobody really inside. With that parentage"—Nell allowed herself a thrust—"it's hardly surprising."

"You've always hated Poppy . . . Mrs. Whitlaw, that is."

"Alan, I don't like your tone of voice."

"And I find yours detestable." He stormed out of the room.

Next morning he did not wait for any messages she might wish him to deliver, but went out and walked, and walked, waving his right arm not to the rhythm of music but to a hammering of points in an argument, the same argument going in and out and round about. His mother hated Poppy, Poppy hated his mother: why should that be allowed to come between him and Rosalind?

They had arranged to meet for a few minutes only in the afternoon, outside Hengler's Circus building where Rosalind and a young woman from the American Chamber of Commerce were to listen to visiting American evangelists Moody and Sankey, whose revivalist hymns were causing a great stir and some fashionable amusement throughout the country. It was tacitly understood that Alan would be here to convey, though not in so many direct words, the impressions his mother had formed of Rosalind.

As he approached, her friend moved a short distance away but unabashedly watched as Alan and Rosalind talked.

In all the things he had repeated aloud or in his head while pacing the streets, he had not rehearsed what he would tell her. Now it came out: "Rosalind, would you consider marrying me?"

The crowd converging on the circus building jostled him to one side. When he had fought his way back he set one hand against the wall beside Rosalind's shoulder. Her unperturbed gaze was disconcerting. Without uttering one hurtful word she had it in her power to hurt him so much.

"This is hardly the right place to consider any such thing," she said.

"But I have to know. I mean, is there any reason why you *wouldn't* consider it?"

Rosalind pondered. "No, I can't say there is."

"You're not waiting for anyone else? Even a vague someone else who might come along?"

Rosalind glanced at her friend nearby as if debating whether to seek her advice. Then she said, "No, I guess not."

"Then I'll do?"

Rosalind reached up to touch his arm just once. "There's nobody I've met I like better. And you do have a lot of money, don't you? Or will have."

He was taken aback. "You mean you've set yourself a figure?"

"Oh, no, my dear." She said "my dear" so lightly, but it restored the brightness to the sky. "Just that mother would be so disappointed if I married a pauper. Marrying for money has been a family joke for a long time. Only not quite a joke."

"After her own experiences I'd have thought your mother would prefer you to marry for . . . well, not just for money."

"What experiences?"

"Oh, I thought . . . " He realised the danger. "I got an idea, somewhere, that she'd had some sadness in the past."

"She never told me."

"I don't know where I got the idea. But I still think she'd be happier if you married for love."

"It would be nice," said Rosalind equably, "if I could do both."

"Yes," he said. "So you will marry me?"

"You'd better have a word with mother first."

The pendulum was swinging faster between joy and despondency. Poppy must surely have some inkling of his probable intentions by now; but that was not the same as his declaring them outright, straight to her face.

Cravenly he approached Uncle Edmund first.

They were in the old counting-house when he broached the subject. Whatever Poppy might or might not suspect, it came as a complete surprise to his uncle. Edmund, perhaps because of Nell's self-imposed seclusion, was even more preoccupied with business nowadays than ever before.

He assessed Alan's fumbling declaration with the fairmindedness he would have brought to any unexpected twist of fortune on the quays or in a Gresham-Bostock captain's report, letting his informant wait until he was sure of his judgment. For Edmund Gresham did not care to change his mind once it had been made up.

"Your mother knows about this?"

"She's met Rosalind."

"And approves?"

"She doesn't positively disapprove," said Alan carefully. "And she'll like Rosalind even better when she really gets to know her."

"Mm. Well, I suppose there's something to be said for keeping the firm in the family. Better my stepdaughter than some invader."

"Uncle Edmund, I wasn't looking at it like that."

"The firm comes second in your calculations?"

"No. It's all part of the same thing, really. I do want to pull my weight better. If I can marry Rosalind—"

"So that's one of the conditions of working harder?"

"All part of the same thing," Alan repeated.

He had an eerie sense of Jesse taking him over, making him bolder, steadying him on the right course.

"I tell you what we'll do," said his uncle, smiling with a touch of envy. "Come to the house tomorrow evening. Give me time to put it to Rosalind's mother. And that'll give you time to make sure you have a sound case and can express it convincingly."

Alan spent the interminable waiting hours repeating, to Poppy's imagined frown and accusing eyes, "I love her, I love her." It was the best argument he knew: the only one that mattered.

When he reached Falkner Square it was Edmund who opened the door. His expression boded no good. "I ought to warn you, my wife's not best pleased."

Poppy was waiting in her drawing-room almost as Alan's mother had sat awaiting Rosalind's entry. There was no sign of Rosalind herself.

"Close the door, Edmund."

"If Alan would prefer to talk to you alone—"

"No. *I* prefer that we settle this between the three of us. So we know what we talk about and there is no more silliness."

She waved him to a chair facing hers. It was like the one he had sat in when last facing her, but with a wider gap between them—a nicely calculated gap, perhaps. She waited for him to speak. Until this moment it had not occurred to him to choose how he would address her. "Mrs. Gresham" sounded stilted: the surname was his own. As for "Aunt Poppy"—no, not after that previous occasion.

He said, "I believe Uncle Edmund's told you I want to marry Rosalind."

She was a rigid, unyielding statue.

"I can make her a good husband. I know I can."

He tried not to let himself be mesmerised by the dark dead slits of her eyes.

"I'm proposing to take a more active part in the company. Rosalind will have everything she needs."

You felt that cockerels, rams, slaves, captives, weeping children ought to be sacrificed before that implacable face.

He said, "I love her."

Edmund was standing by the window with his feet apart, hands behind his back. He often stood like this in the office while handing out decisions, praise and dismissals. Here in his own home his stance was somehow no longer a commanding one.

Poppy said, "You cannot marry my daughter."

"But I love her. And I think she loves me, and I can make her happy."

"It is not possible."

"I'm not poor"—Alan leaned forward, intensifying and concentrating everything he had said to the air since yesterday—"I'm prepared to do anything for her. She'll have everything she wants."

"So romantic."

"If there's been some misunderstanding in the past between you and my mother, I'm sorry." He talked to her but looked past her, desperately, at Edmund. "I'd have thought you could forget the past and think only of Rosalind's future . . . her happiness."

"It is of Rosalind's future I think."

Edmund hunched one shoulder forward. "You know, my dear, if you've any real objections you ought to put them fairly to Alan and let him answer them."

"I say there will be no marriage. That is enough."

"It's not," cried Alan.

Now he wished Edmund were not in the room. Without Edmund present he could have flung in Poppy's face her own jibes about jealousy. He would have denounced her determination to wreck her daughter's happiness from sheer spite.

Edmund said, "Perhaps, Alan, if you gave it a little time, so my wife may get used to the idea—"

"I shall not get used to it," said Poppy.

"I think you're being a bit dogmatic, my dear." Edmund's "my dear" was so weary and patient and so unlike the blithe "my dear" that Rosalind had offered Alan. "Unless there's some truly insurmountable obstacle—"

"There is. But I do not wish to say it."

The flesh between Alan's shoulder blades prickled. A cold sweat started from the back of his neck. Poppy was lying. He could not imagine what objection she was contriving, but was sure she had every intention of saying it after she had played him like a cat dabbing at a mouse.

"Of course it's up to you to decide what's best for your daughter," Edmund said, "but I think you owe it to Alan to explain. He's man enough to take it sensibly."

"And you?" said his wife. "Are you man enough, also?"

"I don't see how it affects me."

"Perhaps not. It was in the past, before you and I, so perhaps you do not mind. You are not very sensitive."

"You'd better come out with it."

Poppy said, "It is forbidden Alan and my Rosalind marry. They are too close. The church does not allow."

"We're cousins by marriage," Alan protested. "No more than that."

"More than that."

"How could we be?"

The sloe eyes opened full at last. With her back to her husband, Poppy stared derision at Alan. "Your father. You do not know about his past, and about me?"

Edmund strode to the back of her chair. "You can't feed the boy's mind with—"

"You were so anxious for the truth."

Something ticked in the wainscotting. Alan heard the tick of a drop of saliva caught in his own throat.

"It was over," said Edmund, "before Alan was born."

"You asked for truth, and you know that it was not so."

"Then before Paul Whitlaw married you. Poppy, you know Rosalind wasn't born until after—"

"Until after Mr. Whitlaw had been persuaded to marry me and remove me to America. But when was she conceived? A farewell present from Malcolm, you could call her."

"You're lying," said Edmund.

"Why should I lie?"

"Because . . ."Alan began and could not finish. Not with Edmund here. Not to make it worse for Edmund. And if he got rid of his uncle or came back tomorrow, or the next day, to catch Poppy alone, what difference would it make how he denounced her, or what she admitted or refused to admit in private?

"So I am not lying" she said. "And there will be no marriage. Because Alan's father was Rosalind's father."

"I don't believe you," said Alan.

"You also, you do not wish to believe? Then ask your mother. And if she also doubts, I give her dates and times. I tell her the nights Malcolm was away from her, and once reminded she will remember, because I am so right in my details."

"Damn you," roared Edmund, "you wouldn't dare."

For the first time she deigned to turn and look full at him. "But you know me, my *dear*. Of course I will dare, if I must." When she had taken her fill of their silence she went on, "So it is settled, yes? Alan, you do not

279

see Rosalind again. If you try to meet her, I tell your mother why it must not be. Tell her, who so sadly lost her daughters, that her husband gave me a daughter. Tell her that even after she is so clever and arranges to be rid of me, her husband still came back to me, until I was no longer there."

"You're inventing it," breathed Alan.

"Then you must tell her why I invent such a story. I do not think it possible you tell her, no?"

When he stumbled off into the twilight he swore that yes, he would tell his mother. He would be honest and bring it all out into the open so that lies could be thrown aside and the truth of his love remain. But the evil whispers chased him down into the brawling city: *If she also doubts, I give her dates and times . . . of course I will dare . . . I do not think it possible you tell her . . .*

He tried to imagine what Uncle Edmund was saying to that woman, or she to him, now he had left them. And could not.

I'll marry Rosalind, he swore to himself. It's all lies, Poppy made it all up, its only purpose was to wreck our happiness. When Rosalind is of age, when I can take her away and marry her . . .

I tell your mother why it must not be.

I'll tell Uncle Edmund the whole truth, about why she wants to destroy me.

And after hearing this, on top of everything else he has heard about his wife, he'll stand by me?

Alan reeled on down streets splotched with gaslight and a scattering of lanterns carried by men who had been drinking or were on their way to drink in some of the darker, cheaper alleys. He cursed aloud, and two Irishmen cursed cheerfully back. He vowed he would take Rosalind away, save her from the wickedness of her mother, and they would deny every slander and deny anything Poppy dared to say to his mother.

He thought of Nell crouched in on her grief, and swore at her, too: cursed her self-indulgent grief and her deification of a man who was dead and could neither be helped nor harmed any more. I'll go home, sit down, *tell* her . . .

He found he was shuffling, drunk without having touched a drop of drink, past the entrance to the Gresham-Bostock Hotel. His eyes stung with tears. He could not let himself be seen in there; could not go anywhere. As he swung away across the street, someone called his name. A haunting, urgent voice. It was real, not a taunt out of his own despair.

Louisa had pushed open the main door and was running after him.

"Aren't you coming in to see how well I'm working? You haven't been for ages."

"I'm sorry. I . . . I've been busy. I . . . " He pretended a sneeze, and hastily wiped his eyes.

"I saw you outside." She must have come recently through the kitchens: he could smell vegetable water and a hint of frying fat in her hair. "Please don't just go past." When he tried to look away she unceremoniously trapped his cheeks between her hands and pulled him round. "Alan, whatever . . . ? Please, do please come in."

"I'm in no state to—"

"I'm off duty this evening. Come and sit with me. And I'll tell you how I'm getting on." When he did not reply, she said, "Or you can tell me all about it, whatever it is. If you want to. Or don't, if you don't want to."

ON IMPULSE Edmund made a short detour and headed for the gate into Bostock Gardens. It was twenty minutes since he had left Poppy at home, and another twenty before he was due to call on Nell. He needed a breather.

The park-keeper, sweeping up leaves, straightened his broom as if about to present arms. He showed every sign of wishing to indulge in respectful conversation. Edmund swerved away and took the path leading to the shelter. From the bench he had a view of the back of Jesse Bostock's head. The wooden figurehead was concealed by the plinth, but he could see it in his mind's eye as clearly as when he and Malcolm had stared at it on opening day and remembered Poppy, who had gone away.

And who was now back.

Last night as he reached their bedroom landing she had walked along it naked, as he had seen her do in Malcolm's day. In the doorway she had looked back once, and he almost expected her to say "Good evening" in the accent she had long since lost, and to be inviting and mysterious once again. *The more you strip her down, the more mysterious Poppy becomes.* The only mystery that remained was that of his own obsession: why had he hoped for so long, and what had he ever hoped to find?

When he followed her into the bedroom she was erect before the looking-glass, studying herself without vanity and without suggestiveness.

Only when he had turned half away, avoiding the double image of her, did she speak.

"You haven't touched me for nearly six months."

"No? I haven't been counting."

She walked round the bed so that he was forced to look at her. The bone had always drawn her fine, smooth skin closely over itself, but now the skull seemed laid almost bare, and her lips were pulled back from her teeth.

"Six months," she said. "When I sent that ridiculous nephew of yours packing. Would that have anything to do with it?"

"What an absurd idea."

"It is, isn't it? Because, after all, you'd known about Malcolm for a long time."

"I didn't know about that particular . . . " He stopped himself.

"And did that matter so very much?"

"Not in the least."

Poppy's left leg bowed towards the edge of the bed and she let herself roll forward and over, as smoothly and enticingly as ever. Under the diffused light from the gas globe her triangle of pubic hair shone like oily seaweed.

"It will do you good to prove it," she said, "for your own sake."

She watched with coldly contemptuous eyes as he crouched over her, kissing her and urging himself to want her—to take her and be done with it, for his own sake. If she had closed her eyes, or murmured to him even in that deadest of voices, and wrapped her arms round him, perhaps he could have pretended that there was still something loving to bind them together. But she lay unmoving. Until, when he could summon no response to that lean and lovely body, she reached up and began trying to arouse him with ignominious, mechanical tugs and squeezes. He knew she was hoping to fail so that she could have the excuse to sneer at him.

When he lay back, unable even to look at her, she said coldly, "Perhaps you'll be good enough to put out the light."

He twitched between tortuous dream and half-waking inquisition—a self-inquisition that repeated the same questions over and over again, then twisted them into a new torment until he longed to get out of bed and to walk through the night until he was exhausted.

In the morning the inquisitor became Poppy. At the breakfast table she said, as if she too had been lying awake mulling over their problems and finding no comfort, "If you can't be a real husband, at least you must work harder at being a provider."

He thought of the endless bills from milliners and dress shops, of the new gig she had cajoled from him, the redecoration of rooms decorated only a year before, and her indifference to the household accounts.

"What do I fail to provide?" he asked incredulously.

"It is what you may fail to provide if things go on as they are doing."

"What things?"

"This Atlantic Waterworks Company, or whatever you call yourselves."

She knew perfectly well that their joint venture with the Wylie Palace Car Company was registered as the Atlantic Bridge Company, but it always suited her to feign indifference. It was only when she wanted to buy something for herself that she suddenly displayed a shrewd knowledge of their financial standing.

He said, "What's that got to do with my failing to provide for you?"

"Nell and that boy of hers. Holding on to those blocks of shares, collecting their dividends and leaving you to do all the work. Running to and fro at that woman's beck and call—what sort of profession is that for a man . . . a real man?"

"Without Nell's inheritance we could never have—"

"Yes, her inheritance. But what about what *you* contribute? She and Alan between them still basically control the company. And what if one day, out of sheer pettishness, she decided to force you out?"

"Why should she want to?"

"I don't know. That's the point. Neither of us knows what she's spinning, there at the centre of her web. We don't know what mood she may be in tomorrow or the next day. And Alan—would you call him reliable?"

"He's gone to pieces since Rosalind went away, drinking around the town and disappearing for nights on end."

"And he has a major interest in the business? How would he stand if there were trouble, if those American partners showed signs of collapsing?"

He crumbled the edge of a slice of toast between his fingers. "Where've you heard that, about the Americans?"

"At one of our whist parties. Some of my friends have heard things. Their husbands have been asking them—"

"Asking them to ask you to ask me, so that they can gamble on 'Change?"

Poppy laughed happily.

"You're not really interested in the firm," Edmund said. "Not interested in whether we put more capital into the Wylie partnership, or shift our assets elsewhere, or take a chance here and make a mistake there. All you want is to do Alan down. And through him, Nell."

"I am saying only that you must get control of Alan's shares."

"If you were so anxious to get your hands on them"—he threw his napkin down and pushed back his chair—"you should have let him have his Rosalind. Then we'd have had them in the family."

She watched him to the door. "You must do something about it."

"I'll do what I think is best for the company."

"That's what I mean. I'm glad we agree on something, Edmund. Because if you don't soon act, I might tell the ladies over our next few rubbers some things you wouldn't want them or their husbands to hear."

Edmund said, "You hate us all, don't you?"

She smiled one of her rare unforced, spontaneous smiles. It was answer enough.

He sat in Bostock Gardens and hated himself almost as much as she did.

Other men envied him Poppy, just as he had once envied Malcolm and Paul Whitlaw. They saw his wife spending lavishly on clothes and dreamed, as he had often dreamed, of stripping them from her. She shone in Liverpool society and enjoyed the prestige of being the wife of a leading citizen. And for some time in bed, in return for his name and money, she had coolly done whatever he wanted of her—and then, at the start, he had wanted many things. She was calculatingly sensuous and compliant: just what any husband could ask for. But time and that impersonal compliance had drained him. She was nothing but a slow, implacable appetite for food and warmth and luxury and admiration—and now, in some way he could not fathom, for vengeance. She would suck a man dry yet pass on with no sign of having won any satisfaction from him or having changed in any degree whatsoever.

It was time to go. Edmund got up and made a circuit of the outer path. Even from a distance he saw that there was something wrong with the centrepiece. He took the straight path leading directly to it. Jesse Bostock's head still dominated the plinth. But the figurehead was no longer there. It had been replaced by a black-painted anchor.

The park-keeper stiffened to attention again as Edmund hailed him.

"Good morning, Mr. Gresham, sir."

"How long has this anchor been here?"

"Oh, must be a couple o' months now. Mrs. Gresham sent orders down about that. Yes, a good eight or nine weeks."

"What happened to the old figurehead?"

"Getting right rotten in patches. But it'll come in useful. Chop it up, make some stakes for the nursery beds over behind the greenhouses. Heart of the wood's sound enough."

Edmund went on to Bostock's Brow.

285

The gatekeeper who saluted him from the sandstone lodge was new—if that was the right word for someone so stooped and prematurely old. Gossip had reached Edmund that the man was a widower; and there had been talk of the steady replacement of Nell's other staff by older servants with no attachments and no romantic intentions. The woman who now answered the door to Edmund was a lean, despondent spinster unlikely to encourage any fleshly dreams or desires under Nell's roof.

Nell greeted him as imperiously as Poppy had dismissed him. "I wanted to get a message to you first thing this morning. But Alan's nowhere to be found. What does he do with himself?"

"I see very little of him."

"I thought he was supposed to be learning the business from you. Now he's out of the house till all hours, refuses to do more than pass the time of day with me. . . . " Nell pulled her skirt tightly across her knees. "What happened between him and that girl of yours?"

"Poppy's girl," he corrected.

"You're her stepfather. You do have some authority there, don't you?"

Edmund had no intention of denying it aloud, to Nell of all people. "Rosalind has been sent to study in Switzerland."

"To study what?"

"Deportment, French, a little music."

"If music's what she needs to study, what was wrong with Alan? At least they'd have had something in common. I suppose your wife didn't care for the idea. Is that why—"

"It all seems to have fallen through," said Edmund carefully. "Passing infatuation, you know." When Nell did not answer, he said, "Did *you* want them to marry, then?"

"I can't say I did."

"Then all's well."

"Is it, indeed? When he seems to be running wild?"

Edmund switched his coat tails to either side of his chair. "That wildness"—he was glad of such an opening for what he had to say—"could seriously damage the company in the long run. Perhaps even sooner than we think."

"So you do know something of what he's up to."

"I know what the market is up to. And I'm not sure it's wise to let him control such an influential block of shares."

"Oh, dear. You've really got something to tell me." Nell made an obvious effort to summon up interest. "I suppose you'll have to get it off your chest."

"We're in this together. We have to be."

"All right, all right. Go on."

"In his present state, if Alan chose to unload his shares on the market, or cause confusion in any negotiations to take us over or save us being taken over—"

"Is anyone proposing such negotiations?"

"There are some disturbing things in the wind."

"And I have to know about them?"

"Yes," said Edmund, "you do have to know. And you have to care. When we were a real partnership, when we ran Gresham-Bostock together, we managed splendidly. And there was Jesse growing up, ready to step in when the time came. Now I'm on my own."

"Alan will never put his heart into it?"

"Never. Any more than his father did."

"I won't have you speak of Malcolm like that."

"Nell, be honest. You and I did it all, and—"

"Malcolm at least gave *me* the strength to do what had to be done. Just by being Malcolm."

"But now you've given up."

"You're strong enough, Edmund. I leave it all to you."

"Not strong enough. Not by half, not as things are at the moment—wondering when the props may be kicked away from under me."

"I don't understand what you're asking."

Nell had refused ever to have Poppy in this house. How could she be unaware that today Edmund had brought her in?

He felt her presence at his shoulder, ensuring that he carried out her orders. The exasperating thing was that there was so much truth in what she had put forward. He tried to cling to the truth and forget the mouth through which it had come.

"We've got along pretty well so far," he said, "because high costs imposed on American shipping by their own legislators has made it more profitable for companies like our partners to invest in British vessels and British management. And during this recent slump they've been even more dependent on us. But things are taking a turn for the better internationally—which could mean a turn for the worse so far as we're concerned, if we don't take action now."

"We give better service, as we've always done. That's what has kept us ahead, and it'll go on keeping us ahead."

"I wouldn't bank on that lasting. American recovery has given a big boost to the emigrant trade."

"So much the better for us."

"And a lot of others. The Danes and Germans are taking a larger slice every year, and there are more and more sailings direct from the Clyde. And the French government is offering its shipping lines a huge navigation bounty for new ships built and put into service. They'll all be competing with us far too soon."

"We've never been scared of competition."

"But the rules of the game are changing. Now the money's flowing again, the Americans are beginning to move in on entire companies. We've been protected till now by their rule that only American-built ships could fly under the American flag, so it suited shippers to do all those partnership deals with us. Now Congress has passed an act enabling British-built ships to be granted American registry. Inman's have already found that promises of continuing brotherly cooperation soon get broken. All the operations are becoming one hundred per cent American."

"One can hardly blame then for waking up at last."

"No, but it won't be to our benefit. Even the best fleet commanders taken over with British liners are demoted unless they agree to apply for intention papers of American citizenship."

"Since we don't intend to sell out to any American organisation, I see no cause for alarm."

"The Wylie Company," said Edmund, "is close to bankruptcy. Word's already getting around. Pullman have been doing their damndest to drive Wylie out of business, and look like succeeding. So Wylie's trying to realise its assets. Including its holding in our Atlantic Bridge Company. Whether it puts its shares on the open market, or passes them on to its own purchasers, or lets one of the railroads pick them up, we could be in trouble. Especially if they fell into the hands of a railroad company like the Pennsylvania, already backing its own Atlantic fleet."

"We still hold control—you, Alan and I."

"And you think Alan's reliable?"

"I'm beginning to see. You want him to surrender his shares."

"Or let me buy him out."

"So that he can have a small fortune to squander on his follies?"

"So that I can be given a freer hand."

Nell studied him sceptically. "But why you in particular? Why should we not split them between us, you and I? What game are you playing, Edmund?" Before he could reply she amended it: "What game does Poppy want you to play?"

"I want you to think about it," he hedged. "Look through the latest reports from Baxter in New York." He put them on the table at his elbow. "When you're ready to talk about it again, let me know. But it needs to be soon."

There was a sudden agitated rapping at the door, and without waiting for an invitation a maid ran in.

"What do you mean by this, Chalmers? I didn't give you—"

"I'm sorry, ma'am. Please. But it's Lady Speke. I think she's . . . I think . . . " The girl dissolved into a fit of hysterical sobbing.

Edmund was on his feet. He led the way upstairs, then hesitated, not knowing which was Julia's room. Nell joined him, pointing to a half-open door. They went in together. He had half-expected to see the old woman sprawled on the floor, or slumped across her bed. Instead, Julia was sitting bolt upright on a low chair with a high back, her eyes staring peevishly ahead and her mouth open, complaining that someone had been cruel enough to interrupt her in the middle of a complaint.

"I'll send for the doctor," said Edmund. "It's still Rathbone, isn't it?"

Nell nodded mutely.

"I'll be as quick as I can," he said.

Not that there was any real hurry. Julia was beyond the need of a doctor. Strange, he thought, that she should have gone so swiftly and with so little fuss. One would have expected her to lie complaining in bed for several years, summoning Nell or the servants every ten minutes, grumbling and having a contrived seizure two or three times a month. Instead she had been summoned away without even a few seconds in which to protest.

He met Nell again two days later, not at all where he would have thought to find her. She was standing, in heavy black mourning once more, in the open doorway of the Gresham-Bostock Hotel with her back to the street. Inside cowered Goffin, the manager. He bobbed thankfully away when Edmund came on the scene.

"I haven't seen you out of doors," said Edmund, "since . . . for goodness knows how long."

It was hard to tell whether it was the very fact of this foray into the outside world or her recent haranguing of Goffin that had left Nell breathless. She virtually stammered, "Came to arrange funeral breakfast. N-not . . . not at home. Couldn't bear it. Hotel's not full this time of year, can use small dining-room."

"If you'd asked me I'd have got someone to make all the arrangements for you."

"Decided . . . do it myself. And what do I find? What do I find?" Nell drew herself up in a towering rage. "That girl—after all we did for her—to find her like *this*, and nobody paying any attention."

"Like what?"

"With child. Assistant manageress, and one look at her and I knew she was pregnant. What is this establishment supposed to be—a hotel or a brothel? Fleecing men of their money—is that going to be a new feature on our booking programme?"

"I'll speak to her."

"You'll not."

"Nell, you've got too many things on your mind. Leave this to me."

"I'm leaving it to nobody. I've already dismissed the shameless little hussy."

"But who's going to carry out—"

"Thrown her out!" cried Nell so wildly that two men on the far pavement looked back at her, "bag and baggage. It's disgusting. Disgusting!"

He tried to lead her inside, but she pulled away and began to walk briskly towards the stableyard entrance where her carriage was waiting.

Was the mere sight of a young, pregnant woman still so much of a pain to her?

14

"YOU SENT her away?" Alan swayed in front of his mother, the taste of beer foul in his mouth, and anguish fouler in his head. "Threw her out? Louisa?"

She was wearing black again. Forever black, always in mourning, for his father whom she had loved, and now for her mother who these last years had been no more to her than a dismal wraith moaning its way along corridors and drifting from corners in Bostock's Brow.

"You threw Louisa out like some . . . some . . ."

"Some waterfront harlot," said Nell. "Which is what she appears to have become."

If she had stood up he would certainly have struck her. But she remained seated in black dignity, daring him to criticise her or have any opinion of his own, any need, or any knowledge she didn't already have.

He said, "She's expecting a child? That doesn't mean she's been out with any sailor or docker who happened to fancy her."

"Who else would fancy her?"

"If Louisa was genuinely in love with someone, or sorry for someone—"

"Sorry? I never heard such rubbish. At least she didn't try that sort of excuse on me. She brazened it out, in fact. If only she'd had the grace to say who the man was, or ask for help, I might have been more lenient."

"She wouldn't say because she didn't want to hurt you."

"How could she have hurt me?"

"I'm the father." Alan's eyes bleared with drink and impotent anger. "It has to be me."

"How can you say such a thing?"

"There wasn't ever anyone else. I'd swear to that."

Nell's face was ashen. "You? Is that what you've spent your time doing? Whoring. Drinking and whoring."

"Where did she go?"

"I don't know and I don't care. She's gone, and that's an end to it. But to think that *you* . . . and how many others do you suppose, how many did you share her with?"

"I want to know where she's gone."

"Back to America on the first steamer, most likely. It's a pity she ever crossed our doorstep."

"You were the one who wanted her to stay. As long as you needed someone's shoulder to lean on, someone to fetch and carry—"

"That policeman was right all along. He knew her for what she was. I trusted that disgraceful little slut, and this is how I'm repaid."

"Trusted her?" he wept. "Only the way you'd trust a pet dog when it fawns on you. And then kick it out into the street when you get bored with it."

"You'd better get out of this room, Alan."

"Yes, and out of this house."

He left without so much as a change of clothing. When he had found Louisa he would return to collect anything he needed. Or would bring her back and insist that she stayed.

First he had to find her.

There was so much of Liverpool he knew. But also there was many a square mile unexplored. Add the known to the unknown, and the task of finding someone who had chosen to disappear into that tangle of streets and alleys was a daunting one.

She might already have set off homeward across the Atlantic.

He went first to the hotel.

"Where did Miss Fenwick go?"

The manager was slyly glad to have some recompense for the dressing-down to which Nell had subjected him. "I'd have thought after the special interest you been showing her, Mr. Alan, you'd be best qualified to know that."

"I'm asking you a question, Mr. Goffin."

"And I don't know, and that's straight. Mrs. Gresham came here and caught us all unawares, see, and then there was this to-do and next thing

292

I know Fenwick's down here with her bag packed, and off without so much as a thank you. Leaving me in a fine mess, an' all."

"Nobody has the slightest idea where she might have gone?"

"Not the slightest," said Goffin with some relish.

Alan went to the American Line and Cunard booking offices, and even to the Gresham-Bostock office, though he thought Louisa would hardly have chosen to travel on that line. Passenger lists were unreliable: it was not difficult to get a last-minute berth in the steerage without any name ever appearing on a list. And since Louisa had left the hotel in such a flurry, without asking for a penny or arguing the pros and cons of quitting without notice, she would perhaps not have the fare on her. She could work her passage as stewardess. He did another tour of the major offices, using his name to win immediate cooperation, laced with a few salty jokes. There was no trace of her having been hired. She might have gone under an assumed name; might even, in desperation, have stowed away.

No. He would not believe that she could have left Liverpool so secretly and finally.

He turned to the streets and courts, the lodging-houses, the bars and cocoa rooms and shops where a girl might look for a temporary job. In her condition it would have to be temporary.

Heads shook. There had been no one answering to that description, no.

It was midnight before he gave up, and then only because tiredness had twice let him stumble into places he had already visited before. He must have a night's sleep. But he was not going home, for that or anything else, until he had found Louisa.

Like her, he had flung out with little in his pocket. Not enough for a reasonable hotel or lodging-house. They would of course put him up without question at the Gresham-Bostock Hotel; but his mother would be there in the doorway in the morning. He found a seedy room behind Paradise Street and curled up in a stinking old blanket. His feet ached and his mind was lurching out of one dark alley into another, but he was unable to sleep. He thought of Louisa's bed in her little room at the top of the hotel. Of how he had crept up there, sometimes desperately and sometimes in warm anticipation. He had accused his mother of treating Louisa as no more than a pet dog. Had he been so very much better? After that first time when he had cried out his pathetic miseries in her arms, she had always been there when he wanted her, soothing and loving and uncomplaining. She was always eager to take him close, draw his head between her large breasts and clamp him contentedly between her wide thighs. Her pleasure was flattering, easing the anger and drunken

293

self-pity out of him. Whenever he appeared without warning—and that was usually how he had come to her—her eyes shone like those of an adoring, one-man bitch eager to leap up and lick him, whining with joy when he settled beside her and stroked her.

And now his loving little bitch was pregnant. He ought to have guessed. She had hidden it from him and from the hotel manager and others, but not from his mother's searching eyes. Louisa was carrying his child. The prospect scared him. He hadn't thought that far ahead and wasn't ready for it. But even more scaring was the thought of what might happen to her without him. She must be wandering, hurt, like an injured mongrel driven out of the house on to harsh, hostile streets.

A mongrel bitch's unwanted puppies were usually drowned.

No, she wouldn't do anything dreadful. Even now she might be trying to get in touch with him at Bostock's Brow. He sat up in bed. But there was no point in hurrying home. She wouldn't do that, either. Whatever he might not know or only half-know about her, of that much he was sure.

In the morning the dawn was slow to break. The early spring days were still lengthening only gradually, grudgingly. When Alan went out into the streets again he walked through a tarnished silver haze in which the outlines of buildings sharpened slowly from night into day. He was out and about too early. The street cleaners were busy, and some groups of men clumped down towards the docks or off to the ironworks; but the world in which Louisa might be working was only just waking up.

"Good morning, Mr. Alan."

There was a semi-respectful wave across the street from a Gresham-Bostock employee whose name Alan did not recall. The man had probably seen him before at this hour of the morning, or perhaps heard of his wanderings from others who had. There was no hint yet of a general alarm, of his mother sending out messages that he must be brought home. How many nights would it be before she realised that he was in earnest, that this time he would not be stumbling back in due course to Bostock's Brow? Not without Louisa.

A few of the waterfront pie shops and stalls would be open by now. It was barely possible—no more—that she might be working in one. And he had a few coppers to buy himself a pie, even though he was not hungry.

He went the whole length of the docks from Wapping to Clarence and at the end admitted that he was simply marking time, with no idea of his next move. The city was too huge, there were too many people, too many boltholes. She had gone.

But not of her own free will. His mother had thrown her out. Louisa would not demean herself by going to Bostock's Brow in search of him. But might she not have left a message in the hotel?

Which Goffin would certainly pass on to Nell, wanting no further trouble.

He was near the corner of the street. Walking up to the hotel entrance he hesitated. When Louisa came out, had she turned down towards the water's edge or up to the warehouses and railway and the huddled houses beyond? Something urged him to continue up the slope. But he had been up and down so many of these slopes yesterday. They would all blur into one again, as they had done then.

He pushed open the hotel door and went in. He did not approach the reception desk until he was sure Goffin was nowhere in the immediate vicinity.

"Has anyone left a message for me?"

The sallow, blue-chinned man at the desk was new to him; and he to the man. "What name would that be, sir?"

"Gresham. Alan Gresham."

"Oh. I'm sorry, Mr. Gresham, we haven't . . . I didn't recognise you."

"You wouldn't. We haven't met before. And it would suit me best if you've no recollection of our meeting now."

"I'm sorry, sir, I don't quite—"

"Is there a message for me?"

The man turned to the room pigeonholes and took out at random a number of waiting envelopes. Then he turned over some letters stacked on the shelf below the counter.

"Doesn't look like it, sir. If anything comes in later in the day, you'd like me to put it aside? I'll keep a special lookout for it, you can rely on me, Mr. Gresham."

Alan went back to the street. He turned up the slope without conviction. When he had gone forty or fifty yards there was a scurry of feet along the pavement behind him.

"Sir. Mr. Gresham, please—Mr. Alan."

A girl had been sent after him to say there was a message after all. It had been lying there all the time, hidden under carelessly scattered papers, coming to light the moment he left the hotel.

He waited for her to catch him up.

She was a thin girl in a scuffed, shiny black dress and a white cap. Her face was peaked and older than her years, and along one jaw was a raggedly healed scar. She looked scared but determined.

"I saw you as I was laying for breakfast," she gasped in a hoarse whisper, looking back over her shoulder. "I had to come after you."

"You've got a message for me."

"I been told to give no messages, not to you nor anyone."

"By Mr. Goffin?"

"By Miss Fenwick!"

"Then you know . . . you do know? You know where she is."

The girl nodded. He caught her shoulders in gratitude, but she wriggled away and looked back again, shaking her head.

"Please, Mr. Alan. You're not to let on. She said I wasn't to breathe a word, least of all to you."

"But you're breathing it."

"She was good to me, was Miss Fenwick. The only one who was. And I think she needs you and you'd better get to her. She'll break her heart, honest, if she gets on that boat and leaves."

"Which boat?"

"Whichever one she can afford. When she's saved up."

"She's working, to pay her fare?"

"Not just the fare. She's worried, y'see. Not knowing if they'll let a single girl aboard if they can spot she's expecting. And who's to look after her at the other end? 'Course, she could write and get a letter from her brother saying who she is and what he's prepared to do for her, and it's her own country she's going back to anyway. But she don't fancy that."

"The longer she delays—"

"Yes, well. That's why she's working in this dressmaker's place, see? And making some clothes for herself as part of her wages. So she can have a Mother Hubbard cloak and some other bits and pieces, all very smart and stops anyone seeing the way she is."

Alan laughed unsteadily. He could not control it, could not stop laughing, until the girl took his arm and shook it, begging him to be sensible and not get her into trouble.

He gulped. "I'm sorry. I don't know how to thank you. I . . . ." He fumbled in his pocket where there were only two pennies left.

"I'm not asking for nothing. Just go and find her and make it right, that's all."

"Where is she?"

"It's a place called Stallman's, in Duke Street. You can't miss it—it's written up big outside."

He found it easily enough: a board lettered in yellow, one of four on a pitted brick wall broken up by long windows. On the step he paused, hearing the chattering treadles of sewing machines through a side door and from the floors above. Could he march into the workroom and confront her—force her to come away at once? When she had forbidden her friend to tell anyone where she was. When perhaps she would not want to be shamed before her new workmates.

When he was not even sure what he was going to say.

He retreated across the street. On the far side, almost opposite the tall, prison-like building, was a public house. The barman was swilling water over the step, and the floor of the bar was still damp and smelling of caustic as Alan went in.

He spent the rest of the morning there, standing with his back to the counter so that he could see over the frosted glass along the lower half of the window. By noon he was familiar with every stained brick on the building opposite, with the two sheets of cardboard wedged into two broken window panes, and with the slow shifts of daylight across the brick and glass. Work would go on inside until shadows of buildings on this side of the street fell too deeply across those windows. It was rare for any garment maker to waste money on gas or oil lamps. Daylight was used until it was impossible to see by it.

But there must surely be a break in the middle of the day? The women could not work right through from dawn to dusk.

Behind him the barman said, "Got your eye on a little bit of what you fancy, over there?"

"I'm waiting for someone. If she's working today."

"He lets 'em out for two quick breaths round about half-past. You'll have to move fast if you want a quick one up the entry."

Promptly at half past twelve a score of women, most in cotton dresses and mob caps, came out on to the pavement. Some slumped back against the wall and raised their faces to the sky, rubbing their eyes and stretching. A few sat on the step and unwrapped hunks of bread and cheese. When another group clattered down from an upper floor, one strolled away to stand on the corner of a cobbled alley alone, pressing her hands into the small of her back.

Alan set his glass down and went out. He was on the kerb beside her before she saw who he was.

"No! I didn't want you to . . . I don't want . . ."

Her eyes were pink with tiredness. She kept one hand behind her, still, as if seeking the solidity of the wall.

"Why didn't you leave some word for me?" He was so glad to see her, so weak with the knowledge that she was still here, that it came out as a shaky, querulous accusation.

"There wasn't anything it would have helped you to know."

"But after what—"

"After what your mother said to me, I just wanted to be off. Better for you, as well as for me."

"How could it be better for me?"

She made a move to rejoin the other women, who were beginning to stare and snigger. Alan caught her arm. He felt it tighten in protest, then surrender as she had so often surrendered.

"Please," she said. "Alan, please don't. I did the right thing. I didn't want you to try and find me."

"Because my mother spoke abominably, do you have to cut *me* out of your life?"

"Yes," said Louisa simply.

"But that's not fair."

"Not many things are."

"To go off without a word, leaving me without any idea . . . what did you think I'd do?"

"I didn't know you'd want to do anything."

"You're going to have a child."

"I'm not asking you to—"

"It's mine."

"Oh, so you're sure of that, are you?"

"Yes," he said. "Quite sure."

Her lips trembled. She had comforted him so often, but now when he reached out to take her other arm and stop her trembling, she would not be comforted.

"Alan, I didn't tell your mother whose it was."

"I know that."

"I felt I owed her that much."

"And what about what you owe me?"

"I've told you, I'm not blaming you for any of it, I'm not asking you to feel responsible. I'm not asking you for anything."

"Why not?"

She made an effort to draw herself up. Her smile was infinitely sad, infinitely loving. "Please let me go. I'm sorry I let things happen as they did."

"I'm not. And you're coming home with me. Now."

"I don't think I'd be very welcome."

"Louisa, you're going to marry me."

Three or four of the women were trying to edge closer, not to miss any of what was going on.

"That's noble of you," said Louisa in a fierce undertone. "Very correct, I'm sure. But your mother wouldn't like it."

"We're not discussing what my mother likes."

"In the end we'd have to. Do go back to her before things get too bad, Alan. Please. I beg you. That's your world, and she's the ruler of it, and

298

you'd be silly to throw everything away."

"I'm not going back. Marry me, and I'll look after you, and—"

"Do you love me?" She was clear and quiet.

"Louisa, I will love you. I promise."

"You promise you'll try. You can't honestly promise more than that. And I'm not sure it'll do."

"I'll look after you," he said again.

"I could look after myself better than you could." She was smiling again, trying to make him laugh with her.

"I love you, Louisa."

"No," she said. "No, you don't."

But that night, when he said it again, and over and over again, she laughed in sheer exhaustion and said, "No, not yet you don't. Maybe you never will. But I . . . oh, God, I suppose I've got enough for the two of us."

"You'll marry me?"

She was silent for a long time in the darkness of the cramped little room to which she had taken him. Then she said, "If I had any pride or even a scrap of common sense I'd send you away. But I can't. You'll never get by on your own, will you? So I'd best take you on, I guess." When he pressed his head down to the tightness where his child was growing within her, she murmured, "I guess I'll take you on any terms."

THE SELECTION of Scottish airs skirled to its conclusion, and there was a sprinkling of applause around the grand saloon. The two violinists stood up and bowed, the cellist inclined his head, and the pianist bent over the keyboard until his spade beard almost touched the white notes. A bass note that had thrummed like a bagpipe chanter below the Scottish melodies continued after the instrumentalists had stopped: the boom of Atlantic rollers along the sides of the ship.

The quartet was joined by the second mate, who fancied his prowess on the banjo, and they played some Stephen Foster successes. A number of passengers tapped their feet. A few elderly ladies pursed their lips. This was hardly suitable fare for first-class passengers on a White Star liner and went ill with the white and gilt décor of the saloon, with its coffered ceiling and white pillars and pilasters. The moment the bouncy syncopations finished, a steward was sent forward with a request. It was one that came at least three times an evening, and then usually had to be followed by an encore: a piece called *In the Gloaming*, which Alan felt he could have played in his sleep.

His hands shaped the phrases automatically. He and his fellow players put a wealth of feeling into each nuance without actually feeling anything at all.

Liverpool was four days behind them.

One of the first things he had noticed when going ashore this time was a poster announcing a new series of Philharmonic Hall recitals sponsored by the Gresham-Bostock Foundation. Was his mother hoping that one day he would be unable to resist, would attend out of curiosity, and be seen and identified and coaxed home? Last trip there had been a different poster, inviting young pianists to compete for Gresham-Bostock scholarships. She would surely not have been optimistic enough to expect him to come forward and enter? Having grown a beard and bought American clothes, he felt well disguised and was ludicrously tempted. To be able to win, and get away with it—a taunting mystery figure! But he was not going to be tempted.

One of his violinists, who like himself served as a steward also, had brought aboard a copy of the *Daily Post* with the small advertisement, on a page facing the shipping intelligence, which had been appearing regularly for eighteen months now. It requested Mr. Alan Gresham to get in touch confidentially with Mr. Edmund Gresham, when he would hear something to his advantage.

"To your mother's advantage," Louisa had said when the advertisement first appeared and he mentioned it to her.

"And if it weren't? If it were a genuine attempt to make things up, and take you into the family and forget the past?"

"I wouldn't forget."

"Not even for Margaret's sake?"

She looked at him across the cot and the baby's bright button eyes. "Would you want me to? Do *you* want to go back?"

"No."

"I thought not." She kissed him: one of her moist, full-lipped, greedy kisses that made up for all the noise and dirt and smells of the streets and back yards hemming them in.

The second mate, relinquishing his banjo, was bowing attentively over one of the middle-aged ladies. Her head bobbed to the music, or to his words, or both. She kept glancing past him at Alan. Rings on three of her fingers caught the light as she tapped her knee or put up a coy hand to wave away a joke or compliment from the mate.

He came back at the end of the piece and leaned over the piano as Alan embarked on the inevitable encore.

"You could do yourself a bit of good with that one."

Alan did not look up, pretending that it needed complete concentration to find notes that by now he was incapable of mislaying.

"She's a widow," the mate went on. "Not a bad looker if the lights aren't too bright. You wouldn't find it too difficult to give her what she wants."

"I don't think I would fancy it," Alan sang to the melody.

"It'd be worth your while, if you ask me. Taken quite a fancy to you. Come on, now, that's what we're here for—to please the passengers. The old man won't be too pleased if you let one go begging."

There had been other hints and offers like this, from older women and younger women. Some were so bored after three or four days at sea that they would pay any extras in order to be entertained, startled, even bullied. Every ship's officer, steward, musician and deckhand recognised those special desperate cases who had come aboard with nothing but that in mind.

"Not for me," said Alan.

"Think of the presents you can take home to the fireside. A few nice little souvenirs, money in your pocket. Something pretty for the wife. You *are* married, aren't you, Pooley?"

They had in fact married solemnly and correctly as Gresham in Southport, but thereafter called themselves Pooley. No one with the name of Gresham would last long on shipboard without someone asking if there was any connection with the G-B line, and then the rumours would drift back to Nell. Pooley was a name they had adopted as a joke rather than a purposeful choice: a scrap of Liverpool argot, it was easy, ordinary and attracted no attention.

"Well?" said the mate.

"I'm married," said Alan, "and that's one good reason for doing my job and nothing else."

"Your wife would never know."

But she would have done. Alan could have played along with those women, east to west and west to east, month in and month out, choosing the likely ones as shrewdly as the captain and mate always did, and brought Louisa more comforts, which she deserved. But she would have known at once. Was that all that restrained him? He played a wrong chord, modulated hastily to cover it, and thought of Louisa waiting for him, and knew that it was not.

The *Balearic* ploughed on; he sat at the piano in the dining saloon and the smoking room, and sometimes quickened the tempo of his playing so that the ship would pick up the rhythm and go faster, and they would reach New York ahead of time and he would stride all the sooner off the East River quay and on to the streetcar and at last up the steps of the house.

It was a clapboard building on a brick foundation that plunged down

302

into a deep, narrow area. A Polish family with four children lived in the basement with two shadowed windows looking out on to the area below the railings, and strung vast signal halyards of washing across the back yard from clothes posts to spikes halfway up a telegraph pole. Hoisting the weekly wash above the junction of rickety fencing was a major operation, usually accompanied by a chorus of shouting and wailing and ancient Slav curses. Alan, Louisa and their baby daughter lived on the ground floor, with two other families above them. The narrow hallway was wedged with perambulators and two battered bicycles, one of them used by a lad from upstairs to get to his work as a newsboy. There were lingering smells of cooking, sometimes enticing but more often stale.

Each time Alan returned from an Atlantic crossing, as now, he hesitated on the steps to the front door and swore that he would somehow get Louisa and the baby out of here, to something better, a place worthier of her. But by the time they got round to talking seriously about it, it was time for him to turn round and set off again.

Today, he had to squeeze to one side of the hall to let Mr. Grodzinski from the first floor pass on his way out. The jumble in the hall was the same as ever; the smells were the same; and the greeting the same. "It was windy out there, Mr. Pooley? So noisy it was again?" Mr. Grodzinski remembered his single one-way crossing of the Atlantic in an emigrant sailing ship, had no intention of ever setting foot on a deck again, and looked on Alan with a mixture of respect and ridicule because of his continual shuttling to and fro across those abominable waves.

"I see you got a visitor." He paused on the top step, with a cloud of dust swirling up to envelop him as a four-horse pantechnicon clattered past. "Good news I hope for you."

Alan reached slowly for the latch. He wanted no visitors, least of all when he was just home. He longed to be with Louisa again, shutting out everything and everyone else. Impatiently he opened the door and strode through to the parlour overlooking the street.

George Fenwick said, "Good. I was hoping you might be due back about now."

Louisa got up from her chair and held out her arms. They were thinner now, and her breasts had lost some of their proud thrust after feeding Margaret when their own food had been scarcely adequate, carrying Margaret with her while she tried various part-time jobs; there was still the patch of discoloured skin beside her left temple where a clumsily unloaded crate of fruit had knocked her over while she was working in Washington Market; but he went weak in his bowels with tenderness whenever he came home, walked in and saw her again, and held her again.

George coughed. "If you'd like me to come back, say twenty minutes from now? I can't leave it too much longer. Got some things to settle in Brooklyn."

Louisa released Alan, and they sat down.

"Nice to see you again, George." Alan tried to make it sound cordial. Last time Louisa's stepbrother had been here it had been to deliver a homily on Alan's need to settle down and do something better for Louisa and face up to his responsibilities in this new world.

"You remember our little talk?" said Geroge now.

"I do."

"You did get round to applying for American citizenship?"

"I did."

"Fine. That's a start, I'll say that. And you've thought about the railroad job I mentioned?"

Louisa said, "George, do I have to tell you again that Alan—"

"Let Alan tell me himself."

Alan said, "It's kind of you to use your good offices on my behalf, George, don't think I don't know it."

"It's on Louisa's behalf. I want to see her settled some place worthy of her."

"So do I."

"Then you're going a mighty strange way about it. Look, Alan, when are you figuring to come along to the depot and see my supervisor? He's got an interesting proposition to put to you, that I do know."

"I wouldn't want you to get into trouble because of praising me too highly."

"Hell, you've got to make *some* kind of move. How long do you reckon to drudge on banging away at that piano of yours, away from home most of the time, with Louisa on her own and no prospect of anything ever getting better? Maybe getting worse. When they want a change and find themselves another piano player, where does that leave you? Pounding out muck in a sporting house—is that what you want, when there's so many better things just waiting for you to come and see?"

Alan shared a rueful grin with Louisa. Of course George meant well and of course what he said made good sense. There had to be a better future than this for Louisa and little Margaret. But not by George Fenwick's patronage.

"I'll level with you, Alan," George said. "If I get in trouble it won't be from overpraising you, but from not getting you along for . . . for an interview."

"But why should you be?"

Louisa broke in sharply: "Have you been writing to Mrs. Gresham back in Liverpool?"

"Would I do that when I promised you not to?"

"Has she been writing to *you* again?"

George hesitated, then confessed, "Two or three more times she's sent to ask if you've shown up yet, and if Alan's with you."

"And you replied?"

"How could I? I don't know anyone called Louisa Fenwick, do I? Or Alan Gresham? Only the Pooleys. I wouldn't cheat on you. I don't tell anybody where you are, or anything, even if it does get me in a hole."

There was no mistaking his sincerity, mixed with the irritation they both caused him. Whatever might be driving him at the moment, it was no cunning scheme to deliver Alan up to his mother. Alan knew how ungrateful he must appear. But something in him went as solid and resistant as a jammed sheave when employment with an American railroad was mentioned. He was applying for citizenship; when he knew what was right for all of them he would somehow take Louisa and Margaret out of these surroundings; and there was no question of his ever turning back to his family's maritime religion. So why not accept help and good prospects when they were offered? It was no good. He jibbed.

Impossible, irrational, that he should still be postponing the moment when he cut his last tie with Liverpool.

Louisa said, "George, what's this hole you've gotten into?"

"Just that I'm expected to produce Alan. He's taken an interest in Alan for some reason, and I tell you, once he gets a notion in his head he worries at it until he gets his own way. That's how he's got where he has."

"*Who?* Who are we talking about?"

"Kellaway," said George unhappily. "At least, that's what he calls himself now. But I'll swear I knew him once under another name. Like you—another Englishman fixing himself up with another name to hide something."

"And what's your Mr. Kellaway hiding?"

"You don't ask a man in Kellaway's position that kind of question. But I'm as sure as can be that he's the one who was on the ship with us, when your mother brought us across." His face softened. He shrugged at Alan, remembering Nell and loving the memory. "He was up to no good then, from the moment he spotted her. Name of Hesketh then, I'd swear to it."

"Hesketh or Kellaway," said Alan, "what does he want with me? He doesn't know my real name, does he? *Does* he?"

"Alan, he has ways. I didn't mean to say anything, and I'm sure

305

I . . . look, ever since he set foot in this country I guess he's found ways of getting what he wants and finding out what he wants. They say he started by selling prospectuses for oilfields and finding just the suckers who would buy, and just the right big names to tempt them with. Only when they'd paid over the money they found there wasn't any oil there. Then he got himself into financing railroads that never got built, though that didn't stop him taking a fortune out of the set-up. And when it looked like he'd overreached himself, he was bailed out by bankers who set him to buying up a whole network of lines—rail and sea—and tying them into a nice neat consortium. He's no fool, I've got to hand it to him. He's seen it all and done it all."

"And this," said Louisa scornfully, "is the man you want Alan to go and crawl to?"

"I'm not saying he's not good to work for. You get on his right side, he'll treat you right."

"I'm sorry if you've got yourself into an awkward situation," said Alan, "but I don't think I've anything to offer your Mr. Kellaway—or Mr. Hesketh."

"Look, I know it's not a good time, you just getting home an' all. You know where to find me. Sleep on it and come see me tomorrow and we'll talk it over, right?"

When he had left, Louisa said, "I'm sorry. I did try to get him out of here before you showed up."

He reached for her and held her again, and kissed her.

"You'll be hungry," she said.

"That's so." He kissed her and would not let go.

"I got us a fine piece of steak specially for tonight."

"Extravagance."

"I want to keep you strong." Her tongue dabbed at him between her lips.

When she had gone into the kitchen recess he sat back and contemplated the edge of the cot for some minutes. Then he prodded a small heap of newspapers in the corner by his chair. One had been laid slanting across the top, folded as if to pick out one item for his attention. It was surely not Louisa's usual reading matter: births and marriages.

Names sprang out at him. Rosalind Whitlaw, daughter of Mrs. Edmund Gresham and the late Paul Whitlaw, had been married a week ago to one Henry Updyke II.

Louisa stood in the curtained opening to the kitchen, a pan in her hand.

"Do you mind?"

"It means nothing," he said wonderingly.

"You're sure? I didn't know if you'd sooner not . . . if you'd . . . if I ought to say something. Or not."

"There isn't anything to say. Odd, isn't it? A couple of names on paper—and neither of them matters."

His immediate hunger was not for food but to take her to bed and slowly, lingeringly, lovingly prove it.

In the morning the three of them went for a leisurely walk through sultry streets. They stopped for ice cream at a barrel on a corner, under a tattered umbrella. Margaret struggled up in the perambulator, fell back, struggled up again. Her eager eyes strained to follow the striped brightness of an awning over a coffee stall, a trio of birds on a wire, a dozen flashes of colour and movement. Each with a hand on the perambulator, Alan and Louisa pushed contentedly along a route they had evolved this last year without calculation or compass. Then they squeaked to a halt. A street that had been here a month ago was now only a gash across the city, where yet another railway cutting was being gouged out by immigrant labourers swarming in daily from their East River shanty towns. It took five minutes to find a reasonable detour; and on the next corner they were rewarded by the triumphal strains of a five-piece German band.

Louisa caught his eye. Their hands pushing the perambulator edged closer together.

"I could put on a German accent," Alan suggested, "and take up the saxhorn."

"And then I still wouldn't see you enough, because you'd be out all night and every night playing in one of the Bowery beer gardens."

Her cheek nuzzled his. Margaret stared straight at them and chuckled.

"But George is right," he said out of the blue.

"No, he's not."

"We can't stay in that place much longer. It's not fair to you."

"Have I complained?"

"No, my love, but—"

"Please say that again."

"No, you haven't complained, but—"

"The other bit."

"My love," he said.

"As long as you say it like that and go on meaning it, I don't care where we live."

"But I care. There has to be something else. Only not done George's way."

"No," she said. And she added, "My love."

They circled back, past the smell of stale-beer dives and under bridges and towering scaffolding. Behind a steamed-up restaurant window someone was grinding away at an accordion, its wheezing harmonies clashing with those of an Italian organ-grinder further down the street. Everywhere there was music, had to be music, of a kind. Many months ago, looking for a shore job, he had applied for a post at the Metropolitan Concert Hall. But their regular orchestra had already been dismissed. The grandiose building had been a failure in spite of its musicians and its celebrated roof garden. As a theatre it was a worse failure. Now there was talk of turning it into a skating rink. And what else was there for him? As George had frankly said, the sporting houses . . . garish dance halls . . . at best, dull café tinklings as a background to the tinkling of cups and saucers and cake plates.

If I could afford my own piano, and time for regular practice to get me back where I used to be . . .

There must be enormous possibilities, even without a career on the concert platform. Even on board ship. The increasingly luxurious liners would sooner or later demand increasingly lavish orchestras. Already the Germans had bands playing on deck in the morning, and accompanying hymns on Sunday with sonorous brass. The saloons or music rooms could be expanded into dance halls for the evening. Large orchestras, famous professional orchestras, travelling with the ships could alternate—appearing in some New York theatre for a week or two, playing their way back across the Atlantic, fulfilling engagements in Liverpool and London, building up international reputations for themselves and the shipping line.

He laughed aloud.

"What is it?" asked Louisa.

He did not dare tell her that in his mind he was playing at being an entrepreneur on a scale of which George would surely have approved.

They took a wrong turning and found themselves in a dead end, barred by an inlet from the river into which had been tipped rubble, old cartons, boxes and household rubbish from the neighbouring tenements. When they retraced their steps he caught a flicker of movement from the corner. A young man too flashily dressed for this quarter had turned on his heel and apparently succumbed to the attractions of a pawnbroker's window. He wore pale grey trousers and a tightly buttoned cutaway jacket, but what caught Alan's attention was his straw hat. Surely he had seen that twice before this morning? At least three times, now he came to reflect. So they were being followed?

308

He said nothing to Louisa but set a circuitous course for their return home. Through stalls of a street market and through clothes hanging from a rack outside a Russian tailor's he glimpsed the man again, dodging in and out, half-concealing himself in doorways or pretending interest in random windows.

It could hardly have been a man put on to them by George. George had no need to have them shadowed. George knew where to find them—and was waiting for Alan to come and find *him* today.

He wondered if one of his mother's employees had at last, somehow, picked up his trail.

When Louisa had first got in touch with George and he had come to see them after Margaret's birth, it had been on the understanding that he would not disclose their whereabouts to anyone else. He was the kind to stick to such a promise. But he had asked why in God's name Alan didn't find some way of making up with his mother . . . and surely Alan had money due to him through the Gresham-Bostock company, and wasn't it right he should claim it and use it for his wife's benefit? It was Louisa who had finally said that if George didn't shut up she'd be sorry she had ever sought him out.

"Wherever are we going?" demanded Louisa as Alan forced the perambulator round a tight turn into a long, narrow alley.

It was hard to move fast with the perambulator without arousing Louisa's suspicions, but he managed a devious route that in the end seemed to baffle their pursuer. Alan did not espy him again during the two days remaining before he rejoined his ship. Nor did George come to see them; and he did not call in on George and agree to see Mr. Kellaway.

The day was close and humid as he turned on to South Street and made for the East River quay where the *Balearic* lay. Some girls in skimpy cotton frocks flaunted themselves in front of the taverns, and a man stripped to the waist was sprawled across two crates by a mooring bollard.

Looking even more relaxed and summery, the young man with the straw hat stepped in front of Alan.

"Mr. Gresham, if I could have a word with you."

"My name's Pooley. Sorry."

Alan tried to brush past. A hand caught his arm, and before he could shake it free another man had moved out of an alley and clamped his other elbow tightly against his side.

"We only want a chat, Mr. Gresham. There's no need to make a fuss."

Alan sagged, then tensed again. He threw the man to his left against the wall, and spun round to lash out with his fist.

George ducked out from the alley and said, "Please, Alan."

"So you did give our address away."

"I didn't. No, I swear I didn't. They had to find you their own way, and they're not too pleased about that or about me. Please, Alan, I'm in enough trouble already on account of you. Won't you just go along and listen? Just listen, that's all."

"Sure, that's all." The younger man tipped his hat back to its correct angle, but kept one hand ready to grab Alan again if necessary.

"If I miss my ship . . . "

"You won't regret it."

When they steered him down the alley from which they had recently emerged, he wondered if they were going to set about him in the gloom. But they came out at the far end, crossed a street, and led him into an office block above railway sidings. George left them at the door and backed thankfully away.

A hydraulic lift carried them up to the fifth floor.

Flowers in a vase on an ormolu table in the small entrance hall to an apartment reminded him, with their drifting scent, of the pot-pourri long ago in his grandmother's home. An inner door opened. The young man took off his straw hat and waved him in with a brief bow; then retreated, closing the door behind him.

A man stood in the middle of a red and green carpet with his arms folded. He was broad and craggy, with a wizened face and a few trailers of white hair lying across his broad bald head as if pasted down in careful symmetry. He stuck out one large hand.

"So we've found you at last, Mr. Gresham."

Alan dumped his bag unceremoniously beside him, but did not take the proffered hand. "Pooley's the name."

"Well, yes, we know all about that. And mine's Kellaway, Mr. Gresham."

"Pooley," Alan repeated.

"Plenty of folk in New York like to hide behind assumed names. Good reasons, eh?"

"I don't know *your* reasons for hiding, Mr. Kellaway. Or was it Hesketh?"

The seamed face puckered evilly in on itself. The man's chin shook, and his head jutted forward as if to lower in attack.

"Where did you pick up that idea? Who told you that kind of crazy—"

"And who gave you the wrong idea about me? Pooley's the name, and I've got a ship to catch."

Abruptly Kellaway—or Hesketh—hunched himself to one side. Somebody sitting behind him had been almost concealed until now by his squat bulk.

He said, "This *is* the one, isn't it?"

Poppy got up slowly and advanced on Alan. She put up her long fingers to pluck experimentally at his beard.

"It suits you. I'd hardly have recognised you but for the voice." She nodded at her companion. "Oh, yes, this is Alan Gresham."

He said, "Then sit down, Alan. We have a proposition to put to you."

Three

Hull Down

1

NELL WAS countersigning cheques when Edmund arrived. From the little stack of leaflets beside her, and the corrected proof of an outdoor band recital programme, he guessed she was paying another series of bills arising from her musical patronage. As he came up the drive the scent of roses had been heady in the still air. No smoke puffed from chimneys of the terraces below. A dark plume from the sugar refinery rose unwavering but lazy. The library windows ought to have been open on to the day; but when he entered he found the curtains drawn, shutting out not merely the sunlight but the view of the river, and Nell sitting with her back to them.

"Sit down, Edmund. I'll not keep you a minute."

He chose an armchair across the room, studied the weave of the curtain against the brightness outside, and hummed abstractedly.

"Whatever is that silly little tune?" asked Nell without looking up.

"One of the latest street jingles. About those two cotton shed fires by Hornby Dock. Scurrilous stuff about the insurance—but everybody's chanting it, and it has one of those infernally catchy tunes that plague you for days."

"Hm."

Nell's pen scratched another signature.

Edmund said, "All the philanthropy in the world won't bring Alan back, you know."

She made a point of reading very slowly through an itemized account for the recital marquee she had funded for the great Liverpool Shipperies Exhibition in Wavertree Park. "I've never made any effort to bring Alan back," she said flatly. "You're the one who keeps running that advertisement in the paper."

"You don't try to trace him directly, no. But what's all that"—he waved at the papers on her desk—"if not an offering to the gods?"

"We've always played our part in local charity."

"A libation," he insisted, "in the hope they'll listen and give him a following wind homewards."

She looked up at last. "You've come here to pick a quarrel, Edmund?"

"I've come here for decisions on the whole future of our enterprise. Without ships and passengers, there'd be no money to spare on philanthropy."

He pushed himself up from his chair and went to the window, looping back one of the curtains so that he could gaze out over the rooftops. In this stuffy room he needed a reminder of the river traffic and the reality of the outlying ocean and all he had come here to talk about.

"And how's your wife?" asked Nell coolly.

"Well, thank you. Back from New York only yesterday. She's been over for Rosalind's wedding."

"Rosalind. Ah, yes. Now, if only . . ." Nell stopped. "Tell me, why *did* your wife snatch the girl away from my son? And how?"

"It's not worth bothering with now."

"I'd still like to know."

"You'd better ask her."

"You know I'd never bring myself to that."

"Then forget it. There are more important things to settle today."

"You really are in truculent mood, Edmund." Nell shielded her eyes against the brightness. "I do wish you'd come away from that window. I can't see you properly."

He went back to his chair.

Nell pushed her papers to one side. "Well, now. What's so very important? And has your wife's recent return from America anything to do with these fidgets of yours?"

"We have to face up to it sooner or later, anyway."

"Face up to what?"

"The question of whether we find a new way of financing Gresham-Bostock—whether even, it's worth trying—or whether we sell out."

The sun sent the shadow of a fold of curtain halfway across the carpet between them. One bunched loop blended with an urn in the pattern to make a puffy caricature of an old man's head. If you wished to see it as Jesse Bostock's head, it was not too difficult.

Nell said, "Your wife wants you to sell out?"

"We're not talking about Poppy."

"Oh, but I think we are. What's behind it all?"

"Poppy has shares in the firm, true. I made some of mine over to her a few years ago. After proper consultation with you."

"Am I denying it?"

"But they don't give her any power to overrule the two of us. Even if I added her holding back to mine, she and I still wouldn't have a majority holding."

"Which you want?"

"I only want us to look at the matter fairly and squarely now, Nell. In the interests of all of us."

Nell rested her arms on the desk and leaned forward in a travesty of solemn attentiveness. Once her eyes would have sparkled, and at the mere mention of selling out she would have let fly with an exuberant broadside. Now she simply looked tired and cynical, listlessly daring him to go on.

The deep glow of her hair had faded over the years to a brindled tawny and sand mixture, with intrusive streaks of grey. He remembered her so clearly as a fine, radiant young woman with expansive gestures and a tendency to plunge from boldness to shyness and then leap up again without warning. Now in her early fifties she was handsome rather than beautiful, and the impetuous grace of her body had been disciplined within severely formal dresses and jackets—a body and mind corseted by dour willpower. The power was still there, in spite of her years of withdrawal. That seclusion, too, had been wilfully restrictive: just as her devotion to good works and charitable functions at which she herself never appeared—an invisible, unsociable Lady Bountiful—had been calculated, rigidly administered, rigidly and unalterably marked out.

She had detached herself for so long from the everyday business of the company. Yet her approval was needed for every move. He knew ten times more about the Gresham-Bostock operations than she did now; yet she retained the power to disturb him and put him forever on the defensive. If he was to win her over now, he must state his case clearly and incontestably.

But when he thought of winning, it also seemed to him that they would both be losers.

317

He could not falter now. Before him was Nell. Behind him in Falkner Square he had left Poppy; but had brought with him the cold, contemptuous demands on which she had insisted.

He said, "I see no way that we can retain our independence. The big combines are moving in on us. While you've been sitting here relying on our original ideas to keep us forging ahead with only an occasional trim of sail here or there to suit a temporary change in the weather, men out there have been forging powerful new alliances—and gobbling up the smaller fry into their monopoly. What Bismarck has been doing to the German states, the American barons are doing to independent companies on land and sea—drawing them into a conglomeration that could dominate the whole market."

"We've talked about this before. We're not small fry. And we've avoided the predators smartly enough so far."

"We've talked about it before," he agreed, "but the boarding parties haven't been so powerful before."

"Who are we talking about this time, then?"

"Principally a financier called Jeremiah Wolcott Groman. Years ago he moved into steel, and when he'd virtually cornered that he began buying up railroads, one after another. Somewhere along the line it must have dawned on him what we've always known—that shipping lines and railway lines are extensions of one another. So now he's turning his attention to the sea. He's bought the whole capital stock of two American lines, frozen another one out by some tricky wharfage deals, has made an offer to a British line and hopes to grab a German one as well. And our New York associates tell me he now has his eye on Gresham-Bostock."

"I'm sure you're capable of handling the matter."

It was not so much that Nell's attention was wandering as that she had no driving urge to get to grips with such matters. She expected from Edmund a brisk presentation of pros and cons on which she would graciously give a ruling and then return to her other occupations.

"This responsibility's too great for one director only," he said. "We have to decide whether it's in any way possible to continue on our same course, or change tack altogether, or—"

"Or throw ourselves overboard in mid-ocean," she derisively took up his metaphor.

"Look, Nell. To combat Groman's bid to buy us out or squeeze us out we'd need to raise capital by putting our still-unissued shares on the market. And we'd have no way of ensuring that they weren't all snapped up by a Groman nominee—giving him a big enough say in the management of the company to alter our whole family concept of it. And if we try to go on without any extra finance, I doubt if we've got the strength. Wylie sold out last year, and I have a feeling those Atlantic Bridge shares were picked up by the consortium."

"If Alan were here—"

"If Alan were here and chose to sell off his holding, the balance could be dangerously tipped."

"Yes, I see. If your wife and Alan were to turn against us—"

"A situation hardly likely to arise. But I'd like to know just where Alan is and what he *would* do if it came to a battle."

"So that's why you've been advertising for him."

"I've seen the danger of something like this for a long time."

"And your wife?" said Nell like a prosecuting counsel. "How anxious has she been for you to continue that advertising? And what tricks has she up her sleeve—and what does she propose to do with her shares?"

Edmund took a shaky breath. "I won't deny that Poppy wants us to sell out."

"So she may become a lady of leisure, unsullied by the grime of coarse commercialism? So there'll be no risk of business battles and expenditure of energy and money, maybe ending in penury. She doesn't want to end up as the slavey of a bankrupt husband—is that it?"

"You don't have to make it sound so selfish, Nell."

"Don't I? Come to think of it, perhaps that's not the only motive. If your wife were to sell out and persuade you to do the same," said Nell thoughtfully, "I believe she'd want to do so in such a way that the very name of Gresham-Bostock would be obliterated. She would love to destroy us—you included, Teddy."

"You're making too much of it, Nell."

"I may have lost interest in many of the company's affairs in recent times," said Nell, "but I've not lost my senses."

"I'm here," Edmund attempted, "to work the whole thing out rationally with you."

"To persuade me that we may as well give up. However you may dress it up, that's basically what you're saying."

He could not remain still under that sceptical gaze. Once more he got up and went to the window.

The river was dominated by the great sad hulk of the steamship *Great Eastern*, reduced to servitude as a floating fun-fair under the auspices of Lewis's department store, garish lettering on its hull and on waving banners promising acrobats and gymnasts, military bands and equestrian displays. So much for the dead, disillusioned Brunel's grandiose dream. And so much, before long, for Gresham-Bostock.

He felt the slow lash of Poppy's peremptory scorn across his neck, and said towards that vista of lost grandeur, "Nell, there can be no decision without you. Nobody can force anything on you. But since the company has no future without you, and you've chosen to play no active part for a long time, may we not just as well strike our colours? I'm tired, Nell. I've lost the will to go on steering this craft."

"And your wife will give you no peace until you sign off."

"Give me one good reason for going on," he said. "One good reason for not selling out. One reason why you think we could survive on our own. Or why we should even try."

Nell stared into the empty space on the desk before her. She found no reflection in the scuffed morocco panel.

"I can't give you one," she said.

"So we sell?"

"What does it matter?"

"You can name your own price. Make a fortune, devote it to all the good works, the concerts—start enjoying yourself."

For a moment he thought she would laugh. But all she did was scratch one finger musingly into the slit between morocco and wood. "I'm sure you're right," she said indifferently. "There's nothing to hold on for."

It was over so quickly. He had known what had to be done and had come here to do it, yet could not believe they had so dully, defeatedly agreed. So many years of work, of struggle, of achievement—and now the two of them in this sunny room had agreed on surrender before the first battle in the threatening war had even been joined. He was relieved, but lost and empty.

"So I'll draw up the figures."

"I leave it to you."

"I'll let you know exactly where we stand, and what price we can bargain for. And we must find out what to do about the shares in Alan's name."

"You'll know what to do."

Nell came across the hall to let him out. In their silence, with nothing more to say, they were both startled by the jangle of the bell-pull just as she was about to open the door. A maid came hurrying along the passage beyond the green baize-covered door, but Nell put her hand on the knob and turned it.

The young, bearded man on the step stood quite still.

Edmund stared into the beard, sure he recognised the set of the mouth. Then into the familiar eyes—the warm, sensual, unreliable, restless eyes of his brother Malcolm, yet with a grey intensity that was Nell's legacy.

Nell said, "I'm sorry, I don't think we—"

"Alan," said Edmund. "It's Alan."

He stood back. Alan Gresham walked past his mother into Bostock's Brow.

"You said his name was Hesketh?" Nell tasted an old nausea on her tongue. "You're sure of that? The same Fred Hesketh?"

The memory of that foul man was somehow more vivid and immediate than the presence of this stranger before her. Here was her son Alan, but he was taller and leaner than she remembered, and bearded and older, and he had not kissed her as he came in or said more than "Hello, mother." She longed to reach out and touch him. But it was a habit she had lost. When he was little she had loved to put one arm round him and one round his brother Jesse and hug them close, yet even then it had not been as easy and natural as it was to touch and embrace her husband. She had loved Malcolm's touch, hungered for it, wanted to touch only Malcolm, even, sometimes, flinched at the unexpected touch of her children. With him there had always been the catch of loving breath and the delicious skim of fingers over flesh, lips over lips. Without him there had been nothing but cold, clutching pain: not just the first shocking pain of loss, but a lasting ache of physical revulsion, a prickliness, a drawing back from the touch of a hand or the most casual brushing of shoulders in a crowd. Now she wanted so much to put her arms round Alan. For him to make the first move and come to her.

He would not. And she could not.

He said, "The fellow calls himself Kellaway. But George Fenwick remembers him as Hesketh. And from the way he reacted when I used that name, I'd say it was real enough."

"He was hateful. Despicable."

"I think he harbours an old hatred against you, too, mother."

I will get up and kiss him. We can talk later. Nothing is more important than this. Alan's home. I will get up and go to him.

And he will turn away.

I'll say I'm sorry, I behaved stupidly, he should never have been allowed to go away as he did, he must sit down now and play the piano and somehow it will all be as it was . . . or as it ought to have been.

Edmund said, "You'd better tell us the whole story, Alan."

The bearded stranger with the serious, courteous voice said, "I was tracked down by this Hesketh's underlings. They forced me to go and see Hesketh. I might have fought them off if it hadn't been for George. Things would have been made very unpleasant for George if I hadn't gone along. Anyway, whatever Hesketh was when you knew him, mother, he's doing nicely for himself now—working on behalf of a financier called Groman."

"We know about Groman," said Edmund.

"On Groman's behalf, Hesketh has instructions to buy up the Atlantic Bridge Company and the whole Gresham-Bostock concern."

"That, too, we guessed."

"He offered me a quarter of a million for my shares."

"Dollars?"

"Pounds."

Nell thought of the money that she might expect from the sale of her own shares. Edmund would do well; she would do magnificently. They could live out their lives not merely in comfort but in luxury. Give up the struggle, and turn to less arduous occupations. It was what they had been talking about such a short time ago. This news confirmed all that Edmund had been saying.

She nodded across the drawing-room, and Edmund went to pour Alan another glass of sherry.

She said, "And you accepted?"

"I . . . didn't commit myself. I told them there'd be trouble if I didn't rejoin my ship, and once I reached Liverpool I'd claim my shares and see about transferring them—if I decided in favour of their offer."

"And you've decided? You're accepting?"

"It depends on you. The more I thought about it the more I knew I had to come and tell you what they're up to. So we all know, and it's all above board."

323

"You came back," she marvelled. "And . . . that girl. What does she think about it? I mean, if you're still with her. If you . . . "

"I married Louisa," he said. "Thank God."

It was impossible that he should be grown up, should have stormed out on her and now have a wife. But he was a stranger: she could believe anything about a stranger as cold and remote as this one.

"And she knows what you're doing?"

"I had no chance to tell her. I was nearly late for my ship as it was. Tomorrow I'll write to her."

"Tomorrow?"

"When I know what I have to tell her."

"What do you think she'll say? You coming back here, and—"

"Whatever it is, she'll say I've done right."

"You're so sure of her?"

"Yes," said Alan, "I'm so sure."

The confidence in his bearing showed Nell how he had grown up, grown far beyond her.

"You still haven't told us in so many words," she said, "what course you're proposing to take."

Edmund offered, too eagerly, "With a payment of that size you could set up your wife and family . . . you have a family . . . ?"

"The child Louisa was expecting when mother threw her out was a girl."

A granddaughter, thought Nell longingly.

"You could set up your wife and daughter," Edmund resumed, "in comfort. Set yourselves up where you like, take up your musical career again, hire your own halls, devote-yourself wholeheartedly to what you really want to do."

"That's exactly what they told me."

"But still you came home to—"

"To give you time to decide on your own position."

"After you've sold out."

"Is that what you want me to do?"

"We have a choice?" asked Nell quietly.

"If I'd been sure my own benefit was all that mattered, I needn't ever have bothered to come and warn you."

Edmund said, "We're not blaming you for thinking of yourself. We're all having to do that right now. Your mother and I had already decided—"

"Wait!" said Nell. "Please, Edmund. There was always this one factor we couldn't be sure of. We didn't know about Alan."

"You must surely know now," said her son. "If you *want* to know."

324

A warmth such as she had not experienced for years began to glow within Nell like the warmth of a fine brandy in her stomach. She looked at her son and through him saw the ghost of Malcolm, but a ghost growing more substantial and resolute; and at last, amazed, found she could think of poor, weak, entrancing Malcolm without pain.

"Alan, are you telling me you want us to fight?"

Instead of answering he turned to his uncle. "What about you?"

"If you knew all the facts, you'd know how impossible that is. Your mother agrees with me. We've already made up our minds. We knew Groman would be closing his fist on us sooner or later. Now there's no alternative to selling out while we still have something to sell."

"Aunt Poppy agrees with you, No doubt she's already told you."

Nell felt the intoxication still rising. She was awake, alert, thrilling to danger with all her old instincts. "I was right, then, Edmund. About your wife's influence, I mean."

He hesitated. It was enough. As he fumbled, "Naturally I put the facts to her so I could speak for both of us when I got here," Nell swung towards Alan for confirmation. "But what do *you* know about her?"

"She was there. With Kellaway. Or Hesketh."

"There in New York—planning to sell out?"

"She has already sold."

"She told you so?"

"And told me she'd have no trouble persuading Uncle Edmund to follow suit once she got home."

"Edmund?" said Nell.

He sank deeper into his chair and closed his eyes. "I saw no alternative. I still see none."

"You don't want to persuade Alan to come in with us and fight?"

"Let's be sensible. We'll all do better if we get out now than if we flounder on. We're bound to be beaten in the end. And then they won't be offering high prices to us: they'll dictate their own terms, and pick up the pieces."

Nell rose to her feet. "Since your intentions have been made so clear, I don't think we need detain you any longer."

Edmund flushed. "Half an hour ago you were ready to give in. Now you've been blown in the other direction by some sentimental wind. You're going to try hatching some absurd scheme with Alan. I can see it. Nell, for his own sake—"

"I'm going to listen to him, that's all. If there's some profitable bargaining to be done, it's best for us to settle the asking price between us, isn't it?"

When Edmund had gone she was about to risk a step towards her son, extending a tentative hand, when he said soberly, "Uncle Edmund has his wife's wishes to contend with, you know. Just as I have Louisa's."

"About your wife . . . "

"When you talk to Uncle Edmund you try not to mention Poppy's name. I've noticed. *My* wife's name, mother, is Louisa."

"About Louisa. You said she'd approve of what you've done."

"Just so far. She'll see why I had to come here and let you know what those pirates are up to. But she won't want me to stay and become too involved."

"You've got to stay, Alan. There isn't anyone else. If Edmund deserts, who's going to stand by me?"

"I'll stand by you until it's all settled. And then we'll decide what to do about reallocating my shares, and I'll be off. Back home."

"This is your home."

"No."

"You've got to stay. And you've got to make your . . . make Louisa come. And the little girl."

"She'd refuse."

"You're her husband."

"That doesn't mean I can command her. Not on a matter like this."

"Doesn't it? Alan"—she ventured closer, still excited but touched with fear of this son who was so determined a stranger—"I suppose I've seemed a domineering woman most of my life."

"Yes, mother."

"But it only *seemed* like that. Trying to keep things on an even keel between my father and mother. Then my grandfather and his moods. And then your father, and the whole Gresham-Bostock business, which became more mine than his, and then he was no longer there and . . . Oh, Alan, I've been the commander for so long, and I never wanted to be. Never. All I ever wanted was a man to look after me and tell me what to do and—"

"Mother!" He was laughing. "You're an old fraud."

She felt an impulse to put him across her knee and spank him, and that made her laugh too, and he saw it and they were both laughing and now, at last, his arms were round her and they rocked to and fro.

"I'm not a fraud," she cried jubilantly, "and I'm not all that old. In the prime of life, most people would say."

"So you're perfectly capable of staying on the bridge a while longer."

"With the right crew behind me, perhaps. So I'll ship your wife and daughter over here whether you like it or not."

"They won't come. Louisa wouldn't budge."

"When we've settled Groman and Hesketh and the rest of them"—

Nell would brook no obstacles now, she sniffed the challenge in the air and was eager to take it on and take on everything and everybody else as well—"I'll go and fetch her. Myself. I'll go down on my knees if I have to."

"To get your own way in the end, as usual?"

"No," she said. "To give you the chance of having *your* way, whatever it may be, in the end."

Nell went to the window. The sun had gone round, so that one of the curtains had had to be pulled right back. But the glass was still warm. She twisted the catch and opened the double casement windows. A breath of air fingered one of the papers on her desk, nudging it playfully towards the edge.

Alan came and stood beside her. Awkwardly, with a reluctance she acknowledged and loved, he kissed her behind the ear.

She said happily, "It's time we left harbour and engaged the enemy. What big guns can we bring to bear?"

THE PRESENCE of a woman in the room manifestly perturbed Vice-Admiral Sir Andrew Erdington. The Liverpool Parliamentary Office had found it necessary to indulge in many diplomatic stratagems to bring about this meeting in the first place; there were reservations in official minds before it was even authorised; and the notion of admitting a woman into naval confidence, even when her motives had an undeniably patriotic element, was not at all to an old sea-dog's taste.

Erdington was a pink-faced man with wavy brown hair and a brown beard trimmed smartly in imitation of that favoured by the Prince of Wales. He had placed himself at the head of the table with the Parliamentary Under Secretary of State on his right and a black-suited, black-shod civil servant with a black-lead pencil and black-bound notebook on his left. Nell sat facing them, flanked by Alan and Mr. Visick of the Liverpool Parliamentary Office. The Vice-Admiral looked hopefully at Visick, tacitly inviting him to propound the case that the authorities were called on to consider. But when he had formally opened the meeting, it was Nell who spoke.

The journey from Liverpool to Euston Station had been tiring and unsettling. It was so long since she had travelled such a distance. Half the time she longed for the seclusion of Bostock's Brow; the other half, she berated herself for being so ridiculous. She was only just over fifty, not some doddering old woman afraid of the noise and grit and jolting and

328

speed of a modern railway train. How could she have allowed herself to sink into such a pathetic parody of old age? She tried practising, under her breath, what she would say at the forthcoming meeting. But without the direct stimulus of an audience—or an enemy—she could not summon up the right, clear thoughts. Instead she looked out at green fields streaming away behind, and when the train slowed or stopped, hissing and chafing, at some level crossing, she let her mind wander down a meandering lane that led somewhere, somehow, to Malcolm.

She remembered Malcolm, when they were first married, asking why they didn't sell up and go round the world and enjoy life. If they had done that, he might be alive today.

But there had never been such an "if" in her mind then; and apart from her momentary weakness in the face of Edmund's defeatism, there was none now.

They were met at Euston by Mr. Visick, with a waiting carriage. He was nervous when they shook hands, and stammered on his first few words. Her reputation had preceded her: a reputation so absurdly at variance with all she felt and remembered. Seeing in other people's eyes a fear of her own fearsomeness, she could think of herself only as an uncertain girl of eighteen, aggressive to hide her uncertainties, hard-working to disguise the fact that if once she stopped she would betray her own sense of a lack of any direction. If she raised her voice, people cringed; if she spoke quietly, they were afraid she must be planning something sly and dangerous.

On the station platform a young woman ran to meet a young man descending from the train. Her arms were outstretched, she made no secret of her joy. Nell turned, as the carriage drove away, to glimpse the couple's embrace. *A woman in her early twenties—and I'm younger than you,* thought Nell, *younger and less confident, if only you knew it. I've lived so long and yet it's not long, it has been no time at all, and I'm still younger than you. Don't you see?*

They were driven past the Admiralty in Whitehall, and stopped some yards away. Visick led Alan and herself through Horse Guards Parade and round to a side entrance. Men, thought Nell with a resurgence of derisive confidence: men loving to play at secrets and subterfuges.

And now here she was, installed in this sombre room evocative of one of the little masculine sanctums tucked away in the corners of the Beckwith Club, smelling faintly of furniture polish, cigar smoke and, despite its cleanness, of long-established dust. And she was awake; and ready.

She said, "You'll not be unaware, Sir Andrew, of the growth of American investment in British shipping."

"We've been aware of it, madam, for a long time."

329

"Some of that investment, and the mutual cooperation that went with it, has been beneficial to this country. A number of individual partnerships have cut costs, brought trade to our vessels, employment to our crews, and work to our shipyards. They have also created goodwill between our country and the United States. But now there's a decline in new building. The yards are feeling the pinch."

"You refer specifically, of course, to Merseyside shipyards. Your own special interest, naturally."

"It's in the interest of all of us to keep the yards busy," said Nell. "For the sake of the whole country's economy. And the health of our merchant fleets—and the Royal Navy."

"The one would be poorer without the others," conceded the Vice-Admiral. "Much depends, though, on which is accorded prior place. I'm given to understand, Mrs. Gresham, that you have it in mind to use the Royal Navy to bolster up your commercial operations."

"A slight oversimplification, sir," intervened Visick with a deferential grin.

"Then perhaps one of you will expand."

Edington was obviously hoping that one of the two men would take up the discussion. But Nell intended to remain at the helm.

"We have in mind nothing, Sir Andrew, which is not to the benefit of us all," she said. "Perhaps I may remind you that last year there was a scare over a possible war with Russia, and a lot of talk about a campaign in the Black Sea."

The Vice-Admiral was affronted. Military talk was not the province of ladies. "A scare, madam? There was a controlled exercise in partial mobilisation against a possible emergency, but nobody would refer to that as—"

"A scare," Nell repeated. Mr. Visick bowed his head and winced apologetically. She went on, "At that time the Navy took over a number of commercial steamships and hastily fitted them up as armed cruisers and troop carriers."

"I really do not need telling all this, Mrs. Gresham. The facts are not unknown to me."

"I want you to realise that they are not unknown to the rest of the country, either. And the facts are that many of the ships you commandeered were quite unsuitable, the gun mountings were makeshift, a deal of expensive damage was done in ripping out cabins to build up coal bunkers and shield machinery above the water line, and when the war scare was over there had still been no adequate training of Royal Navy men in the handling of such craft. Will there be the same undignified scramble next time?"

"This meeting was not called in order that a civilian might question the future intentions of the Sea Lords."

"The meeting was suggested," said Nell politely but firmly, "so that we might put to you a proposition that will not profit my family personally, but will profit our company and its employees and our country. And will offer the Navy a properly planned, suitably engineered and efficiently crewed second-line fleet in time of emergency."

Vice-Admiral Erdington stared at her as he might have stared at a hitherto unknown, unidentifiable vessel coming over the horizon towards him at an alarmingly improbable speed.

"I don't think the question of Her Majesty's men-o'-war relying on private enterprise has ever been seriously contemplated."

"Then start contemplating now." Nell was beginning to enjoy the encounter with this braided, bemedalled warrior. She measured her stride, measured the pace of her words, and knew she was capable of anything she set herself. "The Americans have kept our shipyards busy building vessels that fly the Red Ensign but belong in all save registration to the United States. Now they've learnt all our technical skills, they're building more and more in their own yards. And when they want any of our fleets, they buy them up lock, stock and barrel."

"We've still got a healthy number of independent lines."

"Very few. And far from healthy. If Gresham-Bostock are to remain independent and not hand over liners—your potential armed cruisers and troopships, Sir Andrew—into American custody, then we need some subsidy from the British government. I'm not talking about loans, or postal subsidies: we know the mess they've got other companies into. What we put on the table here is a plan for real partnership. Within our own country. Not enforced amalgamation into combine or consortium, but a marriage freely undertaken—and fruitful. We will build ships to a specification agreed between our company and the Royal Navy. They'll be floating palaces good enough to compete with the Germans and American-owned liners flying their own or British colours. The admiralty will ensure that we are paid a regular subsidy so long as we draw at least half our crews from the ranks of the Royal Naval Reserve."

"Damme, you mean you'd engage . . .you'd train . . ."

"Isn't that what's been lacking in the past? We give officers and men the experience they need, they're in tip-top condition if war breaks out, they know the ships and their capabilities, and while we're training them in the national interest we're also paying them. If it becomes necessary to arm the ships, they'll have been so designed that armour plating can easily be attached, the gun mountings are ready to be opened out, the drill is known to at least half the crew, and the whole thing is still in British

331

hands—not diffused through those of holding companies and speculators whose first thought in a crisis will be to get their property out of dangerous waters, not send it *in* where it's most needed."

Vice-Admiral Erdington was endeavouring, with little success, to preserve an impartial demeanour. When he raised another query it was with respect: instead of seeking to confute Nell he was offering a formal objection in the hope that she would shoot it out of the water.

"You've summed it up admirably, Mrs. Gresham. But we haven't been sitting idle since the scare . . . I mean, since the minor disturbance last year. We've reached agreement with several lines that all steamers flying the Red Ensign, no matter what the shareholding of other nationalities, are in effect British territory—armed cruisers on loan until such time as they are required."

"And when the need arises, they will be handed over obediently?"

"We have no reason to suppose otherwise."

"Sir Andrew, I don't believe you and the Lords of Admiralty are entirely unaware of the intrinsic danger. If Britain finds herself involved in a European war—*any* war—do you suppose that American owners of expensive ships, whatever flag they may be flying for financial or political reasons, will simply relinquish them to the Royal Navy? Wouldn't most of them somehow, by pure chance, find themselves in United States ports—and somehow be detained there out of harm's way until the fighting's over?"

"A very cynical view, Mrs. Gresham."

"One which you take yourself, Sir Andrew, unless I'm much mistaken."

"You mustn't put words into my mouth."

"Let's hear your own words, then."

The Vice-Admiral glanced at the under-secretary, who shifted on his chair and leaned across to see what the clerk was writing in his notebook so that he might later, if things grew too embarrassing, order it struck out.

Sir Andrew took command. "In English law, madam, as I've already observed, a British ship is a segment of British territory that happens from time to time to be afloat. You speak of American owners. No such thing: no British ship or any part of it can ever be owned by a foreigner. It's permanently our territory and when we want it to reinforce our mainland resources, we simply ask for it back."

"Legalistically very fine," said Nell. "In actual fact . . . a fiction. Of course no actual British ship is directly owned by a foreigner. But scores of them do belong to companies registered in Britain that are in effect dominated by American shareholders."

"Perfectly legitimate."

332

"Perfectly. But—"

"Those shareholders," said Erdington doggedly, "have no rights over the actual vessels."

Alan leaned forward. "Sir Andrew, if I may. I've been living quite some time in New York. And I make my living on the Atlantic, in a Birkenhead-built liner run by Americans. I know folk over there. I get on fine with them—it's a great country, a great people. All kinds of people. But they're just as proud and patriotic in their outlook as we are, and they've got every right to be. Let's be honest, plenty of them hate us and think the War of Independence is still on, and wouldn't lend us a rowing-boat if we were drowning. And those who do like us—or at worst are neutral—do you think that after watching good American money and effort being put into the building up of a shipping line, they're going to sit by while their most obvious tangible assets are taken away from them? Taken away and used, maybe destroyed, in a conflict involving purely British interests?"

When the Vice-Admiral did not answer, Nell said, "Let us make ourselves plain. The financial interests of my son and myself will be better served if we sell out to the Groman consortium. If we struggle on in the teeth of their opposition we shall have to work harder than ever before, spend more money, defend ourselves against every conceivable attack, and perhaps still end up without a penny. From our personal point of view we'd be fools not to give in now."

"You don't sound as if you intend to give in, though."

"Given the right encouragement, we'll fight on."

The under-secretary put his mouth to Sir Andrew's ear and mumbled something, at the same time stabbing his forefinger at a sheet of figures laid on the table before them. Erdington nodded. Then he looked back at Nell and meditatively twirled one end of his curling moustache.

Beside her, Alan eased himself on to the edge of his chair. Nell put a hand on his knee. They both sensed that they were winning, but it would be a mistake to show either complacency or impatience.

Erdington said weightily, "We have never supposed that these mergers were entirely favourable to British maritime policy. So far we haven't wanted to arouse antagonism. In a world at peace, peaceful financial manoeuvres are neither illegal nor hostile. But if *all* British shipping concerns were to be swallowed up in some foreign amalgamation . . . if there were no resources for us to fall back on when the international climate deteriorated . . ."

Nell waited, hardly breathing.

"So here we are," said Erdington. "To maintain our own freedom of manoeuvre—"

"To maintain that freedom," Nell took him up, "in peace and in war,

333

to maintain our national jurisdiction over our national possessions on the high seas, we must ensure that controlling interest in our Gresham-Bostock company is always held by British nationals. We want an agreed national subsidy, Sir Andrew, and we want it guaranteed over a long period so that we can plan building and sailing schedules far ahead. In return we do what I promised earlier: we build ships according to specifications agreed between you and ourselves, we give precedence in our choice of crew to Royal Naval Reserve officers and men, and train them in a dual role, which the Admiralty and my directors will work out to our mutual satisfaction."

"What subsidy would you think appropriate?" The under-secretary's voice was thin and sceptical, for that was how he had been trained. But his eyes were respectful, and he held a pencil poised as if to begin checking figures the moment she advanced any.

Nell said, "I may take it that we are agreed in principle, then?"

Vice-Admiral Sir Andrew Erdington got up from the table, stalked ponderously round it, and stood above her holding out his hand.

"I think we have to be, Mrs. Gresham. If we're not to have our decks shot away from under us."

THEY MOVED from their different directions towards the old counting-house. A meeting here would attract less attention and be less liable to interruption than one held in the main quayside offices or in Kellaway's Lime Street hotel. Edmund and Poppy drove from Falkner Square; Nell and Alan from Bostock's Brow; the man who called himself Kellaway from his hotel. They arrived within a few minutes of one another: Kellaway last, impressing on them that he was the one whose hour it was and on whom their future depended.

"Make yourself comfortable."

Alan wondered, too late, if Uncle Edmund had another reason for convening the meeting here. On his own familiar territory he would implicitly be in charge of the proceedings and more at ease than elsewhere.

But Alan's mother seemed unperturbed. She lowered herself into the creaking leather of the old couch, patted the ochre bulge beside her to indicate that Alan should join her, and tucked herself into the arm so that she could keep both Kellaway and Poppy in full view.

The two women had attired themselves specially for the occasion. In a new tailor-made costume of olive green cashmere, Poppy was returning Nell's scrutiny impassively. Nell herself sported a tight blue jacket with six rows of braid across her breast, like a military uniform, and the silk-covered buttons had an equally trim appearance. In one appalling instant Alan saw how utterly and mercilessly the two women loathed each other. It was unalterable, deep down, physical. Like a minor ailment swelling into incurable disease, it might have dormant periods but in one encounter could twist viciously to life again. There was no antidote. It would have been laughable if it had not been so savage: laughable in the way that women bickering on committees were laughable, in the way that disputes within church flower arranging rosters were laughable—not laughable when you felt the heat of this scorching, unquenchable hatred.

There they were, the two of them, nodding a barely perceptible nod at each other.

Poppy was flanked by her husband Edmund on one side, the man who chose to call himself Kellaway on the other. The man's air of bullying disdain was as much a garment as Poppy's expensive new outfit.

Nell fired the first shot. "Goodness me, we *have* come on in the world, haven't we, Mr. Hesketh?"

"I'm afraid I don't yet have the pleasure of your acquaintance, ma'am. And my name—"

"My sister-in-law, Mrs. Gresham," said Edmund hurriedly. "Mr. Kellaway."

"The acquaintance never was any pleasure, Mr. Hesketh," said Nell, "and I doubt if it'll improve."

Alan leaned over the end of the couch to prop his brief-bag against it. Hesketh looked piercingly at him, worried by this closeness to his mother. Edmund must already have reported doubts as to which way Alan would jump. There had been two messages sent to the house, asking him to call at the hotel. He had ignored both.

Edmund closed the window. To the usual noises of the street had been added in recent years the screech of wheels and brakes as horse-drawn tramcars slowed on the steepest pitch of the slope.

"Very cosy," Hesketh approved. "Nice and private. Don't want to eat humble pie in public, do we, Miss Bostock? Oh, sorry—Miss Meredith. Always did make that mistake."

"So you do remember me."

"Wouldn't swear to it. I mean, I might say I remembered you as Mrs. Fenwick. Gets so confused, doesn't it?"

"At least we know now what we're talking about."

"Oh, we do indeed. That I'll wager, Miss . . . er, Mrs. Gresham. Let's settle for Mrs. Gresham, shall we?"

"Yes, Mr. Kellaway. If I can settle for Hesketh."

Edmund intervened. "Shall we get down to business?"

336

"I've been looking forward to this," said Hesketh, "for a long time."

It was Hesketh who did most of the talking, but Alan remained conscious above all of his mother and that other woman who sat so still, poised, like an iridescent snake ready to strike.

Just once Poppy smiled an encouraging little smile of complicity, inviting him to remember the promises made to him that day in New York. When he did not respond, her lips remained parted for a few seconds but the smile had fled. He remembered the sensual dab and sting of her tongue, years ago; now its sting would be venomous.

"What Mr. Groman offers," Hesketh was saying, "is mighty generous. Better than you could hope for anywhere else. Isn't that so, Mr. Gresham . . . Edmund? And young Alan here . . ." He probed, as Poppy had done, for a response—and got none. His voice grew harsher. "All right, let's put our cards on the table. We've already picked up the old Wylie shares. We're willing to offer you half a million pounds for your shares, Mrs. Gresham. We've agreed on half a million between Edmund and his wife here. And a quarter of a million for Alan."

"You're wasting our time," said Nell.

"In addition there'd be another million and a quarter for all Gresham-Bostock assets—offices, warehouses, dock facilities. You wouldn't have another care in the world. Live the way you like, enjoy yourselves. It's been hard going, Mrs. Gresham. You owe yourself a rest." Hesketh's face wrinkled in on itself as he looked at Alan again, half-jovial, half-menacing. "And we've already agreed you're all set for that famous musical career of yours, eh? Ready to go a whole lot further. And we take all the cares off your shoulders—every ship, every last building, that headache of a hotel, every ledger, every inkwell."

Each phrase was meant to sound tempting; but from Hesketh's mouth the words came out as spiteful and gloating. Alan could almost see the man's hands clamping on to the Gresham-Bostock flagpole and snapping it; plucking bricks from the terminus until it crumbled and collapsed; tearing the gilded initials off the doors of the hotel; wiping out every last vestige of the Gresham-Bostock name and tradition.

Nell said, "I have no intention of selling."

"You'd be crazy not to. When these two gentlemen have been paid, and with the Wylie shares and Mrs. Gresham's—"

"I told you, I'm not selling."

"I was speaking of the other Mrs. Gresham."

Alan felt the faintest tremor through the couch as his mother tensed. In her own mind she had never really allowed that Poppy, however legally and correctly, could be referred to as Mrs. Gresham.

Edmund said, "Nell, do see reason. We did agree we couldn't fight on in present conditions."

"That was before we knew who the enemy was."

"Mr. Groman doesn't think of himself as your enemy," said Hesketh.

But you do, thought Alan. And Poppy, too, watching his mother, recording her every expression.

Nell said, "Gresham-Bostock is not for sale."

"You can't compete with us," said Hesketh with malevolent moderation, "unless you raise one hell of a lot of fresh capital. Which means putting your unissued shares on the market, and maybe offering more. Which we'll pick up one way or another. And with what we've got, and what we're taking over from these good folk here, including Alan—"

"No," said Alan. "You won't get mine."

Edmund said, "Alan, don't be hasty. Let's get all the details out in the open, have a good look at the situation, and then—"

"I'm not selling."

With an effort Hesketh kept his voice steady—and lethal. "Look. We agreed. A few weeks back it made good sense to you. It's still the only thing that makes sense. In New York we—"

"In New York you put a proposition to me and I said I'd think it over."

"Sure, but we thought you saw it our way and—"

"I've thought it over," said Alan, "and decided against it."

Poppy said, "I told you he was a devious little bastard."

"You can't want to throw your whole future away," said Hesketh. "Let me tell you—"

"Let me, rather, tell you, Hesketh." Nell pushed herself up to her feet and rested one hand on the padded end of the couch. She spoke quietly, raising her voice only when a tramcar rumbled under the window and sent a shudder through the floorboards. "We don't need your money. On the contrary. We're prepared to buy back the Wylie shares, and those that this . . . this lady has sold to you."

Poppy laughed shrilly.

"You're out of your mind," said Hesketh.

"They'll be no good to you—not set against the subsidies invested by Her Majesty's Government."

"Government subsidies? Postal contracts? They wouldn't pay for the refit of a single liner at today's rates."

Nell went on calmly and concisely to explain the understanding reached with the naval authorities. She quoted the terms of the agreement, made no secret of the exact figures involved, and did not take her eyes off Hesketh's slowly reddening, swelling face as she added one relentless clause to another.

Alan became aware of his uncle gently shaking his head: not in denial but in dawning wonderment, an old, comradely admiration.

When Nell had finished, Hesketh sat without a word, slumped forward to gather his thoughts and strength and anger for whatever assault he could launch.

Poppy broke the silence. Her scream was like a terrible siren shrieking an alarm through the room.

"Leave her to it, then. Let her go to hell her own way." She seemed to be getting up from her chair, but remained in a painful, twisted crouch, dragging howls of abuse up from her stomach. "*We* can't lose. *We'll* have sold enough to make her . . . to make it . . . she *can't* win, can she?" Edmund was trying to force her down, but she wrenched away from him and thrust her face close to Hesketh's. "You can still have Edmund's share, can't you? You can still find a way . . . still finish that bitch off, can't you?"

"Oh, yes." Hesketh leered vengefully at Nell. "I'll finish this whole thing off, you see if I don't. And your husband'll get his price all right."

Edmund separated himself from the two of them. "I'm not asking for it any more."

"You don't have to ask. It's settled."

"No." Edmund was smiling—the most candid, free, heartfelt smile Alan had ever seen from him. "Dear Nell," he said. "You're superb. I'm ashamed of myself."

"So you should be," hissed his wife.

Alan had vainly hoped that Poppy would falter at the end: that her own pride would not allow her to demean herself by too crude a show of old hatreds. For the sake of memories his body had to be grateful for, he wanted her to be the mature, knowledgeable, stylish creature he had once enjoyed. A flutter of her hand, a quirk of that mouth that could so entrancingly have launched a thousand ships, and she could bring them all out of this wrangle without bitterness.

But now she was screaming bitterly. "So you should be, so you should."

"You told me he'd do whatever you said." Hesketh turned his fury on her. "Told me we'd got nothing to worry about."

She said, "Edmund, if you don't . . . if you cheat me now . . . Edmund, I'll never forgive you."

"So be it." Edmund was still in a silent, joking, devoted rapprochement with Nell. "I think we may now declare this meeting closed."

"I'll be damned if we do," grated Hesketh. "I'm staying here until you know what the stakes are. I'll stay here in this town until I see your whole rotten business in ruins and you . . . *you* . . ."

"You're not staying," said Nell.

"I'll not leave this goddamn town until—"

"If you don't go back, and go at once, to tell your Mr. Groman the price we're offering for those shares to which you were rash enough to commit him, then your name will be well and truly what it used to be."

Nell nodded to Alan. He leaned over to open the brief-bag and take out the rolled broadsheets. Nell opened them out, took off the top one, and handed it to Hesketh.

He began to read. And growled. And wiped a spittle of rage from his mouth with the back of his hand.

The broadsheet had been printed on bright yellow paper, of higher quality than the usual ballad-monger's wares. This was necessary to ensure the clarity and authenticity of Hesketh's face at the top, finely and recognisably engraved alongside the title in ornate capitals:

A BALLAD OF WENCHING AND WASHING

"I'm told there are two thousand copies in print," said Nell. "One thousand for local distribution, and one thousand for shipment to the United States."

"You wouldn't have the nerve. You'd never dare."

"Oh, but you mustn't accuse me, Mr. Hesketh. I'm merely doing you a good turn by drawing your attention to the dreadful way gossip—or history—gets round Liverpool. Of course it'll all be new to the New York watermen. What a dreadful shock in store for them!"

Edmund reached for a copy, and began to read. There were ten stanzas in all. By the time he had reached the second his eyes were widening, and he gulped.

> There's lots of muck on Merseyside
> Comes floating in on the making tide,
> But here's the tale of mucky Fred
> Who was scoured right clean from his toes to his head,
> Though the bit that proved most hard to clean
> Was the tarnished weapon in between.
>   CHORUS: Rub-a-dub-dub, it's time for a scrub;
>   Go to it ladies, then off to the pub.
>
> Poor Fred was noted for his ardour:
> When young girls screamed he shoved the harder
> But in the washhouse one fine day
> They laid him out and had *their* way;
> And Fred, who says he's now called Kellaway,

340

Got well scrubbed up till his foreskin fell away.
   CHORUS: Rub-a-dub-dub, etc:

They laid his grubby body down,
His yells were heard through Liverpool town
As brushes with their bristles thick
Got working on . . .

"No!" Hesketh snatched it from Edmund and tore it across, tore it again, scattered the pieces and stuttered with rage. "You!" he bellowed at Nell. "You . . . I can just see you . . . Christ, you and your airs and graces, I always knew . . . filthy slut, sitting up all night and thinking up that kind of thing, I can just see you . . ."

"You don't seriously think *I'd* pen such libellous stuff, do you, Mr. Hesketh?"

"Libellous, aye, that's what it is all right. I'll have you in court, see if I don't. Have you for every last penny you've got."

"But I'm not the author," said Nell equably. "And even the printer hasn't put his name on it."

"You'll not get away with it."

Alan said, "I've a mind to set it to music. Wouldn't do for the grand saloon, but there's a fair number of smoking rooms, and some dives down the Atlantic coast, where they'd be yelling for encores."

"This won't make any difference. This isn't going to stop me. The likes of you—you don't ever forget, do you? Never let an honest man ply his trade without finding dirty ways of trampling him down."

"You could hold up a mirror, Mr. Hesketh," said Nell, "and fancy you looked at an honest man?" While he spluttered for an answer, she went on, "Very well, then. Play straight with me, and I'll be honest with you. Give me your word that you'll go back and tell Mr. Groman there's been a mistake. There'll be no sale. But you can get him out of it without loss of money or loss of face. Do that, and I promise I'll do what I can to suppress this ballad sheet."

"Nobody's going to believe all that muck."

"No?"

"It was all a story, there never was anything in it. Nobody remembers it, anyway."

"They can soon be reminded."

"I won't be blackmailed."

"What a way to put it! Now that really *is* a slander, Mr. Hesketh." With

341

sudden briskness Nell said, "Well, I think it's time I seconded Edmund's motion to close this meeting. Mr. Hesketh, I suggest I call on you at your hotel tomorrow morning. We can both think over our mutual interests and round everything off then. You may offer me sherry at eleven o'clock—will that suit?"

As she left the counting-house Edmund made a move to take her arm, then blew her a kiss—an incredible flippancy for Edmund—and stayed circumspectly at his wife's side. Not for the first time this afternoon, Alan felt a twinge of alarm. At a crucial moment Edmund had changed sides and helped win the day. Alone with Poppy, could he be made to recant?

Seeming to pluck an echo of this doubt from the air, Edmund said, "Doing anything for lunch tomorrow, Alan? Perhaps you'd like to join me at the club."

Poppy was erect, pale, petrified into silent and unblinking fury.

Alan led his mother across the street towards the stables and their waiting carriage. Hesketh watched them go. When Nell glanced back and said, "Eleven o'clock then, Mr. Hesketh?" he drew his head down like a tortoise retreating into its carapace, and stumped off uphill. On a corner he stopped and peered round it as if afraid that some newsboy or ballad-monger would be there already selling copies of the broadsheet. From the top of the gradient a three-horse knifeboard tramcar was beginning to squeal down past him.

Edmund was locking the outer door of the counting-house. Poppy stood with her back to him, staring at Nell's retreating back even more malignantly than Hesketh had done.

Then she said something fast and clipped from the corner of her mouth. Edmund reached out to clutch her arm. She dodged away and started across the setts and the glistening tram-track.

The grinding of the brake rose to a banshee pitch. The trace horse stumbled, and the weight behind it thrust it wildly on. Its two followers whinnied with terror. There was the scrabble of hoofs, the howl of the brake and slithering wheels. Something snapped; the horses splayed out; the driver was shouting something hopeless, helpless.

Poppy was kicked inwards and upwards by a flailing hoof. She thrust out despairingly with one arm, but only tangled it in the reins. Then, as Alan turned in horror towards the noise and confusion, she appeared to do a somersault; was lost for a second between the horses; and then was down across the steel grooves as the wheels cut their way through her, chopped through her knees and neck.

The car careered on its way another ten yards before the brakes gripped on the shallower slope, and the terrified horses took the weight behind them.

Alan ran into the road from one pavement; Edmund from the other. They stopped to turn Poppy over. When they saw what was left to them, Edmund turned away and spewed a yellow trickle of vomit down one rail. He lurched a few steps; came to a halt against the handrail of the tramcar step. Choking on his words and his determination not to be sick, Alan said:

"Why did she . . .what made her . . ."

Edmund wiped his lips with a large linen handkerchief that Alan had never before seen removed from his uncle's top pocket. "She . . .was going to tell your mother . . ."

"Tell her what?"

"One last stab. The story about Rosalind. About your father being Rosalind's father."

The driver and conductor were climbing down, shouting. Passengers on the top deck leaned out, questioning and arguing.

"But the story wasn't true," said Alan with cold, uncaring certainty. "Was it?"

"Of course it wasn't."

"You knew—"

"I never really thought it was. But when she went off to Rosalind's I asked, just to be sure. She admitted it was an invention—she told me because it didn't matter to her any more."

"No."

"Does it matter," asked Edmund, "to you?"

Alan thought of Louisa, and their daughter, and the warmth and untidiness and lovingness of their scrappy, mismanaged life. And he said, "No, it doesn't matter."

"But it would have hurt your mother. Poppy couldn't resist one last attempt—one last lunge, taking Nell off guard and : . . ."

There was no more to be said. They turned back towards the bloody sprawl on the Liverpool street, the flesh and crushed bone that had once been Poppy and which now no longer felt or cared or hated.

That evening Nell said, "Someone'll have to stand by Edmund while we're away."

"Away?"

"I'm coming to New York with you."

"Mother, there's no need. Once we're quite sure the Hesketh business is straightened out, there's no call for you to come to America."

"There is. To see Louisa and throw myself on her mercy."

"Mother—"

"And bring you both back here," said Nell. "And then you must have a few sons, and be quick about it."

All at once she began to laugh, and then to cry at the same time. Alan went to her and knelt by her, and she put her arm round his shoulders and went on quietly, helplessly laughing and crying.

"Mother, what's the matter? What *is* it?"

"What I've just said. Just the way it was said to me, years ago. And how cross I was! And now here I am, saying the selfsame thing to you. Does nobody ever break entirely free?"

Alan kissed her cheek, rested his head against her. "No," he said quietly, "I don't suppose so."

ON HER eightieth birthday Nell Gresham returned from a cruise cut short by Great Britain's declaration of war on Germany. The trip had been a present from Alan and Louisa: ironically, it had been German shipping lines who introduced the idea of cruising in the Mediterranean, and now it was the Germans whose enmity meant the cancelling of holidays and a turning for home of British passenger vessels—must urgently, those promised for military conversion in time of emergency.

"Lot of fuss about nothing," grumbled the captain of the Gresham-Bostock *Adela,* only recently taken out of Atlantic service and transferred to the cruising trade. "It'll all be over in three months, from what I hear. Mess our ship up with guns and armour plating, and before Christmas we'll be stripping it all off again."

But some of the younger Naval Reserve officers and ratings were eager to be home, to turn their attention to sea warfare and the challenge of the German fleet.

The *Adela* steamed into the Mersey on a gusty autumn day. Nell stood at the rail, erect though needing her grandfather's silver-knobbed stick to brace her against the roll of the tide across the bar. She drank in every detail. The familiar markers were still there, the pillars and buoys and fort and lighthouses between which the dredged channel wove its way. Traffic was as busy and predictable as ever. Masts jabbed up from the timber docks. Freighters were unloading on to miles of quay. Scurrying out from New Brighton like a water beetle went a ferry-boat. As the *Adela* forged on with regal certainty in midstream, another ferry nudged round her stern towards the Wirral landing.

Everything was surely as it had been when Nell set out on holiday. War was a distant flurry whose ripples could never reach this far. Only as the river narrowed and the docks built up to port and starboard was there any glimpse of change. Rearing above a shipyard wall, two funnels were in the process of having their bright red and white stripes painted over in battleship grey. And men roped down from the rails were hammering grey plates to a Gresham-Bostock steamer within a graving dock.

The engine-room telegraph clanged faintly, imperiously. As they lost way and adjusted to the current, ready for the slow reverse arc into the landing-stage, the sound of music drifted across the water. On an improvised platform beside the upper level gangways waiting the *Adela's* arrival, a wind band was playing a lilting waltz that Nell had never heard before. As the liner thumped gently against the fenders, the music changed to a rousing march, mingled with the sound of clapping and cheering and shouts of welcome from the stage below. Faces were upturned, fingers pointed; some groups of men and women waved vigorously, recognising friends and relations or simply waving in the hope that their signals would be identified and returned. One little girl perched on her father's shoulders was flapping both arms joyfully.

All at once, close to the band, waiting for the gangways to be run out, Nell saw a group of four. They had all come to welcome her—all, of course, save Margaret, away in Newcastle with her husband and Nell's two great-granddaughters. But there was Alan, and Louisa with her arm through his, and the two boys, smiling up and beginning to wave. Boys no longer, really: young men in their middle twenties; but from this lofty viewpoint still seeming too young for the responsibilities they had taken on. Nell leaned over the rail, impatient for them to be close to her: dear Malcolm, dear Robert, schooled so assiduously and with such steady, unfussy affection by Edmund right up to the day of his peaceful death six years ago.

When at last she set foot on the stage, and Louisa and Alan were kissing her and saying, "Welcome home, mother, welcome home," and Robert was attending to her luggage, the band began to play that first tune again.

"You like it, mother?" Louisa's pretty, plump, pink face shone with expectation.

"Very attractive. I've never heard it before."

"It's called the Eleanor Waltz."

"Well, I never! You found it specially for me?"

346

"Wrote it specially," said Alan.

"You mean you—"

"No point in being Gresham-Bostock Director of Music and Entertainments if I can't make our orchestra perform one of my own compositions. Nobody else is ever likely to."

"Idiot," said Louisa adoringly.

Nell looked into their faces, and saw Robert's face through the throng, on his way back to her; and was content. She had to say something to all of them, but it wouldn't come. As the musicians ended the waltz, all she could manage was an awkward, "Such extravagance."

Malcolm was holding out something to her in his cupped hands. "Welcome back, grandma." In the convex glass of a paperweight swam a ship so tiny that she was afraid it would vanish over the horizon of her memory; yet so clear she knew she would never really forget it: the old *Eleanor*, which she had launched so long ago.

"More extravagance," she snapped. "Malcolm, you're supposed to be the sensible one of the family."

"Isn't it a sensible thing to give a present to someone you love?"

As her grandsons moved away, their attention snared by the details of passenger reception, traffic flow, hotel transport and onward train bookings, and comments on the voyage, she wondered again that they should take their responsibilities so seriously at their age. Then thought of herself, and the challenges she had met at just such an age. Too much, too soon.

Alan said, "You'll never let yourself accept that you're loved, will you, mother? And have been, so often, by so many people."

"Oh, stuff and nonsense. Come along, we can't stand about here all day." But as Alan began to lead her along the stage towards the slanting exit gangway, she said, "Alan, do you ever regret . . ."

"What is there to regret?"

"Not going on with your career. You didn't have the chance, you *could* have gone, instead of . . . well . . ." She waved at the crowd and the waterfront and the hull of the ship rising above them.

"Mother, I'd never have been better than a good second-rate performer in something I consider first rate. Better to do what I have done— enjoyed being a first-rate manipulator of good second-rate things."

"You came back to Gresham-Bostock . . . thinking it was second-rate?" she puffed.

Louisa came round to her other side and squeezed her arm. "Alan's already told you why he came back—if only you'd been listening properly."

"And you?"

347

"It took *me* time to accept," said Louisa. "But he was right. Otherwise we wouldn't be here, would we?"

Nell looked straight ahead, then raised her eyes so that the breeze might dry the absurd moisture in them. Through that slight shimmer there was a vision of the blocks and towers and chimneys and streets of her inescapable city. Factories and terraces were piled up along the ridge, and Nell in her mind's eye saw them rolling on for miles beyond. Smoke drifted, sparks of sunlight were reflected from a window far away, and from the side of an electric tramcar on a hill. And closer now, reared against the sky, were the new bastions of the waterfront: the august dome of the Docks and Harbour Board building, and the soaring clock towers and wide-winged birds on the Liver Building.

So much had been lost; but there was so much to replace it. She had seen so much—too much. She had little appetite for any more. There had been the triumphs, and the near-defeats. She had watched Clydeside shipbuilding threatening Liverpool, the Manchester Ship Canal cutting a swathe through trade that Liverpool had too complacently taken for granted; and watched the fatal diversion of so much Anglo-American passenger traffic to Southampton. So many storms weathered; but so many more waiting below that next lowering cloud.

Beyond the moored *Adela* a United States liner was moving downstream. Hoarse salutes were sounded from one vessel to the other. Neutral and undaunted, the American faced the Atlantic with no hazards other than the usual day-to-day navigational problems.

Nell was reassured rather than resentful. There had been rivalries and partnerships between the two countries, there might be others while this war lasted, and when the war was over would be yet more. But the lifeline must never be cut. It had taken many a strain: it must not break. Across those thousands of miles Liverpool and New York must somehow always be linked as loving, cheating, quarrelsome, exuberant members of a family are linked no matter what the disasters and discords. There would be new quarrels, new alliances, new methods and new mergers. Still the tie would hold.

But that's all beyond me now, thought Nell. Aloud, to her son and Louisa and to her grandsons far back along the stage and to the dock gates and gantries and chimneys and floating roadway and all that lived and moved and had its being on and beside that grey, unresting river, she said, "It's up to someone else now."

In Bostock Gardens the pensioner employed as park-keeper now that younger men had volunteered for the wars found, trapped in a crack of the toolshed wall, three slivers of rotting wood. They had once been employed as plant tags in the flowerbeds, but had gone pulpy from being stuck so long in the damp soil. All that remained of the figurehead that had once paid homage at the foot of Jesse Bostock's plinth, they had only one further use. The park-keeper dropped them into the sack he was taking home full of kindling for his grate.